"**Have you forgotten what it was like for us in the beginning?**" Richard demanded. He reached out and caught Sarah around her waist, pulling her to him. "I want you, and you know you still want me."

She struggled, but his grip tightened. "Let go of me, Richard, or—"

"Or what? You'll scalp me? Let me make love to you Sarah, and I guarantee you'll never think of your Indian brave again!"

Sarah went rigid. Her eyes were filled with contempt for him. "Why don't you go back to your whores?"

"Because I haven't felt desire for another woman since you came back to me."

"I did not come back to you. I brought our son back to claim what's his."

Richard laughed. "Liar. You think I don't know what you're feeling. Your lust is as strong as mine, and it always was." He pulled her against him, and she began to struggle.

Her hands flew to his throat. Catching him by surprise, she felt satisfaction when he gasped for breath. She'd mastered him, if only for a brief moment, until he wrenched her hands from his neck.

"You could perhaps prevail over a sheltered Englishwoman, Richard, but not over me. I've lived with the Apache too long. You'll learn what that means if you lay a hand on me again," Sarah promised in a low voice.

Richard smiled. "I've never had to force a woman, Sarah. But I don't believe your ardor is dead. The time will come when you'll beg me to make love to you. . . ."

UNTAMED

JOAN DIAL

BANTAM BOOKS
TORONTO • NEW YORK • LONDON • SYDNEY • AUCKLAND

FOR CRAIG AND GARY

Grateful acknowledgments are made to those dear friends and family members who provided research material (as well as support and enthusiasm) . . . Elaine Rosenberg in Australia, the Robinson family of Yorkshire, Jo Sperrazzo and Luciana Chafin, and, of course, all the Dials.

UNTAMED
A Bantam Book / April 1988

ISBN 0-553-27111-3

Published simultaneously in the United States and Canada

Bantam Books are published by Bantam Books, a division of
Bantam Doubleday Dell Publishing Group, Inc. Its trademark,
consisting of the words "Bantam Books" and the portrayal of a
rooster, is Registered in U.S. Patent and Trademark Office and
in other countries. Marca Registrada. Bantam Books, 666 Fifth
Avenue, New York, New York 10103.

PRINTED IN THE UNITED STATES OF AMERICA

O   0 9 8 7 6 5 4 3 2 1

BOOK I

1

ARIZONA, 1886

A dust devil swept out of the canyon and whirled through the mesquite in mindless frenzy. In the distance the mountains were a silent, brooding presence. The railroad tracks, parallel steel bars that slashed across the dry lake bed, caught the sunlight and returned it like a knife thrust. Sarah blinked, her mind conjuring a different panorama. England, gently green, a sanctuary that beckoned ever more urgently.

She felt a fingernail crack as she gripped the granite face of the boulder shielding them from view. At her side her son watched with growing horror the scene unfolding at Bowie Station.

The soldiers barked orders, prodded, pushed, and herded the formerly proud Chiricahua warriors into the waiting boxcars as if they were cattle.

"I am glad my father did not live to see this peace that Goyathlay made with the white-eyes," Hakan whispered savagely. "Come to Fort Apache so that we may count you, the soldiers said. Instead they disarmed the braves and told them they were prisoners of war."

The situation was even worse than her son realized. Sarah had overheard a soldier mention the eventual destination of the exiles. The followers of Goyathlay, whom the soldiers and Mexicans called Geronimo and with whom she and Hakan had ridden for several months, were on their way to a reservation in Florida. How could these desert-dwellers possibly survive in a swamp? Thank God Hakan had stayed out of sight, following and observing as the Apaches were marched to the fort.

As the band of the Fourth Cavalry formed ranks and began to play "Auld Lang Syne," Sarah covered her ears with her hands and turned away, her long braid of wheat-blonde hair slipping over her shoulder. There were silver strands in her plaited hair, although she was only thirty-six. Her pink-and-white English complexion had long since tanned almost as dark as the wives of the settlers, although not the rich bronze of the *Tin-ne-ah*. She was still reed-slim, and the one way in which her body had failed her was not visible to the naked eye.

"I cannot bear to watch the humiliation of my people," Hakan muttered. "Let us go now. Tomorrow we will return to Mexico."

Sarah's eyes filled with tears as she gave one last glance at the Chiricahuas, packed tightly into the boxcars, and at the vastly superior force of soldiers. There was nowhere left for the nomad Apaches to hide. The last stragglers would be hunted down mercilessly on both sides of the border. She followed her son silently back down the trail to where they had left their horses.

As soon as they were safely hidden in the stronghold, she would explain to Hakan that they could not survive as lone fugitives in Mexico. Then she would tell him of the decision she had made, a decision to return to England. She had been thinking about it since the murder of *Tonsaroyoo*. The sorry spectacle at Bowie Station only confirmed the wisdom of her plan. The Indian agent, Sam Rutherford, would help them.

The rider appeared to be floating above the parched earth, a ghostly wraith against the glare of the midday sky framed by turretlike mesas of volcanic rock.

"Optical illusion?" Philip Merrin suggested, his pale blue eyes squinting in the unaccustomed harshness of the sunlight. Despite the dusty heat, he managed to look immaculate, perfectly pressed and groomed, and properly stoic.

"A mirage," his companion snapped back. "Like this whole damned expedition." Sir Randolph Leighton's polished boot stirred the sand coating the weathered wood platform. "What bloody idiots we are—"

"Yes," Philip interrupted. "I believe we established that in Liverpool, again in New York, St. Louis, and what was that last town? Oh yes, how could I forget *Lords*burg? The fact is, our dear sister-in-law is about to be restored to the bosom of her grieving family. What a lark!"

"For the love of heaven, Philip, must you be such an ass?

If this pathetic woman really is Sarah Merrin, what then? What the devil do we *do* with her?"

"We decide that when we know for certain it is she. How many times must I explain this to you?"

Randolph tipped back the brim of his Panama hat as he stared across the shimmering expanse of mesquite-dotted sand to the red-tinted mesas that rose from the desert floor like pagan monuments. "I see only one rider. Damn, two hours' wait for nothing. If we have to spend another night in that miserable excuse for an inn—"

The two Englishmen walked to the edge of the platform, watching the approaching rider. A plump Indian woman who had been sitting on the only available bench now stirred herself and followed. She stood inches away from Randolph, scrutinizing first him, and then Philip, with an unblinking stare.

Amused, Philip reflected that the woman wasn't the first observer to study them curiously. She probably thought they were an odd pair, not only because of their strange clothes, but also because of the sharp physical contrast between the two of them. Whereas he was tall and lean, fair-skinned and blue-eyed, a complete Anglo-Saxon, Randolph was as dark-haired, swarthy-skinned, and brooding-eyed as any denizen of a Marseilles bar. Added to which, Randolph's bulging muscles and boxer's shoulders indicated, correctly, that he was a man given to much physical activity. The most strenuous exercise Philip was apt to engage in consisted of floating downriver on someone else's punt as he turned the pages of a book.

Under his breath, Randolph muttered to Philip, "I thought all of the aborigines had been rounded up and put on reservations."

"Apparently not. I believe this one finds you attractive, old man. Your beetle-browed scowl perhaps reminds her of her departed Indian brave. Funny how women seem to want to soothe that raging impatience of yours."

"More likely she's eyeing your golden locks and thinking what a handsome scalp you have."

"Apache not take scalps," the woman said quietly. She turned away, her gaze seeking the man riding a lathered horse toward the station.

"I believe we've both been guilty of a breach of good

manners," Philip said, genuinely concerned. "We must stop
assuming that the Indians don't understand our language.
Especially since Sarah has undoubtedly taught her son to
speak English."

"And that's another thing. What do you think their plans
are for the boy? And why wasn't he sent to the reservation
with the others?"

"We'll soon find out," Philip murmured.

The horseman was in sight now. A big man, his brawny
shoulders strained the buckskin jacket he wore, and his trail-
dusted hat was pushed up over a high, intelligent forehead.
About forty, Philip guessed, although the sun lines etched
into the leathery skin might have added a few years to his
age. Despite the man's size, he reined his mount and jumped
to the ground as lightly as a dancer.

"Philip Merrin?" He offered his hand to Philip without
hesitation. "I'm Sam Rutherford, the Indian agent."

"How did you know which of us was Lord Moreland's
brother?" Randolph asked, sounding annoyed.

"The light hair and height," Rutherford answered.

"May I present Sir Randolph Leighton," Philip said, wondering whether to qualify Randolph's position in the family
and deciding to say as little as possible at this point. As the
two men exchanged wary handshakes, Philip added, "I don't
remember mentioning in our correspondence what I looked
like."

Rutherford apparently didn't hear the remark as he was
sizing up Randolph. They looked like a pair of pugilists
about to square off, Philip decided, feeling their instant mutual dislike. Rutherford said, "If you gents will give me a few
minutes to take care of my horse." His eyes met those of the
squaw, and a slow grin spread across his face. Surprisingly,
the woman's solemn countenance broke into a broad smile.
He said something in her language and she giggled.

Philip saw Randolph flush angrily and knew he had assumed the Indian agent had made some derogatory remark
about them. Fortunately Rutherford didn't give them time to
comment, as he led his sweating horse away. The Indian
woman went with him.

"Calm down, Randolph," Philip said. "Perhaps your
fondest wish has come true and Sarah has decided not to
embarrass us after all."

"If the woman in question actually is Sarah Merrin." Randolph prowled the platform restlessly for the few minutes that passed until Sam Rutherford returned, alone.

"Where is the woman who claims to be Sarah Merrin?" Randolph demanded before anyone else could speak.

Sam addressed his response to Philip. "Sarah—The Countess of Moreland—and Hakan have been hiding out in the Cochise stronghold, dodging army patrols for months while waiting for word from England. They weren't about to show themselves without some guarantees about their future. Your letters, sir, have been vague. Sarah thought it best if I rode in ahead to find out why her husband sent his brother instead of coming himself."

Randolph's nose twitched, almost imperceptibly. "Why couldn't she have stayed dead, after all these years?"

"Randolph, will you please let me handle this?" Philip said. "Mr. Rutherford—"

"Sam."

"Yes. We're somewhat at a loss to understand the situation in regard to the boy, Hakan. From what you said in your last letter, he's still with her. We'd understood that your government had made peace with the Apache Indians and that his tribe was to be sent to a reservation."

"True. Geronimo and his people were on their way to Florida when I first wrote to you last year. Look, we'll get in out of the sun a helluva lot faster if you answer my question. Why are *you* here?"

"Sarah Merrin was declared legally dead nine years ago," Randolph snapped. "Surely she didn't expect her husband to still be waiting for her?"

Philip said quickly, "My brother wanted to be sure the woman was, in fact, Sarah. I can hardly determine that until I meet her."

"Why didn't he come himself?"

"Because, damn it all," Randolph said, visibly exasperated, "he's now married to my sister."

Sarah sat in the shade of an overhanging rock, watching her son with a familiar thrill of pride. At sixteen, Hakan was more accomplished as a hunter and horseman than any brave she had known. He moved silently along the ridge, arrow taut against his bow, as he stalked an unseen prey. Straightening up suddenly, he released the arrow and it flashed out of sight. Hakan dropped from the ridge, disappearing from her view.

Nearby, the tethered horses stirred and sniffed the wind. Sarah rose to gather wood to light the campfire in order to cook the game her son had just killed. When Hakan returned he would also expect her to prepare the meat and cook it, just as she would build a wickiup for shelter tonight if Sam Rutherford did not return for them by dusk. Had they still been living in the rancheria, it would also have been her task to tan the hide of the animal. Not for the first time, Sarah felt a stab of apprehension about their chances of adapting to a new way of life.

As she coaxed the campfire to life, she wondered how the years had treated Richard. So many times, over the years, she had thought about their possible reunion. The scene constantly rearranged itself in her mind, like the particles in a roughly shaken kaleidoscope. But her mental images in which Hakan was presented to her English husband were always the same; she knew exactly what Richard's reaction to the boy would be.

And Hakan . . . what would he think of the rolling meadows, misty lakes, and shadowed woods of England? It was all so different from this harshly beautiful landscape. Perhaps, like herself as a girl, Hakan would feel a greater affinity with the wild moors of her Yorkshire home.

Her son reappeared on the ridge, a young antelope slung across his shoulders. He looked down at his mother, his eyes softening with love, and she felt a fierce surging pride in him and, at the same time, a stab of acute sadness, knowing the turmoil into which she was forcing him.

At first he had adamantly refused to accompany her to England. "I will never leave this land, I would rather die," he had told her. But of course in the end he had understood why he must go.

Before he reached her side, they heard the thunder of hooves. A moment later Sam Rutherford's horse came galloping into the canyon. Sarah knew from the tight lines of his face that the meeting with Philip Merrin hadn't gone well.

She took the reins as Sam jumped from his mount. Hakan came to the fire, dropping the antelope to the ground before he approached. Sam said, "He brought a friend with him. A Sir Randolph Leighton. You know him?"

Sarah shook her head.

"They're staying in Willcox. We'll ride into town tomorrow and decide what to do then."

"I've already decided," Sarah said. "We're going back to England."

Sam avoided her eyes. "Ma'am, you'd best think some more about that once you talk to your brother-in-law."

"My husband isn't overjoyed to hear I'm alive," Sarah said. "I didn't expect he would be."

"Sarah—ma'am, it seems you were declared legally dead and your husband . . . married again."

She digested this silently for a moment. "That doesn't change my plans to go to England."

"Why don't you hold off making any decisions until they've met the boy?"

She looked at him, surprised. "You didn't tell them?"

"No. Sometimes showing is a whole heap better than telling." Turning to Hakan, Sam said, "That's a mighty fine piece of game." Sam knew better than to address the boy by his given name. Apache men used given names only under circumstances of extreme gravity, in mortal danger, or in grief. It was permissible to use nicknames, but since neither Sarah nor Hakan had told him the boy's nickname, Sam assumed they no longer wished to use it, probably out of respect for his dead father, Tonsaroyoo, who undoubtedly had given it to him.

Sarah turned her attention to the antelope, slipping her knife from its sheath. Sam said, "Hold up, there. I'll skin the animal."

Watching him prepare the game for roasting, Sarah had a sudden vision of herself as a young bride, presiding over her first dinner party at Merrinswood. She had worn a white satin gown and a diamond necklace, and there had been thirty guests seated at the dining table, where on Merrin silver was served four different types of meat and half a dozen kinds of vegetables. The silver dishes had been of such pure quality that they rarely required polishing. Strange how small details like that stayed in the mind long after shattering pain or emotional upheaval had lost its power to hurt.

Sensing that his mother's mind was again traveling away

from them, her son spoke quietly. "Soon the waiting will be over. Then it will be easier."

She smiled at him. "Please—in English?" Her tone was more pleading than demanding, as befitted the mother of a nearly grown son of a chief.

Hakan stared into the flames of the campfire. "Time enough for English when it must be spoken." The words were no sooner out of his mouth than he turned to her with a rueful smile, his eyes telling her that it had occurred to him that he must put aside his own feelings out of concern for hers.

He touched her arm gently and whispered her Apache name. "*Sons-ee-ah-ray*, forgive your clumsy son. Of course we will speak English. You will be glad to know that I am even thinking in English—well, sometimes, at least. I must not spoil your joy that you go at last to your homeland. I will go also, with my heart and mind open, and speak the tongues of your people."

Sarah lay awake long after Sam and Hakan had fallen asleep, watching the embers of the campfire fade. The stars pierced the sky so brightly they seemed to be within reach, like impossible yearnings.

She wondered if the spirit of Tonsaroyoo was with her tonight. Was that persistent warning voice in her head his? Did her beloved Lone Wolf plead with her not to force their son to leave this land he loved so much?

Sarah tossed and turned and told herself she had no choice.

At dawn the following morning they rode into town. There, they waited for Philip Merrin and his traveling companion in the dining room of the larger of the town's two hotels. It was clear from the outraged glances of the other patrons how they felt about the wearing of Apache buckskins and moccasins in their hotel.

Listening to the whispers, Sarah remembered for the first time in years how often people were judged by the clothing they wore. Fortunately, Sam Rutherford's imposing presence prevented anyone from causing trouble. The mere size and demeanor of Sam, Sarah had discovered, intimidated most men.

Sarah was too nervous to eat and Hakan politely declined

the white man's food. Sam ate a plate of steak and potatoes while they waited. Time ticked by, minute by interminable minute, until the two Englishmen finally entered the dining room.

Her first thought was, how incongruous, yet how impressive, they looked. Handsome, impeccably dressed, they were completely in control of themselves and oblivious to the stares that greeted them.

She would have recognized Philip Merrin anywhere. The charmingly lazy boy she remembered had matured into a man with the same golden good looks, faintly amused blue eyes, heavy-lidded with perpetual fatigue, and a slightly astonished expression—as though he hadn't expected to find himself participating in life, but merely observing it. His physical resemblance to his older brother, Richard, was still quite startling. It was a Merrin family trait that the males all looked alike but were bestowed with radically different personalities. For an instant Sarah had to remind herself which brother she was facing.

As the two men crossed the room, negotiating the clutter of tables, Sarah glanced quickly at Philip's companion. He was about the same age, thirty or so, several inches shorter but burlier of build, as dark as a gypsy, and his features were marred by a downward curve to his lips that suggested discontent. He had glowering eyes that at first had also appeared dark, but as he came nearer she saw they were actually a very deep, almost midnight blue.

Sam hastily wiped his mouth with his napkin as the men approached. Hakan had his back to the door, but when Sam rose to his feet, the boy followed suit, turning to look at the two Englishmen.

From Sarah's vantage point between them, she was able to observe the shocked dismay that appeared on both Philip's and his companion's face. Philip recovered his composure more quickly than the other man, who stared with a mixture of open-mouthed astonishment and horror at her son.

Sam smothered a grin and said, "I guess I don't have to explain to you two gents who this is? His Apache name is Hakan—means 'fiery' because of the red glints in his blonde hair. But, of course, his English name is James Richard Merrin, firstborn son of the sixth Earl of Moreland."

2

YORKSHIRE, ENGLAND, 1887

A thin mist crept tentatively across the bleak moors like a ghostly army advancing on a sleeping castle, but even in the dawn grayness, the walls of Merrinswood glowed with a golden vitality. The local stone that had been used to build the house had mellowed over the years to a rich amber, so that no matter how desolate the day, Merrinswood seemed forever bathed in sunlight.

To the ragged seven-year-old boy who clung to the elaborate wrought iron gates leading to the forecourt, the incongruity of building a house better suited to a French city than a barren moor was lost. Danior had more pressing matters on his mind as he waited for his breath to grind less painfully in his chest. He hadn't eaten for two days and had run three miles to get here.

The Romany tribe to which he belonged would never have dared approach a house as palatial as this one, but as he fumbled with the latch to open the gates, Danior could think of nothing but the pain and terror in Chavi's lovely eyes. She was so alone, so helpless.

Inside the forecourt, he stared at the house, unsure where the tradesmen's entrance would be. There was no sign that anyone had yet risen, but his sharp ears caught the soft whinny of a horse. He wheeled to the right and followed the sound to the stables.

A stableboy, a couple of years older than Danior, raked straw and rubbed sleep from his eyes. He looked up, startled, and raised the rake defensively as Danior approached.

"I mean no harm," Danior said breathlessly. "Just tell me how to get to the tradesmen's door of the house."

The boy looked at him disdainfully. "They don't want no gypsies a'calling. You'd best be off and right quick about it."

Danior fixed the boy with what he hoped was an unblinking stare. Blue eyes faltered slightly under the onslaught of his own dark gaze. Chavi had once told him his eyes were like black mirrors that, depending on his mood, reflected all the hopes and dreams and even the fears and secret horrors right back to whomever he stared at. "If you don't tell me where the door is," Danior said slowly, "I'll put the evil eye on you."

The stableboy bit his lip, obviously wavering, then pointed to a neatly trimmed hedge on the far side of the cobbled stableyard. "Go through the kitchen garden. You'll see the tradesmen's door after you pass the toolsheds. But they'll chase you—whip you too, most likely."

Danior ran toward the kitchen garden, then whirled through it along a path tamped into the earth, feeling the desperate urgency of time passing, fearful that it was already too late to save Chavi.

Spring vegetables, dew-washed and fragrant, distracted him briefly, and he resisted the urge to pull a carrot from the row to still the gnawing ache in his belly.

An archway of rambling roses not yet in bloom led to a cobbled yard. Ahead was an iron-studded door, over which hung a weathered sign proclaiming this entrance to be for tradesmen. Danior raised the brass knocker, shaped like a hawk in flight, and let it fall. The echo rattled from wall to wall across the stillness of the estate.

Seconds later the door opened and his eyes met a formidable expanse of starched apron. Looking up at the woman who towered over him, he saw her sharp, wrinkled face, her hair hidden under a mobcap. Snatching his own tattered cloth cap from his head, he said quickly, "Begging your pardon, mum, but could I please speak with Lady Moreland?"

The woman's thin nostrils seemed to clench. "How dare you come here? Who put you up to this? Be off with you, boy, before I fetch a footman to—"

Danior didn't wait. He ducked under the woman's arm and darted into the kitchen. Pausing, he glanced about. Several young scullery maids were preparing breakfast while half a dozen better-dressed servants sat around a large scrubbed-wood table in the center of the flagstoned kitchen floor.

Before the outraged scream of the woman at the door could alert anyone, Danior ran to an inner door on the far side of the room, wrenched it open, and plunged into a long hallway.

He heard the servants coming after him as he raced along the corridor. It led to another door which connected the servants' wing with the main house. A more luxuriously carpeted corridor led to a massive pair of carved doors, and beyond them, a vast hall that seemed to expand in all directions, upward to a giant domed ceiling, sideways through ornate arches to staircases, and into long vaulted corridors.

For an instant Danior was bewildered, unsure which direction to go. Then the sound of muffled footsteps behind him spurred him on. He chose the largest of the staircases and went flying up the thickly carpeted steps toward the floor above.

A young maid, dressed in black with a white apron and carrying a silver tray bearing a teapot and cups, had just reached the top of the stairs ahead of him. She turned and saw him coming and screamed, dropping the tray.

Cups and saucers, toast rack, teapot, and all slid over the polished bannisters and crashed to the marble floor below. The sound of breaking china must surely have awakened the devil himself, Danior thought, but only one door on the floor above opened.

A woman appeared, pale as a nun, with heavy sable-brown hair hanging in thick plaits and wearing a cambric nightgown. Danior knew instantly that his luck hadn't deserted him. From Chavi's description, this had to be Jean Merrin, the Countess of Moreland. Those dark blue eyes, gentled by violet shadows like the boundless and fleeting beauty of a summer twilight, could belong to no one else.

"Her eyes," Chavi had said, "are so kind, so full of compassion. She'll help me. I know she will. But be gentle with her. I don't think she's strong. There's such a weariness about her, as though she must drive herself to do what others do easily."

Jean Merrin's luminous eyes widened still further as she saw Danior, but there didn't seem to be either fear or contempt there. At that moment a pursuer from the kitchen caught up with him and he felt a large bony hand close around his neck.

Danior's head was jerked back viciously and his thin young body was hauled into the air as effortlessly as if he'd been a trapped hare. He looked into a face so devoid of expression it might have been made of stone.

At the same moment a soft voice said, "Put him down, Barlow."

Barlow of the granite countenance did not relax his hold. "Milady, it's a gypsy lad. Filthy and germ-laden and bent on mischief—"

"Did you hear me, Barlow?" Her voice, although gentle as summer rain, was surprisingly firm.

The man's hand released him and Danior went sprawling on the floor, inches from the hem of her cambric nightgown. From his worm's-eye view Danior could see that the Countess's feet were bare, slender and white, with blue veins and pale pink toenails. She must have jumped straight out of bed to investigate the noise, he thought.

"Please, milady," Danior cried. "It's Chavi—she's dying, I think, and she needs you. She said you'd come."

Lady Moreland drew a deep breath. Looking up at her, Danior saw that her lips parted and her eyes closed, perhaps in horror, or in mute acceptance of the news. She said, "Take him downstairs to the breakfast room. And please be quiet. Don't arouse the entire household."

Bending over Danior, she added in a sympathetic tone, "Barlow won't hurt you. I'll be down to talk with you in just a few minutes."

"No! No, Chavi can't wait, she's in terrible agony. We must go to her now."

"I must dress first," she reminded him gently, then disappeared back into her bedroom.

"Come along, boy," Barlow said, his voice cracking like a whip.

Danior picked himself up and followed the man down the stairs. He was taken to a room that seemed almost to be a part of the garden. As Barlow ushered him through the door, giving his ear a painful tweak in the process, Danior saw a wall of diamond-paned glass framing a pleasing arrangement of trees and shrubs.

The door closed with a thud behind him and he was left alone. To his right was a glass-fronted cabinet containing china, pewter, and silver items. His first thought was that one of those pieces would never be missed and could be sold to buy food and a shawl to keep Chavi warm while she

suffered through her slow ordeal of death. He took a step
toward the cabinet, feeling his heart begin to drum against his
ribs.

Jean dressed quickly, slipped a warm coat over her wool
dress, and picked up hat and gloves before going to the inner
door that adjoined her husband's bedroom. She hesitated for
a second, then turned the knob and went into the room.

Richard's bed stood on a dais in the center of the room,
shrouded by a velvet canopy, like a dark galleon rigged to sail
across a foggy sea. He lay on his back, still fully dressed, one
booted foot hanging over the edge of the bed. His mouth was
open, his sensually full lips curving in the secret smile of a
slimber whose dreams reflect his hidden desires.

She crossed the room silently and stood looking down at
her husband for a moment. Then here hand drifted as though
with a will of its own toward his mouth. Her fingers grazed
his lips lightly, felt the warm breath escaping between those
white feral teeth. She drew back her hand, clenching her fist
to her breast as though to keep it safe.

Other men might have seemed vulnerable in sleep, but
not Richard. Not even in this fully-dressed drunken stupor
of a sleep. No doubt last night he had managed to drive off
his ministering valet, who had not even dared remove his
master's boots.

Did Richard drink himself to oblivion to escape the boredom of his marriage to her? Jean feared so. She had never
been a match for him, her frailty of body and spirit seemed
almost an insult to his robust health and overpowering presence. His untethered masculinity had terrified her from the
start, and in her secret heart she had not been sorry when she
could present him with an acceptable reason to end their
physical relationship. If only Richard were able to love her in
the same way she loved him, purely, spiritually, untainted by
lust . . .

The memory of the wild dark eyes of the gypsy boy
intruded on her thoughts, persuading her to set aside her
own troubles and concentrate on the desperate problem at
hand. She tapped Richard's cheek lightly. He stirred but
didn't awaken, so she slapped him a little harder.

He opened a bloodshot eye and regarded her for a second. "Well, well . . . my dear wife. To what do I owe this

nocturnal visit? Surely the noble madonna isn't in my chambers because she's succumbed to the needs of the flesh?"

She felt herself flush with hurt and anger and the humiliating suspicion that, because he was aware of the depth of her love and need for him, he enjoyed trampling on her feelings. "One of the Romany children is here. He says the girl named Chavi is dying."

Richard groaned and sat up, his hand to his forehead as though to keep it in place. "What has some blasted gypsy to do with us?"

"*Chavi*," Jean repeated coldly. "Don't you remember? I awakened you only to tell you that I'm going to her." She spun around and fled from the room, hearing his muttered curse.

Danior almost jumped out of his skin as the door opened. He shoved the small silver pitcher into the pocket of his ragged jacket before turning to face Jean. She was dressed to go out, her frail body swathed in several layers of coats and capes. Behind her stood a housemaid holding a cloth-wrapped bundle.

"The carriage is being brought around to take us to Chavi. Tell me, what is your name?"

"Danior, milady."

"Very well, Danior. We've brought you some breakfast. You can eat it on the way."

The maid thrust the cloth-wrapped parcel into his hand. He almost fainted with joy as he sniffed the warm yeasty odor of new-baked bread.

As he followed the two women out of the room, he wished there had been an opportunity to return the stolen pitcher, but now he didn't dare. He felt guilty, too, that all at once the urge to devour the food overwhelmed his desperate concern for his sister.

Outside in the forecourt, a groom held the head of a pair of docile-looking mares harnessed to a brougham. Lady Moreland spoke to Danior. "You shall sit with the driver and direct him where to go."

The groom helped his mistress into the carriage, closed the door, and then turned to Danior, his expression clearly annoyed at having a ragged gypsy as a companion.

Danior climbed up onto the driver's seat outside the

closed carriage, and had already unwrapped a thick crust of bread and wedge of cheese before the carriage rolled down the drive toward the gates.

"Coombe's Woods," Danior mumbled to the driver between mouthfuls of bread and cheese.

The wheels of the brougham and the legs of the trotting horses were lost in ground mist as they passed through the gates of Merrinswood and traveled down the narrow lane bordered on one side by farmland and the other by rolling moors. The air was chill, the moors not yet fully awake after the long hard winter.

How quickly the three miles to Coombe's Woods were accomplished in the carriage, Danior thought as he saw the shadowed copse of trees rising from the mist. The warm bread and cheese lay comfortingly inside him, but as the driver reined the horses to a halt, Danior's fears for his sister returned and he was shaking as he jumped to the ground.

Lady Moreland looked around in surprise as the driver handed her down from the brougham. "I don't see any caravans, Danior," she said. "Are you sure this is where your people are camped?"

"The caravans moved on last autumn, milady," he answered.

"But—where is Chavi?"

"There's an old tumbledown cottage. I'll show you." He wasn't sure whether to offer her his hand, so instead led the way through the trees, trying to select the easiest route around downed branches, dead logs, and drifts of decayed leaves.

When they came to the clearing where three walls of a stone cottage stood, he heard the Countess's swiftly indrawn breath. There was no roof to the walls, and his sister lay on a bed of dried leaves and ferns.

Chavi's bloated body twisted this way and that as spasms of pain ripped through her. Her long dark hair was a damp tangled mass framing her sweat-streaked face, and her lower lip was bitten raw. A low moan of agony escaped her and she clawed at her belly as if demons were inside her.

Her eyes swiveled slowly in the direction of her brother, then found Lady Moreland. Chavi gave a great shuddering sigh.

"We're here, Chavi, we're here," Danior cried, rushing to her side and dropping to his knees.

As swiftly as he'd moved, Lady Moreland reached his sister at almost the same instant. "Oh, my poor dear girl," she said softly, picking up Chavi's hand and massaging it. "Danior, quickly, gather wood and light a fire, then fetch some water from the brook. I see a pot over there that we can heat it in." To her waiting driver, she added, "Go directly to the village and get the doctor. Bring him back here and tell him we'll need a carriage large enough for someone to lie down in. Go, man—hurry."

"She's dying, isn't she?" Danior said, feeling tears sting the backs of his eyes again.

"No, Danior, Chavi isn't going to die. She's about to give birth to a baby," Lady Moreland responded calmly. "And we must help her because it's almost time."

3

Sarah stared at the unfamiliar reflection in the mirror of her hotel room in New York. With her hair coiled into a bun and a lacy jabot at the throat of her ivory silk blouse, she appeared to herself to be a slightly stern stranger, intent upon some important quest and not about to be hindered in its execution.

Only the calluses on her hands remained to remind her of sixteen years as the wife of a Chiricahua Apache chief and the mother of his favorite son.

Perhaps, too, there was a hunted wariness in her eyes that reflected the desperation of these past months of running and hiding. She was too thin by far for current fashion, but years of hard work and being constantly on the move did not produce indolent curves.

She was glad that Sam Rutherford had decided to come East with them. On the day they were to board a train in Willcox, Arizona, Sam had surprised her by saying without preamble, "It's not too late to change your mind, Sarah. Stay here—make a new life with your son in country you know. Hakan was born here, after all. Your English husband has a new wife, a new family. But even apart from that monumental problem, you'll be ostracized by English society as soon as the word gets out that you lived as a squaw."

"In the same way I'll be ostracized here?" she'd asked. "You're forgetting that Hakan is my English husband's first-born son, his heir to the title and lands owned by the Merrins. It's time I stopped depriving him of his birthright."

Sam had given her a long look of assessment that didn't succeed in masking his growing awareness of her as a woman. "There must have been times during all those years when you could have escaped and made your way to Fort Bowie or a stage station."

"After the first year, when escape was impossible, I didn't want to leave," she said simply, and knew by his slight wince that her answer wasn't what he wanted to hear, despite his liberal views toward the Apaches.

Then he surprised her still further by saying, "Then maybe I'll go East with you. It's time I visited my folks in upstate New York." He paused. "I haven't seen my daughter for five years."

That too was a surprise. Not only did Sam not sound like an easterner, but she'd had no idea he had been married. Sensing the unspoken questions, he went on, "I came out West when I was very young—did a little hunting, trapping, worked for the Butterfield Stage for a while before I got interested in Indian affairs. I married a half-Indian woman. She died when our daughter Bly was born."

"Your daughter lives with your parents?"

"Yes. They didn't approve of either my way of life or my wife. I should've gone back to visit Bly before this. . . . God knows what they've filled her head with by now."

"Was your wife half Apache?"

"No. She had a Kickapoo mother who'd been taken captive by the Navajos. I guess that was one of the reasons I was interested in you and Hakan."

Sam had left to visit his daughter and parents, but he'd promised to return to New York before their ship sailed. Sarah missed his reassuring presence.

Someone knocked on her hotel door and she called, "Come in," expecting the visitor to be her son.

Instead, her brother-in-law, Philip, entered the room. His lazy blue eyes flickered over her briefly and he smiled. "What a transformation! I'd have passed you in the hall without recognizing you."

Unsure how to respond to his comment, Sarah asked, "Is Hakan ready?"

"Randolph and I aren't the world's best valets," Philip answered. "But yes, your son is dressed in a suit and shirt. We even persuaded him that shoes would be more suitable for the ship than moccasins. Randolph has taken him to the barber. I simply didn't have the heart."

"Thank you. Shall I go to them?"

"Let Randolph and the barber handle it. I'd like to talk to you privately, if I may. Your son has been so protective of you I was afraid to suggest it in his presence. Will you join me for a glass of sherry? I'd offer you tea, but the tea in this country is atrocious. I don't know what they do to it."

"Thank you, it's been a long time since I've had a glass of sherry."

Five minutes later, as Sarah sipped her sherry, Philip said, "I must say I admire your fortitude. A lesser woman would simply have given up the ghost under such an ordeal."

"The Apaches treated me kindly, in their own way."

"I wasn't referring to the Apaches. I meant the ordeal of the past couple of days since your friend Mr. Rutherford departed and left you to the tender mercies of Randolph and me."

Sarah placed her glass on the table in front of her. "You've been very considerate. It wasn't an ordeal."

Philip raised an eyebrow. "You don't think Randolph has been a bit too forceful in suggesting that you should give up the idea of returning to England? I feel I might have acted as a better buffer between you."

"It's understandable. He loves his sister and is afraid I'll make trouble for her." For a fleeting instant the distant Jean, faceless and formless, floated through Sarah's mind. A woman who had borne twins seemed formidable, invincible perhaps. Sarah added, "Besides, Hakan will displace Randolph's nephew as heir."

"When Randolph offered you money to stay here, I thought your son was going to kill him. You handled the boy very well. Averted a nasty incident."

"I merely persuaded Hakan that he must make allowances

for Randolph's lack of good manners." She knew from the flicker of amusement in Philip's eyes that he was contemplating the comparison of manners between a boy he considered to be a savage and an English gentleman. Sarah, who had lived in both cultures, had her own views about which was more civilized.

Philip stretched his long legs out in front of him and stared into the rich amber liquid in his glass. "The wine reminds me of the color of the walls of Merrinswood. Do you remember?"

"Yes," she answered softly. "I never forgot."

"Tell me, how was it that Hakan was accepted as the chief's son? I mean, after all, a fair-haired, blue-eyed Apache must be unusual, to say the least."

Sarah was too far removed from the mores of English society to be embarrassed to answer. "The Apaches do not believe a woman can become pregnant from a single act of intercourse. They believe pregnancy is cumulative . . . it takes many times of being with a man to conceive a child."

Philip's mouth twitched slightly and he blinked. He was either amused by the information or astonished at her candor, she decided. Perhaps both.

"I was only a few weeks along when I was captured," she went on. "Seven months passed before Hakan's birth. In the Apache culture, if a woman is with more than one man before the birth of her baby, then each man is partly the father of the child."

"Fascinating. And your son's physical differences to his Indian father were totally discounted?"

"To the Apache, a man's character is more important than what he looks like. Hakan was his Indian father's son by virtue of his courage. Even as a little boy he was brave and fearless. The Apaches knew that Hakan's courage had come from their chief . . . certainly not from his white-eyes father."

Interest flickered over Philip's features. "Are you inferring that old Richard disgraced himself in their eyes? That he was cowardly?"

Sarah pushed the wineglass away. She'd forgotten how alcohol loosened the tongue. "I'm uncomfortable talking about Richard when he isn't present."

"Tell me, what really happened sixteen years ago? I honestly believe Richard thought you were dead."

"What did he say happened?" Her tone was measured, careful not to betray any hint of emotion.

"That a band of Indian raiders attacked the stagecoach in which you were traveling. That the driver managed to get into a rocky gulch and hold off the attackers for a while. During the night—when apparently the Indians are too afraid of evil spirits to fight—Richard attempted to go for help. By the time he'd wandered around the desert for a while and was found by some prospectors, it was too late to save anyone aboard the stagecoach."

"He told you my body was found?"

Philip looked uncomfortable. "It seems the Indians attacked the stagecoach as vengeance for a raid on one of their camps when soldiers killed their women and children. The passengers on the stagecoach were mutilated, their bodies burned."

Sarah was silent, contemplating Richard's story. She knew the years had a habit of dulling the edges of memory, and people sometimes arranged events in their minds the way they wanted to perceive them. Richard, for all his other faults, had never been a liar. Perhaps this was merely the way his family, including Philip, had dealt with the long-ago event.

"What really happened?" Philip asked again, leaning forward.

"I was captured. A young chief desired me, although he already had two wives. At first I was little more than a slave, but in time he made me his wife."

Philip shrugged. "So be it. I don't blame you for your reticence. But I do wish you'd corroborated Richard's account of the attack."

Sarah had been watching the door for Hakan's arrival, when she saw Sam Rutherford come into the lounge, leading a little girl by the hand. Sarah waved for Sam and his daughter to join them.

Sam looked different in a suit and starched collar, and not entirely comfortable. The little girl was a rather plain child, but perhaps her scowl gave that impression. Sam introduced her and then said apologetically, "Bly's a bit unhappy about missing school, but I wanted her to meet you and Hakan."

There was a sudden commotion at the entrance to the hotel, where Sir Randolph Leighton was angrily ordering Hakan to return immediately to the barbershop. Her son glanced down at Randolph's hand, clutching the sleeve of his new serge suit. Then Hakan brushed Randolph's hand away from him as though swatting a fly. He strode through the curious spectators in the lobby toward the open lounge where his mother and uncle sat. Sam and his daughter were still standing, the little girl now wide-eyed.

Hakan's red-gold hair still hung past his shoulders, catching the light from the chandeliers overhead. He stopped in front of them, nodded briefly to Sam, ignored Bly, glowered at his uncle, then said to his mother, "If my hair is to be cut, I wish you to do it. I'm not yet ready to trust a white-eyes near my throat with . . . what do they call the cutting tool?"

"Scissors," Sarah replied. "We'll talk about the haircut later. But first sit with us until I've finished my sherry."

Philip raised his hand to motion for a waiter as Hakan and the Rutherfords sat down. Randolph, evidently exasperated, did not join them. Philip said casually, "You're a little old to have your hair cut by your mother, old man. You really—"

"My name is Bly Rutherford," Sam's daughter interrupted. "And your manners are terrible. Just because you lived with the Indians doesn't mean you can go around ignoring people. I thought my father and the other Indian agents were getting schools built on the reservations. Didn't you get taught any manners?"

Hakan looked at her in astonishment. "*My* manners are terrible? Small squaws should be seen and not heard."

"*Have* you been to school or not?" Bly asked tartly. "My grandfather says we've got to stop coddling the Indians— especially the Apache, because they're the most bloodthirsty."

"Bly," Sam warned, "you mind your own manners. Hakan—Lord Moreland—isn't Apache, but you're part Kickapoo, much as your grandfather would like you to forget it."

"No, I have not been to one of your schools," Hakan said. "Nor do I intend to go."

"If you'd lived in England," Philip put in mildly, "you'd have been away in boarding school for the past seven or eight years. I should think your father will want you to make up for lost time as quickly as possible."

Hakan's eyes showed a flash of steel. "I know about the white-eyes schools. Many of the *Tin-ne-ah* were put on reservations, the children sent to schools. My father took us into the mountains of Mexico so we would escape that fate."

To the hovering waiter Philip said, "Please bring the young lady and gentleman a glass of ginger ale. And another carafe of sherry." He turned bemused eyes on his nephew. "Your—Apache—father did you a disservice. A proper education is essential for the fulfillment of one's life."

"It is not the Life-way of the *Tin-ne-ah*."

"It's *our* life's way."

"I know of your Life-way. My father said that you begin to work when you are children, in your schools—and you work there until you are men in order to begin fresh work. You work hard in order to learn to work well. After you become a man your labor of life commences."

Philip smiled. "How do you perceive our life work?"

"You build houses and towns and ships and many goods. Then after you have all this you die and leave them behind. We call this slavery. You are slaves from the time you begin to talk until you die. But the Apache is as free as the wind. We never work. Our wants are few and easily met. The river, the wood, and the plain yield all we require."

Watching, Sarah saw Philip's mouth slacken somewhat. He made no comment, but then what could he say?

The child, Bly, however, jumped into the silence. "What nonsense! You'll never be able to live in our world unless you go to school. I *love* school," she added smugly.

Sam looked at Sarah and said awkwardly, "Her teachers say she's very smart. I guess my folks are bound and determined Bly's going to get the education they thought I should have had, even though she is a girl."

The waiter brought the ginger ale and Hakan took a sip, wrinkled his nose, and put the glass down.

Bly stared at Hakan. "Well, *are* you going to get a haircut? It's far too long, you know."

"Bly!" Sam pleaded. Sarah felt sorry for him. The child was rudely outspoken, but she understood Sam's reluctance to discipline his daughter, having neglected her for so long.

Philip got out his gold pocket watch and looked at the time. "Why don't we have an early dinner so there will be enough time to take care of the haircut? We should turn in early tonight, as we have to be aboard the liner early tomorrow."

"I will not eat fish," Hakan said.

Philip sighed. "Yes, you've made that perfectly clear. Fish are the same as snakes and lizards to you and therefore forbidden. Something about the spirits of bad women, wasn't it? My dear nephew, what are we going to do with you in England? I fear our rather structured society isn't prepared for such a splendid savage."

"He *is* a savage, isn't he?" Bly said gleefully.

Red-faced, Sam rose and said, "Bly and I have already eaten. I'm sorry we can't stay until the ship sails tomorrow, but I have to get her back for school."

Sarah stood up and embraced him briefly. "Good-bye Sam. Thank you again for everything."

"You know how to find me—if you ever need me."

Sarah was touched by his concern. She had a feeling that his remark would sustain her on what was bound to be a journey riddled with doubts and fraught with tensions.

Halfway across the Atlantic, the Cunard liner wallowed in heavy seas, which kept many passengers belowdecks and caused an epidemic of *mal de mer*.

If the boy named Hakan—Randolph couldn't bring himself to think of the wretched creature as Richard's son—felt seasick, he was too stoic to show it. But he kept to himself, spending most of his time in his cabin. Philip, looking green and ill, also secluded himself in his stateroom, leaving Sarah and Randolph alone.

Randolph watched Sarah steadfastly pacing the deck outside the windows of the main salon. The wind had whipped strands of her light hair free of the heavy woolen muffler wrapped about her head and shoulders, and she leaned into the gusts like a slender willow bending the wrong way; which, he reflected, was exactly what she was doing with her life.

He disliked the ambivalent feelings he had toward the woman. He wanted to hate her, but found himself curiously intrigued by her. There was about her that indefinable air of . . . dignity was the only way he could describe it. True dignity, the kind that was only achieved by a noble spirit. He sensed intelligence and a resolute determination beneath her detached exterior in the way one sensed the tensile strength of a tough fabric. Jean would be no match for this woman.

On a sudden whim, he pushed open the salon door and went out on deck. The icy chill of the wind took away his breath for a moment, and he grabbed the damp rail for support as the ship rolled in the giant swells.

When Sarah had completed her circle of the deck and returned to where he stood, she nodded to him briefly. He spoke loudly to be heard over the whistle of wind and hollow roar of the ocean. "You've never asked about her—about my sister, Jean. Have you no curiosity about Richard's wife?"

Sarah regarded him with a probing stare. She replied, "I have great sympathy for her."

She continued to walk and Randolph followed her progress until she disappeared down a companionway. Damn. *Damn*. Why couldn't she have been an imposter, or a madwoman, or anything other than what she was? Why couldn't she have been blown overboard and lost at sea? She and her damned changeling son.

Randolph turned back toward the salon, the thought hammering at his brain. Perhaps . . . oh, God, was he capable of it? The sweet, tormented face of his beloved sister was never far from his thoughts. Orphaned before they were ten years old, he and his twin, Jean, were bonded together in a way that few others could understand. There was nothing she wouldn't do for him, and as for his love for her. . . .

Shivering, Randolph hurried into the salon. Sarah and her offspring hadn't reached England yet. They would be at sea for several more days. Who could tell what might happen?

4

Chavi was floating, somewhere over the moors. There was a bank of purple heather down below her, and she longed to sink into it and smell the fragrance of the earth. But she knew she was being borne away to hell. Already, fiery demons were tearing at her vitals.

She thought perhaps she saw her little brother's face, his

lips moving in a silent plea for her to return to him. Such a pinched little face, so hungry, so loyal. A seven-year-old boy shouldn't be witness to her shame. But when her father had cast her out of the tribe and the painted caravans had moved on without her, Danior had run away and returned to take care of her, and she hadn't known how to send him back. Nor had she wanted to.

Danior thought she had a tumor growing in her belly and she had prayed so hard that he would never learn that her malaise was caused by the seed of Lord Moreland.

Chavi thought, too, that she caught a glimpse of the sad, sweet face of Lady Moreland, but perhaps that was an illusion within the dream.

Voices intruded, calling to her to do something—but what? She didn't care; she was too weary.

The images of memory came and went. Lord Moreland, astride his big black horse riding pell mell across the moors, hounds in full cry, and the poor wee fox running for his life.

Lord Moreland's mount balking at a rain-swollen brook and sending his rider flying from his saddle. Herself crouching in the shallow water washing her clothes and finding a golden-haired god of a man suddenly sprawling in front of her. . . .

"Where were you, gypsy girl, when I needed you to tell my fortune?"

"Fortune, sir?"

"Warning me that I should be careful crossing water today."

They had laughed together as though they were equals.

The caravans had spent the summer camped along the river. The women traveled to the village and farms, telling fortunes, selling the wooden clothespegs made by the men. The men did odd jobs, helped with the harvest.

Chavi's mother had died giving birth to Danior, and their father had never forgiven the boy for living when his beloved wife had not. Chavi was their housekeeper, and because she looked so much like her mother, her father found her presence a constant trial. He was an embittered man, their father, a man who would have made a pact with the devil himself if he could have exchanged both of his children for his dead wife.

Perhaps that was why it had been so easy to slip away to

the woods to meet Lord Moreland. Perhaps that was why Chavi had needed him so much. Lord Moreland was powerful, strong, wise, and full of laughter; so different from the silent, brooding man always ready to crush the joy of life out of her. How wonderful to have a make-believe father who would talk to her and explain things to her the way Lord Moreland did. He'd been so kind, so loving.

Until the look in his eyes had changed—and Chavi had been both frightened and thrilled by the new way his blue eyes had caressed her. The summer slipped by like a lovely dream.

"You're so beautiful, Chavi. Your hair is like black silk and I could lose myself in those midnight eyes."

"Please don't touch me there."

"Why not? It makes me happy. And you like it, you know you do."

"Please, sir, don't—or I shan't come back here."

She had looked down at his hand, its skin so fair with tiny golden hairs like a sprinkling of sunlight, stroking the honey-colored skin of her breast. Fascinated, like a rabbit cornered by a ferret, she watched his hand bring the dark center of her nipple to a tiny peak of almost unbearable ecstasy.

"*Oh, Chavi was a gypsy . . . and she lived upon the moors,*"

Delighted, she heard him insert her name into the poem, in place of Meg Merrilies. His wonderful voice whispered in her ear, and all the while his hand worked a spell on her.

"Please . . ." she begged.

"Do you know your Keats, Chavi? *Her bed it was the brown heath turf, And her house was out of doors.*"

He pulled her down on the soft summer turf and she could not resist. "*Her brothers were the craggy hills, Her sisters larchen trees, Alone with her great family, She liv'd as she did please. Do you, Chavi? Do you live as you please?*"

She hadn't been able to get up and run away, not even when his other hand reached under her skirts.

"I—have to save myself—for my husband," she gasped as he found the searing core of her needing and wanting.

"Darling girl, the little I take from you won't be missed by any lout of a gypsy husband, believe me."

Then the words hadn't had any meaning for her. Nothing

had had any meaning beyond her own throbbing flesh. Nothing except that he was touching her, and his body joined with hers in the way she desired, and the golden gorse and purple heather and the green, green grass and the sky and sun and everything were part of her and part of him and the two of them together.

The blossoms had died and cold winds were blowing down from the north to herald the winter on the day she had taken all of her courage in her hands and gone to the great golden house of Merrinswood.

But at the iron gates her courage had faltered and she'd lingered there a while, hoping to see Lord Moreland come galloping across the moors.

Lord Moreland didn't come. A carriage bearing a pale, lovely woman rolled up the lane and came to a halt. Eyes of deepest violet-blue regarded her gravely. "Are you looking for someone, my dear? May we help you?"

Tongue-tied, Chavi had hung her head.

The lady with the lovely eyes said, "I am Jean Merrin, Lady Moreland. Are you camped with the gypsies by the river? What is your name?"

"Chavi, milady." She bobbed a curtsey and at the same time saw that there were two children in the carriage, a boy and a girl about Danior's age. The little girl's appearance didn't register on Chavi's numbed brain as she stared in startled recognition at the boy. The same fair hair touched with auburn, the same lake-blue eyes, the same handsome features. He was Lord Moreland's son, and the little girl was his sister. The lady with burnished brown hair and the sad blue-violet eyes was Lord Moreland's wife, his Countess.

Why hadn't Chavi conjured them up in her mind before? Why hadn't she known how wrong it was to steal—if only for a fleeting moment—what belonged to his wife? In her shame, Chavi could only stand there and wish for a bog to swallow her.

"Well, Chavi, you haven't told us how we may be of assistance to you."

"Nothing. I—I don't know why I come here, mum."

She turned, ready to flee, and Lady Moreland called after her, "If you need anything, Chavi—if you're in trouble, you can come to me. Please remember that."

When Chavi's pains began and didn't diminish for two

nights and a day, she had remembered the kindness in the lady's eyes and sent Danior to fetch her.

Had she come? Was it truly her kind face that Chavi saw, or was it only part of the nightmare of fear and pain into which her recklessness had plunged her?

Gentle hands touched her and a voice, soft but insistent, urged, "Push, Chavi—push with all of your might. Help your baby. Push, push . . ."

Someone moaned, then whimpered in hopeless anguish. Was it herself? Ministering hands mopped her brow. "Good, good. Keep it up. It will soon be over, Chavi. This is the worst of the pain. Push, harder . . ."

One long, never-to-be-forgotten pain that had no beginning, no end, a mortal wound that was killing her . . . Then, astonishingly, it eased, and she heard the thin wail of an infant's first breath.

"Chavi, oh, Chavi, you have the most beautiful daughter. Lie still, there'll be a little more pain as you pass the afterbirth."

Struggling to raise eyelids that seemed made of lead, Chavi felt the sweet weight of a tiny body upon her breast. Her arms closed around her daughter and she sighed, unsure whether to be happy or sorrowful that the two of them were still alive.

Jean faced her husband in his private study. He hadn't risen when she entered the dark-paneled room, and she ignored his invitation to take the armchair at the opposite side of the fireplace, preferring to stand for an interview that she knew would be painful.

With her diminutive height, it wasn't often she had an opportunity to look down on Richard, and if ever there was a time she wanted that advantage, it was now.

"From the look on your face," Richard drawled, placing his brandy glass down on the table beside him, "I'd say we're in for another of those wretched oh-you-swine-look-what-you've-done-now talks." He paused, then added with an elaborate charade of casual interest, "Surely the ship from America can't have docked at Liverpool yet?"

"You don't remember my coming into your room early this morning?" Jean asked, knowing quite well that he did.

"Oh, yes," he answered offhandedly. "Something about gypsies, wasn't it?"

"Not gypsies, one gypsy girl. She can't be more than fifteen or sixteen years old. Her name is Chavi. She gave birth to your daughter today."

He stared at her for a long time, waiting for her to continue, his face a mask. He wielded the weapon of silence in a manner more deadly than some men battered with their fists, but for once she found the strength to wait him out.

At length he said, "What utter nonsense. Surely you don't believe some itinerant—"

"Yes," Jean said, "I do. Actually, Chavi hasn't accused you of being her baby's father, but I knew of your affair with her last summer. You boasted of it during one of your drinking episodes with Randolph and he told me about it. The gypsy girl came here, to Merrinswood, four months ago. I think she came to ask for your help, but unfortunately it was I who found her at the gates."

Richard shrugged and picked up his brandy again. "A girl-child, you say?"

Jean knew what he was thinking. She said, "Pity the child wasn't a boy. He'd undoubtedly have inherited all of the physical traits of Merrin males—you all do, don't you? A fact that makes it difficult for the rest of the world to know which of you is a villain and which a hero. But your daughters are much more individual. This one is, too. A beautiful, black-haired, olive-skinned baby who will probably have the dark eyes of her mother."

He closed his eyes as though already bored with the subject. "My dear Jean, since I'm a normal male and you're unwilling to fulfill your wifely duties to me, you're hardly in a position to complain about my little peccadillos. Do I have to remind you that refusal of conjugal rights is grounds for divorce?"

She felt the color drain from her face but managed to keep her voice level. "That's not fair. You know very well that Doctor McGreal—"

"Yes, yes, your dour Scot and his dire predictions. A convenient method of keeping me out of your bed while he lusts after you in the realm of his fantasies but isn't man enough to put them into practice."

"I refuse to get into that ridiculous discussion with you again, Richard. The question is what we're to do about Chavi and her baby."

"Perhaps you'd better tell me what you did today and then we can go on from there."

Jean's hands tightened on the folds of her skirt. He might have been discussing the results of a casual mating of his favorite stallion. Anger welled up inside her, threatening to erupt in a violence of which she was physically incapable, yet somehow knew she could find a way to express. Oh, if only she could have been as indifferent to him as he was to her.

"I helped her with the birth. There was no one else. Your daughter was born where no doubt she was conceived . . . on a bed of ferns in the woods."

His eyes swept over her, grudging admiration registering in his speculative gaze. "You performed the duties of a midwife? How droll!"

She went on, "Doctor McGreal has taken Chavi and her baby into his house."

Instantly, his expression changed. "Ah, the saintly doctor. Of course, he would rush to aid the unfortunate, wouldn't he? What would you have me do, pay him a substantial fee?"

As much as she wanted to defend Andrew McGreal's motives, she knew better than to fall into the trap of discussing them with her husband. Ignoring the comment, she said, "As soon as she's able to travel, I'd like to send Chavi and the child to live somewhere far from here. You must provide the money for their support."

"Is that all?" He laughed. "I'm surprised you didn't want them to come and live here at Merrinswood. We could have founded a proper menagerie, with Sarah and her Red Indian son and a couple of gypsies. Do you suppose we could import a few Abyssinians also?"

"Stop it!" Jean said, her voice trembling. "How can you be so unfeeling? Can't you know what the very existence of your first wife—and your gypsy mistress—does to my pride? I could wish them dead if I were to allow myself. But they are both women to whom you owe a debt. I will remind myself of that fact and pray for the strength to endure the consequences of your actions."

"How sporting of you, old girl." Richard drained his brandy glass, reached for the decanter, and added in his most infuriatingly disinterested manner, "Do whatever you will with the gypsies and I'll foot the bill. But if you imagine for a moment that I'll welcome Sarah and her half-breed here—"

"The cable from America—" Jean began.

"I won't meet with Sarah or the boy," Richard snapped, his studied lethargy vanishing in a flash of chilling anger. "Don't mention the possibility to me again. In the eyes of the law she's dead. Our marriage, my dear Jean, was legal, not bigamous. Sarah has no claim on me. Philip will handle the matter and set them up in a small house somewhere. That is"—Richard's sensual lips curved into a sly smile—"if that hotheaded brother of yours allows him to bring them to England."

5

Hakan moved with surefooted ease across the heaving deck of the vast ocean liner. Darkness shrouded the ship, and those passengers who had acquired what they called their sea legs were engaged in their various games or dancing in the brightly lit common rooms belowdecks. Unaccustomed to either the harsh artificial light or the tribal rites of the whites, he walked to the stern, enjoying the solitude of the night.

Five days out of New York and the worst of the squalls had passed, but great swells continued to roll over the gray surface of the sea, causing many of the passengers to refuse their food and remain in their cabins. Hakan had battled the same malaise at first, although he would have died rather than let anyone know.

After a couple of days, the Englishman Randolph approached him and suggested that his belly would churn less miserably if he were to get out on deck in the fresh air and fix his eyes on the horizon, which did not pitch and sway like the ship.

Surprisingly, this proved to be true. But it troubled Hakan that Randolph—brother of the woman who had taken the place of *Sons-ee-ah-ray* in his English father's wickiup—had been the one to tell him how to end the seasickness.

To do a favor implied friendship, but Hakan was well aware that Randolph Leighton was his sworn enemy. Therefore, the favor was double-edged and its value had to be carefully weighed. Hakan had learned from bitter experience that the forked tongue of the white-eyes was no myth. His own father, weary of the endless battles, and longing for peace for his followers, had been lured to his death under a flag of truce.

A slight sound intruded upon Hakan's thoughts and he tensed, pausing to look back over his shoulder. Shadows moved, timbers creaked, and the engines drove the great vessel through the water. But there was no sign of any other passenger abroad in the night.

It seemed to him that since he'd left his cabin to wander about the ship eyes constantly followed him, often felt rather than observed. A nagging, persistent sense of danger refused to leave him, and he knew it was always prudent to respect such warnings.

When he reached the stern he leaned on the rail to watch the wake of the ship cut a frothing silver path to the dark horizon. It was as if the bright ribbon of his life connecting him to the shore he'd left behind was stretched so far that it must soon break, and Hakan felt an aching sadness overwhelm him.

The skin on the back of his neck suddenly tingled and he cursed inwardly that he'd allowed himself that moment of distraction. There was no other warning before his attacker hurled himself out of the darkness. Arms went around Hakan's waist, lifting him from the deck.

He felt himself pushed over the slippery rail. The wind whistled in his ears, and below him the dark writhing mass of water beckoned.

As his ribs hit the rail, he bent his body, flung his arms forward, and felt his hands touch the damp circle of a life preserver. At the same instant he kicked backward with his feet and felt his heels connect with soft flesh. There was a grunt of pain and his assailant fell away from him.

Hakan swung himself back onto the deck, landing on his feet with the precision of a cat. He turned to face the man who now clutched his stomach and gasped with pain. The yellow glow of a lantern illuminated Sir Randolph Leighton's contorted features.

They stared at each other, all pretense abandoned. Randolph was heavier than Hakan, with a man's fully developed muscles, but the boy had the advantage of height and lifelong physical conditioning. Without the element of surprise, Randolph faced a formidable opponent, and they both knew it.

Randolph's fists came up, then he lunged, but missed Hakan's jaw. Hakan circled him, arms curved at his sides in readiness. It was clear now why this man had wanted him to spend more time out on deck.

"You never should have been born—you hear me?" Randolph said between ragged breaths. "I would have been doing you a favor. Have you any idea of what awaits you in England? You'll be hated and despised by everyone you meet. You're a savage. You don't belong with civilized people."

Hakan continued to move around him in a diminishing circle, knowing that prolonging the anticipation of a blow was an efficient way of immobilizing an enemy.

"If you don't care about yourself," Randolph cried, "then think of what will happen to your mother. In the eyes of our society she's a whore—"

In a flash, all that his mother had urged him to forget, all that she had strived to teach him about how he must behave in his new life vanished. Hakan's blood ran pure and true. He was of the *Tin-ne-ah*. He was Apache. A low growl came from his throat and he sprang, fastening his hands around the man's neck, determined that his enemy would die.

The sound of footsteps running across the wooden deck and his mother's voice crying, *"Hakan! No!"* made him slacken his hold.

Only the use of his given name stopped him from throttling the man. An Apache must heed such use of his given name, which was never uttered aloud unless the moment was of the most earnest gravity.

A second figure emerged from the shadows and his Uncle Philip appeared. Hakan's hands were still around Randolph's throat.

Philip said quietly, "Why don't we all go inside where it's warm and talk this over?"

"This man tried to kill me. A cowardly attack when my

back was turned," Hakan said. "We have nothing to talk about."

"Let him go, please," his mother begged. "Philip—take Randolph away, quickly. Leave us alone."

Philip grabbed Randolph's arm. "Come along, old man. Let Sarah take care of the boy. You look as if you could use a stiff brandy."

Hakan looked into his mother's pleading face and released his hold on Randolph, who was immediately dragged away by Philip.

Sarah closed the space between them and put her arms around him. Hakan said, "He tried to push me over the rail."

"You must be on your guard against him in future," Sarah said. "But you must also remember what I told you about English laws. You cannot take vengeance personally. You must allow the law to deal with him."

"And where is the law now? Is the law here, on this ship?"

"We could report the incident to the captain, but I think it would be better not to."

He was silent, fighting an inner turbulence that refused to subside. After a few moments his mother's arms fell away and she stood back, waiting. "Randolph is afraid of us—of what we're going to do," she said. "He's just shown us how afraid."

"He said we shall be hated in England."

"I expect he's right."

"Then why do we go there?"

"You know why. Come on, let's walk around the deck until your blood cools down."

They strolled side by side, and Hakan's eyes searched the night. His mother asked, "You're not afraid he'll come back?"

"No. It is this vast sea that fills me with awe."

"Think of it as a desert," she suggested. "In a way it is. A desert is a place without fresh water, as is the ocean."

"How wise you are. When one can compare the unknown with something familiar, it becomes less troubling."

"The sea isn't quite as rough this evening. Perhaps tomorrow we can begin to study the books we bought in New York. We must continue your lessons."

Hakan bit back a protest, knowing that his mother would

not be deterred by it. There had been subtle changes in her since she had cast off her squaw's buckskins and turned herself back into a white-eyes woman. Her determination was strong and her will unflagging to fashion him into an Englishman.

Or perhaps the change in her had begun on the day the small party of braves had found the butchered body of her husband. The braves had brought her a prisoner from the fort, a white-eyes soldier, so that she could torture and kill the man. This was the Apache way. The squaws of fallen braves were given prisoners to kill in order to exorcise their grief. But *Sons-ee-ah-ray* had refused to kill the man. Perhaps that was the moment she had resumed her old identity. Perhaps that was when she had decided she would make her son into a powerful white-eyes chief.

"Yes, we can look at the books," he told her. "I'll learn what I need to know in order to deal with your Englishmen. They won't call me savage, I promise you."

She stopped and took his hands in hers for a moment, looking at him with a fierce and loving gaze. "You are inferior to no one. Never think that you are. It's going to be difficult and bewildering when we reach England, but don't let anything or anyone intimidate you. You are the son of two great chiefs. You were born to lead, never to follow. Never bow down to any man."

He slipped his arm around his mother's shoulders to shelter her from the cold wind. "I'll have you to teach me the English customs I need to know. All of my days of walking the earth, I have been learning the wisdom of the Life-way. I will be a great chief, I promise you."

He thought her eyes misted a little, but perhaps it was the biting chill of the wind. She said, "Do you remember Hell's Canyon?"

The seemingly abrupt change of subject, he knew, would have a purpose in his mother's mind. Her thoughts were never the random images of most of the women he'd known. He answered, "Yes. The first time I saw it I thought it was a place of no life. Great boulders, barren sand, sheer walls of granite—like a dried-out split in the earth. No plants, no animals. A desolate place."

"And then, three or four years later, when we were again in that part of the country, do you remember the transformation? There had been a heavy snowfall in the mountains, much rain that year, and new washes were cut into the hills. The life-giving water rushed down through Hell's Canyon, and where it flowed the desert willow and mesquite and many kinds of plants grew. There were hundreds of birds and the birds had brought more seeds to scatter."

"There were deer and antelope, and we camped at the mouth of the canyon," Hakan said, caught up in the magic of memory. "And my father killed a mountain lion and made quivers for our arrows from its hide."

"In a few short years, the barren canyon was transformed into a place of beauty," his mother said. "Life is like that, too. When I'm not here with you, always remember that the bleak and barren times will give way to new wonders, new paths to tread that will bring joy and happiness."

"But you *will* be here with me to remind me of the rebirth of Hell's Canyon," he said in sudden alarm, afraid she had perhaps seen some omen that told her they must soon part.

"Yes. Yes, of course I will. Come on, let's go and unpack the books. I found one about the Arizona Territory."

They went to her cabin and Hakan was pleased with the pictures in the book, but when his mother read the words her eyes clouded and she angrily snapped the book shut.

"What is it?" Hakan asked, wanting to look at the pictures again. There had been a photograph of a particularly beautiful Chiricahua maiden, dressed for the Puberty Ceremony, and his eyes wished to linger upon her.

"Lies," his mother said, brushing her fist across her eyes. "Lies about the Apache."

He looked at her in surprise. "But you knew this was a trait of the white-eyes. How many times have they deceived us?"

She sighed deeply. "It's still hard to bear. You and I are white-eyes, by birth at least. Perhaps some day someone will write the truth about the *Tin-ne-ah*."

There was a tentative tap on the cabin door and when Sarah called, "Yes? What is it?" they heard Philip's voice asking if he could enter. Sarah responded and Hakan's uncle's face appeared around the door, wearing a conciliatory smile.

"I've come to apologize to you, old man. Randolph has

been properly told off and he's full of remorse. I think perhaps he'd had one too many after dinner."

"Attempted murder is too serious a matter for a mere apology," Sarah said. "And why hasn't he come here himself?"

Philip came into the cabin, closing the door behind him. "I believe he's afraid of your son. Look, it could get a bit messy if you were to bring charges—things are going to be difficult enough when we reach England without adding to the complications. Is there some way I can make it up to you?"

"Yes," Sarah said unexpectedly. "You can send a cable to Merrinswood and have Richard meet us in Liverpool—alone. No solicitors with legal precedents or petitions are to accompany him. I want a private interview with my husband."

Philip looked relieved. "Of course. I'll speak with the wireless operator at once. There should be enough time for Richard to get the wire and be in Liverpool when we dock."

"There's something else," Sarah went on. "Sir Randolph, you said, is Richard's estate steward."

"Yes. Richard hired him at the time of his marriage to Jean."

"I believe it would be a good idea for Randolph to start looking for another position," Sarah said, and even her son who knew and loved her was faintly chilled by the raw determination in her voice.

6

Doctor Andrew Donald McGreal listened carefully to the chronicle of symptoms recited by the well-dressed woman who sat on the other side of his desk.

"Palpitations, nervousness, insomnia . . ."

His surgery was crowded with patients today, but this particular one would be able to pay him for his services. He felt a certain whorish resentment about that. It was unfair that those who needed him least should occupy most of his time. Besides, he was anxious to clear out the surgery before Lord Moreland arrived to visit his gypsy mistress.

A sheet of glass protected the top of his desk, or perhaps it had been placed there by the secondhand dealer in a futile attempt to disguise nicks and scratches in the oak surface. Andrew's reflection gazed up at him from the glass, accusingly it seemed. As if to say, what happened to the bright, hardworking young man who was top of his class and was going to heal the world? Look at him, kowtowing to the rich so he could afford to treat a few of the poor.

In the dark glass his face was neither handsome nor ugly. It was an ordinary face with a high forehead, somewhat gaunt cheekbones, and—although it had been only his mother's opinion and therefore was discountable—sensitive eyes. Still, Jean—he now allowed himself to call Lady Moreland by her first name, at least in his thoughts—had once commented that her eyes were like windows that shone brightly, so that a troubled traveler might find his way to a safe haven. He had been happy for weeks remembering the remark and the shy way her own beautiful eyes had glowed when she made it.

He made appropriate comments to his wealthy hypochondriac patient, wrote her a prescription for some nerve medicine, and managed to get her out the door and into the hands of Mrs. Tremayne, who was his nurse, receptionist, and housekeeper.

Mrs. Tremayne, who hailed from the balmy Cornish coast and was perpetually cold in this bleak northern clime, was a no-nonsense widow of indeterminate age who had organized his life eight years ago when he arrived to set up practice in the village of Merrin Quarry, the ink on his diploma still wet.

She whisked the rest of his patients in and out with her customary efficiency, then came back and announced, "Your lunch is ready, Doctor McGreal. I've put it in the kitchen so we can keep the sitting room tidy in case his grace should arrive early."

"I'll just pop upstairs and visit Chavi first, Mrs. Tremayne."

She frowned. "Your lunch won't stay hot if you waste time talking to the girl. And you've quite a number of house calls to make before your evening surgery. Lord Moreland coming over is going to mean you'll be late getting started."

"Yes, thank you, Mrs. Tremayne." Her efficiency warranted his allowing her to mother him a little. As he reached the door, she called after him, "The seat of your trousers is getting shiny, Doctor. You'll be needing a warmer suit before winter. Your appearance—"

"Yes, I agree. I must see to it one of these days."

The third stair creaked and he stepped over it, in case the baby was sleeping, although he was well aware that newborns didn't require absolute silence. But Chavi and her baby were his sacred trust, deserving of special care. They were here as a favor to Jean—a woman who had brought a little light into that secret part of his mind where his loneliness dwelled.

There were four rooms upstairs. Chavi was in the smallest bedroom at the end of the hall. Pushing open the door, he saw that the baby was feeding energetically. Her small pink fist opened and closed against the darker skin of her mother's breast. Chavi's long black hair fell loosely about her slender shoulders and she gazed down at her child with a madonnalike wonder that Andrew felt few fifteen-year-olds in her position would have exhibited.

To preserve her privacy, he immediately withdrew, but Chavi called out to him, "Oh, please come in, Doctor. She's finished feeding."

He waited a discreet moment to enable her to button her nightgown, then stepped into the room. She gave him a radiant smile that broke his heart. She was so young, so very unworldly and vulnerable. Damn that womanizer for taking his careless pleasure with an innocent child!

"How are you feeling, Chavi?"

"Much, much better. I'd like to get up, please. I'm not used to lying abed."

The Romany women probably didn't lie around for long after childbirth, but he didn't want her looking too robust for Lord Moreland's visit. He said, "You're going to have a visitor today, Chavi. I want you to remain in bed when he comes."

Her almond-shaped eyes widened. "My father?"

"No, I'm sorry. No one seems to know where the caravans have gone."

"My little brother, Danior?"

"Danior was taken to Merrinswood, remember? I told you yesterday. He'll be taken care of until you're both able to travel."

Chavi's eyes clouded. "If my father doesn't come for us, we shan't be able to go back, Danior and me."

"Don't worry about anything now. You'll be taken care of, one way or another, I give you my word. Your visitor, Chavi, is Lord Moreland. He'll be here soon. Would you like me to remain with you when he comes? I believe it would be a good idea."

She bent to kiss the pulsing soft spot on her baby's tiny head, and said in a low voice, "I'd rather talk to him by myself, if you don't mind, Doctor."

"Very well. Mrs. Tremayne will bring up your lunch and I'll see you later on."

Andrew hurried down the stairs, feeling his anger return. In the split second before she had lowered her head, he'd seen the way Chavi's eyes lit up at the mention of Merrin's name. The same way Jean's eyes lit up. Damn it all, what did women see in a man who treated them so abominably?

At the back of his mind a voice whispered what they saw in Richard Merrin. A physique worthy of a Greek god—despite his dissipated ways—and a face a master sculptor might have imagined carving when he'd reached his zenith as an artist. Jean had once told him that Richard Merrin had courted her with a single-minded dedication that had, quite literally, swept her off her feet. What chance had there been for a naïve gypsy girl?

Before Andrew had finished eating Mrs. Tremayne's Cornish pasty, he heard carriage wheels grind on the cobbled street of terraced houses, and looked through the window to see Richard Merrin alighting from a gleaming brougham.

He heard his housekeeper's footsteps on the polished wood floor of the hall as she answered the doorbell. She would show Lord Moreland into the sitting room and take her time before announcing him, he knew, to allow the doctor to finish eating. Mrs. Tremayne constantly chided him for being too thin. At six feet two, he probably could have comfortably carried a few more pounds.

At least, he thought as he got up to go to the sitting room, he was tall enough to look Richard Merrin straight in the eye.

The Earl of Moreland paced restlessly back and forth in front of the sitting room fireplace, making the somber room seem even more colorless and spartan than it was. "Ah, there you are, McGreal. Where is Chavi? I don't have much time, so let's get on with it."

"Before we go upstairs," Andrew said, trying to keep his tone impersonal, "I'd like to know what it is you intend to say to her. I must warn you that I shan't stand by and allow you to bully my patient."

Merrin gave him a disarming smile, and for an instant Andrew reluctantly felt the charm of the man. He wondered how many women had been caught and lost in the full force of that smile. "My dear doctor, I simply wish to assure the young woman that she and her child will be provided for. I even brought a small gift. Not that I'm at all sure the infant is mine, you understand. You know how these gypsies are."

"The ones I've met have been as chaste as any well-bred Englishwoman," Andrew said. "Chavi is not much more than a bairn herself. A gentleman wouldn't have taken advantage of her."

"Oh, for God's sake, spare me the sermon. I didn't have to come here at all, did I? My long-suffering wife, with your help, was adequately taking care of the problem."

Any illusions Andrew might have had about Richard Merrin feeling remorse for his actions were immediately dispelled. "Perhaps," Andrew said stiffly, "it would be better to allow us to continue to do so? You may raise false hopes in Chavi."

"*Us?*" Merrin repeated, his blue eyes crinkling in amusement. "You feel somehow allied with my wife in this matter, I take it? Though it was she who acted as midwife, not you."

"And you, sir, acted contemptuously. The seduction of a child, and a gypsy at that, too ignorant and afraid to defend herself from your advances. How could you in all conscience have carnal knowledge of a child?"

"Carnal knowledge, old man?" Laughter bubbled near the surface of Merrin's voice, further infuriating Andrew. "Lord, I hope your medical experience is less archaic than your vocabulary. But then, I'm an incurable optimist. I already know that your standard treatment for your female patients is to cater to their hysteria."

Andrew battled an overwhelming urge to thrash the man,

but went on. "I agreed to act on Chavi's behalf to ensure that she and her baby are provided for. I understood from your wife that you would instruct your bankers to make such provision. I further understood that I was to send Chavi and the child to a place that would be unknown to you."

Merrin's pale blue eyes glinted like a rapier. "Yes, well, we'll see about that." The deceptively casual tone again aroused fears in Andrew that Jean had underestimated her husband's reaction to her plans for taking charge of the situation.

"I'll take you upstairs," Andrew said, turning to the door.

"Are you still in love with my wife?" Richard Merrin's voice struck him like a whip.

Andrew spun around, clenching his fists at his sides. "I won't dignify that accusation with a reply."

Merrin laughed. "But my dear fellow, you just told me all I needed to know."

"When the twins were born," Andrew said, knowing that his Scottish burr had returned, a sure sign that he was losing control of his anger, "and you allowed the midwife to maul your wife rather than calling me when it became obvious the birth was too difficult—"

"Yes, yes. We've been over that. You frightened Jean with dire predictions of what would happen if she were to share my bed."

"I pointed out—to both of you—that another pregnancy could prove fatal to her."

"And to Jean that meant she no longer had to fulfill her marital obligations to me."

"I also suggested that an operation—"

"No, dammit. I'll never allow you to use your butcher knife on my wife like some diseased brood mare. You'd better lead the way up to Chavi's room and on the way remember whose fault it is that I must turn to the likes of her for my satisfaction."

Andrew had to remind himself that little would be gained by anyone if he were to give in to his urge to strike the man.

Richard looked down at the young girl who lay on the narrow bed. On the floor was a large basket in which an infant slept. Behind him, the red-faced Scottish doctor, who looked as if he should be wearing a kilt and leading ten thousand wild highlanders into battle rather than tending the sick, shuffled his feet angrily.

"Well, Chavi, how are you?"

Her pinched face had softened somewhat, in that way that pregnancy and childbirth brought about. "Quite well, thank you, sir." Her eyes glanced proudly at the basket. "It's a girl, sir. I haven't named her yet."

Turning, Richard stared at the doctor until he left the room, then pulled a slim leatherbound volume from his pocket. "I brought you a present. Keats. Do you remember?"

"Yes," she answered, blushing. "You put my name in his poem. But sir, I don't know how to read."

He felt foolish, but dropped the book on her bed. "No matter. You know the words. I also brought this." He dangled from his finger a slender silver chain holding a filigree pendant. It was a delicate butterfly with tiny sapphire eyes.

"Oh, sir! It's lovely!" She clapped her hands in childlike pleasure.

Richard said, "Lean forward. I'll fasten it for you."

His hands brushed aside her silken hair, and he remembered the afternoons in the woods when he'd made love to her. How beautiful she was. Her hair was darker than Jean's, but he wondered now if there was some slight similarity between them that had attracted him. As though the gypsy were perhaps a rough copy, an unfinished sketch, an untutored facsimile of the real woman. But perhaps that was only in his imagination. The gypsy would be a beauty one day soon, whereas Jean's allure lay only in the false promise of her eyes. The exotically foreign almond-shaped eyes of the girl bore no resemblance to the wide indigo eyes of Jean, but then, neither did they regard him with that disconcertingly direct and honest gaze. Chavi's eyes adored him unconditionally. They worshiped him, and dammit, wasn't that the way it should be?

Why the hell hadn't she disappeared at the end of summer with the rest of her tribe? Instead here she was, along with her bastard, to cause trouble. Richard was well aware of the scandal, possibly even legal complications, that McGreal might precipitate. Especially when the lovesick doctor found out about that other woman and her child who were en route from America.

Richard thought of the cable he'd received from the ship

and wondered again how Jean would react to the news that her beloved son had been displaced as heir to Merrinswood. There was no telling what she might do, and he certainly didn't intend to let her have any more ammunition to use against him.

The gypsy girl was gazing at him expectantly. He said, "Chavi, you'll be staying here with the good doctor for a few days. Then I'll send someone for you and the baby."

Her eyes opened wide with delight. "You . . . you're going to take care of us yourself? I thought—her ladyship said—"

"Oh, you're going to be well taken care of, my dear. But I want you to keep our plans a secret. Not a word to the doctor, or my wife if she should visit you. Promise me?"

She nodded solemnly, clutching the volume of Keats to her breast as though it were a Bible to swear on.

Richard said, "The person I'll send for you will bring a pair of earrings that match the pendant I just gave you, so that you'll know he represents me. Do exactly as he tells you, you understand? Now I must go. I have some pressing business to attend to."

"Sir, would you tell me what you want me to name our daughter?" The last words were uttered shyly, but with such pride that he was almost irritated enough to retort that the little bastard should have been drowned at birth. Instead, he was silent, as though giving the matter careful thought.

At length he spoke. "Let me see . . . since she will no doubt have your raven hair and dark eyes, I should think it appropriate to name her Brenna. It's a Celtic name meaning 'raven maid.' The raven, you see, was a bird highly esteemed among the ancients."

Chavi gazed at him, awestruck. "Oh, sir, that's a lovely name."

He waved his hand airily as he departed.

At the front door the doctor awaited him, his face as bleak as an arctic blizzard. "I'd be obliged if you'd not come here again. I've neither the inclination nor the time to waste on you."

"Waste your time?" Richard raised an eyebrow in a way he knew was guaranteed to burst blood vessels in his opponents. "You doctors constantly amaze me with your arrogance. You're tradesmen selling a service, nothing more. And

a rather poor service it is, most of the time. Your victims get
better in spite of you, rather than due to any result of your
fumbling treatments. You get into the filthy and disgusting
trade of lancing boils and chopping off limbs because you're
not clever enough to be merchants."

It was amusing to witness Andrew McGreal battle with
himself to retain his composure. He said, "I trust you were
honest with Chavi. That you didn't hold out any false hopes."

Richard looked at the doorknob expectantly, and as he
knew he would, McGreal opened the door for him. Pulling
several bank notes from his wallet, Richard handed them to
the doctor. "This should cover their food and lodging until
we make other arrangements."

He was amused to see Andrew McGreal's frustration as
the carriage rolled away.

The coachman knew their next stop. Richard didn't usually visit the office of his solicitor, preferring to have the man
come out to Merrinswood, but today he wanted to be assured of absolute privacy. At his solicitor's office the senior
partner, Hilliard Stoughton, ushered him into his private
study.

Stoughton reminded Richard of a particularly unpleasant
headmaster who had presided over his prep school, a hawk-
nosed individual with a penchant for wielding the cane more
than necessary. But Stoughton not only handled the affairs of
the Merrinswood estate and holdings, he also—discreetly—
took care of other matters for the Earl of Moreland; the
sometimes awkward results of his drinking, or the payment
of gambling debts.

The solicitor's oily smile as he waved his client to a chair
disguised what Richard knew the man actually felt about
him. Pay people enough money and there was little they
wouldn't do to ensure the rewards continued.

He said shortly, "What about my first wife? What about
Philip's cable asking me to meet the liner in Liverpool?"

Stoughton's forefinger stroked a bushy white eyebrow.
The gesture inevitably heralded gloomy news. "Sarah is still
your legal wife."

"What? Dammit, man, I waited seven years before marrying Jean. I thought after that length of time Sarah was
presumed dead."

"You neglected, however, to have her declared *legally*

dead. Since I wasn't your solicitor at that time, I can't speculate as to why that wasn't done. Your first marriage is still valid."

Richard swore for a full minute. Stoughton waited for him to wind down, then added, "I'd recommend that you do indeed meet her in Liverpool. You can tell her that you intend to file for divorce in order to marry Jean."

The full implication of this suddenly hit Richard. He leaned back in his chair and considered the situation, several possibilities flashing across his mind.

The solicitor went on. "You unquestionably have grounds. Desertion, for one. Then there's the matter of adultery. The courts love adultery. She lived with a savage, bore him a son."

"I'm not at all sure I'd want a lot of dirty linen washed in public," Richard said. "There's one other thing I've learned from Philip. The boy, it seems, was conceived by Sarah *before* she fell into the hands of the savages. He's my son."

Stoughton's white eyebrows moved up his domelike forehead. "How can he be sure of that?"

"Oh, come, man. You've seen the portrait gallery at Merrinswood, you've met the twins. Isn't little Robbie the spirit and image of me—of all Merrin males? Apparently, the boy Hakan might be myself at his age. Blue eyes, fair hair, over six feet tall with my rather striking features."

"That puts the cat among the pigeons, then. He's your heir, no matter what you do about his mother. Tell me, what do you want to do?"

"Nothing, for the time being. I'll go to Liverpool and meet the liner. I'll decide what's to be done after I've seen them. But there is something I need done immediately."

"Anything at all."

"Find me a man who will do a job and vanish afterwards."

"You're asking me, a lawyer, to be an accomplice to something illegal? Your Grace, while I appreciate—"

"Shut up and listen. I merely want him to take the gypsy girl, Chavi, and her baby away somewhere. Out of the reach of my wife, who will enjoy having me squirm for the rest of my life if the girl and her bastard's whereabouts are known to her. My life is complicated enough at present with Sarah being resurrected. I don't need any further problems." He paused, giving Stoughton a sharply meaningful look. "I need a man whose discretion is absolutely assured."

Stoughton considered for a moment. "Very well. I can no doubt find someone recently released from prison who is desperate for money."

"Have him meet me at the inn at Carisbrook in a couple of days. I'll take a room under my usual nom de plume."

Two days later, the innkeeper tapped on Richard's door. "Mr. Tomlinson, sir? There's a"—he lowered his voice ominously—"a *person* here to see you."

"Send him in," Richard called, disentangling the arms of the barmaid and uncoiling himself from the bed. The girl giggled and pulled the sheets up over her nakedness.

Even Richard, who prided himself on his savoir faire, recoiled at the appearance of the man who entered the room. Behind him, from the depths of the disheveled bed, the girl gasped in horror.

"Christ in heaven!" Richard exclaimed, unable to contain himself. "What happened to you?"

The man held his head high, so that the gaslight fully illuminated his horribly disfigured face. Among the welts and weals and partially healed scars, a pair of intensely burning eyes, dark as stormclouds, looked steadily at Richard. "A knife fight in a foreign port. I understand you have a job for me."

Despite the laconic reply, Richard noted the cultured voice, hinting perhaps of an Oxford or Cambridge education, and was surprised it could have come from such a cruelly distorted mouth. Could another human being wielding a knife have created such a monster? Surely this man's features must have been deformed to start with.

Richard cleared his throat. "There's a bottle of brandy on the table. Help yourself while the lady dresses and leaves us."

"I don't drink," the man said. He walked to the only chair in the room and sat down. Richard noted the way the man moved, proudly, with perhaps a military bearing. His first assumption that a knife fight in a foreign port indicated a seafaring career was mentally revised.

Reaching for his dressing gown, Richard said to the barmaid, "Go on, get out of here." She didn't need to be told twice. Casting terrified eyes at the visitor, she flung on her dress, gathered up her undergarments and shoes, and fled.

As the door closed, Richard asked, "Do you have a name?"

"Why? Are we to be friends?"

"Taciturn wretch, aren't you?"

"I've been told you'll pay well for discretion. I'm quite sure you're using an assumed name. Why should you know more about me than I know about you?"

"Very well. Shall we get down to business?"

"Before we do, there are a couple of things you should know. First, I won't kill for you. Secondly, if you think you can trace me later through your solicitor, you're mistaken. Stoughton got in touch with a man just out of prison. He—and most of the other ex-convicts he approached—decided that to do the dirty work of a lawyer was probably to ask for a knife in the back. I happened to overhear Stoughton's request and offered him my services. Now, while I doubt he'll ever forget my face, the fact is he has no idea who I am or where I came from."

"You're quite a trickster, aren't you?"

"What is it you want done? And how much are you willing to pay?"

Richard hesitated. The man's clothing was too old and ragged to offer any hint as to his origins. The frightfully scarred face bore the unmistakable pallor of years in prison, and certainly would make any prospective employer recoil in horror. Yes, this man was perfect for the job.

Pouring himself a stiff brandy, Richard said, "There's a village about ten miles from here. I'll give you directions. There's a doctor there named McGreal. In his house is a gypsy girl and her newborn infant. You're to get them both out of there without anyone—especially the doctor—knowing. The girl will cooperate with you when you show her this."

He opened his portmanteau and pulled out a small velvet case. Snapping it open, he revealed a pair of silver filigree earrings in the shape of tiny butterflies with sapphire eyes.

"And when I get them out of the doctor's house?"

"I don't want to see either of them again, ever. Since you apparently have some qualms about killing, perhaps you have a suggestion?"

"They could be taken to a large city. London, perhaps. If the girl is attractive, and I suspect she is, there are ways for her to support herself and her child."

"No," Richard said at once. "There might come a time when she'd be able to make her way back to Yorkshire to haunt me, I'm already in that situation with a woman I thought was long dead. I'd need a better guarantee from you that I'll never set eyes on her again."

The man's twisted lips moved, curving in a travesty of a smile. "A different country then? Somewhere far away."

"You have somewhere in mind?"

"Australia."

Richard blinked. "She certainly wouldn't find it easy to make her way back from there. But—"

"To put your mind at ease, I'll tell you that if I had the price of my fare, I'd go there myself. To a sheep station in the Outback—remote, isolated, inaccessible, away from the horrified stares of everyone who encounters me. A place, by the way, where women are a rare and precious commodity, and men desperately seeking wives might overlook a bastard child."

"Yes," Richard said, thinking that to a man as hideously scarred as this one, any woman would be an impossibly precious commodity. How much would the cheapest pair of steerage passages to Australia cost? Probably not much more than he planned to pay the man in the first place. "But how would you persuade her to board a ship with you?"

The burning eyes bored into his. "You leave that to me."

Oddly, as Richard handed over the silver earrings, he felt a momentary pang of pity for the gypsy girl.

7

The great ocean liner sailed up the River Mersey on a rain-swept summer's day. Hakan stood beside his mother watching the dismal miles of docks pass by, feeling the cold dampness of the air bite into his bones. If it were this cold in summer, then what must the winters be like? He chided himself that a man did not spend his energy pining for places and people that were forever lost to him, but nevertheless his blood yearned for the warm desert winds of his homeland.

His mother said, "It seems so long ago that your father and I stood on the deck of a ship as we sailed for America."

Your father. She meant the Englishman. Hakan said, "Your Grand Tour. Your honeymoon."

Sarah seemed transfixed by the ugly port city they were passing, but perhaps it was into her own memory she was staring. She said tonelessly, "Other men toured the Continent or the Greek Isles. Or they took their wives to Italy for their honeymoons. Your father wanted to see America. I thought we'd spend a few weeks in New York or Philadelphia or Boston. But no, your father had a schoolboy's urge to see the wild frontiers of the West."

"Schoolboy's urge?" Hakan repeated, puzzled. Had the Englishman been a schoolboy at the time?

"I suppose that was unfair. Perhaps I should have said that as a young man he fancied himself an adventurer. But he shouldn't have taken a nineteen-year-old bride into such dangerous territory."

"The Apache take their women and children with them wherever they go," Hakan pointed out.

She turned to look at him, her gray eyes reflective. "Which is probably what eventually brought about their downfall. They were doing battle with soldiers who were unencumbered by women and children."

"The soldiers were too many. We were too few," Hakan answered shortly, his mind filled with questions without answers. Not the least of which concerned his mother's intentions regarding her first husband.

She had explained that, unlike the Apache who may take more than one wife, in England a man was allowed only one woman. Hakan already knew that the contempt he felt for a man who abandoned his woman to his enemies would be difficult to hide when he met his English father. Even harder to bear would be the sight of his mother with the man.

The Apache placed great value on a woman's chastity, but if her husband were killed, his brother or other male relative was obligated to take her to be his wife. The only surviving member of Hakan's father's family, a cousin, had been exiled to Florida with Geronimo. Since Sarah had refused to go with him as his wife, choosing to return to her first husband instead, Hakan was afraid this meant she intended to resume her role as wife to the Englishman, because it was the Lifeway for a woman to share her life with a man. Hakan's skin crawled at the possibility. His Apache father had loved Sarah so much.

The Chiricahua Apache did not place a high value on squaws, not even bothering to give most girls a name. Only the most beautiful, or clever, or valued for some other attribute were favored with a given name. His father had called his mother *Sons-ee-ah-ray*, which meant Morning Star, and because the Apache hated the night and welcomed the dawn, it was the greatest compliment he could have paid her.

"*Sons-ee-ah-ray* is as warm as the earth at midday, as gentle as the first rain, as courageous as any of my braves," his father had told Hakan. "But she is also as tricky as a coyote." He had thrown back his head and laughed. "In this one woman I have a dozen or more people to deal with, and I never cease to find another hidden inside of her."

At Hakan's side on the rolling deck of the ship his mother asked, "What are you thinking that brings a smile to your face?"

"I was remembering my father."

She stared straight ahead, into the steadily increasing rain. "It's good that you remember him, for then he will never die."

For a few minutes she was silent, no doubt lost in some reverie of her own. Then she said suddenly, "But don't forget what I told you: You are to make no comparisons when you meet your English father."

"There is no need to tell me this many times," Hakan said, not wanting to think about his upcoming meeting with the man whose seed had given him his blue eyes, fair skin, and yellow hair.

"I'm sorry. I'm a little on edge about arriving back in England after all these years."

"Don't be. No one will be allowed to harm you. I will protect you."

Thunder rolled up the river, followed by a jagged flash of lightning. A little boy who had been running around the deck dodging his nanny, now stopped in fright and began to cry. Hakan reached down and gathered him up into his arms.

"Hush. Little warriors are not afraid of a storm. Has no one told you about the Thunder People? The lightning is only their arrows."

The child stopped crying and listened, wide-eyed.

Hakan went on. "Once the Thunder People were our friends and their arrows killed game for us. But human ingratitude caused them to withdraw their aid. Thunder and Wind quarreled and the earth suffered floods and then droughts. But then Thunder and Wind arranged a meeting, with Sun as a mediator, and now they use their power to keep the earth as before."

When a clap of thunder exploded overhead, following a flash of lightning, the child shouted, "I saw the arrow! I saw Thunder People's arrow."

His nanny came panting along the wet deck, her expression horrified when she saw her charge in the arms of "the wild Indian," a name Hakan had overheard whispered whenever he appeared. He was sure it had been given to him by Sir Randolph, who had stayed out of their way since the night of his unsuccessful attack.

Before the woman had time to open her mouth and scream, Hakan placed the little boy on the deck at her side. Glaring at him, she dragged the protesting child away. Hakan and Sarah exchanged glances, which didn't require words. He took her arm to lead her down the companionway. At the same moment the ship nudged the dock.

The confusing bustle of disembarkation, of officials and baggage examination, all made more tiresome by the constant drumming rain, was over.

Waiting for the arrival of Lord Moreland in the tearoom not far from the landing stage, Hakan let the name *James* echo about his mind. He supposed he must accustom himself to being called James. The English, it seemed, were quite careless in their use of given names. Not that it mattered, since only the use of his real name, Hakan, would alert him to a serious situation. His mother had explained that their English family name was Merrin, but his father was called Lord Moreland because his title was Sixth Earl of Moreland.

The rain ran in a solid sheet down the windows of the tearoom, steam forming on the inside to mercifully block the view of the dreary street. Outside, gray skies hung low over gray slate roofs, and the streets were filled with scurrying people wrapped in drab clothes, their faces as gray as their weather. It was as if the whole world had been drained of color.

His Uncle Philip ordered another pot of tea and said, "We'll give him a few more minutes, then hire a cab to take us to the hotel. Perhaps he didn't receive my wire in time."

"You told him to come here if he missed us at the dock?" Sarah asked. Philip nodded. She said, "Then we'll wait as long as necessary."

"I must say your patience is astonishing."

Her eyes were as serene as twin lakes, and just as unfathomable, Hakan thought. She replied, "Achieving what one seeks is often just a matter of waiting long enough for it. People give up too soon."

"Another bit of your Apache folklore, old girl?" Philip asked with a laugh. Sarah didn't appear to be insulted by either the question or his calling her "old."

"No. My own philosophy of life."

They talked, back and forth, and Hakan knew that Philip, in his lazy drawling manner, was baiting Sarah. But she continued to toss the gauntlet back with her customary skill, and in the end, Philip found himself outmatched.

Although Hakan didn't understand all that Philip said, his uncle's remarks often brought a smile or laughter to Sarah's lips. Therefore, he decided, his uncle must be a witty and lighthearted man. Hakan liked his father's younger brother. His uncle Philip was almost as carefree as a young squaw: his attitude seemed to be that life was only a game. Nothing was to be taken seriously, he seemed to say, because, in the end, what did it matter? Hakan wondered if his English father would display the same temperament. If he did, Hakan knew he would have to keep reminding himself that a man who abandoned his woman to his enemies was no man at all.

"Another cup of cocoa, James?" Philip asked.

The beverage was much tastier than tea, and Hakan responded, "Yes, thank you." James, he repeated to himself silently. He was James Merrin now, and this damp cold gray place was his home. It was inconceivable to him that any man could value it enough to fight and die for it. Sarah had shown him a map which she said showed all of the earth. Most of the land masses were depicted in red ink. The red, she said, represented the British Empire. Now it became clear to Hakan why Englishmen had gone out and conquered territories far from their homeland, even America, before the Yankees came. The English were fleeing from this dismal gray place of their birth.

The door of the tearoom opened and a gust of wet wind blew in, bringing with it a tall man dressed in black. He swept a hat from his head, and his black overcoat contrasted strikingly with his golden hair. Blue eyes with an unmistakable flash of flint in them searched the room and rested first on Philip, who now appeared to be a faded and worn copy of his older brother. Richard, Lord Moreland, was more vivid, more compelling in every way. Every eye in the room swiveled in his direction.

Sarah's conversation died on her lips as Richard made his way through the clutter of tiny tables to where they sat, moving with long impatient strides. Philip said in an undertone, "On your feet, James, at once."

James rose, whereas Hakan would not have. Out of the corner of his eye he could see that his mother had turned very pale, even though her skin still bore faint traces of the sun's-gilding. Philip greeted his brother with a handshake. Then Lord Moreland bowed to Sarah. He didn't smile, but his eyes devoured her. "Welcome home, Sarah. I trust the crossing was smooth?"

"As a matter of fact, it was quite rough," she answered.

"And about to get rougher, I daresay?" Richard's tone seemed light, joking, and Hakan felt a seed of anger take root, but James ignored it. Was he forever to be split into two like this? His Apache self battling his English self?

His father turned to him, giving him a piercingly appraising glance. He held out his hand. "No need to ask who you are." When James failed to take his outstretched hand, his father dropped it to his side and turned to Sarah. "What do you call him?"

"My son can answer for himself. He isn't mute," Sarah said. "And please sit down, Richard, there's no need to direct everyone's attention to us."

"My dear Sarah, don't you remember that it's impossible for a Merrin male not to attract attention? Three of us must surely be more than most ordinary mortals can stand."

Philip smiled and said, "Especially in view of our extreme modesty." Sarah's expression was still unreadable.

Hakan said, "James."

His father turned to him. "I beg your pardon?"

"I am called James."

"How do you do?"

"How do I do what?"

Richard's eyes rolled upward. Philip said quickly, "I suggest we go to a hotel immediately. Our clothing is wet and we could all use a hot bath."

Sarah said, "I agree. We can't talk here."

"There's one thing I can say here," Richard murmured as he pulled out her chair for her. "When all's said and done, you're still a very handsome woman, Sarah."

In the hotel bedroom, Sarah fastened an errant strand of hair back into the coil on top of her head. The pins holding her hair in place felt heavy, uncomfortable, and she longed for the freedom of braids swinging free over her shoulders. But the feel of fine lawn underwear against her skin was pleasant.

As she smoothed her skirt over her hips she allowed herself a moment to recall the sensations and pleasures of the flesh that the rush of activities these past weeks had taken from her life. She sighed, thinking how long it had been since she'd felt a human touch on her skin.

Was it the presence of Richard in the next room that brought back those yearnings she had forced herself to forget? She longed for the feel of the hard length of a man lying close to her, his whispers and his laughter in the darkness, the sweet fusion of bodies and minds in that most mystical of all human bonding.

Why had simply seeing Richard again filled her with need? How could she even associate such needs with a man she'd grown to hate? He'd worn well, that much she had to admit. He was more handsome than she remembered, now that the blank look of youth had gone. Would he be an even more accomplished lover than he had been then?

Quickly, as though the thought might give way to the act, she forced her mind back to what must be said and done with Richard, silently rehearsing exactly what she intended to say and throwing a veil over what she could not, would not, say.

For one devastating second a picture intruded in her mind of a Chiricahua chief standing motionless against a sky slashed with scarlet as the sun descended behind the awe-inspiring mesas of the southwestern desert. A bronzed and beautiful man, fully in tune with nature, taking care that his footsteps did not mar the earth they trod, so that when he moved on to new hunting grounds, new pastures, nothing left behind had been changed.

Tears pricked at her eyes and she blinked them away. He was gone forever, and, she suspected, so was his Apache Life-way. Herded like cattle onto reservations far from their hunting grounds, treated like ignorant children, dependent on the crumbs grudgingly distributed by men who knew nothing of them or their culture and branded them all as bloodthirsty savages, how could they survive? No, she mustn't think of that now. Now she must think only of the welfare of her son.

Sarah went through the adjoining door to the sitting room, where Richard sat gazing morosely into space. He stood up and crossed the room toward her, stopping inches away to stare at her with a quizzical, almost mesmerizing intensity.

Looking around and realizing he was alone, she said, "Where are Philip and James?"

"They went down to the dining room. I wanted to see you alone."

"Could we sit down, then? I'm not sure I want to continue standing here while you look at me as though I were a ghost."

"Aren't you?" He slipped her arm through his to lead her to a chair. She was able not to tremble at the unexpected way her skin, through the satin of her long-sleeved blouse, reacted to the warmth of his hand.

"I'm no ghost, Richard. Although I'm sure you wish I were." She sat down while he remained standing, looking down at her.

When he spoke there was a certain honest wonder in his voice that disturbed her, because Richard had always been too devious for honest feelings. He said, "You're the same, yet different. Older, and yet in some strange way, younger than I remember. You've acquired a certain . . . finish that is forever going to separate you from other Englishwomen of your class. It's exotic and quite attractive—not a gloss exactly, but some undefinable veneer that hints of untamed qualities beneath the composure. I do believe, my dear Sarah, that you'd be quite capable of slitting my throat if the occasion seemed to warrant it."

"You're absolutely right," she answered coolly. "But at the moment I'd prefer to simply talk."

He gave a mocking bow, took the chair opposite hers, and leaned forward, his chin supported by one hand as though he were studying a particularly intricate portrait. "So what's to be done about this tangled web we've woven, Sarah? You know about Jean, of course."

"Yes. Philip told me she bore you twins. How old are they?"

"Robbie and Emily are eight years old. Born a year after I went through what I thought was a legal marriage to their mother."

"I won't stand in your way in regard to a divorce, I want you to know that. So long as James is named your legal heir—which, of course, he is."

He leaned back, his eyes still fixed on her face. "I'm curious. Why did you wait so long to resurrect yourself from the dead? Why now?"

"If the last of the Apaches had not surrendered I wouldn't be here. It was a choice of going with my husband's people to sicken and die on a reservation in a Florida swamp or coming here. The lesser of two evils."

"Your *husband*?"

"I considered him so. Don't you feel Jean is your wife?"

"Touché."

"You saw for yourself that Hakan—James—is your son. You didn't deny it. The moment you saw him there was recognition on your face. The physical likeness is quite uncanny, isn't it?"

"Tell me, how was it, living with a savage? Do they make love like us, or is it some sort of animal rutting? Is that what kept you with him? Are there other children—little half-breeds running around somewhere?"

"I never had another child."

"But you did cohabit with the Red Indian?"

She gripped the folds of her skirts, her knuckles white against her tanned hands. "Where is this conversation leading? What purpose does it serve? We're here to talk about James. He's your heir and he should, of course, live at Merrinswood. Although I suppose it will be necessary to send him away to school until his education is complete."

"I see. You have it all planned. What else?"

"Sir Randolph Leighton attempted to kill your son while we were at sea."

"You don't say! That wasn't my idea."

"We don't have a witness, so it would be difficult to bring charges against him. However, I must insist that Randolph is asked to leave Merrinswood."

"So—I'm to take a wild Indian home and present him to my wife as my son and heir, and I'm to dismiss my estate steward. Anything else?"

"You are to give me your word that James will be treated decently. In return I'll be as unobtrusive as possible."

"And what about the past, my dear Sarah? What about the few blissful weeks we were bride and groom? Shall we ever discuss that time? Or that fateful ride in the stagecoach?"

For an instant a fog rolled through her mind, threatening to obscure all her rational intentions, but she was able to control it in time. She shrugged. "I don't see that it would serve a purpose, do you?"

"You don't want to know what happened back there in the Arizona desert—why I couldn't get back to you in time? Am I to be condemned without a trial?"

"You saved yourself. The fact that you did so after we quarreled—"

"Dammit, your bloody ankle was broken when the stagecoach went over. You couldn't walk. Have you forgotten?"

"Did you send a search party after me? No one ever came looking for a missing bride. I assumed you were glad to be rid of me. As I was glad to be done with our marriage."

He jumped to his feet, eyes blazing, and for an instant Sarah thought he might strike her. But he controlled himself with a visible effort that showed he was angry with himself for allowing her to arouse such strong emotions in him.

Taking a deep breath he said, "Believe what you like, but I thought you were dead."

He walked over to the window and looked out at the rain clouds hanging low over the row of exclusive shops on the opposite side of the street. Without turning around, he said,

"You've been informed, I take it, that legally we're still married?"

"I knew that all along. Do you wish to discuss the terms of our divorce now, or would it be preferable to engage solicitors first?"

Richard spun around, a crafty grin on his face. He watched her expression carefully as he replied, "You chose to come back into my life. Therefore you, my sweet, have no grounds for a divorce. And as for myself . . . well, I'm not at all sure I want to remain married to Jean. I don't know if I want a divorce, Sarah."

8

Only the silver filigree earrings, delicate butterflies with sapphire eyes, dangling from the fingers of the man at the window prevented Chavi from screaming in fright.

Clutching her baby to her breast, she clenched her teeth to keep from crying out as he dropped into the room, the heavy velvet draperies falling back into place behind him.

She had lit a candle for the baby's midnight feeding, and the small flickering flame illuminated the cruel scars that distorted the intruder's face. The poor man had been brutally disfigured in some ghastly accident, and Chavi chided herself for showing horror at his appearance, which he certainly hadn't chosen for himself. Besides, he was her beloved's messenger, and if Lord Moreland had selected him for such an important mission, then the man must be trustworthy.

"Good girl, no noise now," he said, his voice surprisingly cultured. "I've come to take you away from here. The man who sent me said you'd recognize these."

He handed her the earrings, and she tried not to shudder as his hand brushed hers. "Yes," she whispered. "I've been expecting you. My name is Chavi. What's yours?"

He hesitated, his eyes flickering over the baby, then answered, "You can call me Lysander." If it hadn't been for his hideously deformed face, she might have imagined a hint of amusement in his voice, but no man who looked like that would find anything to smile about. He added, "The doctor was called out to visit a patient of his about half an hour ago, and his housekeeper is asleep. But we must be very quiet. Get up and get dressed as quickly as you can. I'll take care of the baby."

A protest sprang to her lips when he reached for Brenna, but his touch was gentle and sure. The baby was lifted to his shoulder and his big hand patted her back to bring up the air bubbles she'd swallowed.

God in heaven, Chavi prayed silently, help me not be afraid of this man. He means us no harm. She jumped out of bed and went to the oak wardrobe that housed the clothes she'd been wearing when she'd come there. A cotton gown, a couple of torn petticoats, and a threadbare shawl, all of which had been washed in strong carbolic soap by Mrs. Tremayne. Chavi pulled them on over the nightgown the doctor had provided, then fished in the bottom of the wardrobe for her shoes.

When she turned around, Lysander had Brenna on the bed and was expertly changing her nappie. Chavi had never seen a man do such a chore, and watched in astonishment when he then wrapped the infant envelope-style in a blanket, tucked in her feet, and left a flap to fall over her face to protect her from the night air.

"You must have babies of your own, sir," Chavi said.

"No more talking," he said gruffly. "Just listen. There's a ladder at the window. I'll go down first, carrying the baby. When I'm on the ground, you come down. There's a wind tonight, but I'll steady the ladder. Not a sound now—if we wake the housekeeper I'll have to knock her over the head. You don't want that, do you?"

Chavi shook her head, praying that Brenna wouldn't cry out. Strangely, Chavi had no fear that he would hurt the baby, but she didn't doubt he meant what he said about knocking the housekeeper over the head. She sensed this man would have his way in any situation, no matter what. Still, Lord Moreland would no doubt be waiting for them, close by, so she could endure the company of his terrifying messenger for a little while.

"Do you have any other possessions?" he asked, looking around the bare room. She picked up the leather-bound volume of Keats on the bedside table. The filigree pendant was still around her neck.

"That all?" She nodded and he muttered something under his breath she didn't catch.

Chavi stood at the open window and watched him descend to the alley below, the baby tucked inside his coat. Since her room was at the back of the house, there was little likelihood there would be passersby at this hour of the night, but nevertheless she prayed that no one would happen by, because God help them if they did. Lysander's gentleness with the baby didn't fool her one bit. This was a man with nothing to lose; every instinct Chavi possessed told her that he placed little value on life, his own or anyone else's.

The wind whipped her skirts as she backed slowly down the ladder. Her legs felt wobbly and unused, although she'd been up and walking about her room for several days. She jumped when she felt Lysander's hand on her arm, steadying her as she reached the ground. He muttered, "All right, I won't touch you again. Come on. This way."

They hurried along the dark streets, Chavi running to keep up with his long strides. The baby slept inside his coat. When they reached the village square a hansom cab was waiting for them, and Lysander helped her into it.

Moments later they were rolling through the shadowed countryside and Chavi had regained her breath sufficiently to inquire, "Where are you taking us, Lysander?"

"To a place where your fancy man is going to meet you," he answered. "I'll tell you all about it when we get to the railway station."

"Railway station!" Chavi repeated in alarm. "But—"

"You're going to a new life in a new country. You didn't think you could live with an aristocrat here, did you?"

"No—" She broke off, wonderment filling her. She was to *live* with her beloved? He was giving up everything—his home and family—in order to go to a new country to be with her? And to think she'd doubted his love for her! She felt ashamed, humble with love for him, but so happy she wanted to sing. She pushed aside the troublesome thought about

Lord Moreland's deserting his wife and other two children for her. They'd be all right, they'd have the great golden house and all he'd leave behind.

"Which country—where?" she asked, excitement pounding in her chest.

"I'll tell you that when we get to the ship. The less said now, the better. Your lover has powerful enemies who might try to intercept us. So we're to be discreet about who we are and where we're bound."

"Enemies?" Chavi gasped. "Lord Moreland has enemies?"

"Lord Moreland, is it?" Lysander digested the name in silence for a moment, then said, "Members of his family, you see, who don't want him to leave the country with you."

In her joy at her imminent reunion with her beloved, she had forgotten a very important member of her own family. "Wait!" she cried. "Stop the cab! We must go back for my little brother."

"What are you talking about? What brother?"

"Danior. Lady Moreland took him to Merrinswood. Oh, what will happen to him when they find out Lord Moreland has run off with me?" She turned and tugged at the hansom door, almost succeeding in getting it open before Lysander seized her wrist.

"Calm down, girl, you'll wake the baby. I forgot to tell you. Your brother is already on his way to the ship."

Danior crept into the darkened breakfast room, glad that a pale sliver of a moon sent fingers of light through the diamond-paned wall of glass framing the garden. The sparse light reflected on the glass-fronted cabinets as he inched silently across the polished wood floor.

He patted his shirt pocket, reassuring himself that the silver pitcher he'd taken that first day he came to Merrinswood was still there. His heart thumped painfully and his mouth was dry. In the week he'd been here there had been no opportunity to come to the main house and return the stolen pitcher.

Although the sweet-faced Countess had wanted a place found for Danior in the servants' wing, her husband had refused to allow it.

"If you must collect strays, then this one goes to the

stables," Lord Moreland had said. "My stablemaster can always use another boy and gypsies are good with horses. After all, they're experts at stealing them, aren't they?"

The stablemaster and the other stableboys had made Danior's life miserable, with cuffs to the ear and curses and endless work. He'd been so tired when he finished at night that he'd fallen to the straw, too exhausted to think about bringing back the pitcher until tonight.

He hated being here, but Her Grace had told him it would only be for a short time. Soon he'd be reunited with Chavi and her baby and they'd live together in a little house.

Danior wasn't sure he relished the idea of staying forever in one place, in any kind of a house. That wasn't the Romany way. But there'd be time enough to worry about that when he was with his sister again.

His fingers closed around the brass handle of the cabinet door and he pulled it open. He was shaking so much that when he pulled the pitcher from his pocket it slipped from his fingers and crashed to the floor.

At the same moment the breakfast room door opened and the room was flooded with yellow light from a lantern. Barlow, the butler, and the frozen-faced housekeeper loomed over him like great black bats.

The housekeeper said, "Just as you suspected, Mr. Barlow."

"Indeed. We've caught the little thief in the act. It's just as I tried to point out to Her Grace. Gypsies are thieves. It's their nature, they can't help themselves."

Although Danior tried to elude him, Barlow's bony hands grabbed him, pulling one arm painfully behind his back. "Not a sound, gypsy, or I'll snap your neck like a chicken's."

"But sir—" Danior began. Barlow's other hand closed around his throat, cutting off his air. Danior choked, gasped for breath when the pressure eased, and didn't say another word as he was dragged from the room.

They took him back into the big kitchen.

"What shall we do with him until morning?" the housekeeper asked, her cunning little eyes filled with pleasure. Her name was Mrs. Braithwaite, and it had been she who'd opened the tradesman's door to him that morning he'd come for the Countess. When Her Grace had brought him back after Chavi's baby was born, Barlow had growled at the housekeeper, "A pity he got past you, isn't it? Now we're to have a smelly gypsy on our hands."

No doubt both the housekeeper and the butler had been waiting for an opportunity like this. Danior tried to keep from shaking at the prospect of what might be done to him.

Barlow said, "Go and wake up the stablemaster and tell him to come here at once. I'll keep an eye on the boy."

After she'd gone, Barlow thrust Danior down onto one of the wooden chairs. "Don't move so much as an eyelid, you understand?"

Danior nodded. A clock ticked on the mantlepiece over the fireplace. The fire was out and the room was filled with the chills and shadows of the night. There seemed little point in trying to explain that he'd been trying to put back the pitcher. Since he'd stolen it in the first place, he was a thief, just as they said.

After a moment Danior cleared his throat and said, "Please, sir, what will happen to me?"

"You, boy, are going to a reform school. That's what we do with thieves. And this time there'll be no Lady Moreland to intercede for you. By the time she wakes in the morning you'll be on your way with the stablemaster, who'll be just as glad as we are to be rid of a thieving gypsy."

Reform school! Prison for little boys, where brutality ruled and they learned to be hardened felons. Danior's blood froze in terror. His teeth clamped down over his lower lip to keep from whimpering like a baby. Bad enough to be forced to live in the stables here, but to be locked away from sun and sky, from the rolling moors and the endless winding highways. . . . For a gypsy, that was worse than death.

There was a whispered conference between Barlow and the stablemaster a few minutes later, while the housekeeper stood watch over Danior. Then he was dragged outside and flung over the back of a horse, the stablemaster mounting behind him.

They galloped off into the night. Danior's thin body jolted until his teeth rattled with each step the horse took. A cold breeze whistled in his ears and he was numbed with fear. But somewhere in the back of his mind a small voice strove to be heard. *You can't let them lock you up. You'll die.*

He had to do something now, when there was only one man to deal with rather than many. He was lying facedown

over the saddle and he turned his head into the wind to try to
see where they were.

The shadows of trees and hedgerows flitted by with frightening speed. Then the shape of a barn hove into view, telling
him that they were passing the first of the tenant farms. The
stablemaster was riding across the open fields rather than
down the lane to the village. That meant that soon they
would come to a fence or a gate and have to stop.

But as they approached the far boundaries of the Merrin
farmland, the stablemaster dug his heels into the flanks of the
horse to urge it to gallop even faster. He was going to jump
the fence, rather than stop.

Danior bent his head, burrowed his face into the horse's
silky hide, and in the instant they were airborne, bit into the
animal's flesh as hard as he could.

Everything was tossed awry. The crescent moon and the
night clouds spun around to where the dark earth should
have been. The horse screamed as his hooves struck the
fence. Riders and horse tumbled in different directions.

Danior was thrown backward and landed on his feet, then
rolled over to escape the crashing bodies. There was a thud
and the stablemaster cried out in pain.

Danior scrambled to his feet and ran.

Barlow led his mistress to the breakfast room the following morning and pointed to the open china cabinet, the silver
pitcher lying on the floor where Danior had dropped it. "We
caught the lad red-handed. We left everything as it was, so
you'd see for yourself."

Jean shook her head and sighed deeply. "The poor little
soul must have been desperate. I'll speak with him now,
Barlow. Where is he?"

The butler's face was impassive. "He ran away last night,
milady. The stablemaster went after him, but unfortunately
his horse threw him and he had to give up the search."

Jean's hand went to her throat. "Oh, dear heaven! Is the
stablemaster hurt?"

"A twisted ankle and a few bruises. Nothing serious."

"You must organize a search party to find Danior, at
once," Jean said. "The poor child must be terrified."

"Yes, milady. But I believe our chances of running down

a gypsy are not great. They'll know every hiding place on the moors."

"Start with Coombe's Woods, the old tumbledown cottage. I'll be in the nursery. Please let me know the minute the boy is found, Barlow, and treat him gently. I'm well aware of the superstitious whispering belowstairs about gypsies being unlucky."

"Yes, milady."

Jean went upstairs, her heart heavy, imagining the gypsy child's terror as he ran from his pursuers. At the same time she was disappointed that he'd stolen from his benefactors, and she dreaded having Richard find out about the theft. Fortunately, he was still in Liverpool. In his usual inconsiderate manner, he hadn't informed her when he would return.

She constantly created pictures in her mind, imagining his reunion with Sarah. Despite the fact that Richard had told her many times that his brief marriage to his first wife had been ill-advised and stormy, Jean knew him well enough to recognize that he was excited and intrigued with the prospect of meeting her again after all these years.

Jean's constant worry since that first letter from America arrived had been that Richard, despite his assurances to the contrary, might use the reappearance of Sarah to bow out of his marriage to her. If that happened, what would become of Robbie and Emily? To say nothing of herself and Randolph. They had no income of their own; as orphaned children, they had been dependent on the charity of a maiden aunt, who upon her death—after Jean's marriage to the Earl—had left all of her worldly goods to her church.

Opening the nursery door, Jean was greeted with a babble of chatter from the twins. "Morning, Mummy! What a pretty dress! Robbie nudged my arm and made me spoil my picture."

"I didn't, honestly. Emily's just trying to get me into trouble."

"Mummy, can we go for a picnic today, can we, please?"

"Now, children, we must remember our manners," their governess, a plump and rather plain young woman named Charlotte, chided.

The twins hurled themselves into Jean's arms and she hugged them, loving the warm tangle of arms about her neck and the sweet scent of their breath as they pressed kisses to her cheek. Robbie looked so much like his father that it broke her heart, because Robbie's golden good looks masked a sensitive and timid nature that he had inherited from her, as well as a delicate constitution, which Richard found intolerable in his son. Emily's hair had none of her twin's golden glints, being more mousy than fair, and her eyes were a more subtle shade of blue. Unfortunately, she had also inherited her mother's undramatic features, and seemed to be developing a sharp cutting edge to her personality that said in later life she would demand homage if it were not freely given.

"Darlings, if the weather stays fine and you finish your lessons, then we'll have lunch in the summerhouse," Jean said.

Emily wrinkled her nose. "*That's* not a picnic."

"It will have to do, dear. We mustn't go too far away, in case Daddy comes home today."

Robbie clapped his hands. "Oh, I do hope he comes home today."

And so did she, Jean thought as she hugged him again. She couldn't stand much more waiting, wondering. Would he bring Sarah and her son here? Surely he wouldn't humiliate her so.

A moment later there was a sharp knock on the nursery door and Barlow appeared. Jean looked up questioningly, hoping that the gypsy boy had been found.

But Barlow announced, "Doctor McGreal is here, milady. He says it's most urgent that he speak with you."

9

The sun broke through the clouds as the train from Liverpool snaked through the gently rolling countryside of Lancashire. Hakan sat on the edge of his seat, watching the pastoral scene. How green, how very, very green it was. So beautiful . . . until the train passed through an ugly little industrial town. How could they have done this to their lovely land? Stained bricks, slate roofs, and chimney pots belching black smoke. Occasionally a chimney stack soared into the air higher than a hawk's flight and this, Sarah had explained, was a factory chimney.

"There are many mills here in Lancashire. They weave cotton and wool into fabric. To make clothing."

"They don't tan hides?"

"Oh, yes. But they use the skins for shoes and bags."

"Saddlebags?"

"No. Very few people ride their own horses except for sport."

Hakan noticed that the elderly gentleman seated in the compartment with them had lowered his newspaper and was listening to their conversation. Catching his eye, Hakan smiled. He had also smiled and greeted the only other passenger when they entered the compartment, but the man evidently hadn't noticed, because he'd made no response. Now the elderly man hastily raised his newspaper again.

"Sir," Hakan said. "You seem to be interested in the subject my mother and I are discussing. Perhaps you have something interesting to add to what she told me?"

The newspaper descended about an inch. The man looked flustered and said, "I'm sorry."

Hakan was perplexed. Why had the old man apologized? English customs were proving to be even more difficult to understand than Sarah had indicated. Hakan couldn't understand either why his English father, having insisted that both he and his mother travel to Merrinswood, had then departed with his uncle and Sir Randolph Leighton, leaving Sarah and Hakan in the gloomy seaport. After a few days, which were spent buying clothing, his mother said they would travel to Yorkshire and find a country inn at which to stay until they could go on to Merrinswood. Confused about the delay, Hakan was told that his father must make certain arrangements in advance of their arrival.

Sarah said, with a slight edge to her voice, "I forgot to warn you that the English are extremely reserved. They don't usually address strangers."

The old man, looking even more embarrassed, folded up his newspaper. "Ah, you're visitors here? Where are you from?"

Now he was friendly, talkative. Allowances were apparently to be made for foreigners. Introductions were made. He was the owner of a cotton mill which received raw cotton from America. He had been in Liverpool meeting with the shipping company. The man commented, "Forgive my saying so, but neither you nor your son sound like the other Americans I've met. Which part of the country are you from?"

"We are from the Southwest. We are Apache," Hakan answered pleasantly.

The man turned red, sputtered, and rose to retrieve his bag from an overhead luggage rack. There was amusement in Sarah's voice as she pointed out that the conductor had not yet announced the next stop.

Sarah gazed out of the train window, mesmerized by the rhythmic grinding of wheels on track as well as the sight of the English countryside after so many years. She'd forgotten the gentleness, the tranquility of meadows and woods and sparkling streams. It was still the same, yet subtly different. Like Richard. What was his intent? Was it a game he was playing with them? Could he be cruel enough to amuse himself by having his two wives confront one another? Did he think perhaps they'd fight over him? Knowing Richard, the answer could be yes.

He had refused to discuss any plans until, as he put it, "All of the players are assembled at Merrinswood."

One admonition surprised her. He said, in a tone that was too offhanded, "By the way, outside of the family, no one knows what happened to you. Everyone in England believes you were killed in an accident on our honeymoon. Why don't we keep your sojourn with the Red Indians to ourselves? I don't see that it's anybody else's business that the Apaches carried off my bride, do you?"

How could such a secret be kept once Hakan took up residence at Merrinswood? Sarah worried that either Richard didn't expect his son to remain for long, or that he didn't understand their son's pride in his Apache upbringing. Apparently Richard had never even bothered to find out which group of Indians had attacked the stagecoach. They had not been Apache, but Comanches, a party of renegades who had escaped from their Oklahoma reservation and were cutting a bloody swath through the settlers of the Southwest.

Sarah leaned back against the starched antimacassar adorning the back of her seat and closed her eyes, remembering once more the journey that had irrevocably changed her life.

The Arizona Territory in the spring of 1870 . . . Settlers were spreading west, and President Grant's Board of Indian Commissioners had decided that "civilizing" the Indians on reservations would be cheaper than fighting them. Bands of the nomadic Apache, fiercest of all the Indians, were roaming the Southwest in a desperate attempt to evade being put on reservations.

Sarah and Richard were traveling to California by way of Arizona. When they came to the end of the railway lines, they had boarded a series of stagecoaches.

There had been heavy rains, flash floods, and the trail had been washed out. Somehow the unthinkable happened, and their stagecoach driver found himself in strange territory, hopelessly lost. Almost immediately, they encountered the war party of Comanche braves.

They came over a ridge, the sun behind them, about twenty in the party; stripped to the waist, faces daubed with war paint, eagle feathers adorning scalp locks; their lances glittering in the sunlight. In the instant before stark terror overcame her, Sarah had marveled at the barbaric beauty of the braves.

One of the other passengers, a pale and bespectacled young journalist who had told them his name was Otis Prouther, immediately suggested to Sarah that she should crouch on the floor of the stagecoach. "They don't appear to have guns," Otis said calmly, "but until the driver gets us to cover we might catch a few arrows."

Richard stared at the approaching warriors in fascination, as though they were there merely for his entertainment. "Splendid! God, they're marvelous," he murmured.

Otis helped Sarah to the floor, where the motion of the wildly dashing coach was even more nauseating. The early weeks of pregnancy had been troublesome, and it seemed that everything made her sick to her stomach. She wrapped her arms around her knees and leaned her head on them, to keep from losing her dinner.

"Can we outrun them?" she asked Otis.

He looked down on her with a grave expression that said

he was contemplating what might happen to the only female passenger on the coach if she were taken alive, but he answered, "Oh yes, we've a good team of horses and an excellent driver."

"How will they attack, do you know?" Richard asked.

"They'll try to surround us. Then they'll ride in a circle to draw our fire. You won't see the braves, they'll disappear behind their horses as they pass by. You'll just see a hand grasping the withers of the horse or a foot showing above his back. But their arrows will come at us faster than the eye can see."

"But we could shoot their horses," Richard said, horrified.

"That's what they want us to do. Run out of bullets so they can come in and finish us off. Look, sir, I—if I were you, I'd give your pistol to your wife."

"Even if Sarah knew how to shoot," Richard said, "I'm not carrying a pistol on my person. I do have one in my trunk, but it's lashed to the top of the coach."

Otis reached under his seat, pulled out a battered carpetbag, and fished out a revolver. "It's loaded," he said as he offered it to Sarah. "You probably won't need it, but—"

She shook her head. "Thank you for your concern, but I won't kill myself if we're caught. Where there's life, there's hope, isn't there?"

Richard said, "Oh, I see, a fate worse than death and all that rot."

Sarah bit back an angry retort that she would have welcomed death if it would have meant only her own end. But there was a new life growing inside her. She hadn't told Richard that she suspected she was pregnant, not after the episode in the saloon. She thought perhaps she'd never tell him. She'd leave him at the first opportunity and he'd never know she was carrying his child. It was the only way she could think of to deal with her sense of betrayal and hurt.

"Aren't we getting a bit melodramatic?" Richard went on. "The driver has a rifle and the guard has a shotgun. There are four of us in here, and I see you're all armed." To Otis he added, "Give me your revolver. I'm a crack shot."

Ignoring him, Otis leaned precariously out of the window and aimed a shot at the Indians who were rapidly gaining on the coach. The other two male passengers were at the opposite window, also firing, but a moment later the guard who rode with the driver appeared at the open window, swinging upside down. He yelled, "Save your ammo until you can hit one of 'em."

There was a hissing sound over Sarah's head and a grunt of pain. She looked up to see an arrow imbedded in the shoulder of one of the men. At the same time the war whoops of the Indians became bloodcurdlingly distinct as they rode alongside the stagecoach.

Struggling to stand up in the rocking coach so that she could help the wounded man, Sarah felt dizziness overcome her. She heard someone shout, "He's heading us into the canyon—hold on!"

The coach rocked more violently than ever. The squeal of a falling horse heralded disaster as a wheel hit a boulder and went careening away from the coach. For a split second they seemed to hover on the brink of some unseen chasm. Then the coach went over. Sarah was tumbling in space, her body battered with blows from unseen objects. Something struck her head in the instant before she fell into a black void.

The sound of gunfire had pulled her back to consciousness. Her eyes felt heavy-lidded, her body strangely not her own. Turning her head slightly, she saw the stagecoach down on its side, the six men behind it, firing in the direction of the fearful sound of thudding hooves and war cries.

As the scene came into focus, she realized they were in a narrow canyon with steep rocky sides. The stagecoach and dead horses formed a barrier between them and the Indians. All of their horses, she saw, had been killed by arrows.

Waves of dizziness passed through her as she struggled to her knees with some idea of helping load the weapons. As she tried to stand up her right leg buckled and she sprawled on the ground again, her body screaming at the new assault of pain. Her ankle was either badly sprained or broken.

How long did she lie there? Long enough for two of the stage passengers to die. Otis had run out of ammunition, and Richard, having snatched up the guns of the fallen men, quickly emptied them.

Only the guns of the driver and guard protected them. The shadows grew longer and the sun dipped toward the jagged mountains carving a horizon on the darkening sky. The guard clutched at his chest as an arrow hit him, then fell, mortally wounded.

Twilight was brief, a fleeting pause between day and night. Minutes after the sun disappeared, the Indians stopped the attack.

Exhausted, Richard and the others dropped to the ground and rested for a moment before the driver turned his attention to the dead men, pulling their bodies away from the coach. He said to Richard, "See to your wife. She's hurt."

There was a wild, exhilarated light in Richard's eyes as he crawled over to where she lay. "Looks like you broke your ankle, old girl." He pulled off his cravat to bind her foot.

Otis came to them and began to ease her shoe from her rapidly swelling foot. "They'll probably leave us alone until morning. They don't like fighting at night."

"Then this is our opportunity to escape," Richard said.

The driver materialized in the shadows beside him. "They don't like to fight at night, but they ain't going to let us just walk out of here either." It was then that they saw that he too was wounded. A dark stain soaked his sleeve. The arrowhead was still imbedded in his upper arm, although he had broken off the shaft. He eased himself down beside Sarah and turned to the two men. "We might have a chance if one of you could get to the stage station. They could send word to Fort Bowie."

"I'll go," Richard said at once.

Later, it occurred to Sarah that he hadn't asked which direction he should take. Nor had he returned when the first silver streaks of dawn peeled the night back from the sky.

With the daylight came a horde of red warriors, their ponies leaping over the barricade of dead horses. Sarah's last memory, as she attempted to roll out of the way of pounding hooves, was the death cry of the driver. Then a blow to her head brought unconsciousness.

When she awoke she was lying on the ground in an encampment, her arms and legs bound with strips of rawhide. Nearby lay Otis, also bound, and she was so relieved to see that he was still alive that tears sprang to her eyes. Her joy turned to horror when she realized that he had been only temporarily spared in order to endure a slower death.

Sarah sat up. Now memory was a present, living thing, not just pictures from the past, because her emotions, terror, revulsion, and horror were in the here and now. A small cry escaped her lips.

Immediately she felt a hand on hers, warm and reassuring. Bewildered, she turned to look at Hakan, and saw, beyond his concerned face, the compartment of the English train. "You were asleep—dreaming something bad?" he asked.

"I'm all right," Sarah said, her heart pounding. "I was remembering being captured by the Comanches, and what happened to us before they traded their prisoners to the Chiricahua Apache."

10

Jean paced nervously around the threadbare and somber sitting room of the doctor's house while Mrs. Tremayne went to fetch him. Jean's heart felt as leaden as the storm-tossed clouds that raced past the window. She was filled with such despair that the fragile veneer of her composure threatened to crack at any second.

Andrew came to her at once. No matter how busy he was, his face always lit up when he saw her. It was a particularly endearing characteristic of his, Jean thought. She wished, not for the first time, that she could have met Andrew before the Earl of Moreland had burst like a comet into her sheltered life.

As the doctor greeted her, his compassionate gaze quickly assessed her distress, and mistaking the reason for it, he asked, "I take it the gypsy boy wasn't found?"

"It seems that I managed to frighten away Danior, and you have lost his sister. We're a fine pair, Dr. McGreal, aren't we? Apparently we endeavored to help people who didn't want our help."

His eyes seemed to reach out and touch her, to soothe away some of the hurt and pain she had locked up inside. "I thought we'd decided that we were friends, that you would call me Andrew."

She felt color creep up over her face. "Yes—of course, Andrew. I hoped perhaps you would have heard from Chavi."

"I can't help feeling that she wanted to rejoin her people," Andrew said. "Although I'm disappointed to think that she'd leave in the dead of night, without a word to either myself or Mrs. Tremayne."

"Yes, you're right, I'm sure. I'm more worried about the little boy. How will he find his way back to the Romany caravans?"

"Perhaps he and Chavi had a prearranged meeting place?" Andrew suggested. "You mustn't worry about them, Jean. They're gypsies. Nomads. They're used to wandering about the country."

Mrs. Tremayne arrived with a tea tray and a stern glance at Andrew that was intended to remind him that his morning surgery would be starting soon. Jean knew he must be surprised by the early hour of her visit, but was too polite to inquire as to the reason. By now his sensitive mind would have recognized that there was a great deal more on Jean's mind than the missing gypsies.

After Mrs. Tremayne departed, Jean picked up the slightly tarnished silver pot, but Andrew said, "Better let me do that. You're shaking like a leaf and you're very pale. What's wrong, Jean? You can tell me."

She said, "Richard's first wife and his son are coming home."

He blinked. "But—I thought she was killed on their honeymoon."

"No. She's been living in America. Richard wasn't even aware that he had a son by her."

He handed her a cup of tea. "Was it a case of amnesia, or what?"

The tongs trembled in Jean's fingers as she attempted to pick up a sugar cube. "I wanted to tell you all about it, Andrew, but, well my brother suggested we keep it quiet until he and Philip went to America to determine if it really was she."

"I wondered about their sudden departure. I take it the woman is not an imposter?"

"She is Sarah Merrin, Countess of Moreland. And I am

Jean Leighton, a spinster with two illegitimate children." All of her pent-up anguish seemed to be uncorked by her speaking the words. Her hands flew to her face as she struggled to hold back a flood of tears.

Without being completely aware of how it happened, Jean found herself seated on a shabby leather settee beside Andrew, his arm around her shoulders as her tears fell on the worn lapel of his coat.

When at last her choked sobs subsided, Andrew asked, "Has Richard told you what he intends to do about the situation?"

"No," Jean whispered, gratefully accepting the handkerchief he offered and dabbing at her eyes. "I'm such a coward. I'm not sure I have the courage even to meet Sarah and her son. They'll be here in a few days. I really want to drop off the face of the earth . . . but instead I came to you, my dear friend."

"I'm glad you did. Jean." He paused. "You know you can count on me for anything you need. Anything at all. Anytime."

She realized that his arm was still around her, and suddenly embarrassed, she sat up straight. His arm dropped to the back of the settee. He said quickly, "The honorable thing to do, of course, is for Richard to divorce his first wife and legalize his marriage to you."

"He's already told me that he has no intention of suing for divorce. There's never been a divorce in his family and . . . well, it's unthinkable to men of his class."

"But surely, under the circumstances. Perhaps he didn't mean it. Knowing your husband, he's probably enjoying the sheer drama of the situation."

"The scandal, if the news gets out, will be awful. I couldn't bear for the children to—God, Andrew, what shall I do?"

"Tell me exactly what Richard has told you."

"Only that Hilliard Stoughton, his solicitor, will be present when everyone's future will be discussed. I don't know when that will be."

She didn't add that Richard had enjoyed tormenting her about what was to become of her, threatening everything from installing her in a back-street love nest to selling her into white slavery. He had reminded her that she had lived with him without benefit of marriage, and was, therefore, eminently suited to a career as a fallen woman.

Andrew said gently, "If you wish, I'll come too. I can at least offer moral support."

She was so grateful she clasped his hands in hers and felt him tremble slightly at her touch. "Thank you," she whispered, hoping he couldn't sense her feeling of unutterable dread about what might happen. Her fears were elusive, fragmented, impossible to put into words. Her husband wasn't behaving very differently toward her than he had since the birth of the twins. His infidelities and drunken binges had become part of her life. But a new element had been introduced into his attitude toward her that made her fear where his excesses might lead. She wished passionately she could confide in Andrew, but her shame was too deep.

Richard had returned from Liverpool in a state of barely concealed anticipation, the same kind of anticipation she had seen him exhibit when he was about to take some risk or encounter a dangerous situation. Two years ago he had gone on an African safari and had had the same expression when he'd departed.

Upon his arrival home after meeting Sarah, he had taunted Jean with sadistic pleasure. Entering her bedroom uninvited, he came to her bed. "Sarah is more excitingly beautiful than I could have possibly imagined," he said, looking at Jean with an expression that said he found her plain by comparison. "A challenge," Richard added. "She presents a challenge in a way that you, my sweet, never did. You were simply too pathetically grateful that you and your brother had been rescued from an impoverished background and were assured a place in society, that your children could grow up in the lap of luxury."

"They're your children, too," Jean had said in growing alarm.

Richard lolled back on her bed. "I've been in a state of intense arousal for two days. Seeing Sarah again made my blood churn. I'd forgotten how exciting she is." He patted the quilt beside him in invitation. "Will you satisfy my needs, Jean, or shall I go and find a woman who will?"

She had gasped, shocked by his crudeness, unsure if he merely wanted to flaunt his sexual appetite before her or if he really meant that he wanted her to service his desire for another woman. In either case, his cruelty appalled her. "Please," she whispered. "Don't humiliate me so."

"But my dear, I'm not asking you to risk pregnancy. There are other things you can do. Must you be such a prude? After all, you are, in the eyes of society, a scarlet woman. A whore, my dear. It's time you learned a few whore's tricks, don't you think?"

Memories of the ugly events of the evening and her own desperation brought a hot stain to her cheeks. But worse was the dread of what he planned to do tonight. He'd hinted this morning that since she was now willing to fulfill his physical needs, he'd stored up a whole host of sexual fantasies.

"Jean." Andrew's voice interrupted her reverie. "I'll cancel my morning surgery and take you home. I don't want you to be alone, even for a short time."

She shut out the memory of the night before with Richard, deeply ashamed of what had transpired between them. But she had lived through the ordeal and would survive whatever tonight would bring. There was no need to add to her own sense of degradation by confiding in Andrew. "No . . . no, I'll be all right. Your patients need you."

He stared at her, concerned. "Are you sure you're not ill? You're deathly pale. Perhaps I should at least take your temperature?"

"I'm not ill, really."

"What are your brother's feelings about the situation?"

"Randolph has been asked to leave Merrinswood. I don't know what happened—he's so angry he didn't want to discuss it with me. He's moving to a room in a boardinghouse in the village today. He was so furious that Richard would simply let him go after all these years that I didn't dare tell him my fears—" She broke off, not wanting to put those fears into words. The picture in her mind was of two golden-haired children who now bore the stigma of illegitimacy.

She rose reluctantly. "There's a question I'd like to ask. Could he . . . could Richard simply turn his back on us—on the twins and me?"

Andrew's sensitive lips compressed, and it was clear from his anguished expression that he felt her hurt and humiliation. "My knowledge of all of the nuances of the law is limited, I'm afraid. But, well . . . as far as I can see, you're his common-law wife. As such, I don't believe you have any legal claim on him or his estate. Neither do your children. But I think you do have a moral right to expect . . ."

Jean didn't hear the rest of what he said. Her mind was filled with the vision of two innocent children and what might become of them. Robbie and Emily had to stay at Merrinswood no matter what happened to her. It was their birthright.

As the carriage went up the driveway toward the house, Sarah leaned forward, not wanting to miss a single detail of the grounds. How lovely the trees were against the summer sky, how soft the late afternoon sunlight. The turf of the lawns had the velvet sheen that only years of rolling could produce.

The first time she had come here it had been early spring, and hundreds of daffodils and narcissus had added their golden aura to the richly gilded stone of the house. Had she fallen in love with the house first? Or with the golden-haired Richard?

But love was akin to hate, and she was no longer the young ingenue who had been dazzled by it all. Besides, she wouldn't be staying. She'd been surprised when Richard suggested that she come.

"But your wife, Jean—"

Richard had shrugged. "It was her idea. She wants to meet you."

Sarah had thought rapidly that she would also like to meet Jean and her children; that Hakan would not have to undergo the ordeal of arriving at Merrinswood alone; that perhaps if they all sat down together to discuss the future, a fair and equitable solution might be possible for all concerned. She didn't for a moment believe that Richard really wanted to resume his marriage to her—that was a game he played to throw her off-balance. But provisions would have to be made for his other children after Hakan was named heir to the estate.

Hakan sat beside her, his clear blue eyes registering his surprise at the sheer size of his heritage.

"All the land that you can see, and more, belongs to your family," she said.

"Surely one family cannot need so much land?"

For a moment Sarah wondered if she had waited too long.

Was it possible for Hakan, raised as a nomad with no ties to any one piece of land, to now feel the territorial thrill of ownership of a vast estate? Enough to fight for it, if necessary? Oh, he was Apache, he was a fighter—but a guerilla fighter, not one versed in the intellectual machinations of legal battles. She had no doubt that the formidable Jean would fight for her young son's rights.

"The house is made of gold," Hakan said, as they drew closer.

"No, it's just mellowed stone that aged to that rich amber."

"It is very large."

"Yes. And quite beautiful. I'd forgotten that a house could possess such grace."

The carriage stopped and Sarah saw that a footman was positioned at the bottom of the terrace steps to await their arrival. He was young, a stranger to her. She supposed few of the servants who had been at Merrinswood sixteen years ago remained. But after they alighted and went up the steps, followed by the footman carrying their bags, the front door was opened by Barlow, the rather unpleasantly impassive butler who had been with the family when Sarah had married Richard.

"Welcome home, milady," he said, with no welcome in his eyes. She could see that he was making a visible effort not to stare at Hakan. Barlow added, "His Grace was called away on a matter of extreme urgency. He asked me to express his regrets and tell you that he will return shortly. He thought you might like to rest after your journey."

"Is Lady Moreland here?" Sarah asked, unsure how to refer to Richard's present wife and deciding to use her own title.

Barlow's eyes were fixed on a spot over her head. "No, milady."

"I see. Very well. Have our bags taken to whichever rooms have been assigned to us. Then send the housekeeper to the breakfast room. I want to take James on a tour of the house."

The butler stood still, his lips slightly parted but his face still blank.

Sarah pulled off her gloves and hat and handed them to him, then asked, "Is something unclear to you, Barlow?"

"No, milady." He turned to obey with obvious reluctance as the footman crossed the marble-floored hall and went up the main staircase.

His mother felt great pride, Hakan knew, as she showed him the house. For her sake he tried to express proper interest in room after room, treasures and still more treasures. How could one family require so much? Sarah seemed to have forgotten the simple life she had lived as wife of *Tonsaroyoo*.

Hakan never uttered the name of his Apache father aloud, as there was a taboo about disturbing the dead, but he was never far from Hakan's thoughts. Yet his mother had begun to speak of *Tonsaroyoo*, which in the white-eyes' language meant Lone Wolf, and told Hakan that it was only a superstition that saying the name of a dead person brought forth his ghost.

She seemed to believe that it was as easy for him to slip into the role of white-eyes as it had been for her, forgetting that he'd had little preparation other than being taught the language and a rudimentary knowledge of the history and geography of both England and America. His mother had also taught him simple mathematics, in order to deal with pounds, shillings, and pence. She'd complimented him on having a good head for figures, but hadn't explained the need for the paper banknotes and cumbersome coins. A barter system worked just as well.

As they followed Mrs. Braithwaite, an old woman who wrinkled her nose as if she smelled something bad, he carefully observed certain items that would guide him back to the door leading outside, marking a trail in his mind.

The housekeeper turned to look at him, then said to his mother, "It's a marvel how you two can walk on a marble floor and not make a sound."

"Do today's manners permit personal remarks, Mrs. Braithwaite?" Sarah asked.

The woman turned red and muttered an apology.

Hakan tried to be helpful. He pointed out to the housekeeper, "You would make less noise when you walk if you would breathe through your nose. When I was small we used to run several miles each morning with our mouths full of water. This taught us to breathe correctly."

Mrs. Braithwaite's tiny eyes blinked rapidly and, ignoring

him, she asked his mother, "Will you be wanting to go belowstairs, milady?"

"Not today. When his Grace returns no doubt he'll have Barlow assemble the servants in order to present his son to them. What we'd like now is to be shown to our rooms so that we may change our clothes. Inform the stablemaster that we'd like two horses saddled and ready for us in fifteen minutes."

To her son, Sarah said, "I've a surprise for you. Come and see what I bought for us in Liverpool."

In the spacious second-floor room that was to be his, Sarah presented Hakan with very strange looking leggings, boots, and coat. "It's for riding," she said. "Your father suggested I buy it, as well as a riding habit for myself."

"Habit . . ." Hakan repeated, searching his mind. "That is a tendency to act always in the same manner."

"That too. In this case it's a garment. Shall I ring for a valet to help you into your riding clothes?"

"No!" Hakan said, in alarm. "I'll do it myself."

"Hurry," his mother said. "I want you to see as much of the estate as possible before your father returns."

As Hakan suspected, he was required to ride a saddled horse. How could Englishmen tolerate these uncomfortable clothes *and* a saddle? he asked himself despairingly. Why did they make it so difficult for themselves to enjoy being one with their ponies? He longed for the freedom of soft buckskin leggings and only a blanket between him and the horse as they set off across the cobbled courtyard. His mother was even worse off, as her "habit" consisted of a long black skirt and her saddle forced her to sit sideways on her mount.

Once they left the grounds, which were beautiful but too orderly and tamed for his taste, and found themselves in open fields bordered by either hedgerows or low stone walls, Hakan felt a glimmer of interest.

"This is Merrin farmland," his mother said, as her mare cantered beside his. "The Merrins farm some of it themselves, and the rest is leased to tenant farmers."

They passed small cottages, barns, sheep grazing on a hillock, cattle filling a meadow. Then all at once they were out in wild, untamed country, rolling treeless hills with low-growing brush over which blue-tinted mists floated like ghostly veils.

As if in unspoken agreement, they gave their mounts their heads and raced with the wind across the misty blue-green moors. For the first time since leaving Arizona, Hakan felt alive. He was grateful to his mother for recognizing that he needed to be astride a horse again, and for standing up to the sullen Barlow and crafty-eyed Mrs. Braithwaite in order to make it possible.

When at last his mother suggested that they must return to the house, he was reluctant to go, but began to see that his life in England might not be quite the ordeal he'd imagined.

This feeling vanished when he learned that he had to change his clothes again in order to eat dinner. The English, it seemed, were obsessed with changing their clothes, having different types of garments for every conceivable activity.

The meal was served in a dining room as big as a canyon, with enormous artificial lights that glittered like huge clusters of stars. Only he and his mother responded to the dinner gong. Barlow had set places for them at each end of the long table, and they were separated by a towering centerpiece of fresh flowers that were fragrant, but blocked their view of one another.

"Are we to dine alone, Barlow?" his mother asked.

"Yes, milady. His Grace has not yet returned."

"What about Philip? Isn't he here?"

"He doesn't reside in the main house nowadays, milady."

"Where does he reside then?"

"In the guest house, milady."

"Would you please send someone to inquire if he'd like to join us for dinner?"

"He has also left the estate, milady."

Hakan couldn't see his mother, but could well imagine her exasperation at this exchange. However, she merely instructed the butler to begin serving, but to omit the fish course.

Later, when they'd finished eating, she led the way to another vast room, this one completely lined with books. Hakan gasped at the variety and number of books, running his hand over smooth leather and other textures, carefully sounding out the shorter titles. His reading lessons had not yet progressed to the point that he could decipher many of the gold-embossed words, but all at once he was curious about the knowledge contained in so many books.

"The library was always my favorite room," Sarah said, pulling a volume from a shelf and caressing it with her hands. "I saved it for last."

"So many books—for just one family," Hakan said.

His mother took the book and sat down in a leather armchair beside a crackling coal fire glowing in a marble-faced fireplace. She surveyed him over the book, which she clutched to her breast. "A strange homecoming, a strange evening altogether. I suspect your father planned it so to intimidate us."

Hakan eyed a sheepskin rug placed in front of the fire, and although he knew he was supposed to take a chair, he sank cross-legged to the floor. "Perhaps something happened that caused his absence. Perhaps it was not planned."

Sarah gave a small, unreadable smile. "How long, I wonder, will you be able to remain so generous in this selfish society?"

Before he had a chance to reply, the library door burst open and a little girl bounded into the room. She was a plain child, but as fleet-footed as a deer, with darting eyes that were filled with suspicion.

"I want to see the wild Indian!" Catching sight of Hakan seated on the floor, silhouetted against the leaping flames of the fire, she skidded to a stop. "Ooh!"

A plump young woman in a brown dress came panting into the room. "I'm so sorry," she said breathlessly, to no one in particular. To the child she said, "Emily, you are a very naughty little girl. Come back to the nursery at once."

"You are the governess?" Sarah asked.

"Yes, milady. My name is Charlotte. I do apologize for Emily's rudeness."

Rising to his feet, Hakan held out his hand to the child. "I am called James. It's true I am Apache, but I am not wild. I am glad to meet you, Emily."

The little girl approached him cautiously, but there was disappointment on her face now. "You look very ordinary to me. Just like my brother, or Daddy."

"Emily!" The governess exclaimed, her large bosom heaving. She seized the child's hand before she could place it in Hakan's, and the two of them departed as hurriedly as they'd arrived.

There was silence in their wake until Sarah remarked

thoughtfully, "The little girl is one of twins, like her mother. It's interesting that Emily defied her governess to come and see us while her brother Robbie didn't."

Hakan had almost, but not quite, forgotten about Sir Randolph Leighton. He, of course, was the twin brother of the child's mother. They hadn't seen him since the ship docked.

Sarah said, "Sit down—in a chair this time, please, and let me read to you for a while. It will help both of us relax so we can sleep tonight."

He thought wistfully of the wild rolling moors, and wished it were possible to sleep under the stars, but dutifully sat in the chair at the other side of the fireplace. His mother opened the book and said, "This is a novel by Sir Walter Scott . . ."

The following morning Sarah managed to hide her apprehension from her son when, following a leisurely breakfast and a stroll around the gardens, there was still no sign of either Richard or Jean.

Curious now about the mother of the plain-featured little girl, Sarah led her son to the portrait gallery, hoping to find a picture of Jean. As they walked past the long row of Merrin males and their ladies, Sarah thought again how strikingly similar the physical characteristics of the men were.

When they reached the far end of the long gallery she stopped, looking up at a large portrait of herself as a young bride. Had she ever looked as eager as that?

"It's you," Hakan said, pleased. "How very young you were! But you're more beautiful now."

"Thank you," Sarah murmured, glancing back down the long row of oil paintings. She remembered every single one of them, identifying each generation of Merrin brides from their looks and dress. There was no painting of Jean. She had been Richard's wife for eight years, yet he had never commissioned an artist to paint her portrait.

Remembering his mocking words in the Liverpool hotel about not being sure he wanted a divorce, Sarah decided it was imperative that she learn the true nature of his relationship with Jean as quickly as possible.

The portrait gallery ended at the top of a curving flight of stairs leading down to the marble entryhall. They were halfway down the staircase when they heard heavy footsteps crossing the hall from the direction of the front doors.

Sir Randolph Leighton, his swarthy face suffused with an angry flush, came striding into view. He stopped abruptly when he saw Sarah and Hakan.

"Damn you." The words were flung at them like a whip. "Damn you both to hell. This is all your doing. By God, if anything's happened to my sister I'll see you pay dearly—"

"Sir Randolph!" Sarah cut him off. "How dare you threaten us? We haven't even met your sister yet."

"Nor is such a meeting imminent, madam," Sir Randolph said. "Because Jean has disappeared. She's been missing since shortly after she learned that you and your misbegotten son were coming to Merrinswood."

11

Chavi watched Lysander shoulder his way through the crowd of embarking passengers on the quay. She felt sorry for the way people averted their eyes, or worse, showed their horror at his appearance.

Standing on the steerage deck of the steamer, she wrapped her shawl a little tighter around the baby, who slept contentedly against her breast.

Lysander was alone. Chavi bit her lip with worry. There was so little time until the ship sailed. Before he reached her side she blurted out, "Where is he? Oh, what could have happened to him?"

"There was a wire from Yorkshire," Lysander said. In the bright daylight his scars were so livid that she felt a physical pain when she looked at them. "Your brother isn't sailing with us. He'll travel with your fancy man."

"Don't call him that!"

"What? Your brother?"

"Don't tease me, please. You know who I mean. Oh, I'm so worried about Danior. I never should have left Yorkshire without him. And I feel terrible about not thanking Doctor McGreal for taking care of me."

"I told you—we had to keep our journey secret."

"But the Countess took Danior home with her. What will become of him when she finds out her husband is leaving her?"

"Surely you trust his lordship to keep his word?"

The sarcasm in his tone wasn't lost on her, but she had to believe the best would happen, because the worst was unthinkable. She sighed. "If Lord Moreland said he'd bring Danior, then he will."

Lysander propped his elbow on the rail and looked at the waterfront buildings. He rarely allowed her to look at him full face for more than a few seconds. His profile would have been striking had it not been for the cruel distortion of his scars. "Have you seen our accommodations?"

"I've seen some narrow bunks down in the hold. Very dark and crowded. I believe I'll spend as much time out in the open as I can."

Lysander laughed. Sometimes he had a musical laugh that surprised and charmed her, but more often it was full of sarcasm, as it was now. "Gypsies," he muttered, and there was no need for him to elaborate on how he felt about her people. "Well, I for one have seen enough departures from dreary seaports. I'm going below to sleep."

As he turned to go she said, "Lysander . . ."

"Yes?"

"You said it will take weeks and weeks to sail to Australia."

"That's right. We'll go through the Suez Canal. There'll be many a foreign port along the way. Maybe we'll even be able to go ashore in some of them."

She drew a deep breath. "Would you . . . would you teach me how to read?"

His eyes burned like coals in his ravaged face. "So that you can read the volume of Keats his lordship gave you?"

"So that I won't be so ignorant," she answered. "So that when I meet him again he'll . . . admire my mind."

"As much as he admires your body, you mean?"

She wrenched her gaze from his, unnerved by his contempt. "I never knew, before I met him, how ignorant I am. I don't want him to be ashamed of me."

Surprisingly, his tone softened. "Listen, gypsy, you're going to be a beautiful woman one of these days when some of those gaunt hollows in your face fill in. A man would be a fool to be ashamed of a woman as lovely as you'll be."

He turned to leave and she put out her hand, resting it on his arm. "Will you teach me to read?"

For a moment she thought that she felt his arm, though it was strong as an oak branch, shiver slightly under her touch. Then he said abruptly, "Why not? I can be a Pygmalion as well as a Lysander."

She watched him push through the passengers thronging the deck to wave to their relatives on the quay, and she was saddened by the way they cringed at the sight of him and moved hastily aside. From the back he looked so splendid, tall and broad-shouldered, carrying himself like a king, his dark brown hair waving softly on his well-shaped head. If only a person didn't have to look into that horribly disfigured face, she thought. Or listen to his caustic remarks. He spoke as if he hated the whole world and clearly preferred not to converse with anyone at all if he could avoid it.

Now that she knew Lysander was accompanying her to the far side of the earth only because he was emigrating to Australia himself, she felt less obligated to him. But there were moments when, despite his terrible demeanor, she felt compassion for him. Perhaps it was because he was gentle with the baby.

As the passengers pressed in around her to lean over the rail and call their good-byes to friends and relatives who had come to see them off, Chavi decided to go below until the ship sailed. After all, there was no one on the quay to wave to her.

Australia! She still couldn't believe it. At first she'd been a little afraid to board the steamer with Lysander, and had protested that she would wait and travel with her beloved. But Lysander explained that Lord Moreland wished her to get his house in order before he arrived. It seemed natural enough that a man of his position would want his comforts in place ahead of him.

What was perplexing was Lysander's reaction to her agreeing to go. Instead of telling her she was showing good sense, he'd curled his parody of a mouth into a sardonic grin and said, "I knew a gypsy wouldn't be able to resist treading strange ground."

When the ship began to wallow in the treacherous storms of the Bay of Biscay, Chavi would have gladly trodden any kind of ground at all. None of the steerage passengers, nor, probably, any of the others, were allowed on deck. Great waves washed over the ship and everything was tied down, except the passengers, who clung in abject misery to their bunks.

The stench of vomit and urine, the moans of the seasick emigrants and the wailing of children all added to Chavi's ordeal. She would have simply given up living had it not been for the fact that Brenna needed her milk.

Lysander took care of the infant when Chavi wasn't actually nursing her. At first a crew member had tried to stop him from entering the women's quarters, but Lysander had simply lifted the man off his feet and tossed him aside like a rag doll. After that, no one stood in Lysander's way.

Since he had arranged for all of their necessary travel documents, which he had not shown to her, she knew only that he had adopted the surname of "Smith" for all of them. Lysander Smith; it sounded quite noble and certainly didn't go with the fearsome man who used it.

Then one morning they awoke to clear skies, calm seas, and brilliant sunshine. Lysander came for her and said, "Come on, gypsy, you're going to live after all. We'll go on deck and feed you, then we'll begin your lessons. Fetch your volume of Keats, as it's the only book we own."

They found a spot on the crowded steerage deck, and Lysander spread a blanket for them to sit on. Chavi laid the baby across her knee and looked up at him expectantly. A stiff ocean breeze, already balmy with the hint of tropical warmth, blew her long hair about her face.

Lysander stood looking down at her for a moment, then suddenly reached out and caught a handful of her hair in his fist. She froze, feeling revulsion and fear, yet knowing that it would be a serious mistake to let him know how she reacted to his touch.

Slowly, he pulled her hair away from her face, up into a tangled knot on top of her head. "At what age do gypsies put up their hair?"

"The Romany women don't usually put up their hair. Why?"

"You want to learn to read. Would you like to learn to be a lady, too? A lady grand enough to go anywhere with his lordship?"

She caught her breath. "You mean like the Countess?"

"No, I mean more beautiful than any highborn English lady. But just as socially accomplished."

"Oh, yes!"

He loosened his hold on her hair. "I'm going to transform you, gypsy. You're going to be a lady. What do you think about that?"

She cocked her head to one side and tried to see beyond the ugliness of his features to the man inside. "I believe you could do it, Lysander, because you're really a gentleman, even if you pretend you're not."

He jerked his hand away from her as though he'd been bitten. "If you believe I'm a gentleman, then you're a fool as well as an ignorant gypsy. I'm just as ugly inside as out, I assure you. Think of me as the devil himself and you'll not be far off the mark."

Chavi felt as though acid had been flung at her, his growling voice was so abrasive, but she forced herself to give him a cool stare. "You won't succeed in frightening me, Lysander, so give up. Gypsies aren't afraid of bogeymen. You're forgetting, mothers scare their children by threatening them with *us*."

Scowling, he dropped down beside her on the blanket and snapped open the book.

"Lysander?"

"What is it?"

"Did Lord Moreland ask you to turn me into a lady?"

He threw back his head and laughed, the most chilling laugh she'd ever heard. She shrank back, away from the sound, away from this terrible man, and the baby stirred and began to whimper.

"I'm going to teach you how to survive in a world where there will be plenty of Lord Morelands panting after you. I'm doing it for my own amusement, nothing more. As you said, it's a long way to Australia, and there's time to kill. Now let's see, where shall we begin? Do you at least know your alphabet?"

Chavi shook her head. Lysander looked down at the printed page and began to read aloud, his voice surprisingly soft and gentle. *"Thou still unravished bride of quietness, Thou foster child of Silence and slow Time . . ."*

Chavi listened, a captive of his resonant voice, and Brenna drifted off to sleep again, lulled by the sound. It didn't matter that neither mother nor infant understood what the poem was about.

After a while Lysander stopped reading. "I'm going to teach you the sounds the letters make. There are only twenty-six, although the vowels serve a double purpose. We'll begin with the consonants."

Chavi gave a small sigh.

Lysander glanced sideways at her. "What was that all about?"

"I was just wishing Danior could be here so he could learn too."

Danior watched in enchantment as the organ-grinder's monkey danced to the lilting tune. The little animal in the striped jacket and straw hat darted among the crowd like an agile, miniature old man.

It was market day and the square was filled with vegetable stands and vendors hawking every conceivable item. It was a good day for a hungry gypsy boy to slip into the village unnoticed and perhaps find something to eat. Danior had existed on stolen apples for several days, apples which were too green and had given him a terrible bellyache. But he had a more important mission today than merely appeasing his constant hunger. He was searching the faces of the milling crowd looking for one he might be able to trust.

Coming upon the organ-grinder, Danior had been so captivated by the monkey that he didn't notice his owner until the man stopped turning the handle of the organ mounted on a pushcart. As the music died, the monkey whipped off his hat and pranced about, trying to collect coppers from the crowd.

The street musician, who would earn a little more by sharpening knives and scissors, was a stooped, slightly built man with skin almost as dark as Danior's, and brown velvet eyes as soulful as a saint's. He called to the crowd, urging them to go home and fetch their dulled blades and he'd put a fine new edge on them. He spoke in heavily accented English that was pleasantly singsong.

The onlookers began to drift away now that the entertainment was over. The organ-grinder had waited too long to start the music again and lost his crowd. He began to turn the handle again, but it was too late, the audience was gone.

Danior recognized the notes of the new melody, a hurdy-gurdy rendition of an old Scottish folk song. The Romany caravans had spent a couple of years north of the border and Danior remembered the words to the song. Without knowing quite why he did it, he opened his mouth and sang the words in his clear soprano voice. *"Row merry boats, like a bird on the wing, over the sea to Skye. Carry the lad that's born to be king, over the sea to Skye."*

A shawl-wrapped farmer's wife stopped and turned to look back at him. Several other women returned, then a couple of men. One of the vendors selling cucumbers and watercress left his stall to come and listen.

The organ-grinder's eyes met Danior's, and it seemed in that instant that each knew they'd come to this place to meet. The monkey, however, realizing the crowd's attention was now focused on a usurper, scampered over to Danior and bit him on the leg.

Danior yelled in pain and the organ-grinder bent and grabbed the monkey, scolding him in a foreign language. Several of the watchers laughed and dropped coins into the hat before moving on.

The organ-grinder said, *"Scusi*, Alphonso is jealous of you. I'm sorry he bit you. Here, let me see your leg. Oh, it's not so bad." When he spoke he seemed to hold on to the end of his words, so that "leg" sounded like "legga."

Danior peered into the man's face, wondering if he could be a Romany, too. Before he could inquire, the man asked, "You're a gypsy, aren't you? What are you doing all alone, a little fella like you?"

"Are you one of us?" Danior asked.

The man smiled. "No, I'm Italian. My name is Pasquale. But you can call me Pas. What's yours?"

"Danior."

"Well, Danior," Pas said, taking the hat from the monkey, *"Sia detto fra noi*, we probably wouldn'ta gotta this if you hadn't come along. How you like to have supper with us?"

Danior couldn't believe his luck. Not only had he found the man he was seeking, but he was to be fed, too.

A couple of women brought their carving knives to be sharpened. Then Pas went to the butcher's stall and bought a string of sausages. They stopped at a vegetable stand and bought overripe tomatoes on their way out of the square.

"I'm new in the north country, Danior," Pas said as they trundled down the road, the monkey on Pas's shoulder. "Where can we go to make a fire and cook our supper?"

"Out on the moors there's lots of places to hide. But you must watch out for the bogs, they can swallow up a horse."

Pas gave him a quick sidelong glance, but made no comment.

Danior was able to contain his eagerness to ask the favor of his new friend until they were camped in a rocky hollow, replete with a tasty meal the organ-grinder cooked in a single pot over a fire. He had combined the sausage with doughlike strands that he called pasta and immersed the whole in a sauce made from the tomatoes.

"*Buono appetito*, young man who sings like an angel," Pas said. Danior had never tasted anything so delicious.

When they finished eating, Danior said, "My sister is in the village."

"Ah," Pas said, "I thought perhaps you'd run away from your people. But what's a gypsy doing living in a village?"

"She's at the doctor's house. She had a baby. Our father said she couldn't stay with him any more. Now the caravans are gone and I need somebody to go to the doctor's house and tell Chavi where I am."

"And why can't you go to the doctor's house yourself?"

Danior looked into Pas's kind face and decided he could trust him. He told the whole story, accompanied by the excited chattering of the monkey, who had awakened from a nap and was enraged to find the usurper for his master's affections still with them.

"Well, Danior," Pas said when he'd finished, "I'ma glad to hear you were going to put the pitcher back. You mustn't never steal. It'sa not worth it. I'll go and see the doctor tomorrow morning. You can sleep here with me tonight."

Danior nodded, his eyelids already heavy.

Pas said, "You have a beautiful voice, little one. Is there any sound more heartbreaking than a young boy's singing? P'raps it's because we know how fleeting a sound it is. So soon gone." Then he began to sing softly himself, in his soothing foreign tongue, and Danior drifted off to sleep, feeling that today had been the best day he'd had since he'd been separated from Chavi.

The following morning, Danior waited at their camp while Pas took Alphonso into the village again. They decided that the risk of running into one of the Merrinswood servants was too great for Danior to go back to the village, now that market day was over.

When at last he saw the pushcart trundling toward him, Danior ran to meet Pas.

"I'm sorry, little one. She's gone. Your sister isn't at the doctor's house no more. I pretended I'd run into the caravans and your people asked me to find out how Chavi was. The housekeeper said she'd run off in the middle of the night."

Danior felt as if all the lights in the whole world had suddenly been turned off. He turned away so that Pas wouldn't see the tears that filled his eyes.

A gentle hand touched his shoulder. "P'raps your sister found her way back to the gypsy caravans. Don't worry. We'll catch up with them. You stay with me tilla we do. You can sing while I play, and I'll teach you to dance, too. Alphonso is getting old; he dances only when he feels like it. I think maybe you and me, we're *anima gemella*—twin souls."

Alphonso chattered angrily and Danior, despite Pas's reassurances, felt afraid. He wanted to stay with Pas, but a nagging premonition of danger refused to go away. The boy sensed that this man was as much an outcast as himself, and together they'd be in more danger.

But that day it seemed that every farmer's wife they approached had nothing but dull knifes and useless scissors, and Pas did a brisk business sharpening blades. He told Danior he'd brought him luck for sure.

Eager to help, Danior carried knives back and forth from kitchen to pushcart. Once he reached for a knife in a leather sheath, thinking it was one of a batch he'd carried out, but Pas said, "No, not that one. That's the one I keep to coax them. I don't want you never to touch that one. See . . ."

He withdrew the lethal-looking blade from the sheath and then pulled one of the hairs from his head. Holding it between thumb and forefinger, he sliced it cleanly in two with a swoosh of the knife. Danior blinked in amazement.

Pas said, "This one would chop off your finger if you

touched the blade. I honed all of the edges, and the point, tilla they're like razors, so I can show the women what good work I do."

Danior stared, fascinated, as the blade caught the golden sunlight and turned it into cold silver fire. He'd be sure never to touch that particular knife. It was evil, he could tell.

12

Sarah looked up as Richard entered the library. It was after midnight, and unable to sleep, she had spent the evening trying to lose herself in a book. "Has your wife returned?"

"I don't believe she'll be back."

"But I understood that Randolph was going to see if she'd returned to the seaside resort in Lancashire where they lived as children—" She broke off. "I never should have come here. This is my fault. Richard, I want you to know that I—"

"Jean is a blasted ninny," Richard interrupted. "This is nothing more than a ploy for attention. God, how I hate a desperate woman. Is there any more unappealing creature on the face of the earth?"

Sarah jumped up, the book sliding from her lap. "I shall be leaving tomorrow. Perhaps—wherever Jean is—she'll hear that I'm gone and come home. It *is* her home, you know. I regret invading it."

"Sit down, Sarah. I just found this on her dressing table. Read it." He handed her a folded sheet of paper, then took the other armchair.

The letter was written in a childishly round script:

My Dear Richard:
  Since I am no longer bound by what I believed were my marriage vows, I am leaving you. I have not been happy,

as you're well aware, for some time. I release you from any obligation toward me, and would prefer that you do not try to find me.

However, I feel that the twins are Merrins, whether or not they legally bear your name, and they belong with you. Robbie is almost old enough to go away to boarding school, and I expect you could also find a suitable girls' boarding school for Emily. Perhaps I shall be able to see them again at some future time, when they are old enough to understand.

Yours,

Jean

Sarah refolded the letter. "Has she returned to her aunt in Lancashire, do you think?"

"Her aunt died years ago. Randolph thought the local vicar might know where Jean is. I'm sure she'll be in touch with her brother soon. They're very close."

"You were gone for so long. We believed you were searching for her."

"Did you now? You attributed more concern to me than I possess. Jean ran off, that was her choice. We're all separate and individual animals, Sarah. I don't subscribe to the 'my brother's keeper' philosophy."

"What have you told the twins?"

"That their mother hasn't been feeling well and is going to spend the winter in a warmer climate. No doubt there will be letters for them in due course. I'd really rather talk about you and your Apache son."

"Hakan—James—isn't Apache."

"No? He's more Apache than English. Do you really expect me to tame him?"

"I thought perhaps tutors for a while, then a good prep school."

Richard laughed. "I have a better idea. Your Apache chief brought the boy up to be an Indian brave. As soon as he's old enough he could join the army."

Sarah felt a coldness begin at the pit of her stomach. "I didn't bring him to England to put him into the army. The Apache have been hunted down like animals, slaughtered, herded onto reservations—"

"But Sarah, you just informed me that James isn't Apache.

What you seem to be overlooking, my dear wife, is that he is also my son. I now have a say in his future. Of course, I might be persuaded to change my mind about the army . . . it all depends." He regarded her with a sly smile.

Only a single lamp burned in the room, and in the semi-darkness it seemed that she could feel Richard's lust and her own ambitions for her son squaring off like phantom warriors. Richard's open sexuality had been in evidence throughout a tense dinner, when Hakan and Philip had been present. Richard's eyes had never left Sarah, examining every detail of her face and body with thinly disguised sensual interest.

She asked, "What do you want, Richard? I'm tired of playing games."

Laughing softly, he got up and went to a glass-fronted cabinet to select a bottle of brandy. "Will you join me in a nightcap?"

"No, thank you."

After he'd filled his glass he brought it to her chair and perched himself on the arm, his thigh grazing her elbow. "I want you to resume your role as my Countess. I want you to be my wife again, in every sense of the word."

Sarah sat very still, not moving even when he allowed one hand to stray to her shoulder, his fingers sliding into her hair and releasing several pins. "Why?" she asked.

He laughed again. "Why? Many reasons. You are, after all, legally the Countess of Moreland. You've succeeded in driving off the wife I had, and our rather closed society is hardly going to sit still for me marrying yet another woman. I surely don't have to remind you that divorce is unthinkable to members of our class?"

"Richard, how long do you think it will be before one of the servants gossips in the village about Hakan—James—and me? The whole story is going to be common knowledge very quickly."

"I've thought of that. I think the best way to handle it would be for you to have suffered from amnesia."

"And Jean? What will you tell everyone about her disappearance?"

"The same thing I've told the children. I didn't tell you earlier, but Jean took all of her jewelry with her. She isn't destitute, by any means. Believe me, Sarah, in a few weeks the hue and cry will have died down and everyone will have forgotten she was ever here, masquerading as my wife. She was never really meant to be, you know. She and Randolph are hardly of our class."

"Then why did you marry her?"

He shrugged. "Why, indeed? A man whose wife mysteriously dies on their honeymoon . . . doesn't have an unlimited choice of replacement brides. At least, not from among our rather exclusive group."

Yes, Sarah thought, that would be true enough. The members of the upper crust of British society to which Richard belonged were relatively few in number. Her mind raced even as her skin crawled with revulsion at his touch. No matter what, Hakan must inherit the estate, even if she had to sacrifice herself to Richard's lust. But perhaps it wouldn't come to that. For now, it would be best to hear him out.

Richard went on, "I need a wife to help me run the estate, rear three children, see to the servants, the entertaining, and all the other myriad duties a wife performs. Not least of which, of course . . ."

His hand encircled her neck and turned her face toward him. She felt his breath, faintly scented with brandy. Then his lips brushed her mouth, withdrew, returned to nibble playfully at her lower lip.

She jerked her head away. "Jean has been gone for less than forty-eight hours. How can you put her out of your life so quickly? It's as if she never existed for you."

"Perhaps she didn't. Oh, there was a certain wistful charm to her nine years ago when I first met her. She's quite plain, but has rather lovely eyes. Very dark blue, so that at first they appear to be brown. I imagined there was more in her eyes than there actually was. Poor dear proved to be colder than an iceberg in bed."

"I don't want to hear any intimate details," Sarah warned, starting to get up out of her chair.

His arm restrained her. "Jean's gone and she isn't coming back. Let's examine the situation logically, shall we? You didn't really expect to leave your son here while you went on your merry way, did you? He reminds me of an Alsatian dog I had once—handsome, intelligent, but unpredictable. Sooner or later, he's bound to get into trouble. He can't live as an Apache here, yet that's all he knows. Wouldn't you prefer to be here to keep an eye on him?"

Sarah leaned back, her breath slowly escaping her compressed mouth. She wanted to wipe her mouth to remove the taste of him from her lips. Her mind endeavored to deal with the picture of Hakan's future that Richard painted. It was true that her son had not been brought up to fit into English society. She had never believed they would ever return to it. It was clear that Hakan needed her, at least for the next few years until he was fully grown. Sarah, aside from Hakan, had no family of her own. Her father had been killed in a hunting accident. Her mother died a year later. As their only child, Sarah had inherited their estate, but she had no idea what had become of it in the last sixteen years. Presumably it had passed into Richard's hands. For a fleeting moment Sarah thought of the good years with *Tonsaroyoo* and the Apaches, when life was simple and beautiful and there had been no need for money.

She said, "I can't make any decisions immediately. For one thing, Jean might return."

Richard uncoiled himself from the arm of the chair. He said nonchalantly, "No doubt there will be some word from her shortly that will set your mind at rest about her welfare."

Sarah was halfway across the room when Richard called after her, "Tell me, did you bring any of your . . . Indian squaw's clothes with you? I should like to see you wearing them."

Jean struggled to the surface of consciousness, hearing a banshee shriek that was like no mortal sound she had ever heard before. Shadows loomed over her, menacing, indistinguishable, and rough hands gripped her arms, dragging her to her feet. Vague shapes occupied the darkness around her, but she was too bewildered to recognize her surroundings. Surely this must be a continuation of the nightmare?

A tortured sobbing broke out, almost obliterated by the continual shrieking. The sobbing was worse, a measured sound that played on the nerves like blood pumping from a wound.

She was hoisted into the air; someone had her feet and a man with a barrel chest held her shoulders. They were carrying her off, along a dank corridor lit by a faint gaslight, then down a flight of stairs. She was aware of their heavy breathing, of their footsteps falling on uncarpeted wood.

The shrieking and sobbing grew muted, the darkness

became more intense. A door was unbolted, then a blast of cool night air struck her face.

Dear God in heaven, where were they taking her? What were they going to do with her? She struggled to awaken, to try to remember where she was, but neither her mind nor her body seemed to belong to her. It was as though she were experiencing a high fever and with it weakness and disorientation. Her head was pounding and she was wracked with nausea.

Overhead she heard the rustle of branches and leaves. Then the moon appeared briefly from behind a cloud, shining on the white jacket of the woman who carried her feet.

The next second they began to swing her body, back and forth, back and forth. Suddenly they released her. She flew through the air and landed with a splash in icy water.

As the dark water closed over her head the faces of Robbie and Emily broke through the blurred fog of her senses, and she thrashed with her arms and legs. Her hands struck sticky mud and she thrust herself upward, her head breaking the surface. She was on her knees in shallow water, coated with slimy algae that clung in tentacles to her face.

Gasping for breath, she now saw that a pair of hideous monsters were prancing about on a grassy bank at the edge of the pond. They had grotesque faces and wild hair and were dressed in ghostly white robes. They shouted at her to get out of the water, to stand on her feet and open her eyes and come back to reality.

She crawled from the pond, retching to bring up the evil-tasting water. Hands grabbed her again, and hauled her to her feet. The two monsters had disappeared, to be replaced by a quite kindly looking woman, accompanied by a man also wearing a white jacket. They peered at her, tipping her chin, lifting her eyelids, prodding her body with sharp fingers.

"Now then," the man said, "have you come back to us? Do you know who you are and where you are?"

Memories were returning, and with them fear such as she'd never known before. "I am Jean Merrin, the Countess of Moreland, the mother of the Earl's children—"

The man slapped Jean's face and her head snapped backward. She gasped, choking on bile.

"Shall we throw her in the pond again, Doctor?" the woman asked.

"No. We'll try something else in a few days. Summon the attendants and have them take her back to bed."

Dazed from the blow, Jean collapsed onto the damp grass. From beneath half-opened eyelids she saw the white-coated man and woman walk away. Nearby, under a tree, the two monsters were removing wigs and masks, stepping out of the long white robes. Underneath they too wore white coats and ordinary-looking trousers.

She was carried back into the grim barrackslike building that housed the shrieking, sobbing women and placed on a hard bed. Her wrists were secured to the bed with manacles.

After her tormentors had left, Jean began to shiver violently from cold and shock. She lay on her back and stared into the darkness, trying to make sense of all the distorted pictures in her mind.

Richard . . . The nightmare began, as all nightmares did, with Richard. . . .

"Sarah's coming home, my dear Jean. Get it through your stupid head. She's coming home and bringing her son and heir. I find him rather appealing, in a primitive sort of way. Thank God I'll have a real male to leave Merrinswood and the title to—instead of that little sissy of yours."

Jean had stood perfectly still while everything crashed around her, and in that moment of ultimate despair had committed the fatal mistake. "No . . . no, I won't let you do that. If you even consider disinheriting Robbie, I shan't continue to keep your secret, Richard. I shall make it public knowledge."

"You mean that I sired a gypsy bastard? But mother and babe have vanished, love. Who'd believe you?"

"I don't mean that secret. I mean the one we both know I've kept for eight years."

He had roared with laughter and told her he was teasing her, of course he was teasing her. Didn't he always? Sarah and her son were simply coming here so they could untangle all their legal problems. Even as he reassured her, she had seen the fury in his eyes.

Oh, God, how could she have threatened him so? They hadn't mentioned that terrible secret for the eight years they'd been married, and never once had she considered the possibility that he might have married her in the first place to seal her lips. A wife could not be forced to testify against a husband . . . *but now she was no longer a wife!*

Nothing more was said, but late that night he'd come into her bedroom, not drunk, chillingly sober, and forced her to do unspeakable things.

The following morning she had gone to see Andrew McGreal, thinking to confide in him and ask about the possible consequences of such deviant behavior, but she'd only been able to bring herself to tell him about Sarah and her son.

All that interminably long day Jean had waited with mounting dread for Richard to return. At ten she had retired, lying awake as the minutes ticked by. At midnight her door had opened and he came into her room and tossed a gaudy printed cotton skirt, a bright yellow blouse, and a black shawl on her bed. "Put them on, love. I want you to pretend that you're a peasant who has an insatiable desire to romp with the lord of the castle."

Long ago, when they were first married, he'd liked to play make-believe games. He had made her dress up in various costumes before he made love to her; a maid's uniform, or even a man's suit; occasionally a costume, Little Red Riding Hood or Cinderella. It had seemed harmless enough then, until she began to wonder if he could only be aroused by imagining her to be someone else.

Foolishly, she had donned the gaudy skirt and blouse, stifling the thought that the clothes were painfully reminiscent of what the gypsy women wore.

Her cheeks stung with embarrassment when she remembered some of the things she had been forced to do to satisfy Richard's sexual appetites the previous evening, when he had returned from meeting Sarah; still, none of those activities could result in pregnancy. Putting on the gaudy outfit seemed a way to reassure him that there was a way for her to still fulfill her marital duty to him, a way to wipe out the specter of desertion. Before Sarah was resurrected from the dead, Jean had always known that no matter how many other women Richard had, she would continue to be his wife. But now . . .

He studied her carefully when she was dressed, then reached for her hair and unfastened her bun. Her dark brown hair streamed down over her shoulders. "Hmm, not bad," he said. "A bit pale, of course, but your hair is dark enough and your eyes appear dark at first glance." He fished in his pocket and produced a pair of gold hoop earrings. "Put these on, too. I've got a gold bangle somewhere . . ."

Perhaps she'd acquiesced too easily, because he'd frowned and said, "No, it won't work here. We must go to an inn. Yes, that's what we'll do. With the utmost stealth. This must be a real assignation, fraught with the peril of discovery. I'll get the carriage myself and bring it to the side door. Meet me down there in ten minutes."

Why hadn't she refused? Why had she crept like a thief through the house so that no one would see her dressed like that? There was no need for her to dwell on her reasons, she knew them well enough. She'd been desperate, afraid of abandonment, afraid of what would become of the twins and Randolph. Deathly afraid of what Richard's response to her threats might be. She would have done anything he asked, just for the right to remain with him, on any terms. Dear God, had she no pride at all?

She squirmed on the hard bed, her wrists chafing under the restraints, and shivered in her wet nightgown.

He had taken her to an inn in Carisbrook, where he seemed to be known as "Mr. Tomlinson." Jean remembered the leer of the innkeeper and the musty odor of the bed linen, but very little of what had transpired later. The more she sought to recapture the images of that dreadful night, the more indistinct everything became, as if her mind refused to relive the horrors.

Sometime before dawn she was overcome with sudden waves of dizziness. She recalled begging Richard not to force her to drink any more wine. Then his face seemed to dissolve before her eyes. She was vaguely aware of him wrapping her in a long hooded cape and carrying her from the room.

She must have fainted, because when she came to her senses, briefly, she was in a closed carriage hurtling through the night. She was alone, and assumed it must be Richard who drove the team with such reckless disregard for safety. Although she tried desperately to cling to consciousness, within seconds the blackness again engulfed her.

Several times she drifted in and out of a deep sleep, her mind so confused that she wasn't sure what was real and what was only a dream.

When a sullen dawn broke she awakened to find her head on Richard's shoulder. They were in a different carriage, traveling in mountainous country that was neither Yorkshire nor Lancashire. They saw only one tiny village, which they rattled through at high speed, and then they traveled through miles of forest. Feeling weak and ill, she attempted to question Richard about their destination, but her words died on her lips as they came to an ivy-shrouded wall surrounding a stark brick building. This was no inn, a prison perhaps, or, worse . . .

Her most ghastly suspicions were confirmed when, immediately upon entering a barren hall, two women in nurse's uniforms appeared and moved to either side of her in the attitude of jailers. Richard walked away from her and when she tried to follow, she was restrained by the two nurses.

Richard disappeared into one of the rooms adjacent to the hall, and when he reappeared he was in the company of a heavyset man with thinning hair and a pale, pasty complexion. A young woman walked behind them, carrying a sheaf of papers. The pallid man said, "Hello, Chavi. My name is Doctor Voigt."

Chavi? Jean spun around to look at Richard. This had to be some monstrous joke. Richard's expression was solicitous. "Doctor Voigt is a specialist in the . . . problems of the mind, Chavi. He's going to help you get well again."

Jean looked down at the gaudy skirt and blouse she wore, felt the gold hoops on her ears and her hair hanging loosely about her shoulders, and saw in a flash of enlightened horror how Richard had planned to remove her—and the threat of what she knew about him—from his life.

This was a mental asylum, and Richard had just committed her. He had told the doctor in charge that she was a gypsy who imagined herself to be The Countess of Moreland. Now everything she said and did would confirm the allegation that she was suffering from delusions. That she was out of her mind.

13

Andrew McGreal watched from the window as Sir Randolph Leighton unlatched the garden gate and walked up the path to the house. What unlikely allies they were, Andrew thought as Mrs. Tremayne admitted the visitor. The mantelpiece clock chimed ten. Andrew felt unutterably weary. It had been a long, hard day.

When Randolph had first come to see him, it had been with an angry accusation that Andrew must have known what Jean planned to do, since he was the last person to speak with her before she'd disappeared. Andrew hadn't been able to conceal either his shock or distress at the news that Jean had left, and her brother had soon been reassured.

As Mrs. Tremayne showed Randolph into the sitting room, Andrew was struck again by the similarities—and differences—in the twin brother and sister. Both had dark blue, expressive eyes—hers so filled with compassion, his openly hostile—framed with thick black lashes and well-defined eyebrows so that the eyes dominated the faces. Randolph's features were a coarser, dark-skinned version of his sister's. Jean had a very slightly olive-tinged complexion, but she was usually so pale that one didn't notice. They could both easily be mistaken for foreigners, from some Mediterranean country perhaps. For Andrew, it was part of Jean's charm, along with a strange, almost unearthly expressiveness, a look of powerful empathy, while at the same time her own nature was concealed by her shyness. Surely no one who received the full force of one of her soulful looks could forget her, or that spiritual yearning her eyes revealed.

Randolph dropped heavily into a chair, disregarding such social niceties as a handshake or greeting. "She didn't return to the Morcambe area. I spoke with the vicar and everyone who knew us when we lived there. Richard found a letter from her, telling him she was going away and asking us not to search for her. He wouldn't let me read the letter."

"Do you believe such a letter exists?"

"I can't believe Jean would run off without at least telling *me* where she was going. Can you remember anything she said to you that morning that might offer a hint?"

Andrew pressed two fingers to the furrow between his brows. He'd been over every detail of that conversation with Jean many times. "To a solicitor, perhaps, for advice?"

Randolph shook his head. "I've asked every lawyer for miles around. I've been to every railway station, but no one remembers seeing anyone remotely resembling Jean board a train."

"The police—" Andrew began.

"I tried. They tell me that a woman who runs away from home is none of their affair."

"I don't believe Jean ran away," Andrew said. "Not without a word."

"She was distraught that Richard was bringing Sarah back to Merrinswood. I don't know, it's possible that she couldn't face anyone. And I was so full of my own troubles, perhaps she felt I'd abandoned her, too."

It was typical of Randolph that no matter what someone else said, he would take the opposite view, frequently switching from one opinion to another during the course of a discussion. Andrew asked, "What are you going to do now?"

"I shan't rest until I find her. But I've got to earn a living too."

"Jean told me that your knighthood was conferred upon you for contributions in the industrial field."

"I invented a couple of gadgets to make life easier in the Lancashire cotton mills. I was employed in a mill and loathed the work. I suppose I'll have to go back when I run out of money."

Andrew could well imagine Randolph's dismay that his manner of living was to be so drastically reduced. As Lord Moreland's estate steward, Randolph had enjoyed a way of life only slightly less pleasure-filled than his employer's. Andrew said, "I'll do anything in my power to help you find Jean, you know that."

Randolph's dark blue eyes seemed even more malevolent than usual. "That damned woman and her savage of a son— it's all their fault."

Andrew felt an inner chill at the expression on Randolph's face. "The village is agog at the news of her return," Andrew said. "You know, of course, that everyone believes Jean has simply bowed out of the picture?" He didn't add that, despite the sixteen years that had elapsed, Mrs. Tremayne had relayed to him that Richard and Sarah's love affair and marriage were remembered in stormy detail. Apparently, they had both been handsome, strong-willed people who had both battled and loved with a passion that had rocked Victorian society with its sheer heat.

"Apart from any other consideration," Randolph said slowly, "Jean would never have left her children. She worships the twins." A look of real fear passed over his face, and although he didn't give voice to what was on his mind, Andrew knew that he was afraid Richard might have somehow contrived to do away with her.

As much to reassure himself as Jean's brother, Andrew said quickly, "We must find her. We mustn't give up."

Richard stood at the window of the private mental asylum with Dr. Voigt, watching Jean on the lawn below. She sat on a deck chair under the shade of a venerable oak, her hands folded on her lap, her head back against the canvas of the chair, her eyes closed. Her hair looked a little untidy and she wore a simple cotton frock, but she was clean and apparently calm. There was little to distinguish her from the other women who strolled about the grounds in twos and threes. Except for the uniformed nurses and attendants who patrolled among them, they might have been at a garden party. Unlike the poor wretches stored in squalid filth in public institutions, these were women of upper-class families whose physical needs were met by a large "hospital" staff. Richard eased his conscience with that thought.

Dr. Voigt's slightly accented voice said, "She hardly looks like a gypsy at all now, does she?"

Richard gave him a sharp glance of assessment. "My dear fellow, she never did. That was, I believe, part of the problem. You must know that many gypsies are fair-skinned, even blue-eyed. The stories of changelings are rooted in that fact. Tell me more about the treatment you've been giving her."

"We attempted to shock her back to reality. Although in

many asylums this treatment has been discontinued, I still feel that in some cases it can be effective."

"What was the result in Chavi's case?"

"At least she no longer insists that she is your common-law wife."

"I'm not sure I approve of your shock treatment. What does it consist of?"

"Oh . . . various things. Sometimes nothing more than a loud unexpected noise. A gunshot, for instance. There is an Austrian neurologist who is currently working on a new type of shock therapy. He believes if an extract of tubercle bacillus is injected into a mentally disturbed patient, a potentially curative fever might be induced."

Richard swallowed hard. "What I really had in mind for her was simple custodial care."

Voigt's bloodless countenance was briefly disapproving. "As you wish, of course. But without treatment, you could be saddled with the financial burden of her care for a long time. She's a comparatively young woman. Of course, you could transfer her to a public institution. After all, she's not really your responsibility."

Could that have been a veiled hint? Richard wondered. How much of what he'd told Voigt had been believed? Jean must have demonstrated skills and education that were hardly those of an itinerant gypsy. Richard regretted passing Jean off as one. He'd considered saying she had been his children's governess, but at the time he'd committed her, he hadn't been able to resist forcing Jean to switch places with her gypsy protégée. There seemed to be a grand irony in the device. Not to mention punishment for Jean's daring to threaten him. Richard had had to concoct some weird delusion for Jean to be suffering from, so why not the gypsy story? It sounded a great deal more bizarre, and therefore convincing as evidence of derangement, than passing her off as a lovelorn governess. Besides, if anyone took the trouble to check on the story, the real gypsy was far away, while the Merrin governess was still in residence.

He was silent for a moment, as though considering the possibility of taking her out of Voigt's private nursing home. Might as well let the doctor worry about losing his patient.

"I don't think it would be a good idea for you to see

her," Voigt said suddenly. "She's calm now and you might set her off again."

Richard hadn't been about to suggest it. Her screams when he left her that first day had been disturbing. Frowning, he realized where this conversation with Voigt was leading, since the doctor now wore the slightly contemptuous expression of one who knew he had the upper hand. He said, "Your grace, perhaps we should be frank with one another? You obviously don't want me to continue to treat her or do anything to cure her of her delusions. What, exactly, do you want?"

"I told you. Custodial care."

"For how long?"

"For as long as necessary," Richard snapped. "Dammit, if it's payment in advance you want, it's yours."

"I take it she's not to be allowed any visitors?" The doctor's colorless eyes glittered with greed.

"No visitors. I don't want anyone to know she's here. I expect that little service will cost me extra?"

The doctor smiled. "As long as we understand each other."

As soon as Lord Moreland left, Dr. Voigt hurried downstairs and went outside. Crossing the lawn, he was accosted several times by women who clutched at his arms or babbled incoherently at him. One of the nurses, a newly hired young woman named Brigid O'Connell, who had a shock of bright red hair and was probably only weeks off the Dublin steamer, approached him just before he reached Lord Moreland's gypsy.

"Dr. Voigt, sir," she said in her soft brogue, "I was wondering about Miss Chavi, sir. Would you be after looking at her now?"

"You did very well, nurse. She looks quite peaceful."

"She's asleep, Doctor. Poor thing is exhausted, that she is. Tis a miracle she survived the pneumonia, frail as she is. But it's not that I'm worried about."

Voigt gave the nurse a pale-eyed stare. "You aren't paid to worry, nurse."

He had reached the oak tree under which the woman named Chavi sat. For a moment he stood looking down at her. With her eyes closed, she was a plain-looking woman. He looked at her limp hands, with their long tapered fingers and oval nails. When she had first arrived, her fingernails and toenails were equally well taken care of, but, of course, his grace could have had a ladies' maid attend to her personal grooming. She had a slightly foreign look, but she was no gypsy. Not that it mattered. His Lordship would pay through the nose for her care, and for the discretion of her keepers. Voigt reminded himself piously that he had endeavored to shock the poor creature back to reality, thereby fulfilling his Hippocratic oath.

The doctor put aside any doubts he'd had about this patient. After all, her wild hysteria upon her arrival spoke for itself. They'd had to calm her. The shock treatment might have worked had they been able to repeat it several more times. As he recalled, there had only been two or three of the treatments before she'd caught pneumonia.

Leaning over her, he tapped her cheek. She didn't stir. He pinched her wrist, leaving a blue imprint. Her large eyes, dark as midnight, opened slowly. She made no sound, nor did she move.

"How are you today, Chavi?" he asked. She regarded him with an unblinking stare.

"There you are, you see, Doctor?" He'd forgotten the presence of the Irish nurse, who went on, "She never speaks. She just sits, wherever I put her. She never moves, poor soul. I haven't been able to get her to eat, neither."

He turned to look at the nurse. "You're new, aren't you? What happened to the nurse who was taking care of her ward?"

"She was dismissed, Doctor. For stealing."

"I see. Very well, nurse. I'll explain how Chavi is to be cared for and how she is to receive nourishment."

"Doctor, sir, I've never taken care of mentally ill people before. Please, tell me what's wrong with her?"

He pursed his lips. "We are all called upon to solve problems, nurse. To make certain adjustments in life. The mentally deficient are unable to do so. Some people kill themselves rather than face their problems. Others, like this woman, commit emotional suicide. She has withdrawn into herself and refuses contact with the outside world. We may never be able to bring her out of it."

14

Hakan pushed the textbook away and stood up. "This is designed to drive a man mad."

His Uncle Philip laughed. "You may be right. Frankly, I've never had the slightest need for geometry since I left Cambridge."

"Then why do we bother with it? Today is a fine sunny day and my mother tells me that winter will soon be upon us. We should spend such a day outdoors."

"My dear nephew, much as I agree with you as to the complete irrelevance of geometry, nevertheless we must persist with the lesson. You have, by last count, sent four tutors running. I am all that stands between you and some ghastly cramming school, where they will hammer knowledge into you eighteen hours a day."

Hakan prowled about the study, feeling caged, trapped. "My head is bursting."

"Very well. Go and ride your horse like a madman across the moors for a while. Release some of that pent-up physical energy. But I warn you, we shall have to make up the lesson later on. And don't let your father see you leaving."

"He's gone to London on business."

"Did your mother go with him?"

"No. She is in her room, writing in her journal. She is always writing in her journal nowadays."

"Perhaps she's trying to make some sense of things. It must be disconcerting for her to find herself the object of her husband's . . . obsession again, after all these years."

"My mother writes of her life with her true husband. My Apache father. My mother was . . . devoted. Is that the word?"

"A wonderful word." Philip gave him a deceptively lazy

stare. "You're lonely here, aren't you, James? You've been isolated from young men your own age. We must remedy that situation. I'll speak to your father about having a weekend hunt party."

"Hunt?" Hakan's interest was caught immediately. "We need fresh game for food?"

"Not really. I'm not much of a hunter, but I believe most game is out of season now. I meant fox hunting."

"The fox is eaten?"

"Good lord, no! It's hunted for pleasure."

"Englishmen kill for *pleasure*?" Hakan took a step backward, away from his uncle, who didn't seem at all shocked at what he had just revealed. "I do not wish for you to organize such a hunt. The Apache kill only for food. Even then, we ask forgiveness of *Y'sun*, the Great Spirit, that the animal must die so that we might live." He turned and strode from the room.

Hakan ran up the main staircase. On the upper floor he paused for a moment outside his mother's room, wondering whether to invite her to join him in an invigorating ride. He was troubled about the change in *Sons-ee-ah-ray*. Shadows had appeared under her eyes and she seemed withdrawn. It was, of course, the unnatural life-way of the English that caused this lethargy. Hakan wondered how much longer his mother would remain in this magnificent prison. Especially since Sir Randolph Leighton had lost no time in spreading the story of where and how Sarah had been living the past sixteen years. When Lord Moreland invited guests to a homecoming party, many people sent their regrets. Sarah had shrugged and said quietly, "It's to be expected."

But his father had been furious. "This will never happen again, I promise you. The first thing I shall do is call on everyone who refused our invitation and explain that you suffered from amnesia during that period. If apologies and social visits are not forthcoming, I'll find a way to ruin anyone who insults us."

Although Sarah had protested, his father had been adamant. It was difficult for Hakan to associate this man who bridled at such an insignificant slight to his wife with the man who had abandoned his bride to his enemies.

Hakan was concerned too, as his Uncle Philip had indicated, about the strong undercurrents between Sarah and her

English husband. The tension between them was as sharply defined as the rumble of thunder heralding the approaching storm.

He went into his own room, thinking that when his Apache father was alive *Sons-ee-ah-ray* would not have hesitated to let him, or anyone else, know what was troubling her. To conceal her feelings meant that she was brooding about them, and when at last she allowed them to escape, what would be the consequences?

As he changed into his riding clothes and went out to the stables, Hakan decided that he had been so wrapped up in his own misery that he had not considered the fact that his mother must be feeling the same yearning for days past and forever gone.

The stableboy brought his favorite horse, a spirited chestnut stallion. Today, instead of the customary gallop across the moors, Hakan guided his mount through the main gates of Merrinswood and rode down the lane.

The nearest village was called Merrin Quarry, and had sprung up about the stone quarry owned by the Merrin family, which had produced the golden stone from which their mansion was built. The quarry was no longer worked, and the moors were beginning to heal the wound, forming a new skin of grass and gorse and heather. The village consisted of a steeply rising street of shops, a blacksmith, a church, an inn called The Rose and Crown, intersected by several streets of row houses, each connected to its neighbor. Aged brick and slate and stone that had stood here for many years. The concept of a permanent rancheria was as baffling to Hakan as his mother's belief that it was a good thing for him to inherit the ridiculously opulent estate of his English father.

Unsure what to do with his horse on this, his first venture into the village alone, Hakan rode to the blacksmith's establishment. The blacksmith, sweating over his coals, looked up and asked, "Need shoeing, does he?"

"No horse needs iron on his hooves," Hakan responded. "Better to get rid of your artificial surfaces that wear out the hooves."

The blacksmith wiped his hand across his brow and blinked. "Beggin' your pardon, sir?"

"I wish to leave my horse with you."

"Very good, sir. I'll put him in the stable."

Hakan knew that he was watched as he walked away.

He looked in all the shop windows as he passed by. At the end of the street was a shop filled with all manner of goods. Over the doorway hung three large brass balls, and a sign that read *Pawnbroker*.

Three well-dressed young men, perhaps a year or two older than Hakan, stood outside the shop, in angry conversation. "Ruddy old thief," one of them, a muscular red-haired youth, said. "I told him I'd be back to redeem that watch. He shouldn't have sold it."

"Oh, come on, Charles, you popped that watch months ago and forgot about it," one of his companions remarked. "You never think about such things when you're losing. Or when you're winning, for that matter." The third member of the trio laughed, obviously adding to Charles's annoyance.

Hakan caught a glimpse of a piece of jewelry that flashed with blue fire amid the clutter of the pawnbroker's window. A butterfly brooch, fashioned of delicate threads of silver, with eyes made of brilliant blue gemstones. He turned to examine it more closely and at the same instant the young man called Charles stepped backward, colliding with him.

"Dammit, man, why don't you look where you're going?" Charles exclaimed, his face turning an angry red.

"It was you who was not looking," Hakan said.

"Why, you insolent bugger. I should teach you a lesson in manners." His arms came up in front of his face, fists clenched in a threatening pose. His two companions backed away.

Hakan didn't wait for the inevitable swing of the fist to his jaw. He knew about the white-eyes method of attack. As Charles lunged, he was winded by a shoulder in his middle, then found himself hoisted up in the air and sent crashing into the glass of the shop window. The sound of shattering glass, the outraged shouts of the two spectators, and Charles's cry of pain brought the pawnbroker running into the street.

A rotund, bald man, he surveyed first his broken window, then the furious Charles rising unsteadily to his feet. His two friends stared in amazement at Hakan. "Bloody madman," one of them said. "Flew at Charles like a savage."

The pawnbroker spun around to glare at Hakan. "What's the meaning of this?"

"The meaning? I don't know. I defended myself against this man. He was about to strike me."

"Wait a minute," one of Charles's companions said, peering at Hakan. "I'll wager I know who this is. It's Lord Moreland's so-called long-lost son. It's the flamin' Apache. Who let him out of his cage without his keeper?"

Although he felt his blood begin to bubble in his veins, Hakan controlled his anger at the insult. Ever since Sir Randolph Leighton attacked him aboard the ship, *Sons-ee-ah-ray* had warned Hakan not to allow himself to be provoked by mere words.

Charles had cut his hand on the broken glass and now held it up, dripping blood on the pavement. "Get the constable, pawnbroker. We'd better get this creature behind bars before he does any more damage."

Looking from one to the other, the pawnbroker said, "Wait a bit—he said you struck the first blow. And I know you, Master Charles, you've got a nasty temper."

"I never touched him, did I?" Charles appealed to his two friends for corroboration. They said, "That's right. The wild Indian simply picked him up and threw him into your window."

The pawnbroker asked Hakan, "Is that right? Or did he hit you first?"

"He did not get a chance to hit me. But it was his intent," Hakan replied.

The pawnbroker looked at his smashed window again and shouted to a passerby, "Fetch the constable—quick."

Sarah looked down at her journal. The pen slipped from her shaking fingers and landed on the closely written page, creating an inkblot. No matter how many times she'd attempted to write more than the bare facts of what happened those first days after she and Otis were captured by the renegade Comanches, inevitably the memories proved to be too terrifying to relive.

The horrors endured by the young journalist, Otis Prouther, were as distressing to her as her own mistreatment. Yet both of them had survived, and even more miraculously, she had not lost her baby.

She was unsure why she felt compelled to write of her years of living with the Apache. Perhaps because memories were already fading and she felt a desperate need to cling to them. Or perhaps the time would come when her son, or perhaps one of his descendents, would need to know the truth of her life. The bare facts of what happened never really explained anything, and sometimes a person's actions needed to be examined in light of the circumstances, pressures, and reasoning at the time.

Otis had eventually been tied to a stake, branches piled around his feet and a fire lit. Forced to watch, Sarah had screamed and begged them to spare him. Hadn't he suffered enough? He'd run their gauntlet when they beat him with sticks. He had been humiliated by the squaws, been used for target practice, the arrows piercing nonvital parts of his body.

Even as the smoke of his funeral pyre rose, a painted medicine man suddenly burst into the midst of the group, and leaping over the burning branches, released Otis and dragged him clear of the flames.

Otis was carried to a wickiup and two squaws applied a healing linament made from aloe pulp and other herbs to his burned and tortured skin, then wrapped leaves over his wounds. Much later, Sarah had been astonished by the way his skin healed without scars.

The medicine man proved to be an Apache shaman. Apparently, the Comanches traded goods and captives to a Chiricahua clan who had a stronghold in the nearby mountains, although they roamed freely across Arizona and Mexico. The Apache didn't usually spare white-eyes males, feeling they were more trouble than they were worth, but the slightly built Otis had impressed the visiting shaman with his courage in the face of certain death, and the shaman took this to be an omen that the man would be useful to his people.

Sarah blotted the page of her journal and flipped forward to where she had begun to write about the Chiricahuas.

We had been misinformed about the situation in the southwestern United States, believing that most, if not all, of the Apaches had been rounded up and put on reservations. Also, many Apaches had become scouts for the army, and in fact, it was their own people who eventually brought about the downfall of the *Tin-ne-ah*. In fairness to Richard, I am compelled to state this fact. Otherwise he surely would not have insisted we travel through that part of the country.

Several days after Otis was saved from the flames, we saw intermittent plumes of smoke rising from the crest of a hill several miles away. This apparently was the signal from the Apaches that the Comanches might approach their stronghold.

At that time I was still dazed with the shock of all that had happened, and my broken ankle, which had been bound up by the Comanches, did not permit me to walk. I rode in front of one of the Comanches, and Otis was placed upon a woven-branch stretcher that was pulled by a horse ridden by the Apache medicine man. The Comanches had two young Mexican girl captives also, but since they could not speak English and I was unfamiliar with Spanish, we were unable to communicate with one another. Otis told me, during the one brief conversation I'd had with him following our capture, that the Comanches had escaped from a reservation, and so would keep moving. He also said that they would probably trade me to the Apaches, who used slaves to build their wickiups, harvest fruits and nuts during the summer when they stayed in a rancheria, tend their ponies, make the mescal they liked to drink, and so on. Otis didn't remind me, nor did he need to, that I could also expect sexual advances.

We were met at the mouth of a canyon by a party of Apaches. How can I describe my first sight of them? I had thought the Comanche were impressive, but the Chiricahua had what I can only describe as a fearsome, terrifying presence. They were magnificent, invincible, beautiful in a heart-stopping way that filled me with a fear it would be impossible to describe. It was easy to see why the very name Apache struck terror into the hearts of both settlers and soldiers. Otis told me that for every Apache brave killed, probably hundreds of whites had died. That the total number of Apaches in existence, in all of the various clans, was a mere fraction of the number of whites. The Apache, he said, were guerilla fighters who had no equal on the face of the earth.

The deliberations, "dickering" as Otis later called it, seemed to go on forever. I was too faint from the heat of

the sun and from the continuing nausea of early pregnancy, not to mention my fear, to be much aware of the
negotiations for our trade.

Later, we were taken to the Apache rancheria, consisting of a number of wickiups, which are oval-shaped lodges
made of branches and hides. There was also a ramada that
Otis referred to as a "squaw cooler," which was used for
outdoor cooking and dining.

At the time, not many details registered in my numbed
mind. But just before I was placed inside a wickiup, I
looked up and saw a man standing on a rounded boulder
at the edge of the rancheria. He was much taller than the
other braves, perhaps almost six feet tall, with thick black
hair that seemed surprisingly well-groomed, falling in a
smooth mass to his shoulders. He wore a buckskin shirt
decorated with blue beads, leggings, and his moccasins
were high-topped, reaching to just below his knees, but
his clothes did not catch my attention as much as his
splendid physique. He seemed almost to be a part of the
mountain, etched against the sky like a monument to the
beauty that all mankind had once possessed in our days of
innocence. His features were finely chiseled, with an intelligent brow and high cheekbones, and his eyes . . .

Of course, I was too far away to see his eyes in that
first moment of awareness. When I saw *Tonsaroyoo* at
close range, several weeks later, I was intrigued that his
eyes were not the flat brown of many of his people, but
rather seemed to glow with golden glints deep within their
depths, as though the light came from inside his soul.

Sarah looked up from her journal, feeling her own eyes
mist with tears. At the same instant someone knocked on her
door and she heard Philip calling, "Sarah? May I come in?
I've some distressing news, I'm afraid."

Her brother-in-law came into the room wearing, for him,
a distraught expression. "It's James, Sarah. My fault. I
shouldn't have simply let him run loose. But I thought he
was just going for a ride on the moors."

"Where is he?" Sarah demanded, hearing a drum begin to
beat somewhere at the back of her head.

"We've just been informed that he was arrested by the
village constable."

Sarah's breath caught in her throat. A vision of Apache braves herded into boxcars flashed across her mind. "On what charge?"

"Assault . . . and vandalism."

Sarah rose to her feet, angry beyond reason, but before she could rush from the room, Philip caught her by the shoulders and stopped her. "Richard is already on his way to the village. Let him handle it."

"Richard? He's in London."

"No, he returned an hour ago. Sarah, we don't know exactly what happened yet. Let's keep calm until we have all the facts. Come down to the library and we'll wait for Richard to get back."

The dinner hour had come and gone. Philip and Sarah waited, tense and silent, until they heard footsteps in the marble hall, and Richard's voice calling to Barlow to inquire as to the whereabouts of his wife and brother.

Sarah jumped to her feet as the library doors opened. She let out her breath slowly as she saw that her son was with Richard.

"Thank God!" Philip exclaimed. Sarah stifled the urge to rush to Hakan's side and throw her arms around him, knowing that such a display of emotion in front of the two older men would make him feel like a prodigal child.

"Here's your errant son, Sarah," Richard said, his tone amused. "I've paid for the damages and talked young Charles Pettigrew out of pressing the assault charges."

Sarah looked into her son's eyes and conveyed the silent message that explanations should not be made now. Hakan's expression showed that he was still puzzled and angry. She said, "You both missed dinner. You must be hungry."

Richard laughed. "I see. You'll brook no postmortems in my presence. Well, my dear Sarah, let me tell you how I view the incident. James was accosted by that red-haired young bully, defended himself, and accidentally broke a shop window in the process. I'm proud of him. So spare the boy any lectures. Now—let's all go and have dinner."

"I've already dined," Sarah said coldly, feeling inexplicably shut out. "I'll speak with you tomorrow, James. Good night."

She went upstairs, but was still too agitated to even consider sleep. On an impulse, instead of going into her own room, she went to the twins' rooms. Robbie and Emily had separate rooms connected to what had formerly been their nursery and was still referred to as such, but was actually used as a schoolroom. Their governess, Charlotte, occupied a room across the hall.

Sarah had tried to befriend the motherless children as much as their protective governess would allow, especially the little boy. Whereas Emily was a self-sufficient child who seemed to have inherited her uncle Randolph's surly disposition, Robbie was a pale shadow of his sister. A timid, sickly boy, frail of build and perhaps even frailer in spirit, he had developed a pronounced stammer since his mother's departure.

Emily was already asleep when Sarah tiptoed into her room. She crossed the darkened schoolroom and quietly opened Robbie's door. He sat in the middle of his bed, a candle precariously dripping wax onto the opened page of the book he held. His mouth opened in a horrified gasp as he saw Sarah.

She said quickly, "Oh, I didn't mean to interrupt your reading. I know I hate people barging in when I'm lost in the magic of a good book. I'll go, if you like."

"I-I-I . . . Charlotte s-s-said I wasn't t-t-to read in bed." Robbie gulped out the words.

"Oh, I think reading helps one relax and sleep. Although I do think we should light your lamp. That candle looks a bit dangerous. We wouldn't want to start a fire, would we?"

She pulled the gaslight down from the ceiling, but Robbie said, "I'm f-f-finished reading. Thank you."

"What are you reading?" She went to the bed and took the candle from him, placing it on the bedside table.

"It's a b-b-book about S-Spain." He closed the book and handed it to her. There was no need for him to tell her why he was studying the illustrated book. He'd already inquired of her where a person who wanted to spend a warm winter might go.

Sarah's heart turned over with compassion. "You miss your mother very much, don't you?" He nodded, tears glistening on the soft sweep of his eyelashes. Such lustrous eyelashes for a little boy, she thought. "You'll hear from her soon, I'm sure. Perhaps she's been too ill to write? Your father told me she hadn't been feeling very well."

"She always came to k-k-kiss us g-good-night. Why d-d-din't she . . ."

Sarah gathered him into her arms and rocked him back and forth, not knowing what to say to comfort him. Eventually he fell asleep against her breast, and she laid him down gently and covered him, blew out the candle, and quietly left the room.

Glancing at the clock on the nursery wall, she saw that almost two hours had passed. They should be finished with dinner by now, and feeling the pangs of hunger herself, she decided to go downstairs for a snack.

She was halfway across the hall when the door to Richard's study opened and a beam of light fell across the marble floor. He stood silhouetted against the flickering red glow of the fire. "Sarah, may I have a word with you?"

He remained in the doorway as she passed him, her arm brushing against his chest. He seemed to engineer physical contact with her at every opportunity.

"If it's about James—" she began as he closed the door behind her.

"It's about you and me, Sarah." Except for the brightly burning coal fire in the hearth, the room was not lit.

A half-empty brandy glass stood on a small table beside the fireside chair, and as Richard moved toward her, it was clear he'd had several drinks. Although he never became falling-down drunk, or even ridiculous or aggressive as some men did, still he exhibited a dangerous casting off of restraints after a number of drinks, as though the darker side of his nature were in complete control.

He was between her and the door and she had not realized she was backing away from him until her legs touched the armchair. "There's nothing more to be said about you and me. I'm no longer your wife. If you wish me to leave—"

"Dammit, Sarah." He was in front of her now and his arm snaked out and caught her around her waist, pulling her close to him. "Have you forgotten what it was like for us in the beginning? It can be again. I want you, and you know damn well you want me."

She struggled, but his grip tightened. "Let go of me, Richard, or—"

"Or what? You'll scalp me? Maybe that would be preferable to freezing me out. One of these days you should get out your buckskin dress and moccasins and wear them for me. Oh, yes, I know you still have them. I had your maid go through your baggage. Did you keep them to remind you of your Indian brave? Let me make love to you, Sarah, and I guarantee you'll never think of him again.''

Sarah felt her body go rigid. She didn't move, but her eyes locked with his and she hoped he could see the contempt there. "Why don't you simply go to Carisbrook to one of your whores?"

"Because I haven't felt desire for any other woman but you since you came back to me."

"I did not come back to you. I brought our son back to his birthright."

He laughed. "What a liar you are. You think I don't know how you're feeling, right now at this minute? Your lust is as rampant as mine. It always was, that's what I loved about you."

"Your conceit astonishes me. What I feel for you is revulsion, as I did when you humiliated me by taking a dance-hall girl to your bed in that awful saloon in that little New Mexico town." She knew it was a mistake the second she brought it up.

One of his hands went to her hair, pulling it free of pins and combs. "The lure of the unknown and different. She was nothing more than a toy to amuse myself with for an hour. If you hadn't come looking for me, you'd never have known."

"And you think that would have made it all right? You killed everything I felt for you that day, Richard. That was the day our marriage ended."

"Yes. You made that clear enough. I was never to lay a hand on you again, as I recall. You feigned sickness for the rest of the journey. Tell me, was your Apache warrior faithful? Did he cleave only unto you?"

Sarah struggled to free her arms from his embrace, and her hands flew to his throat. Catching him by surprise, she felt the satisfaction of hearing him gasp for breath. Squeezing with all of her might, she felt the sharp thrill of mastery over him, if for only the split second until he grabbed her hands and wrenched them away from his neck. The moment he released her hands she slapped his face as hard as she could. He slapped back.

They stared at one another. Sarah said in a low controlled

voice, "You could perhaps prevail over a sheltered English-woman, Richard, but not over me. I've lived as an Apache for too long. You'll learn just what that means if you ever lay a hand on me again."

His hands fell to his sides and he laughed softly. "I've never had to force a woman, Sarah. I shan't want for willing female bodies. But I still want you to stay and be my Countess. You see, I don't believe all of your ardor is dead. The time will come when you'll beg me to make love to you."

15

It seemed to Chavi that their overland train journey across the vast Australian continent resembled, in some ways, the long ocean voyage. The Outback was as boundless and almost as empty as the sea. So few settlements, so few people.

She knew her gypsy soul should rejoice, but this land was dismayingly bleak, bereft of gentle woods and lush English meadows with their patchwork borders of deeper green hedgerows. The Outback seemed inhospitable, as if it were not yet ready to welcome human inhabitation.

Perhaps the sheep station would prove to be more inviting. The mere idea of a *station* sounded so grand. She envisioned a vast farm that would be presided over by Lord Moreland.

Coming to the end of railway lines, they spent one night in a hotel on the edge of the wilderness. Chavi awakened to an eerie, drawn-out howl, like a lost soul crying in anguish. She sat bolt upright in the unfamiliar bed, her body clammy with perspiration. The howling stopped at the same moment she remembered that Lysander had warned her she might hear dingoes.

The cry of the wild dog faded into the night, leaving only

the whispering of the gray-green leaves of a giant gum tree outside her window. The pungent scent of eucalyptus drifted through the open window, not quite masking the dust she had tried in vain to remove before settling herself and Brenna down for the night.

Feeling sleep elude her, she got up and went to the window, hoping to catch a breath of a breeze. This was their last night in anything resembling a town. Tomorrow they would begin the trek across open country, sleeping under the stars until they arrived at the sheep station that was their final destination. She felt excitement stir within her at the prospect of her new life, and was anxious for the night to end.

The following day was spent purchasing the supplies they would need, and Chavi was tired by the time they arrived at a small farm where Lysander was to obtain horses for the last part of the journey.

They were informed that their dinner would be served in an hour. Lysander, greeted as usual by horrified stares, had snapped. "I don't see any women around, so I suppose the meal will consist of another overdone leg of mutton. Chavi, get into the kitchen and cook something fit to eat."

"I will not," Chavi declared. "I've got to take care of the baby. If you don't like mutton, go without dinner."

Lysander took a step toward her and the old man who had shown them to their rooms fled. Chavi looked up into Lysander's livid features defiantly, then deliberately turned her back to him and went to her bed to lay Brenna down.

"Listen to me, gypsy," Lysander said, his voice a low growl, "You've done precious little to earn your keep so far. That is going to change from now on. You'll work for your food and lodging."

She looked back at him over her shoulder. "Not for you, I won't."

"No? Then how do you propose to support yourself and your baby?"

There was more than the customary cruel taunting in his tone; something in his voice filled her with dread. She pulled a pillow from under a dusty bedspread and used it to prevent Brenna from rolling off the bed, then turned to face Lysander. "Lord Moreland will take care of us," she said uncertainly, suddenly filled with doubts.

"What a bloody little fool you are. What an ignorant—"

"Shut up!" Chavi screamed, heedless of who heard her. "Don't you dare insult me again. I'm tired of your name-calling and your moods and your making fun of me. It's not my fault that you're scarred and ugly."

He reeled as though she'd struck him. His mouth opened, then closed again. He turned and strode from the room and she heard him go into his own room, next to hers, and slam the door.

She tapped on his door a few minutes later, and without waiting to be invited, went inside. Lysander lay on the bed, his arms folded under his head, staring at the ceiling.

She said quietly, "He isn't coming, is he? It's all been a lie."

"You were an idiot to believe he would. Aristocrats don't emigrate. Only peasants and convicts and madmen choose to live as expatriates."

"And which of those are you, Lysander? I'd guess that convict comes closest. You're certainly a liar. You've lied to me from the beginning."

"Your fancy man paid our way to Australia to be rid of you and his bastard. There's work for you as a cook at the station if you want it. No doubt eventually someone will offer you marriage. Women aren't plentiful in the Outback."

Chavi sat down abruptly on the edge of his bed, wondering if she'd suspected this for weeks now, but had been afraid to acknowledge her suspicions. So many times at sea she'd seen the scorn in Lysander's eyes, or he'd taunted her for being gullible or stupid. But he'd taught her to read too, and showed her how to dress her hair and watch her manners. How to make polite conversation. He'd taken her ashore in exotic ports and bought clothes for her and Brenna. Had she known, even then, that none of this was for Lord Moreland's benefit?

"The sheep station," she said at last. "Do you have a job waiting for you there too?"

"Why? Will that influence your decision? If so, I'll drop you off and move on. You never need look at my scarred and ugly face again."

"I'm sorry I said that to you, Lysander."

"Don't be sorry. You meant it. Have the courage to stand behind what you say. The sheep station is owned by my brother. He came out here ten years ago and has done quite well for himself."

"Your brother?" Chavi repeated, surprised.

"What's the matter? Did you think I hatched out of a prehistoric egg? That I have no family?"

"You never mentioned that you have a family."

"I'm not sure my brother will be pleased to see me. But I've no doubt he'll be delighted to see you."

"He doesn't know we're coming?"

"I was never certain we'd get this far. What do you want to do, go on or go back to Sydney and make your own way there? I should warn you that the Outback is harsh country, even for a man. In the droughts it becomes a desert and the surface is blown away and piled into sandhills. Then the spring rains come and grass will grow waist high. It's like nature is undecided whether the land should be the Sahara or England. It's good for sheep and that's all it's good for. Men can't live here; they go mad if they pretend they can. They can exist. So can you."

Chavi pleated her skirt with her fingers. "I have to go on," she said. "I can't go back."

"Very well. From now on you'll work for your living. You'll prepare our food and wash our clothes. And you'll light our campfires." He paused. "You'll be a gypsy again, at least until we arrive at my brother's station. Except for the fortune-telling and thieving, of course."

"If I were to tell your fortune, I expect I'd see a very short lifeline on your palm," she retorted.

"My life ended some time ago. This is just some afterdeath dream I'm having."

"Lysander, before we leave here would you help me write a letter?"

"If you're thinking of writing to Lord Moreland—"

"No, I'm not. I want to write to Doctor McGreal. He was kind to me and perhaps he'll go to Merrinswood and take Danior a message for me. Then when I've saved some money I can send for him."

"Fair enough. Now, will you get out of here and see to your baby?"

"If you'll draft me a letter, I'll do more than that. I'll go and make you a nice stew."

"I think you've done that already," he muttered.

They traveled through a land of delicate scrub, here and there punctuated by trees and bushes that were both familiar and strange. Lysander seemed to know the names of all of them. Applebush and bluebush and emu bush and leopardwood and the oddly named budda.

This was the core of Australia, red earth through which rivers had carved channels and cast up black-silt bands like flung ribbons. A land of gray plains rising to the higher red ground that stretched to infinity. There were stony deserts and clumps of closely grown pines, meadows of yellowish grass, and scarred patches of scraped-clean clay like wounds on the flesh of the earth.

They came upon human remains at one deserted paddock, where a man had simply lain down when his strength gave out, the last of his swag scattered about him. Emu and kangaroo ran from the paddock at their approach, and Lysander commented that it was a mystery how they got there.

Their journey took them from one well to another, to water tanks placed there for the benefit of sheep, not man. Chavi, who knew about living from the land, marveled at Lysander's unerring sense of direction and purpose. The only other human beings they saw were a pair of near-naked aborigines walking along a distant ridge, and a boundary rider who stopped and shared a billycan of tea with them and confirmed that they were on the right track to Twelve Mile, which was the name of Lysander's brother's sheep station. Nearly fifty thousand acres, he said, yet only fifty acres were cultivated, due to the problem of irrigation.

"At first my brother's mind turned, as Anglo-Saxon minds will, to wheat. But that black silt along the rivers won't hold water, and besides, every flood would wipe out the crop. The red earth is above flood level and holds water, but if they devised an irrigation system, what to do with a wheat crop? A few acres would supply the back country and the rest would have to be delivered to the world market. The cost of getting it there would be greater than the current price for wheat. So he became a sheepman and ploughed up only enough to grow food for the station."

After several days of solitude, Chavi noticed that Lysander's mood had changed. He seemed to have cast off some invisible coat of armor and his voice and manner softened. She had seen this gentler side of him before, whenever he was with the baby, and she had reasoned that it was probably because little Brenna showed no horror at his appearance. One day on the ship when Chavi had been painstakingly practicing her writing skills, Lysander had held Brenna, playing with her in an unselfconscious way. Chavi looked up to see her baby's hand drift like a tiny star across Lysander's scarred face and come to rest on his twisted lower lip.

Watching, Chavi saw him blink rapidly several times, then he smiled down at the infant and it was the first real smile she'd ever seen him give. For that one brief instant weals and welts and crooked scars seemed to fade away, and Chavi saw only the warmth in his dark eyes and his perfectly even white teeth.

Now, out here in the wilderness of central Australia, it seemed that that transforming smile of his became more frequent, although it was still bestowed on Brenna, not Chavi.

Lysander had acquired a rifle before they left Sydney, and one evening he shot a rabbit for their dinner. As Chavi skinned it she warned him it looked more like a hare than a rabbit and would probably be tough.

"It will be a change from corned beef," he growled.

"First you were sick of mutton, now you're sick of corned beef. You're a hard man to please, Lysander," Chavi remarked cheerfully as she gathered twigs to light a fire.

Brenna, who had been sleeping on the ground, protected by their packs, now stirred and began to gurgle the delightful sounds of a waking baby. Lysander immediately went to pick her up. Chavi said, "You're going to spoil her. She's got to learn to be by herself sometimes."

But he had already gathered up the baby and now rocked her gently in his arms. "I don't believe you can spoil an infant with too much attention. Besides, we all spend too much of our lives alone. We should snatch any opportunity to connect with another human being."

Chavi fastened the rabbit to a spit, preoccupied with the thought that it should have been jugged to make it tender, and didn't notice his long silence until she heard him exclaim in a strangled voice, "Oh, God, we must go back."

"*What?*" Turning, she saw that he was looking down at Brenna with a terrible fear in his eyes. "Lysander, what are you talking about? Go back where?"

"To civilization," he answered hoarsely. "What was I thinking of, bringing her here?"

"Bringing her? What about me?"

"You'll survive. But Brenna—listen to me, gypsy. I've been here before. I saw a beautiful child taken ill at a remote station. The nearest doctor was two hundred and fifty miles away. They drove day and night, changing horses at stations along the way, and when the horses died the parents walked. Then at last, one morning at sunrise they saw the sun shining on the roofs of a hamlet where the doctor lived. They could have been there in an hour . . . but the child died."

Chavi saw that tears were streaming down Lysander's face. She stared in amazement as he cradled Brenna close to his heart and bent to press his lips to the baby's soft dark hair.

His eyes met Chavi's, and seemed not to care that she saw him crying. He went on raggedly, "The child should have lived. But even if he had . . . there are no schools. I saw parents send their children a thousand miles away to school. Parents left with aching hearts and empty rooms. Can you live with that prospect, gypsy? Can you live with the knowledge you're endangering your child because there are no doctors out here? I can't."

Chavi dropped the twigs and rose to her feet. She began to move toward him, and like a drowning man, he reached for her with one arm, pulling her to his chest beside her baby, so that he held on to both of them, as though if he were to let go they would be lost to him.

For a moment no one spoke. Chavi's hand went around his back and she patted him lightly, like a mother reassuring a troubled child. Then she said at last, "It was your baby, wasn't it? Your son who died before you could get him to a doctor?"

Lysander nodded, tears still streaming, washing down the raw furrows of his face in glistening rivulets.

"What happened to your wife?" Chavi asked.

"Our grief destroyed the marriage," he answered in a voice choked with emotion. "She left me years ago. I don't know where she is today."

"Brenna isn't going to die, Lysander. Don't worry so. She's a gypsy. We've been roaming the face of the earth and taking care of ourselves since the beginning of time."

As if awakening from some awful nightmare and being unsure where he was, Lysander carefully placed Brenna in Chavi's arms and drew back from her. He brushed his fist across his eyes and turned away.

*   *   *

Chavi shielded her eyes from the harsh glare of the sun and stared across the red earth to the house built on a slight rise. A group of gums shaded the south wing, and a patch of green lay to the north, testifying to someone's patient efforts to grow a small garden.

Reining her horse, she said, "My goodness, but it looks grand!"

Lysander, who as usual rode with the baby tucked inside his jacket, laughed. "An illusion. It looks like rough-hewn stone, doesn't it? But it isn't. It's a clever imitation made of concrete. Every block made and dried on the station. The house was built entirely by station labor. Floors, roof beams, wainscots—every bit of woodwork done by the station carpenter."

"That makes it all the more impressive," Chavi answered.

"Australians can make something out of nothing. They're experts at making do. They're jacks of all trades. Out here in the bush a man learns to do everything. There's no such thing as a ploughman or a groom or a cook or a shepherd—on any given day a man might be called on to be all of those. Yes, and maybe he'll have to down tools and fight a raging bush fire, too."

"The house is further away than it appears from here," Chavi said. "The air is so clear and sharp."

"You're getting the lay of the land," Lysander said. "Come on, we'll be there in an hour."

"Wait—Lysander, you haven't told me anything about your brother. I don't even know his name."

"What's in a name?" he answered lightly. "I haven't told you mine, either."

"What if he turns us away?"

"It's a bit late in the day to start worrying about that."

"His name," Chavi said. "At least tell me his name." *And does he have a frightful scarred face, too*? She didn't dare look sideways at Lysander for fear he would read the unspoken question in her eyes.

"His name is Dirk. Dirk Chambers."

"Is he married?"

"No. And that's the last question I'll answer. I'm ready for a hot bath and a decent meal." He dug his heels in his horse's flanks and cantered off.

Chambers, Chavi thought as she followed. So that was Lysander's last name, too. No doubt his first name was something other than Lysander. An alias suggested a man with something to hide, but of course, she had suspected that since her first meeting with him. Since that day when he'd told her about his lost son and wife, she'd felt there had been moments when she had chipped small holes in the wall of reserve Lysander had erected about himself. But she still knew so little about him. Where had he been for the last ten years, since his wife ran off? And, more importantly, what had he been doing? Perhaps she'd learn more when she met his brother.

An hour later they reined their horses in front of the house, which had a wooden porch running the full length of it. Two deeply tanned and sinew-thin men who had been unloading goods from a wagon came to take their horses. It was clear from their shocked glances at Lysander's face that they had not met him before.

"Welcome to Twelve Mile, stranger," one man said in the Cockneylike accent of the Australians. "Where you bound?"

Lysander gave him an evil grin, then opened his jacket and produced Brenna. Both men's eyes bulged.

"Take the baby from me, man," Lysander ordered. "And help the lady down from her mount. Then go and tell Dirk Chambers his brother is here."

Chavi didn't wait for anyone's help. She slid from her saddle and went to take the baby herself as the two men gaped in astonishment at Lysander. Chavi had her back to the house and when a voice addressed them from that direction she knew without turning around that it belonged to Dirk Chambers. He had the same resonant, cultured tones that Lysander at his best used; the same undeniably educated, upper-class English that sounded even more foreign here in the Outback.

"Well, by all that's holy. I never expected to see you again. Especially not with a wife and baby. To what do I owe the pleasure of this visit?"

Lysander said, "No visit, Dirk. We're here to stay. And the young lady isn't my wife. Nor is the infant mine. If we're not welcome, say so and we'll water the horses and be on our way."

"As volatile as ever, aren't you, old man? Don't be so quick to cross swords. You're both more than welcome."

Footsteps came down the wooden steps from the porch and Chavi, feeling a strange, prickly sensation in the region of the back of her neck, turned to look at Lysander's brother.

He came out of the shadows of the house, and the sunshine blazed on his face. Chavi stifled a gasp. It was as if she were looking at Lysander before his face was disfigured; as though identical statues had been constructed, their carved faces beautiful, free of blemishes; but one had been smashed and mutilated and the other left whole and magnificent. Dirk was probably a year or so younger than Lysander, with the same splendid physique, princely bearing, intensely burning eyes, and perfect teeth. As he approached her, his handsome face wreathed in a broad smile, hand outstretched in greeting, Chavi felt her knees turn to water.

16

Sir Randolph Leighton walked into the Rose and Crown saloon bar and quickly spotted the flaming red hair of Charles Pettigrew, who was seated in a corner, staring morosely at a tankard of ale on the table in front of him. Randolph slid into the chair opposite the young man, who looked up and said, " 'Bout time you got here. I've been waiting over an hour."

"I was busy," Randolph answered shortly. "I'm leaving for Lancashire tomorrow."

"What do you want of me? I'm only here out of curiosity, I might as well tell you."

Randolph motioned to the barman to bring him a glass of ale. He looked at Charles Pettigrew's hand, lying on the worn wood of the table. A jagged scar, still purple and angry, curled across the back of his hand like a worm that had attached itself to his pale flesh. Seeing the direction of Randolph's glance, Charles said, "That's a legacy of the Apache's sneak attack. I cut myself on the pawnbroker's window."

"I heard about the incident," Randolph said. "That's why

I'm here. I also heard that Lord Moreland talked to your father, and the pawnbroker, and the constable. It seems the only one not compensated for damages was yourself."

"Oh, I daresay the Apache and I will cross paths again. Next time I'll not observe Marquis of Queensbury rules."

"I have a score or two to settle with him myself." Randolph lowered his voice. "And with his father. Unfortunately I'm not going to be here to do anything about it. But I could be helpful to you—if you're man enough to go after revenge for the Apache humiliating you."

"I was middleweight boxing champion my first year in university," Charles declared hotly. "I'd have trounced the bastard if he'd have fought fair."

"Of course you would have. But he won't fight fair, he doesn't know how. I spent several weeks with him and know exactly how you can take care of him. The first thing to do is to get him away from Merrinswood and the protection of his father. I'd suggest a party—a weekend affair just for young people so he'd have to come on his own. Get one of your friends to give it. It would be a bit obvious if you had it at your parents' home. Then have your friend invite young James Merrin."

"What? Turn the flamin' Indian loose on polite society? Lord knows what he might do."

Randolph smiled. "Exactly. Especially if you set a few traps for him. Let me explain . . ."

"Is it diphtheria, Doctor McGreal?" Sarah asked in a worried voice.

Andrew pulled the blanket back up over Robbie's thin chest. The child's breath rattled ominously. "No, no. A bad case of bronchitis. We must keep him in bed. See that the room is kept warm—have the servants keep the fire lit all night, too." Closing his black bag, he looked down at the pinched features of the boy. "You'll be good as new in no time at all, young man."

Robbie gave a wan smile and coughed again, his body wracked by the effort to expel the fluid from his lungs. Andrew signaled Sarah with his eyes that they should withdraw. Sarah bent over Robbie and said, "I'll be back in a few minutes with some nice hot soup and a new book I think you'll enjoy."

Outside the sickroom, Andrew said, "He was never a

strong child, but it almost seems that since his mother left, he's willing himself to become deathly ill."

They walked down the hall to the staircase. "Is it possible Robbie thinks his constant colds and fevers will persuade his mother to return . . . or send for him?" Sarah asked. "I'm not sure it was a good idea for his father to tell the child that Jean is in a warm climate somewhere for her health."

"There's been no word from her then?"

Sarah shook her head. "We keep hoping there will be a letter, for the children's sake. But . . ."

Andrew glanced at the woman who walked beside him. She wore a dress of gray silk with leg-of-mutton sleeves that emphasized her narrow waist, and the skirt gored over her slim hips. She carried herself well, and there was the unmistakable stamp of breeding in her demeanor. He was still surprised, in view of her history, that she had proved to be not only remarkably civilized and startlingly attractive, but also intelligent and compassionate. He'd been prepared to dislike Sarah on sight for having displaced Jean. But having had the opportunity to get to know her—since due to Robbie's constant illnesses Andrew was a frequent visitor at Merrinswood—he reluctantly acknowledged that if Jean had waited to meet her rival, perhaps everything would have turned out differently, for all of them.

In his capacity as physician, Andrew never ceased to be surprised by the family secrets people confided in him, and the Merrin household was no exception. If he didn't learn what was going on from a member of the family, and the child Emily was a born gossip, then one of the servants was sure to fill in the details. Therefore, he knew that virtually nothing was being done to try to find Jean, who had been idolized by the entire staff.

Nor had his own efforts borne fruit. He had so little time to spare, but had visited all of the local railway stations, patiently running down every single stationmaster and porter, as well as every conductor who passed through the area, just in case Sir Randolph had missed someone. But no one answering Jean's description had boarded a train at Carisbrook. Then Andrew began to check stations down the line, in case she had ridden in a carriage to a more distant station in order to evade pursuers. Although that investigation had been equally futile, it had led Andrew to wonder about the possibility that

Jean had left Merrinswood in a carriage. He resolved to question someone in the stables at the first opportunity.

As they went down the staircase at Merrinswood, Sarah said to him, "I've actually wondered if it would be a kindness to write a letter to Robbie—pretending it came from his mother."

"No . . ." Andrew said, "don't do that. If you really want to do something, hire someone to try to find his mother." He decided to follow his intuition with this woman, because there was an aura of integrity and compassion about Sarah that he trusted. "There's something sinister about Jean's disappearance. I know her well and I'm convinced she wouldn't have left without a word to her children. There are agencies, I believe, who will endeavor to find missing persons for a fee."

Sarah stopped, her hand on the carved balustrade. "Yes . . ." she said slowly. "In America there are private detectives, the Pinkertons. There must be an equivalent group here. Do you really feel it would be a good idea? What if Jean doesn't want to be found? After all, she did leave a note stating her reasons for leaving."

"You saw the note?"

"Yes."

Andrew reached into his inside pocket for his wallet. He withdrew a dog-eared slip of paper and handed it to her, feeling a slight flush of embarrassment as he did so. It was a note from Jean, thanking him for taking care of her during her difficult time after the birth of the twins. He was well aware that the fact that he had kept the note for so many years, carrying it next to his heart, would undoubtedly reveal his love for Jean. But he was too desperately worried about her to be concerned with propriety. He asked quietly, "Is the handwriting the same? That was written some time ago, but—"

"No," Sarah said at once. "There are no similarities whatsoever. This is a beautiful copperplate script. The note I saw was written in a childishly rounded style."

Returning the note to him, she added, "How can we get in touch with a private detective?"

Andrew cleared his throat. "I wonder, in view of all of the ramifications, if your husband really wants to find Jean."

Sarah gave him an understanding smile. "I don't think I'll tell Richard about hiring a private detective. I have funds of my own I can use."

❋   ❋   ❋

Brigid O'Connell put a warm shawl around her patient's shoulders and peered into the blank midnight-blue eyes, seeking some response. "There we are then, Chavi, dear. You can sit here until dinnertime and enjoy the fresh air. You're not too cold now, are you?"

One of the other nurses who was passing by said, "O'Connell, why don't you give up? She's never going to answer you. If Doctor Voigt sees you spending so much time with her you'll catch it, I can tell you. There's too many of them and not enough of us as it is."

Sighing, Brigid moved away from the patient known only as Chavi. Walking back to the house with the senior nurse, Brigid said, "I'm after feeling she's no gypsy, that one. She's a lady. I know it in me bones."

"Oh, for pity's sake! What a duffer you are, O'Connell. Don't you know by now that *all* of the patients here are ladies from good-class families? Aristocrats, some of them. Their relatives come up with all sorts of aliases for them, because they don't want people to know there's insanity in their family."

"I don't believe she's insane either."

"Oh? Then why doesn't she speak?"

"I think she's frightened out of her wits, poor soul. Terrible things have been done to her and she's afraid to trust anybody again."

"Why are you so taken with this patient? Out of all of these demented women, why this one?"

Brigid bit her lip thoughtfully. "I dunno. It's something in her eyes, I'm thinking. Sometimes she looks at me with those big dark blue eyes and it's like she's begging me to rescue her."

"You'll get over that after you've been here a bit. You'll get as sick and tired of the screaming and squabbling and soiled beds as the rest of us. Now that I think of it, maybe that's what you find so appealing about Chavi. She's quiet and doesn't make a mess in her bed. She's not much trouble—except for the force-feeding."

Shuddering at the mention of that horror, Brigid resolved to try to detach herself from this particular patient. After all, the poor soul was probably here for life. She'd never had a single visitor, and in the unlikely event that in the future someone attempted to see her, the gatekeeper or reception staff would never permit it. Chavi with the dark haunted eyes had been condemned by someone to a living death.

17

The group of village louts formed a taunting circle around the organ-grinder. "Bloody foreigner! Go on—be off with you. We don't want your kind here."

Pas put up his hand to stroke the tiny monkey, who chattered nervously on his shoulder. Danior gripped the handle of the pushcart tightly, trying not to show his fear. Pas said in his quiet, lilting voice, "We mean no harm."

"We meana no harma," one of the youths mocked, giving Pas a slight shove. Alphonso was almost dislodged from his perch on Pas's shoulder, and screamed in fright.

"Let's get the monkey," one of the others shouted. They were all strapping young men, but had the unnatural pallor of miners. Danior's gaze swept the street. He and Pas had left the rolling moors and were now in coal-mining country. This was a dismal village of terraced houses, packed shoulder to shoulder, and gray slate roofs sloping beneath tall chimneys of blackened bricks. The narrow cobbled streets formed a spider web around the colliery, marked by stanchions, girders, and water towers almost dwarfed by towering slag heaps that glittered malevolently against a colorless sky.

All the signs here were bad. Too many men on the street at midafternoon. Too much hunger in the eyes of the shriveled women and children. The colliery must have shut down and the men were out of work, thought Danior. There'd be no knife-sharpening business for Pas here, no ha'pennies dropped into the hat when Alphonso danced and Danior sang.

"Please—don't hurt the monkey," Pas begged. "He's just a dumb animal."

One of his tormentors poked Pas in the chest with a bony finger. "Bloody foreigners are wot's wrong with this flamin' country. Why don't you go back where you belong?"

In the next minutes everything happened so quickly that Danior wasn't sure of the exact sequence of events. Someone made a grab for Alphonso, who promptly fastened his teeth around a grimy finger and bit down hard, eliciting a yell of pain. The monkey fell from Pas's shoulder and a pair of clogs tripped over the tiny animal. The villagers moved in, shouting and shoving. In the scuffle Danior was knocked to the ground. A fist connected with Pas's jaw. He stumbled backward, colliding with the pushcart, which began to roll down the sloping street.

Seeing his livelihood headed for possible destruction, Pas wrenched free of the hands restraining him and flung himself after the cart. He managed to deflect it, turning its course toward the pavement, but in doing so sent it crashing into one of the villagers.

Scrambling to his knees, Danior saw the men pinning Pas's arms to his sides, pummeling his body with their fists. Danior heard his own voice, raised in a terrified plea for mercy for his friend, and at the same instant heard Pas's frantic command, *"Danior, get Alphonso and run!"*

Danior felt very small and insignificant, but those men were hurting Pas. The boy threw his arms around the leg of the nearest man and tried to drag him away. The man shook his leg, as though troubled by an insect, and Danior rolled into the midst of crashing clogs. A steel-tipped foot caught him on the side of the head and everything rushed away from him into a black hole.

The first thing he saw when he opened his eyes again was Alphonso. The little monkey chattered and danced worriedly around the motionless form of Pas, who sprawled in the gutter. The pushcart lay on its side, one wheel turning slowly in a rising breeze. The street was now mysteriously empty, doors closed, curtains drawn.

With stars exploding in his head, Danior crawled over to his friend. Alphonso turned on him in rage, jumping up and down and baring his teeth, but Danior batted him aside.

Pas lay face down, and Danior carefully raised his friend's head, praying that he was still alive. There was a dark bruise along Pas's jaw and blood dripped from his burst lip, but he was breathing. He moaned as Danior tried to pull one arm from beneath his body.

His gentle eyes flickered open. "Don't," he whispered. "My arm . . . I think they broke it."

"Oh, Pas, what shall we do?"

"The organ—they broke it, too, I think. Let me rest a minute. Then we'll leave."

He was very pale and he had begun to tremble violently. Not knowing what to do, Danior put his arms around Pas's head and held him.

The long shadows of the shortening days of autumn crept over the cobblestones. Alphonso huddled dejectedly beside the overturned pushcart. Somewhere, in one of the shuttered houses, a woman sang a ballad as she prepared the evening meal. Behind the curtained windows the people of the village got on with their lives, oblivious to what their sons, out of their own misery and despair, had done to a passing stranger. Danior had experienced unreasoning hatred before in his short life. He'd seen the gypsy caravans ordered to leave a village, and the Romany people accused of everything from witchcraft to murder. Now he understood that it was not simply that gypsies were disliked and feared. Anyone who was not exactly the same as everyone else, be it because of a different accent or darker skin, was equally unwelcome.

"Why did they do this to us, Pas?" Danior whispered, afraid the bullies might return if he raised his voice. "We didn't do anything."

"They're out of work and they were looking for a scapegoat. Someone to blame for their hardship. In such a situation, it's always the ones who are different from themselves."

Danior wished passionately that he had been big and strong enough to protect his friend. "It isn't fair," he said.

Pas smiled sadly. "Nothing's fair. Don't ever expect it to be."

At length Pas was able to sit up. His arm fell at a strange angle at his side and he winced with pain. "Take my kerchief, Danior," he said, taking a long breath between each word. "Help me fasten it around my neck. We'll make a sling for my arm. Then we'll leave."

Danior did as he was told, so afraid that he might hurt Pas with his fumbling that Pas had to do most of the work himself. "Now—help me up. We must see if we can get the cart up, too. Pick up any pieces that are broken off the organ."

It was almost dark before they righted the pushcart, then with Pas leaning on it for support, Danior eased it out into the middle of the street. He knew that they were in real trouble now. How could Pas sharpen knives with a broken arm? How could they entertain without the organ? Nor could Pas repair it with only one hand. But their most immediate need was for someone to set the broken arm. Danior had once seen a broken leg being set, and although he was unsure exactly how it was done, he knew that it required someone with more strength than a little boy possessed.

Hakan felt free for the first time in weeks. He was one with the wind and sun and sky. How the sunlight shimmered on the red and gold leaves of the autumn-clad trees as they flew by. How sweet the fragrant air tasted! How effortlessly his horse galloped across the open field, unencumbered by saddle, untouched by spurred boots. Hakan's own body felt curiously light, clad once again in buckskins, almost as if it had burst free of some invisible boundary that had been concealed in the stifling riding clothes he'd been forced to wear. His feet, encased in soft leather moccasins, lightly touched the flanks of the chestnut stallion, more by way of encouragement than in any effort to direct him.

At last Hakan's senses felt uncluttered by the peculiar Life-way the English sought to impose upon him. His mind soared free of structure. No thoughts intruded urging him to imitate a certain behavior, or observe incomprehensible rules. In this moment he could express his true feelings, become his true self.

Now at last he was in touch with this land as it really was, not in the way its inhabitants distorted it to meet their strange needs and desires. He sensed eternal forces at work, in universal and timeless harmony. His perception of the world had mysteriously expanded so that, surrounded by the lushest meadows, he could also experience the harshly beautiful landscape of the desert terrain of his childhood. It was simply the other side of this gently green and rainwashed land. If he blinked his eyes he could see and smell and taste the untamed Arizona desert, pale sand glittering in the sunlight, rocky mesas like the bare bones of the earth itself; overlaid by the verdant moors of England. The one superimposed over the other, each existing in its own element and he a part of both. At this moment, with the sun on his shoulders and the wind in his hair, all the energy of the earth was within him. His mind and body were no longer separated, and he was free of all inner conflict, at peace, transcending time and space.

The stallion slowed his gallop as the place called Coombe's Woods drew near. Hakan allowed his mount to choose a path and the horse clearly wanted to explore the dark pathways among the bright-hued trees.

The dense groves of oak and sycamore wore their gaudy autumn colors like overdressed matrons jostling one another at a party. That thought dimmed some of Hakan's joy. He recalled now why he had rebelled that afternoon, casting aside his English clothes and boots to ride bareback across the moors. The party—a weekend affair at the home of one of his father's friends—loomed ahead, waiting for him like an ambush.

"Lord Dunstan has a son a couple of years older than you," his father had said. "Matter of fact, you met him when you had that little altercation with Charles Pettigrew in the village. Young Gilbert is quite an accomplished polo player, you'll like him. I expect he'll invite Charles too—but not to worry, I'm sure he's quite forgotten the incident at the pawnbroker's."

His father had gone on to point out Hakan's need to socialize with his peers, and added slyly, "Oh yes, Gilbert has a rather lovely sister, a year or two younger than you. Her name is Cornelia."

Sons-ee-ah-ray had argued against allowing him to attend the affair alone. "He isn't ready for that," she'd said. But his father then insisted that it was time for her to allow her son to stand on his own feet. Hakan had bristled at the inference that he took commands from a squaw and announced that he would go.

Immediately, his uncle and his mother, and even the twins' governess, and the awful bossy little Emily, began a campaign to civilize him in time for his first social engagement. Hakan's head ached with the constant barrage of admonitions. Don't forget this, don't do that, never say so-and-so. Don't discuss Apache customs or Indian lore. Don't comment on the food. Don't drink too much wine. Above all, don't drink too much wine.

Oddly enough, his father took the opposite approach. "Not to bother yourself unduly about social niceties. Don't let them force a false refinement on you. You're my son—heir to my title and lands and a member of a rather small and elite group. There's enormous power in just being who you are, and don't ever forget it."

"I am the son of two great chiefs," Hakan had murmured.

His father laughed. "Indeed. You've been taught about your Indian chief, now let me tell you about your real heritage. The entire British Empire exists to nourish the ruling classes of England. Our style of life is one of leisure, and I suppose, a certain arrogance. We're here to enjoy life, to see it as a giant canvas upon which to paint our pleasures."

"If this is so, then why must I labor over books and lessons?" Hakan protested.

"To enable you to savor all the nuances, my dear fellow. One can't fully appreciate all that life has to offer unless one first understands what it's all about."

But then his father had become involved in his own pursuits, leaving Hakan to the mercies of his mother and uncle, and Charlotte, and even his valet. Only timid little Robbie presented realistic advice. The little boy, whose handsome features lacked vitality due to his ill health, said shyly, "Wh-when I h-h-have to go to a p-party, I just sit in a corner and k-keep my mouth shut. It soon passes."

Hakan smiled at the child. "Yes, of course. It will pass. I will keep my mouth shut too, and not bring disgrace to the family. Come, we'll go to the orchard and I'll pick a fine ripe pear for you."

"Will you t-tell me another story about Coyote's tricks?"

"Yes, if you'll let me give you a riding lesson. When your cough is better, I mean."

"If I c-could only ride l-like you," Robbie said wistfully. "F-father might l-like me b-better." Hakan hoisted the boy up onto his shoulders and began to tell how Coyote allowed himself to be tricked by the lynx, whose spotted coat he admired, and who told Coyote he could give his pups the spots by covering them with burning sticks.

"G-goodness, I expect that was d-disastrous."

"Disastrous," Hakan agreed. "We learn many lessons from Coyote's foolishness."

He had temporarily forgotten the advancing weekend until late last evening when his mother had come to him, her face gravely troubled. "Don't go to the Dunstan's . . . please don't go. I have a terrible premonition that something will happen to you."

"You saw an omen? Crows? An owl? What?" Hakan asked.

She shook her head. "No omens. Just a mother's intuition."

"I am no longer a helpless child," Hakan had answered gently. "If we still lived the Life-way, I would be a brave now. Don't worry about me, I will be on my guard."

But the strain of trying to absorb the unfamiliar culture, the constant lessons, and now the bewildering mass of information about social functions had taken its toll. Earlier that day when his valet had begun to lay out a formidable array of attire for the weekend, he had rebelled. Before he became James Merrin, heir to an Earldom, he must have an hour or two of being simply himself. Donning his Apache buckskins and moccasins, he'd stormed out of the house and gone to the stables. Startled stableboys leapt out of his path as he burst into view, riding bareback, without bit or reins.

The ride had calmed him, and as he slid from his mount to walk through the drifts of fallen leaves in the woods, Hakan reached a decision. He would go to the home of Lord Dunstan. He would endeavor to comport himself in an acceptable manner. When he returned to Merrinswood he would explain to his mother that he could no longer be a part of the Life-way of the English.

Having reached a decision he knew was right, Hakan felt a great weight rise from him. Glancing upward along the threads of sunlight penetrating the canopy of leaves, he saw that the sun was slipping toward the horizon. It was time to return and prepare for tomorrow's ordeal.

A twig snapped somewhere close by. Hakan stopped, all of his senses alert. The sound had come from behind an aged oak not more than twenty feet away.

Patting the horse lightly to reassure the animal and convey the message that he was to stay, Hakan slipped behind the nearest tree and moved on silent feet in a circle that would bring him to a position behind whatever or whomever had given away his presence by snapping the twig.

Emerging into a small clearing, Hakan looked down at the back of a small boy who crouched beside the oak. The child spun around, as if warned by some inner voice, although Hakan knew he had not made a sound.

The boy was probably not more than eight summers of age, thin, wiry, with hair as black as a raven's wing, and darker skin than most Englishmen. Barefoot, and dressed in ragged pants and shirt, the boy's eyes widened more in astonishment than fear.

For a moment they regarded each other in curious appraisal. This child was like no other Hakan had encountered, and no doubt he in return was equally interested in the Apache buckskins Hakan wore.

Eventually the little boy said, "Please sir, could you help my friend? He's very poorly."

"Who are you? What is your name?" Hakan asked.

"Danior, sir."

"I am Hakan. Where is your friend and what is the nature of his illness?"

"He's further on, into the woods. I'll show you. His arm is broken. He's got a fever too. Started with it a couple of days ago. He's been talking funny."

"Show me the way." The boy put his hand trustingly into Hakan's and led him along a narrow trail bordered by ferns and closely grown saplings.

"Why did you bring your friend here?" Hakan asked. "Why did you not take him to the village?"

The boy glanced sideways at him, as though trying to decide if he were a friend. "I was afraid to. I came here because I was going to wait near the great golden house to see if the lady with the kind eyes would come out. She helped my sister and me and I thought she'd help Pas, too. I didn't know where else to take him. She'll probably send me to reform school, but I think she'll take care of Pas. We haven't any money. I spent the last of it two days ago to buy bread."

The woods and surrounding moors abounded with game, but Hakan supposed the child was too young to know how to wield bow and arrow, or even set a trap. But surely by this age he should have been taught how to find edible plants and berries. How very lax these people were in preparing their children to survive.

Reform school? What did the boy mean by that? The great golden house was Merrinswood, of course. What was this ragged boy's connection to the Merrins? Hakan said, "Perhaps you'd better tell me the whole story. About the lady with the kind eyes and your sister."

He listened in silence as Danior related what had happened. By the time he'd finished they had come to a stone wall that had once been part of a cottage. Nearby was a small wagon, brightly painted and carrying some sort of instruments and machinery, but obviously in need of repair.

Lying on the other side of the stone wall was a man who twisted and turned in the throes of fever. Hakan dropped to his knees beside him, carefully running his hands up and down the man's arm.

Instantly, a strange chattering burst from a tree nearby and Hakan looked up to see a small animal, clad incongruously in a striped jacket. Danior said, "That's Pas's monkey. Don't worry, I'll keep him away. He bites sometimes."

Hakan pulled his knife from the sheath attached to his belt and slit the grimy sleeve of the man's coat. The child watched silently.

As the discolored flesh of the man's arm was revealed, Hakan's suspicions were confirmed. "First, the bones must be fitted together properly so the arm will mend itself. The fever is caused by the torn flesh, which has become infected." He glanced about at the various trees and vines. "Perhaps I can find the herbs I need here. I'll have to break the arm again and reset it, because the broken bones have already started to knit together. Would you prefer that I take your friend to one of your doctors, or do you trust me to help him?"

The boy's dark eyes locked with his, and Hakan understood the probing gaze very well. The child's mind sought to connect with his, to understand his motives for helping them. Danior said, "I think God has sent you to us."

Sarah paced a worried circle around her bed and when the door opened to admit Richard she spun around. "Did you find him?"

"He returned a few minutes ago." Richard wore an amused expression that made Sarah's heart sink.

"Well?"

Richard sat on the edge of her bed. He chuckled. "Resplendent in Apache buckskins, complete with moccasins, his horse sans saddle. I daresay he'd have ripped the shoes off the beast too, if he'd thought of it."

Sarah maintained as calm an expression as she could. "He's bound to rebel occasionally. No doubt having to go to Lord Dunstan's place precipitated this. I really don't think it's a good idea for him to go alone."

"Nonsense. He's not a child. As for tonight's episode, I admire him for doing what he damn well pleased. You and Philip between you have been driving him too hard. What does it matter if he uses the wrong fork or makes some uninhibited remark? He's my son and as such answerable to no one. Certainly not to that crowd of young rowdies Dunstan will have over there tomorrow."

Sarah went to her dressing table and sat down. She picked up a silver-backed hairbrush. "I don't understand you. You were the one who was appalled that I wanted Hakan to live here with you. Now it seems you almost encourage him *not* to learn our ways."

"One's first impressions and ideas aren't always one's best. There's a certain raw vigor to the lad that I like and hate to see stifled." Richard gave her an enigmatic smile. "Perhaps I can relive my lost youth through him. S'truth, what a time I'd have had if I'd suddenly been thrust into society after living like a savage for sixteen years!"

Placing the hairbrush back on a crystal tray on the dressing table, Sarah stared at her husband in the mirror as though observing a portrait rather than the living man. Richard had spent a lifetime indulging all of his own worst traits. He was conscienceless, with no sense of honor or obligation to any individual or the society in which he lived. Knowing this, how could she have brought her son here? How could she expect Hakan not to be influenced by this man?

There was no point in explaining to him again that the Apache Life-way was far from barbaric. Nor would it serve any purpose to tell her husband that she too had been wrong in her thinking about what was best for Hakan. How much mischief parents are capable of in the name of love, she thought, how very fallible. Wanting everything for their children, did they sometimes seek to deprive them of their own choices?

The portrait in the mirror moved. Richard rose and materialized behind her. He ran his fingers through her loosened hair, brought it to his face and inhaled its fragrance. She said quickly, "Please leave."

Richard's hands dropped to her shoulders. His eyes met hers in the mirror. "You were never meant to live a celibate life, Sarah. If we make love, I promise it will be our little secret. You can maintain that cold contempt for me everywhere but in bed."

There was a bellpull beside her and she reached for it to summon her maid. Richard shrugged. "Your loss, my love."

When she was alone, she placed her elbows on her dressing table and buried her face in her hands, nagged by the memory of an incident that had occurred earlier that evening. When Hakan failed to return for dinner, she had walked to the stables to see if he were there, taking a shortcut through the kitchen garden. An owl had suddenly fluttered aloft, only inches from her face. Her own premonition of impending disaster was now confirmed by the worst kind of Apache omen.

18

From July to November, the sheep shearers fanned out across the Australian Outback like an army, traveling to the remote stations on horseback, in sulkies, or even on bicycles. They were lean, hardworking men who had left wives and families behind in the coastal settlements. To Chavi they seemed interested only in clipping the wool, joking with their mates, swilling beer, and eating. How they ate!

Twelve Mile Station had one permanent cook, a grizzled and cantankerous old man, nicknamed Boomer because of his skill with the aboriginal boomerang. According to Lysander, Boomer had originally been transported to an Australian penal colony from a London prison. The shearers also brought their own cook, but as soon as the two men found out that Chavi could cook, they quickly allowed her to do most of the work.

On the last evening before the shearers were to move on

to the next station, Chavi wearily hauled platters of roast mutton and fresh-baked bread to the dining room and pondered on her unrequited love for Lysander's brother, Dirk.

Since her arrival, Dirk had been courteous, but politely aloof. In contrast to Lysander, Dirk seemed almost afraid of Brenna and avoided contact with the baby. His attitude toward them was that of a considerate host whose houseguests would no doubt depart shortly.

Still, whenever Dirk was near, Chavi felt her heart pound, and the air between them seemed to crackle. She had not felt such an immediate and overpowering attraction even to Lord Moreland, who had briefly captured her heart but whose face had now faded in her memory. If it hadn't been for the anger she felt that his lordship had seen fit to transport her and his child to this faraway place, she would have simply stopped thinking about him altogether. But that part of her mind that, when she listened to it, prepared her for forthcoming events, told her that she wasn't done with Lord Moreland yet. They would meet again one day, she was certain.

Dirk was already seated at the head of the table, in conversation with one of the shearers. Chavi's hand went to a tendril of her hair, to push it back behind her ear, before she took her place at the table. Opposite her, Lysander's knowing gaze flickered from her primping hand to the back of his brother's head. Without words he conveyed what a fool she was making of herself, and angered by his contempt, Chavi forcefully pulled out her chair and sat down.

It had been obvious since the moment of Lysander and Chavi's arrival that Lysander was not his real first name, any more than Smith had been his true surname. Dirk expressed amusement at his brother's choice of nom de plume, but addressed him as Lysander without question. Chavi thought that perhaps Dirk, like his brother, was not anxious for anyone to hear Lysander's real name.

Dirk looked up and smiled. "Evening, Chavi. Dinner smells good. I can't tell you how grateful we are that you dropped into our lives. Apart from the excellent meals, the presence of a lovely girl has a civilizing effect on us. How pretty you look tonight."

Chavi tried not to blossom too visibly under the onslaught of his smile and compliment, but knew from the look on Lysander's scarred countenance that she wasn't succeeding. Damn the man, he knew her too well. She passed the platter of meat to her neighbor. "Lysander bought the dress for me in Bombay." She paused. "That's in India."

"Yes," Dirk said. "A sari, isn't it? It looks nice and cool."

"I can't get used to it being spring, this time of year. Seems so strange that the seasons are upside down."

"You think spring in October is strange, wait till you live through a hundred-degree heat on Christmas day," Dirk answered. "I keep promising myself I'll return to Blighty for Christmas, but I never do."

"How long has it been since you went home?" Chavi asked.

Dirk smiled, but she sensed great sadness behind that smile. He said, "This is my home. I love this country. I can't imagine living anywhere else. I'd only go to England to cater to my nostalgia for the Christmases of my childhood. To hear church bells on a frosty Christmas morning . . . to listen to a choir singing in a cathedral of the birth of the Savior." He paused, glancing at the other men in embarrassment. "I'd go for a short holiday, never to stay."

"Oh," Chavi said, feeling disappointed. She couldn't imagine anyone actually loving this bleak landscape and great woolly oceans of sheep. The prospect of spending one's whole life in any one place, for that matter, was a dreary prospect to her. But if that was what Dirk wanted, then somehow she'd learn to love Twelve Mile, too.

Feeling Lysander's mocking eyes on her again, she concentrated on the food on her plate. Probably the reason Dirk, and every other man on the station, had so far practically ignored her, she reasoned, was because of that fiercely protective attitude Lysander maintained toward her and the baby.

The brothers' relationship toward one another was something of a mystery, too. Chavi sensed they were both holding back their feelings, perhaps attempting to make a new start because old hurts were unresolvable. She caught snatches of emotion between them, bitterness, sorrow, even guilt. Neither would divulge anything about the other, of that she was certain, so she made no inquiries. In time she'd uncover their secrets, one way or another.

Those first days, after they arrived at Twelve Mile, when she realized that she had found the great love of her life, her first fear had been that Dirk would be disgusted with her for having borne an illegitimate child. There had been an awkward moment, just after their arrival, when Dirk had inquired about her "husband."

She had said at once, "I don't have one. I've never been married."

There was a stunned silence, then Lysander said, "Chavi is a victim of upper-class lust. An unsophisticated girl who had the misfortune to catch the eye of the local squire. We understand too well about such situations, don't we, Dirk?"

A glance had passed between the brothers that was so heavy with meaning, Chavi felt it from across the room.

Dirk gave a slight shrug, smiled and said, "You're about as subtle as a sledgehammer. Set your mind at ease. No one is going to molest her here."

"I'd stake my life on that," Lysander answered grimly.

Later, when he had carried her bag up to her room, he said to her in private, "I'm going to give you a piece of advice, gypsy. Act like a lady and you'll be treated like one. And in future don't be so damn quick to label Brenna illegitimate. For her sake, if not your own, invent a deceased husband."

"That would be a lie," Chavi said. "But, of course, you don't think it's wrong to lie, do you? You've been lying to me from the minute we met. Well, let me tell you, I'd rather have a thief than a liar. You can lock out a thief, but there's nothing you can do to protect yourself from a liar."

A strangely vulnerable light flared briefly in Lysander's dark eyes, telling her she'd touched a nerve.

As the days passed and her love for Dirk grew, fed perhaps by his studied indifference toward her, Chavi began to look for some sign that he found her attractive. She was sure he did, because it didn't seem possible she could generate such a great passion all by herself.

If she turned suddenly and found him watching her, she was happy for the rest of the day. A smile, a compliment, made her heart fill with joy. Once he touched her cheek lightly and said, "How pretty you are. It's a pleasure to look at you." She had dreamed that night of lying in Dirk's arms forever.

The main reason for his reticence, she quickly saw, was that he was a devoutly religious man who spent much of his free time studying his bible. The contrast to Lysander, who was the devil's own disciple, added to Chavi's admiration of Dirk.

The arrival of the sheep shearers had thrown the entire

station into a turmoil, and no one had time to think of anything else. But now the shearing was done and tomorrow the traveling men would be on their way. In the days ahead there would surely be opportunities for Dirk and herself to draw closer.

She looked around the crowded dining table. Dirk and Lysander were set apart from the other men by their table manners, their cultured voices, their upper-class English demeanor. But somehow Dirk still managed to be a part of the group, enjoying unselfconscious camaraderie with the Aussies, whereas Lysander made the others uncomfortably aware of their shortcomings. She saw men covertly watch the way he broke his bread into small pieces before buttering it, then follow suit. What was it about the man that made others feel they must follow his example? she wondered. It was especially perplexing with these rough and tough Aussies, since Dirk was their employer, and Lysander's status here was no greater than theirs. But Lysander had moved in, just as he had aboard ship, and taken command.

What made the situation even more baffling was the Aussies's obvious contempt for most Englishmen. Chavi had overheard enough remarks about "Pommies" to quickly conclude that they were regarded here as less than useless. The only explanation of their deference to Lysander had to be that they were afraid of him. It wasn't just his scars, there was something else. A raging recklessness that almost seemed to invite others to attack him. Put me out of my misery, it seemed to say, but don't count on me dying easy. I'll probably take you with me.

As though aware of the direction her thoughts had taken, Lysander said, "Come on, gypsy, you're taking the rest of the evening off. You've worked like a Trojan and tonight somebody else can clean up. Go and fetch the baby and we'll take her to watch the sunset."

Chavi glanced in Dirk's direction and Lysander snapped, "You don't need his permission. You've earned a little relaxation."

Dirk said, "My brother is quite correct, Chavi. Run along; Boomer will clear the dishes."

Chavi went back to the kitchen, where Brenna lay in a makeshift cot under the watchful eye of Boomer, who sat at a scrubbed wood table shoving food into his mouth as though it were his last meal. Although there was virtually no class division on the station, Boomer chose to eat alone rather than join the others in the dining room. The old man regarded her balefully from beneath a wiry tangle of gray eyebrows. "How many times I told you to use your head to save your legs? You should've brought an armful of dishes with you."

"I'm going out for a walk," Chavi said, bending to pick up the baby, who gurgled with delight and fastened her tiny fist into the folds of the delicate material of the sari. Chavi wondered if she should have worn it, but the colors were so pretty and she was tired of staid grays and browns. "Dirk said you'd clean up tonight."

"Oh, 'e did, did 'e? Well, one of these fine days he's going to look around for old Boomer and find 'im gone."

Chavi shut out Boomer's complaints and threats, having heard them before. Gathering the baby into her arms, she wrapped the loose end of the sari around Brenna and went outside into the spring evening.

The setting sun daubed the sky with splashes of red and gold and formed a perfect backdrop for the silhouette of the man who stood at the crest of a slight rise at the rear of the house. Chavi stopped in her tracks, her senses quickening. For an instant she thought it was Dirk, but then Lysander turned slightly, and even though his face was in darkness, the scars mercifully concealed, the arrogant tilt of the head quickly reminded her which brother awaited her. But oh, how alike the two were. If they wore masks over their faces, there'd be no way to tell them apart. The same broad shoulders, torsos like tapered tree trunks atop muscled legs. Chavi had overheard Romany women whispering and giggling about their men long before Lord Moreland rode into her life, and now she fully understood their hunger of the flesh. With Lord Moreland the act of love had happened so quickly she was scarcely aware of her own reaction, overwhelmed as she was by his. But now in her mind she had already lain with Dirk, kissed and caressed every inch of his magnificent body. Lost in her yearning for physical closeness with him, she disregarded the fact that she hated this bleak country, the isolation of the sheep station, the lack of female companionship.

She knew that Lysander must want to speak to her in private, otherwise he never would have suggested that they watch the sunset together. Wishing she'd simply refused, she picked her way carefully through the clumps of saltbush, afraid the delicate sari might get caught on the sharp branches. She'd had enough of his lectures. Oh, she was grateful for all he'd taught her, but the price she paid was his attitude that he had somehow created her.

As she approached, Lysander said, "Why did you wear the sari? It's completely inappropriate for dinner."

"What's it for, then?"

"It was a souvenir of our day in Bombay. Meant to be worn in private."

"What good is something pretty if no one can see it?"

"From now on wear one of the dresses I bought."

When she reached his side he automatically took Brenna from her arms. Holding the baby up to the blazing sky, he said softly, "Look, little one. Look at the glory of nature."

"You talk to her as though she could understand you," Chavi said, feeling shut out as she always did when he held the baby.

Ignoring her, Lysander said, "It's all yours, Brenna. This whole world."

"Oh? And who's going to give it to her?" Chavi asked. "Her penniless gypsy mother, or her fearsome friend?"

"My brother is going to give it to her," Lysander said. "Come on, let's walk. I want to be well away from the house for this discussion."

Chavi fell into step beside him, her interest piqued. "What do you mean—about Dirk?"

"He's wealthy. I don't mean just the station here—though God knows he's done well enough with it. He has an inheritance waiting for him back in England. A very large inheritance, I might add."

"Does he know?"

"Oh, yes. He just hasn't seen fit to claim it. The family trustees are handling my parents' estate for him."

"But aren't you the older brother?"

"I was disinherited years ago. Everything went to Dirk."

"I don't understand. You told me that aristocrats and wealthy people don't emigrate."

"Not unless they're forced to."

"Surely Dirk wasn't forced to leave?"

The shock in her voice caused Lysander to laugh in his most sinister manner. "Hard to believe, isn't it?"

"Why? What did he do?"

"Perhaps he'll tell you himself one day. It has no bearing on our plans anyway."

"Was it something to do with . . . what happened to you? I mean, I sometimes get a feeling when I'm with you . . . now, don't laugh at me and say I'm a superstitious gypsy, because I'm not fortune-telling, but sometimes when we're together and quietlike, I sense a terrible, lonely locked-up feeling in you. I think you spent time in prison, perhaps in solitary confinement. And you weren't born with that face. Somebody did that to you. Probably more than one man, because you'd be a match for three or four ordinary men."

"Enough speculation!" Lysander thundered. "Shut up and listen to me. You want my brother, don't you? Don't be coy. I want an honest answer."

"I do like him," Chavi said meekly.

"You'd like to marry him?"

"Yes, but—"

"Shut *up*. The first thing you've got to learn is that if you want him to run after you, you've got to walk the other way. Stop wearing your heart on your sleeve like some lovesick schoolgirl. Do you know the most powerful emotion you can arouse in a man?"

Chavi shook her head.

"*Curiosity*. You've got to hold a little back, make him wonder. A mysterious smile, a faraway look in your eyes sometimes. A soft sigh. A certain vagueness when he asks questions about where you've been or what you're thinking."

"Have you known a lot of women, Lysander?"

"Will you concentrate on what I'm telling you?"

"I'm listening."

"Remember this, you're beautiful enough to arouse unbridled lust in any man, even one whose newfound religious fervor causes him to ignore his baser urges. Getting him to want your body is the easy part. What you have to do is make him want you enough to marry you. Don't give in to him until the ring's on your finger, do you understand?"

Chavi felt her cheeks grow warm. "I'm not a harlot. Just because I let Lord Moreland doesn't mean—"

"Then convince Dirk that you're a madonna," Lysander interrupted. "Like many another good Christian he wouldn't hesitate to seduce a woman he thinks is loose and immoral, but he'll respect a lady. And another thing, learn patience. You're still only a child, even though you've given birth. You've got to be prepared to wait at least a year before Dirk will be ready to make you his wife."

"Do you think he loves me?" Chavi asked shyly.

Lysander snorted. "Women!" He made the word sound like a curse.

The baby cooed softly and Lysander's voice became soothing as he spoke to her, "Not you, little one. You're my little princess."

"Are you going to stay on here?" Chavi asked. Lysander had surprised her by doing his fair share of the work, but then there were no idle hands on the station, not even Dirk's.

"Probably not. I haven't stayed long in one place since . . ." his voice trailed off. "Come on, let's get back to the house. It's getting cool out here and you didn't bring Brenna's shawl."

"Sometimes you act like she's your baby," Chavi grumbled, but she wasn't really cross with him. After all, a year from now he'd be her brother-in-law. She didn't doubt it would happen, simply because Lysander said it would. One thing she'd learned about him, whatever he said was going to happen always came to pass.

As they walked back to the house Chavi asked, "How long will it take for that letter we wrote to Doctor McGreal to arrive?"

"About as long as it took for us to sail to Australia—possibly even longer."

"I'm so worried about my little brother. I hope they're being kind to him. I had such a strange dream about him the other night. He was standing on some sort of raised up platform, all alone, and there was a great crowd of people around him. I can't think what it means."

"Probably that you ate too much cold meat for supper," Lysander said. "And by the way, now that the shearers are gone, we'll resume your lessons tomorrow. You're still a long way from being the lady my brother will marry."

19

The carriage taking Hakan to Dunstan manor drew level with Coombe's Woods. Hakan glanced in the direction of the trees and silently asked *Y'sun* to watch over the sick man. Hakan knew that he had done everything within his power to help Pas. Many times as a boy he had watched the Apache shaman care for sick and wounded men, and except for the differences between herbs available here and in the Arizona desert, he was sure he had faithfully duplicated their medicine.

He had also built a wickiup to shelter Pas and the boy, and had surreptitiously taken them food and blankets from Merrinswood. Later, when this tiresome weekend was over, he would teach Danior how to live from the land. It was interesting to Hakan to find that there were natural people here, like Pas and Danior, who lived free, unfettered lives, although they were woefully ignorant in matters of survival.

The Dunstan estate was a couple of miles to the north of the woods and proved to be much smaller than Merrinswood. The grounds looked somewhat neglected, and here and there a missing brick or crumbling mortar gave the house a slightly shabby appearance.

Lord Dunstan and his son Gilbert greeted Hakan upon his arrival. The older man was portly and red-faced, and mumbled something about knowing Hakan's father for many years. Gilbert regarded Hakan with a supercilious stare, as though confronted by some kind of lower animal. He said, "The others are all out on the lawn. We're going to have an impromptu cricket match. You can join us after you've changed your clothes."

Lord Dunstan said, "Bit late in the season for cricket, isn't it? But then, you youngsters don't care much about tradition when it comes to your sports, do you?" To Hakan he added, "Johnstone will take you up to your room."

Following the butler upstairs, Hakan felt his gloom intensify. He didn't understand the game of cricket, would not be able to participate in it, and had no idea which of the clothes his valet had packed he should change into. His uncle Philip had been convinced that polo would be the sport of the afternoon and had briefed him accordingly. "Gilbert and his friends all play polo. You ride so well you'll be a natural for the game."

The Dunstan's butler opened a bedroom door. "This is your room, sir. Someone will be along shortly to assist you with your clothes."

Relieved, Hakan waited. A few minutes later there was a knock on his door and he called out, "Come in."

The young man who entered the room seemed somewhat bold for a valet. He immediately picked up Hakan's bag and dumped the carefully folded contents onto the bed. "Hmmm, your valet forgot to pack cricket togs. I'll go get some for you." Whistling under his breath, he turned and hurried from the room.

Minutes later he was back, carrying a shiny black top hat, a long striped muffler, a red flannel undershirt, and what appeared to be a leather breechclout.

Perplexed, Hakan said, "But . . . I have seen pictures in the newspapers of men playing cricket. They were dressed in white trousers and white shirts."

"Ah yes," the valet said, "but that was *before* the bank holiday. After the bank holiday this is what's worn. You wrap the muffler once around your neck and let the ends hang."

"Trousers?"

"No, just this." He handed Hakan the breechclout.

"But—"

"As the weather gets cooler," the valet said quickly, "young gentlemen like to prove their mettle on the cricket field by discarding trousers and playing with bare legs."

The valet spoke with an air of authority Hakan had not formerly encountered in servants. Heeding the admonitions of his mother and uncle that he emulate the behavior of the other young men, Hakan said, "Very well. You may go."

"Oh, I'll wait. I was told to take you down to the lawn when you're ready."

Fifteen minutes later, Hakan was dressed in the red flannel undershirt, the breechclout about his loins, and the striped muffler wrapped about his neck. He carried the top hat in his hand, recalling that it was very bad manners to wear a hat indoors.

The valet led him down a different staircase to a room that appeared to be part of the servants' quarters. "A short cut," he explained as he opened a door and they found themselves in a vegetable garden. "You can put on the hat now."

Hakan did so. The clothes he wore felt ridiculous, but no more so than some of the other outfits he'd had to wear. On trips through the village he had seen the local youths playing a game with a ball. His mother said the game was called rugby. For this sport they wore striped shirts and short trousers, above their knees. He supposed the red undershirt and leather breechclout were no more unusual. No doubt the top hat and muffler were gentlemen's accessories for a gentleman's game.

He followed the valet along a narrow path through a copse of trees so thickly grown that the branches formed an interwoven canopy overhead. They emerged into bright sunlight so suddenly that Hakan blinked.

The scene in front of him etched itself into his mind in horrid detail. There were a dozen or so young men clad in white flannel slacks, white wool pullovers over white shirts, two of whom stood with bats poised before triads of wooden stakes. Another player, ball in hand, stopped in his tracks to turn and stare at the latest arrival. Surrounding the players were a number of lawn chairs and umbrellas, under which sat young women sipping glasses of lemonade. Every eye swiveled in Hakan's direction.

For an instant it seemed that everything on earth was silent, as still as a tomb. Then there was a slight titter, followed by smothered giggles. One of the cricket players threw back his head and roared with laughter. Hakan saw it was the red-haired Charles Pettigrew. Everyone joined in the mirth. Hakan felt battered by their laughter, waves of ridicule washing over him. He stood frozen, humiliated beyond endurance, unable to move from the spot. The valet who had betrayed him had now vanished.

Hakan wasn't sure how much time passed before Gilbert detached himself from the white-clad cricketers and walked slowly toward him. Gilbert's face was convulsed with amusement, and when he spoke it was in a strangled gasp. "Come on, old chap, we'd better get you out of here before one of the ladies faints." He attempted to take Hakan's arm, but Hakan pulled free and turned to run back to the house, howls of laughter following him.

Hakan paced in an angry circle, contemplating the actions of Gilbert and his friends. In the split second before Hakan had left the cricket field, he had seen the young man who had posed as the valet joining in the laughter. He was obviously one of the guests, therefore the humiliation had been planned. Hakan was puzzled as well as angry. If they considered him to be their enemy, why invite him to a party?

He felt a bloodlust he hadn't known since leaving the Chiricahua mountains, when he had ridden out to avenge the death of his Apache father. To ridicule a man was worse than killing him, and someone would pay for the events of this afternoon, of that there was no doubt. The question was, how?

"Always keep a cool head," *Tonsaroyoo* used to tell him. "Never act in the heat of anger. Consider every aspect of the situation."

Very well. He realized now that his humiliation must have been in revenge for the incident at the pawnshop. Therefore, Charles Pettigrew and Gilbert Dunstan were the instigators. Hakan had been warned by the police constable that there were laws in this country that forbade the physical punishment of another, which was called assault and battery. This then, was the reason they had chosen ridicule as a means of getting even. He must repay them in kind.

There had been several knocks on his bedroom door, which he ignored, because he knew he was perfectly capable of killing the owner of any mocking face that appeared on his threshold. Now there was a more authoritative rapping, and the door opened.

Lord Dunstan entered the room, but took a backward step at the sight of Hakan. He had discarded the idiotic clothing and pulled on his riding breeches, but remained stripped to the waist. His pectoral muscles were well developed and still tanned, and his shoulders were wider than average. He towered over his host, and with the wild light of

anger in his eyes, no doubt presented a fearsome appearance.
He stopped pacing. He would not vent his anger on this old
man.

Nervously, Lord Dunstan cleared his throat. "Thought
I'd come up myself, my dear boy, and try to explain. I
understand you took a little joke seriously. The lads didn't
stop to think that you haven't been to school here. That
you're unfamiliar with public-school pranks and the hazing
of newcomers."

"Pranks? Hazing? This is the way newcomers are welcomed? With ridicule?"

The older man avoided his gaze. He muttered, "A practi-
cal joke, nothing more. You mustn't let them think it bothered you. It's simply a test of your mettle."

"It is a strange test."

"I have already expressed displeasure with my son over
the incident and he's promised to apologize to you. Please
don't let it spoil your weekend. The way to deal with the
situation is to simply laugh it off. And . . . uh . . . it would
be a personal favor to me if you didn't tell your father about
it. It isn't . . . uh . . . done, you know, to tell tales."

"I don't see what it has to do with my father."

"Quite right." The relief on his face was obvious and
quite revealing. Hakan remembered what his father had said
about the power of rank. All at once the title and property of
the Merrins assumed a different connotation in Hakan's mind,
becoming desirable, perhaps essential, to his future in England. His father seemed able to rise above even the law of
the land, and Hakan, in dealing with people like Charles
Pettigrew and his friends, needed the same power.

Lord Dunstan's glance flickered to the riding breeches
Hakan wore. "We have a couple of rather good horses.
Gilbert is an accomplished polo player. Perhaps you'd like to
ride before dinner?"

When Hakan hesitated, an idea forming, Lord Dunstan
cleared his throat again and added, "If you insist on leaving
now, you'll never be able to face them again."

"I won't leave," Hakan said grimly. "And yes, I will go
to the stables. Perhaps you'll ask your son and his friends to
meet me there?"

"Yes, yes, of course." He paused, one hand on the door.
"There'll be a party tonight and all of the young men will be

laughing on the other side of their faces when the young ladies start vying for your attention. And believe me, they will. Apart from the fact that you're probably the most eligible bachelor in the north of England, you're also an extremely handsome young man."

Impatient for him to leave, Hakan gave little heed to what the man said until Lord Dunstan added, "If you wish me to help you select the proper attire . . ."

"I know which clothes to wear."

Lord Dunstan gave him a long questioning look. "You'll put the hazing incident out of your mind? Believe me, it's better to pretend nothing happened."

How could he pretend nothing had happened? Hakan wondered as he thrust his arms into shirtsleeves. A gauntlet had been thrown down. They had declared themselves to be his enemies. They had planned an ambush. But he had an advantage they did not possess. He was Apache.

All of the young guests, hastily clad in riding attire, awaited him at the stables. He strolled toward them, taking in every detail of the scene. Evidently some of the other guests had brought their own mounts. Gilbert held the reins of a fine bay stallion and Charles was already astride a spirited mare. A groom had saddled Hakan's horse, which pawed the ground impatiently and whinnied as Hakan approached.

He looked around the circle of expectant faces, some still wearing barely concealed grins. He addressed Gilbert. "I understand you were testing my mettle earlier. Therefore I believe in the interests of fair play, I should be allowed to test yours. Do you agree?"

"Of course, old man," Gilbert said, his voice still bubbling with laughter. "Fair's fair."

Hakan fixed his eyes on Gilbert and Charles. "You are accomplished horsemen, I hear. Would you race with me, Apache-style? He peeled off his riding jacket, then his shirt, and a faint gasp went through the watchers, followed by a muffled giggle. Ignoring everyone but his two antagonists, Hakan said, "Have the grooms remove the saddles from your horses. Take off your jackets and shirts—everything but your breeches. Shoes, too."

"I say, what—" Gilbert began.

Hakan flashed him a murderous glance and Charles slid from his mount and took off his coat, handing it to a stable-boy. He grinned at Gilbert. "Come on, let's humor him."

Hakan said, "We will race through the woods and then across the fields."

"Half naked?" Charles asked.

"More of a challenge . . . old boy," Hakan replied. "If you ride through the trees carelessly, the branches will tear your skin. Oh yes, no reins, no bits in the mouths of your horses." He smiled pleasantly. "After all, it's a difficult ride for them too. We wouldn't want to hinder them in any way, would we?"

"Go on, you two," a feminine voice from within the group called. "You were ready enough to dish it out." Hakan didn't glance in the direction of the voice, but noticed that Charles immediately began to remove coat, shirt, and shoes, muttering, "Utter nonsense."

Gilbert had very white skin and was slightly round-shouldered, while the red-haired Charles, although more muscular, had an even paler chest mottled with freckles. Both looked thoroughly uncomfortable without the insulation of well-tailored riding jackets.

Hakan remained standing beside his horse while the other two mounted. They looked down at him expectantly. He said, "Across the fields to Coombe's woods, through the woods and back. You may start at any time you're ready."

"You're not mounted yet," Gilbert said.

"I'd prefer to mount when you're on your way."

"It wouldn't be fair that way." Gilbert turned to a groom. "When we're all in position, shout, one, two, three, go."

Hakan jumped astride his horse in a single leap. A gasp spread through the watchers.

He deliberately waited, giving them a headstart, after the groom yelled, "Go!" Their pale backs flashed forward, following the curve of the drive to the gates, then out across the fields. Hakan followed at a leisurely pace, keeping them in front of him.

When they reached the woods he dug his heels in the flanks of his horse and caught up with them, whirling past them into the trees. He rode in an almost straight line through the woods, lying close to the horse's back and occasionally swinging down low over the stallion's flanks to avoid low-hanging branches. A couple of times he dropped to the ground, his feet barely grazing the humus beneath the closely grown trees before springing back onto the horse and then down on his other side, without ever slowing the fast gallop.

Behind him the grunts of pain, the whirr of slashing branches, and the sound of hooves stumbling over forest debris gradually receded. The more they tried to emulate his method of negotiating the trees, the more trouble they would be in. Hakan laughed and couldn't resist giving an Apache yell. Once again he and his father were riding for the stronghold in the mountains, knowing that the white-eyes who could catch them had yet to be born.

When at last Charles and Gilbert came disconsolately through the gates of Dunstan manor, their white skin crisscrossed with red scratches, faces grazed, hair awry, Hakan was already fully dressed, sitting on the lawn in a deck chair sipping from a frosty glass of lemonade. One of the girls greeted the two losers with a ringing cry, "Where have you been? You look as if the cat dragged you both backwards through the woods. James has been back for hours!"

Stepping out onto the landing after changing into evening clothes, Hakan saw that the guests were all milling around in the hall below, no doubt awaiting the dinner gong. Conversation faded as he walked slowly down the stairs, feeling their eyes on him.

At the foot of the stairs a dazzlingly pretty young girl with flashing green eyes and pale blonde hair detached herself from a circle of young men and came toward him, her hand outstretched. Her skin had the pale translucence of the desert orchid and her lips were full and red as an ocotillo blossom. When she spoke her voice was soft. He recognized her from the group who had seen the spectacle he'd made of himself earlier, but didn't recall if she had witnessed his triumphant ride. "Hello, James. I'm Nelia, Gilbert's sister. We didn't get a chance to meet this afternoon."

At that instant the dinner gong sounded, and for a moment Hakan thought perhaps the sound was inside his head, heralding the arrival of this beautiful young woman. Before he had a chance to say anything, Nelia slipped her arm through his and said, "Will you accompany me into the dining room? I'll introduce you to the others later."

Over her shoulder he caught a glimpse of Charles Pettigrew glaring at him, the scratches on his face still red and raw. Everyone else had faded from Hakan's sight. He had lost himself in the depths of those emerald eyes. Unaware of the food he ate, or the conversation around him, even hers, he could only stare at Cornelia, who had done him the honor of allowing him to use the shortened version of her name. When the meal ended, she led the way to a large drawing room. The carpet had been rolled up and a trio of musicians was assembled at one end of the room.

"Do you dance?" Nelia asked.

"I have been taught a few steps of the waltz."

"Wonderful! That's all you'll need." She produced a small beribboned card. "Let's put you down for the first waltz."

Nelia led him around the room, presenting him to the other guests. Almost all of the young men congratulated him on winning the race and several told him he was a "jolly good sport." The young women were so unlike the Chiricahua maidens Hakan had known that he was at a loss to know how to treat them. Instead of lowering their eyes and perhaps giggling, or withdrawing in some way, these girls looked him boldly in the eye and handed him their dance cards. Only Charles and Gilbert continued to scowl in his direction. They were standing near the musicians in whispered conversation.

"Here are the pranksters and ignominious losers," Nelia announced as she led Hakan toward them. "Come on now, you two, apologize to James. That was a nasty trick you played on him this afternoon. Then you can congratulate him on his horsemanship and all shake hands and make up."

The two regarded her with bland innocence on their faces. "Us? Play a trick?" Gilbert asked, with exaggerated indignation. Charles glared at Hakan and made no comment.

"Gil, you promised—" Nelia began.

At that moment the musicians picked up their instruments and Gilbert mumbled something and turned to ask a girl nearby to dance. Nelia pulled Hakan out onto the polished wood floor. She placed his hand on her waist, let her fingers rest lightly on his shoulder, and smiled up at him.

In a pleasant daze, Hakan began to move to the music, counting in his head the one-two-three steps of the waltz. Nelia was as light as a drifting blossom in his arms, and no matter what he did with his feet, she matched his steps in perfect unison.

When the dance ended she stayed at his side and suggested they have a glass of punch. A large crystal bowl held the delicious beverage and Hakan was so thirsty he drank several glasses. Nelia said, "Watch out, it has a bite. Charles and Gilbert added some ingredients that neither Daddy nor Johnstone know about." She giggled and Hakan nodded, not wishing her to be aware of his ignorance of the meaning of her remark.

The evening flew by. There was always an attractive young woman waiting to dance with him, or have him fetch her a glass of punch. Nelia, who was by far the prettiest, hovered nearby, and Hakan saw her refuse several other invitations to dance.

A curiously unreal feeling of joy had him in its grip. He danced and laughed. Overhead the chandeliers flashed and the girls' satin gowns gleamed pink and blue and yellow.

Once when he went to the punch bowl he was surprised that Gilbert materialized beside him and said, "Here, let me give you a real drink. This stuff is for the girls." He then handed Hakan a glass of a dark liquid that burned its way down his throat, taking his breath away.

Gilbert was watching, so Hakan tried not to choke. He drained the glass and said, "Thank you." Gilbert said, "Oh, you must have another. That was just a sample, to see if you liked it." An even larger glass was then placed in Hakan's hand.

Since his host pressed the drink on him, Hakan knew it was only polite to take it, despite the terrible taste. "It isn't wine, is it?" he asked. "I'd prefer not to take too much wine."

Gilbert laughed. "No, it isn't wine. Drink up."

Hakan did so, forcing himself to swallow the bitter liquid. Gilbert's face, and nearby the flaming hair of Charles Pettigrew, blurred slightly.

"Cheers. Bottoms up," Gilbert said, his voice seeming to recede into the distance. Hakan drank it quickly to get the horrible taste out of his mouth. Then, in order to avoid being offered more, quickly filled a glass with punch for Nelia. Turning, he took a step and staggered, spilling the drink.

Mortified, Hakan grabbed a serviette and bent to mop up the mess, only to sprawl on the floor. What was happening to him? He no longer had any control over his limbs, and when he tried to speak, all that came out of his mouth was a confused and meaningless babble.

Strong arms hauled him to his feet and dimly he heard Gilbert's voice announcing in ringing tones, "Our Apache friend has had a little too much firewater, it seems. We'd better get him up to his room before he starts taking off his clothes again."

Too late, Hakan realized that once again they were humiliating him. In a rage he yanked free of their grasp and charged at Gilbert. Charles Pettigrew's foot went out to trip him, and he crashed to the floor again. Rising unsteadily to his feet, he felt Charles's fist connect with his jaw. Several of the girls screamed, and then he was a prisoner of too many hands to resist. They pinned his arms behind him and hoisted him into the air. Overhead the lights flashed in blinding patterns, his stomach churned, and sounds faded as a strange unnatural slumber claimed him.

Damp cold air on his bare flesh revived him. From the stiffness in his arms and shoulders he had been in this position for some time, wrists tied with rope behind his back, ankles similarly bound. He was completely naked.

In the faint light of a rising moon he saw that he was in a dense copse of trees, lying on the ground. The wild tangle of ferns and vines and the odor of decayed leaves told him he was in Coombe's woods. There was no other place where the trees grew so closely together.

Nearby, two shadowed figures stood watch over him. He heard their voices before full consciousness, along with a fierce headache, returned. Hakan forced himself to lie still and kept his eyes almost closed.

Gilbert's voice sounded worried. "I don't like this, Charles. I think we should find some other way to teach the blighter a lesson. Let's untie him and leave before my father or somebody catches us."

"No." Charles Pettigrew's voice slashed like a knife. "I'm not finished with him yet."

"But if anyone finds out—I mean, this is hardly cricket."

"He didn't play by the rules the day he shoved me into the pawnbroker's window, did he? And what about making complete fools out of us this afternoon? Besides, nobody knows we brought him out here. The others saw us put him to bed after he passed out."

"Let's just take him down to the village and leave him there without any clothes."

"No, that isn't enough for what he did to my hand."

"Christ, but you really are vindictive, aren't you? You're beginning to worry me. Look, I want this to stop, now."

"Go on back to bed, Gil. I don't need you anymore."

"Untie him," Gilbert's voice said urgently. "Before he comes to his senses. Get out of here."

From beneath half-closed eyelids, Hakan saw the shorter of the two shadows disappear into the trees. Charles moved closer and nudged Hakan with his foot. Hakan continued to feign sleep.

Minutes later, his ear pressed to the ground, he heard different footsteps approaching. He knew before the figure emerged from the dark trees that the newcomer was a man, fully grown, stronger and heavier of build than either Charles or Gilbert.

"You brought him? Ah, I see you did. Good work."

Hakan recognized the voice immediately. Sir Randolph Leighton, twin brother of the missing Jean, former estate steward at Merrinswood, discharged because of his cowardly attack on Hakan aboard the ship. Every nerve in Hakan's body tightened.

Charles's voice took on a slightly worried tone. "Look, I want him taught a lesson, but . . . well, you won't go too far, will you? I mean, it's common knowledge how you feel about your sister running off and your nephew being disinherited."

"The wild Indian is no longer your concern. Why don't you just go on back to bed and leave him to me?"

20

Unable to sleep, Sarah rose and turned on the lamp. She put on a dressing gown to ward off the night chill and went to her desk. Her journal was in the bottom drawer, hidden beneath several copies of *Punch*. Placing it in front of her, she allowed her fingers to drift across the leather cover, as though seeking comfort from the memories it contained.

Hakan would be in bed now, the ordeal of his first day at Dunstan manor over. Why was she so sure it had been an ordeal? A nagging sense of impending disaster persisted, disturbing her sleep, filling her mind with nameless horrors. She had even temporarily forgotten that she must find a way to take the report from the private detective to Doctor McGreal. Tomorrow was Sunday. Perhaps after church there would be an opportunity to speak with the doctor in private.

A small china clock on her desk ticked toward four. The hour before the dawn, she thought, remembering other nights when she couldn't sleep and her husband had held her in his arms and calmed her fears.

"Oh, my beloved *Tonsaroyoo*," she whispered aloud. "How I need you now. What am I to do about Hakan? He's caught between two worlds and belongs to neither . . . and all because you came to me in that hour before the dawn . . . so long ago."

A week after she and Otis were traded by the Comanche renegades to the Chiricahua Apache, Sarah had awakened to find herself struggling in the arms of a man whose face she couldn't see. The salty taste of tears and her own tortured sobbing testified to the vividness of the nightmare, but she couldn't remember what it had been about. A voice whispered close to her ear, speaking words she couldn't understand that nevertheless soothed her.

She stopped crying and lay still, memory returning slowly. The previous week had been spent solely in the company of squaws and the Mexican girl captives. Sarah had felt isolated, frustrated by her inability to communicate with them, living in fear every minute that the unspeakable atrocities conjured in her imagination might come to pass.

But so far all that had been expected of her was that she work, despite her broken ankle. There was grain to be crushed on a flat rock, game to be skinned and cooked, hides to be tanned, moccasins to be made; all of which could be accomplished from a sitting position. The squaws were impatient with her clumsiness and slowness in comprehending their mimed instructions. She was slapped and pinched to make her obey. She who had never lifted a finger to take care of even the simplest of her own needs now labored from dawn to dusk as a slave for these savages.

There were moments of black despair when she wished she had taken Otis's advice and killed herself rather than be taken captive. But she told herself the new life growing inside her gave her a reason to endure. At least she had been spared the anticipated horror of rape. Even the Comanches had not violated the female captives, and Otis had told her that from what he'd been able to gather from overheard conversations the braves believed their strength would be dissipated by the indiscriminate spilling of their seed.

"But, Sarah," Otis had warned, shortly after they came to the Chiricahua rancheria, "the Comanche were on the warpath, preserving their strength for battle. These Apaches are at peace, at least for the summer while they stay in the rancheria to harvest fruits and nuts. One of them is going to make you his squaw. Maybe you'll be lucky and they won't touch you until your ankle heals. They appear to be very concerned with caring for their sick and wounded. We've got to try to escape as soon as you can walk."

Although she remained in the ramada with the squaws, sleeping in a wickiup with two of them at night, several times she saw the Apache brave with the golden eyes walking through camp. Once she turned suddenly and saw that he was standing near her campfire, watching her. Their eyes met and held. Sarah felt a small thrill that consisted of equal parts dread and the heady knowledge that this man was as fascinated by her as she was by him. Somewhere, in some almost primal part of her being, the thought surfaced that if she must be possessed by one of these savages, then she hoped it would be that man. His eyes said he was wise, perhaps even kind. Was that possible? No, she was deluding herself. What she saw in his eyes was a raw emotion that had nothing to do with kindness and seemed unerringly able to evoke an equally primitive instinct in her.

Sarah, very much a product of the British upper class, had been astonished when she married Richard to find that, far from being the unpleasant chore she'd been led to believe marital lovemaking to be, the act was intensely pleasurable to her. Richard had laughed and said, "You've got the soul of a whore, my dear. But don't worry, it will be our little secret."

Perhaps her own delicious enjoyment of sex was the reason she had been shattered by the discovery of Richard's infidelity. She knew that among members of their class it was commonplace, perhaps because divorce was out of the question. But the sick shock of betrayal when she caught him with the dance-hall girl, and his unconcerned dismissal of the affair, still had the power to make her want to kill him.

In that hour before the dawn when *Tonsaroyoo* had come into her wickiup to quiet the body-wracking sobs of her nightmare, she had come slowly awake in the comforting circle of his arms, feeling several sensory impressions. The faint scent of sagebrush that clung to his body. The skin of his bare chest, strangely silken, yet seeming to pulse with power. His hands, strong and surprisingly smooth, touched her forehead, pressed lightly on her shoulders, stroked her hair.

Somewhere in the back of her mind conflicting voices argued. I need the touching, the closeness, to drive away the fear. *You can't give in to him, he's a savage.* I don't have a choice. Otis said one of them will take me. If it has to be, better this one, who is so beautiful, with such intelligent eyes. *What a liar you are, you've felt weak every time this man has looked at you.* Perhaps it's the pregnancy that's turned me into such a wanton. *Nonsense. You've enjoyed lovemaking since your wedding night. Admit it, you want this man.*

She hadn't known then that he was Lone Wolf, chief of the clan. Or that he had sent the two squaws with whom she slept out of the wickiup, so that they were alone. Or that his coming to her to quiet her sobbing had probably saved her life. The safety of the rancheria depended upon silence. No sounds must give away their position to lurking enemies. Apache babies were taught from birth not to cry. Mothers would take a crying child and suspend his cradle board from the branch of a tree, far from the rancheria. While he cried, he would be left alone. When he was quiet he would be picked up, held, cuddled, and fed. The infants quickly learned which behavior produced the results they desired. If *Tonsaroyoo* had not come to quiet Sarah's wild sobbing that night, no doubt one of the squaws would have stopped it more violently, perhaps permanently.

Nor had she known then that he already had two wives. After that night, it didn't matter, because he never slept with either of them again, although he cared for them and their children, protected and provided for them.

In that half-awake state of limbo, still caught in the terror of the formless dream, she had reached out to another human being and found at first solace, and then a swift rush of passion, one perhaps an outgrowth of the other.

With Lone Wolf the act of love was both simple and surprisingly complete. He expected none of the enhancements that Richard had taught her, nor did he provide her with any. He took her gently, but insistently, and managed to bring her to a state of fulfillment before his own climax burst from him.

Then, so soon after, he took her again, but this time playfully, chuckling and tickling her and exclaiming over her soft skin and pale hair, at ease with her now because he knew the phantoms of the night had been banished.

She lay in his arms and watched the silver streaks of sunrise gild the sky to the east. Clear bright light spilled over the edge of the earth, bringing a new day, a new life for Sarah.

The first year was not without turmoil. There were times when Sarah vowed to escape, and did in fact run away as soon as her ankle healed. She was quickly caught and returned to *Tonsaroyoo*, who berated her angrily and shook a rawhide whip at her, but didn't beat her. She raged at his expectation of her unceasing toil, which was the lot of all the squaws. Yet there were quiet moments of companionship, too, even before they began to learn one another's language.

Besides, the work gave a structure and purpose to her days that was curiously satisfying. And always there were the cool desert nights when she lay in his arms and the rest of the world was a faraway memory that perhaps had never existed at all.

When her pregnancy became obvious and Lone Wolf showed great joy at the forthcoming event, Sarah was tempted not to tell him who the baby's father was. But of course that was foolish. The child of two fair-haired, light-skinned, blue-eyed people could hardly be passed off as being half Apache.

Eventually she confided in Otis. He too had attempted escape and been caught and punished. But as time passed Otis became more of an Apache than any bronze-skinned brave. When the time came for the tribe to move on, *Tonsaroyoo* and his most trusted braves scouted the trail ahead and Sarah rode with Otis.

They guided their mounts carefully down the steep slope of the mountainside, bound for the lower plains where they would spend the winter. Sarah said, in English, "Otis, the baby isn't his."

"I wondered," Otis replied. "You haven't told Lone Wolf, have you?"

She shook her head. "He's so happy about it."

"He'll still be happy." Otis glanced sideways at her, perhaps thinking how much they'd both changed. He went on. "I have to be blunt, Sarah, so forgive me for it. It's like this, see—the Apache don't believe a baby comes from a single act of intercourse. They think that it takes many times, and if a woman is with more than one man, for instance if her husband is killed and one of his male relatives takes her for a wife, which is their custom, then each man who has coupled with her is equally the baby's father."

"But my baby will probably have golden hair and blue eyes."

Otis squinted down at the sun-hazed valley below, considering. "Tell Lone Wolf soon, Sarah, before you give birth. I don't think it will matter to him. I heard him call you *Sons-ee-ah-ray*—Morning Star. Do you realize what a compliment it is for the Apache to give any name at all to a squaw?"

She told *Tonsaroyoo* that night of his shared fatherhood. He smiled and held her and said, "You have been with me, and only me, for all these moons . . . the child will be more mine than his, and together we will make him ours."

For a moment she had been overcome with emotion and unable to speak. Mistaking her silence, he drew her down onto the blanket and unfastened her braids, letting her hair spill through his fingers. "Like a golden waterfall," he whispered. "I had never seen sunlight until I saw your hair. Your eyes remind me of twin lakes in the high country. I will feel the same awe if our son has such coloring. But golden hair will not give him courage. Blue eyes do not necessarily come hand in hand with honor."

That night she made the decision not to try to run away from him again.

There were times when she questioned her motives, the wisdom of what she was doing, even her growing love for Lone Wolf, but in the end she stayed. Her only doubts were about her son's future.

Then Hakan was born and he was all that she or *Tonsaroyoo* could have hoped for. If Hakan had inherited his English father's physical grace, then the boy was doubly blessed that his courage and integrity matched that of his adopted Apache father.

But the increasing encroachment of white settlers into the southwestern mountains and desert, the dwindling numbers of free Indians, the steel tentacles of spreading railroads, burgeoning towns, and, not least, the hysterical outpourings of politicians and press about the "Apache menace" all heralded the end. Six years after she was taken captive, the fear and hatred of the native Indians was fanned to a frenzy over the annihilation of General Custer and his men by the Sioux at the Little Big Horn.

Sarah knew that Hakan had been born into a doomed nation and the time would come when she must plan Hakan's escape to England. But the strange thing was, she had come to believe that Hakan really was *Tonsaroyoo*'s true son. So she lived a day at a time, not wanting to think that it would all end. Not preparing Hakan for any other life. That was her secret guilt now, a burden she found almost unbearable.

She sat alone in her room at Merrinswood, worrying and wondering how Hakan was faring, blaming herself for something—what?—that had yet to happen.

✳   ✳   ✳

The parishioners respectfully held back until the Merrin family—Richard and Sarah, Philip, Charlotte the governess, and the twins—shook hands with the vicar and complimented him on the sermon.

Sarah had searched the congregation for Doctor McGreal, but he had not attended the morning service. As the family moved toward the two waiting carriages, Sarah said, "I'd like to take the twins for a ride. Charlotte can come, too. Why don't you and Philip go on home?"

Richard gave her an amused glance. "Still on edge about James, are you? Well not much longer to wait now. I'll dispatch a carriage for him at three."

Philip commented, in his perceptive but deceptively soft-spoken manner, "You know, old bean, you two really should try to agree in your attitudes toward the boy. The conflicting messages you each send to him are causing him more strife than his algebra lessons. I'd hate to see him used as a pawn in whatever little marital game you're playing with each other."

"Mind your own damn business, Philip," Richard snapped. "You may have had some small success in tutoring James, but that doesn't give you the right to criticize the way Sarah and I handle him."

"Please, you two," Sarah protested. "Let's not discuss James on a public street. Richard, I do assure you the only reason I want to stay outdoors for a while is because it's a fine clear day and winter will soon be here."

Glaring at one another, Richard and his brother departed in the first carriage. Sarah told the driver of the second, "Take us to Doctor McGreal's house please."

"Oh, no!" Emily wailed. "You can't take us to the doctor, not on a Sunday. I won't go, so there."

"Hush," Sarah said. "Get into the carriage at once. We're making a social visit, that's all. It will take only a few minutes. Then we'll go for a nice ride to the woods."

Robbie said timidly, "M-mother liked the d-doctor. He was k-kind to her."

Charlotte gave Sarah a reproachful look. Sarah knew that Jean had been a popular mistress of Merrinswood, and was sorely missed by everyone. In the case of the governess, who was neither servant nor family member, Sarah sensed a deeper resentment. Charlotte wasn't about to forgive or forget that the present Lady Moreland had been the direct cause of

Jean's leaving. Sarah wondered too how much of Robbie's pain was being fed by the governess.

The short journey to the doctor's house was accomplished in silence. When they arrived Sarah said, "Wait here. I'll only be a moment."

Mrs. Tremayne, bundled in several woollen cardigans, a muffler around her neck, and a shawl over her arms, responded to the doorbell. "Why, Lady Moreland—please, come in."

"Is the doctor in? I realize it's Sunday, but I must speak with him for just a moment. I promise I won't keep him long."

"If you'll just step into the sitting room, milady?"

Andrew McGreal joined her moments later. He wore a fisherman's pullover, baggy trousers, and carpet slippers, which said he was more eager to hear her news than to present himself attired as his profession demanded. "I was going to take the liberty of calling on you tomorrow. I hope your coming to me means that you've had some word of Jean?"

"I'm sorry, Doctor McGreal, but the detective I hired has been unable to find her."

His face fell. "No clues at all as to where she might have gone?"

"I have his written report. I didn't want to take it with me to church, but next time you come to the house I'll give it to you. He has exhausted all possibilities that she might have gone to any friends she had before her . . . before she came to live at Merrinswood. Or that she traveled from the house in any public conveyance. In essence, all he was able to determine was that on the night Jean left, one of the stable-boys prepared a carriage and team for Lord Moreland who drove it himself." Sarah looked away from the doctor's searching gaze, wondering whether to add that the detective's report stated that Richard frequently drove himself to unknown destinations late at night and therefore this had no significance to grooms or stableboys.

"Your husband won't find out the detective has been questioning the staff, will he?" the doctor asked.

"No. He never came to Merrinswood. He obtained all of his information from grooms and stableboys at the local inn on their days off."

"Did he learn where Richard went that night, or if Jean was with him?"

"Even if Richard took her somewhere, he would have picked her up at the house, so the stableboy wouldn't know that. The detective reported that a maid did hear the carriage come to the tradesman's entrance, but when she looked out of her window it was gone."

Andrew turned and rested his hands on the mantelpiece above the empty fireplace. His shoulders slumped in such an attitude of despair that Sarah was tempted to reach out and stroke the vulnerable tendrils of sandy hair that curled over the back of his neck. Without looking at her he asked quietly, "Do you think your husband took her somewhere? Do you think he knows where she is?"

"There is something . . ." Sarah said hesitantly. "I didn't tell the detective—or anyone else, for that matter."

The doctor turned to her and she was surprised by the fierce light in his eyes. "You must tell me anything that might help me find her. Please, I implore you."

Sarah swallowed her pride. "My husband has been known to spend some of his nights at the inn at Carisbrook. It's been his practice for many years, even before his marriage to me." It was something Richard had flung at her that night in Arizona. That he was accustomed to female diversion whenever he desired, that it had nothing to do with his marriage to her, but she might as well get used to the idea that monogamy was for peasants and paupers. She added, "If Richard went there that night, someone would know whether or not Jean was with him."

"How's young Robbie?" Andrew asked abruptly.

"Much better," Sarah answered, surprised at the turn of conversation.

"Good. I'm going away. This is not a sudden decision. I've been thinking about it for some time. I've arranged for another doctor to take over the practice."

"You're giving up everything," Sarah said slowly, "to go and search for Jean Leighton."

"Yes," Andrew said, his smile sad. "I suppose you think I'm a fool?"

"I think," Sarah responded, "that wherever Jean is, she's a very lucky woman to have the devotion of a man who cares more about her welfare than his own."

Returning to the waiting carriage, Sarah ignored Emily's whining and Charlotte's sour looks, and insisted they drive to Coombe's woods before returning to Merrinswood. The only flicker of interest in the outing appeared in Robbie's haunted eyes, which Sarah decided he must have inherited from his mother. Incredible eyes, like dark blue velvet, emphasized by thick black lashes that seemed to absorb all the sadness of the world.

"That w-will be very nice," Robbie said, coughing politely into his handkerchief. "Mother used to t-take us in the carriage with her s-s-sometimes. Father s-said I should have ridden my horse because only women and s-sissies ride in a carriage for pleasure."

"Where did your mother take you?" Sarah asked.

"To the river sometimes." Robbie's soft response was overwhelmed by Emily's strident comment. "Mother used to take baskets of food to those smelly gypsies who camped there. She took our old clothes and toys for their children, too. Father certainly wouldn't have liked it had he known."

"It's a little chilly to go down by the river today," Sarah said. "We'll drive past Coombe's woods instead, the trees are so lovely in their autumn colors."

Sarah was feasting her eyes on the umber and ochre hues of the leaves when she caught a blur of movement among the trees. She blinked, unsure of what she had seen.

Charlotte said, "How odd. I thought I saw an organ-grinder with a monkey in there."

"So did I—he pulled back when he saw our carriage," Sarah said, feeling a sudden coldness in the pit of her stomach. The woods had all at once become menacing. Some part of her mind sent warning messages that all was not well. For an instant Sarah remembered a similar intuitive dread on the day *Tonsaroyoo* had ridden to his death under a flag of truce. "Stop!" she shouted to the driver. "Turn the carriage around and take us home immediately. Driver—hurry!"

Philip was waiting for Sarah, pacing back and forth across the marble hall. He turned in a single swift movement when she came through the door, his usual lethargy forgotten. All of Sarah's fears were confirmed by the look on his face.

She was vaguely aware of him coming to her, then leading her into the library. He poured a stiff brandy, despite the early hour of the day, and motioned for her to sit down and drink it. She took a sip and then looked at him expectantly.

Without preamble, Philip said, "Your son came home while we were at church. He was dressed only in a blood-stained pair of trousers, several sizes too small. When Richard and I arrived, Hakan—I mean James—told us that Randolph Leighton is dead. His body is in Coombe's woods. Richard waited only long enough for James to wash and dress and then the two of them left to go back to the woods. They should be back any minute."

Sarah gripped the cool leather of the armchair and blinked her eyes, hoping it was only a nightmare. But hadn't she known, ever since that day on the ship when Randolph attacked Hakan, that if ever there was another confrontation between them, one of them would die? The hows and whys of their meeting in Coombe's woods when Hakan was supposed to be at the Dunstan manor and Randolph in Lancashire didn't matter. If Randolph was dead, then Hakan had killed him. The question now was, what was to be done about it?

"I've asked for sandwiches and tea to be sent to us here," Philip said. "We don't know how long it will be before they return."

"I should never have brought him here," Sarah said, an icy chill creeping upward from her toes. "He's Apache, not English. If he's attacked he will defend himself, to the death if necessary. He knows no other way. It's really not his fault. Oh, God, Philip, I can't let them take him to prison."

"Richard will never let him stand trial. You know that."

She looked at him. "Do I?"

Philip pulled a chair close to hers and picked up her hands, which were numb with cold. "Remember how we waited for Richard to bring him back from the village jail after he ran afoul of young Charles Pettigrew? We expected the worst then, but Richard took care of everything. We don't even know what happened in the woods today—perhaps it was an accident. Perhaps Randolph isn't dead."

The discussion ended as the library door opened and Richard came into the room. He glanced at Philip. "You've told her?" Philip nodded.

"Where is Hakan?" Sarah demanded, rising to her feet.

"Upstairs. Packing."

"Packing?" Sarah and Philip asked in unison.

Richard addressed his reply to Sarah. "There isn't time for lengthy explanations. Randolph Leighton is dead, apparently. His body was no longer in the woods when we arrived and James refuses to say what happened, how the two of them came to be in the woods, or what happened to his clothes. He was dressed only in a cheap pair of trousers covered in blood when he came home. Luckily, besides Philip and I, only Barlow saw him. If the police come here to question us—and they probably will, since Randolph was my estate steward for so long—it's essential that James not be here. He'll condemn himself with his silence."

"Where are you sending him?" Sarah asked in a small frozen voice.

"The fewer people who know his whereabouts, the better. I'm going up to him now. Philip, if the police come, get rid of them. Say we're out riding or something."

Sarah had to run to keep up with Richard as he flew up the stairs, two at a time. Opening Hakan's door, they saw he was dressed in his buckskins. Richard swore.

"This is all I had when I came to you," Hakan said, with quiet dignity.

"Put on your plainest suit and take an overcoat," Richard instructed. "I'll pack a bag for you myself. Sarah, tell him what will happen to him if he has to face an English jury."

Sarah went to her son and placed her hands on his arms. "What happened? He attacked you, didn't he? It was self-defense, Richard, you know it must have been. Perhaps—"

"Don't be a damn fool," Richard interrupted. "The outcome of a trial doesn't matter. It's having a son of mine stand trial at all that has to be avoided at all costs."

Hakan's tan had faded, leaving him paler than she had ever seen him. She felt a pang of utter sadness that she had taken him away from everything he loved and put him in such jeopardy. His lips were compressed, his eyes defiant. He was not going to tell them, or anyone else, what had happened.

Richard flung a bare minimum of clothes into a valise. "I'll drive the carriage myself. Say your good-byes, Sarah."

Her hands tightened on Hakan's arms. "Haven't you anything to say to me?"

"Yes," he said. "I would like you to do something for me."

"Anything. What is it?"

"Will you take care of a little boy? His name is Danior. The servants here believe he stole something, but when he was caught he was attempting to return it."

Richard cut in, "We haven't much time, James."

Sarah said, "I'll take care of the boy. Where is he?"

"I sent him to wait at Doctor McGreal's house."

"Will you tell me what happened in the woods?"

"Leighton is dead," Hakan said.

"Did you kill him in self-defense?"

There was no response from Hakan, but Richard said, "He's not going to tell you a damned thing. I haven't been able to get anything out of him either."

Hakan looked at his father, who held a dark jacket toward him. Hakan slipped on the jacket over his buckskin shirt. "I'm ready to go."

Sarah hugged her son fiercely, her tears held back only to spare him further distress. "I can't let you go until I know where you're going."

Richard said, "He's going to a small boarding school in the south, under an assumed name. A cramming school. To prepare him for a military academy."

Richard paused briefly, then continued, "On his nineteenth birthday, if by then he's able to pass the entrance exams, he'll enter Sandhurst. After he gets out of the army, this whole mess will be forgotten."

BOOK II

21

Brenna stamped her foot, her dark eyes filled with tears. "I won't go to bed, I won't. He said he'd be here and he'll come, I know he will."

Chavi looked at Dirk for support, but he shrugged, gave her a helpless smile, then returned to studying his Bible. Chavi said, "It's nearly midnight. He won't come in the dark."

In the corner of the living room, the undecorated Christmas tree seemed to wait as expectantly as the ten-year-old Brenna. The little girl had refused to allow them to touch the tree until Lysander arrived. It was just as well, Chavi reflected, since the poor dried-out bit of scrub brush probably couldn't survive more than a few hours of having candles on its branches in the midsummer heat of the Outback.

The heat seemed more intense than ever this year, or perhaps it was her imagination, or her growing disenchantment with her marriage. She realized that she too had been hoping that the dreary monotony of their lives would improve when Lysander returned. But damn the man, he hadn't come. She said to Brenna, "If I promise to come and wake you when he arrives, will you go to bed?"

Brenna considered. "Oh, all right." She started for the door and Chavi said, "Aren't you forgetting something?"

The child returned and kissed her cheek, then went to Dirk and pecked in the air in the vicinity of his face. He murmured, "Good night, Brenna," without looking up from the printed page.

Chavi watched her daughter trip lightly across the imported Persian rug. She moved with the grace of a ballerina and it was a pleasure to watch her. Lysander would see great changes in Brenna this visit. She'd grown so tall, and her long

hair, which she refused to have cut short despite Chavi's
protests that it would be cooler, had bleached in the sun to a
red-gold on top, underlaid with rich mahogany. She had the
darkest eyes Chavi had ever seen, as dark as Danior's. A
gypsy's eyes, and a gypsy's soul, too. How she'd begged
Lysander to take her with him, on this and every other
journey he'd taken. Once, when a naked aborigine passed the
station on one of his endless "walkabouts," Chavi had to
lock Brenna in her room for fear she'd join him, to go
searching for her beloved Lysander.

"I'm going up to bed now," Chavi said, looking across
the room at her husband.

"I'll be along shortly," Dirk responded.

She sighed audibly, but he didn't look up, so, as she had
on many other nights, she went up to bed alone.

Tossing restlessly on warm sheets, she looked back over
seven years of marriage to Dirk Chambers with a feeling of
incredulous disbelief that she'd stayed so long.

That first year Chavi quickly learned that Lysander was
right about his brother. When she stopped gazing at Dirk
adoringly, trying to please him, allowing thoughts of him to
fill her waking hours, dreams of him to disturb her sleep, his
interest perked up at once.

If she wasn't working in the kitchen, or taking care of the
baby, Lysander kept her so busy with lessons, or long rides,
or conversation, that there wasn't time to pursue Dirk. At
dinner, if her glance drifted toward his brother, Lysander
promptly engaged her in conversation. If she ran into Dirk,
in the house or garden, before they could exchange two
words, Lysander would materialize and have some pressing
matter to discuss, or some new wonder to share with her.

It wasn't long before she realized that Dirk was deliberately seeking her out and making concentrated efforts to
converse with her.

Lysander warned, "Remember what I told you. A year.
You've got to wait a year for him. You're too young."

But Dirk was actively courting her and was obviously
frustrated by Lysander's hovering presence. It was Dirk's
practice to leave the station every six months on business
trips that lasted several weeks. When he returned from the
first trip to the coast, he brought her several gifts. Lysander
looked them over with a jaundiced eye.

"You can keep the book of Bible stories and the sewing box. Return the dress and the brooch."

"No!" Chavi protested. "If I have to give something back, let it be the Bible stories and the sewing box."

"They're appropriate for a single gentleman to present to a single lady. The dress and brooch aren't."

"But he knows you bought clothes for me—the sari, for one thing."

"Immaterial. What's past is done. What counts is your behavior today, now."

She'd fumed but gave in. A subtle change in Dirk's attitude toward her was taking place and she wanted it to continue.

Late one evening, Chavi had gone up to bed only to realize that she had left Brenna's shawl down in the kitchen. Having already bade the brothers good-night, she slipped quietly down the stairs and was about to take a detour through the dining room when she overheard Lysander, in the sitting room, say, "She is almost maddeningly enticing, isn't she?"

Chavi stopped in the shadows, intrigued. He went on, "Have you ever seen a more sensually beautiful woman? And she's only just coming into flower. In a year ot two her allure will be formidable."

There was a moment's silence and then Dirk said, "There's a slight . . . commonness about her."

"Of course. That's what makes her so desirable. She's not some untouchable angel—she's of the earth, warm and nourishing as well as being intoxicating."

"Why, my dear brother! You sound more smitten with her than I am."

Lysander's derisive laugh had the usual effect on Chavi. She crept away before he followed it with some cutting remark about her. After all, she knew he was merely selling the idea of her to Dirk in order to provide for Brenna, who was Lysander's only real concern.

The weeks slipped into months. Brenna learned to sit, then to crawl, and finally to walk. Chavi worked and studied and grew restless. The monotony of her days was bearable only because she filled them with dreams of what it would be like when she was finally Dirk's wife. After she'd transformed the somewhat spartanly furnished house into a real showplace, there'd be travel, theaters, restaurants, a town house somewhere where they could entertain, pretty clothes, and . . . best of all, hours of intimate conversation with Dirk and touching, caressing. How they'd laugh and have fun together! She pressed Lysander for information about every aspect of upper-class life in England, and became excited just thinking about returning there as a grand lady.

There was no response to the letter they'd sent to Doctor McGreal, and although Chavi worried about what had befallen her brother, she knew there was little she could do to help Danior while she was ten thousand miles away.

Then all at once it seemed that many problems could be settled simultaneously. Almost a year to the day after they arrived at the station, Dirk came looking for Chavi one morning as she was hanging laundry from a line strung between two gums behind the house. The hot dry wind whipped the sheets and Chavi's hair flew about her face. Dirk had to raise his voice to make himself heard. "I came to tell you I've just heard from the trustees of the Chambers's estate in England. I have to return at once."

"Oh!" was all Chavi could say.

Dirk's bright dark eyes regarded her with the same warm longing she felt so acutely when he was near. Yet despite that raw hunger in his gaze, she was touched by his shy way of speaking to her, which was so unlike Lysander's authoritative declarations. Dirk, who could converse for hours with his stationhands, seemed to dry up in sheer awe when he tried to talk to her. But today it was clear there was something urgent on his mind. "Chavi—you must know how enchanted I am by you. So much so that I hate to go away and leave you. I'm afraid you might not be here when I return."

Some inner wisdom stilled her swift denial. He reached out and caught her hand in his. "Come with me. Come back to England with me."

She'd gone back to the house in a trance, which Lysander quickly dispelled. "You can't go," he said, when she told him.

"Yes, I can. I will!"

"What about Brenna?"

"She'll go with us."

"Think again."

"But—"

"Listen to me. You can't go anywhere with him until you're Mrs. Dirk Chambers. He's leaving tomorrow—no time for him to marry you before he leaves. If you go with him as his mistress he'll never marry you. He'll bring in some abo woman to take care of Brenna and waltz you off to England and that will be that. Get out there now and tell him no, you're shocked he'd suggest it."

In the end she'd understood the wisdom of the advice, although for the eight long months Dirk was gone she thought she'd die of yearning. It was a miracle she and Lysander didn't kill one another during that period. He slipped easily into the role of master of Twelve Mile and that was perhaps why, knowing he'd have to relinquish the role when Dirk returned bringing a wedding gown and a ring, Lysander immediately announced he would leave on a trip before the wedding.

"But . . . can't you wait just a few weeks more?" Chavi asked, disappointed.

"Why? You don't need me any longer."

"Brenna will miss you."

His fierce eyes softened. "I'll be back. Listen, gypsy—about Brenna, you must see to it that Dirk adopts her. Talk to him about it *before* the wedding."

She supposed it was reasonable that, having just returned from England, Dirk did not want to go back there for their honeymoon. Instead they went to Sydney and stayed at a hotel overlooking Botany Bay. Dirk told her about all the strange and wonderful plants Captain Cook had discovered there, but all Chavi remembered later was the perfection of Dirk's naked body in the instant before, disappointingly, he doused the lamp. How excited she was when he lay beside her on their wedding night, and with what eagerness she reached for him. . . .

Only to have him consummate their union too swiftly for her to be able to experience it fully with him. She was left alone in the darkness as he slept, her skin burning and that inner core of her being throbbing with need.

She bit her tongue and kept silent about her disappointment for weeks. Then, when she could no longer stand the feeling of being left clinging to the edge of a precipice, she tried to tell him of her feelings. He was shocked when she requested that he leave on the light and refused to discuss any aspect of their lovemaking. "This conversation isn't proper. No decent wife would instigate it," he said coldly.

If she'd gone to England with him as his mistress, would it then have been all right? she wondered. And would their lovemaking have been more exciting?

Some weeks later when, driven to desperation, she attempted to arouse her husband after he had rolled away from her leaving her in her state of perpetual frustration, he was more specific. "Nice women—good wives—don't behave like that, Chavi. Look, I realize that you came from a background that . . . well, I have made allowances for that. I've accepted that you were taken advantage of, and God knows never once have I criticized you for the life you led before you came here. I thought that you had successfully put that life behind you. This is a new young country and I believed we could make a fresh start. But I see now that my brother's educating you stopped short of instilling moral values into you."

Chavi collapsed onto her pillow, feeling her ardor dissipate. In that one revealing moment she realized that she'd been blinded by Dirk's good looks, just as she'd been blinded by Lord Moreland's handsomeness. How could she have been so stupid, to fall twice into the same trap?

She began to concentrate on her campaign to persuade her husband to take her back to England. But here she ran into an even sturdier wall of resistance. "I spent eight months in England just before we were married. As far as I'm concerned, I never want to go back. I'll take you to Sydney after the shearers have been here."

"There's nothing to do there either," Chavi said. "The only difference is you can do it around other people."

Why hadn't she seen Dirk's style of life for what it was before they were married? He lived and breathed his damned sheep, and when he wasn't riding madly around the station admiring the stupid beasts, or talking about them to the other men, he found his only relaxation between the pages of his Bible.

When Lysander returned to Twelve Mile about a year later, Chavi was so glad to see him that she raced down the porch steps and flung her arms around him as he dismounted from his lathered horse. So effusive was her greeting that she knocked Lysander's bush hat back from his brow, and it was then that she saw there had been a slight change in his appearance. The scars still crisscrossed his face like a monstrous road map, but he was smiling down at her and she saw at once that his lower lip was no longer as hideously twisted as it had been when he'd left.

"What's this?" he demanded. "Can you actually be glad to see me?"

"You're my brother-in-law, aren't you?"

"Where's Brenna? How is she?"

"Taking her nap. She'll be up soon." She cocked her head on one side and squinted up at him. "What have you done to yourself? You look different."

Pleased that she'd noticed, his smile broadened. "I ran into a doctor on my travels who suggested my mouth was being distorted by the scar tissue that pulled it away from my gums. He said that the careful use of his scalpel and a stitch or two might alleviate the worst of it. As you can see, he was right. At least my lips have some semblance of normalcy now."

Chavi cried excitedly, "Oh, Lysander! I think it's wonderful. Do you think he could—"

Lysander interrupted so swiftly that Chavi forgot what she had been about to suggest. "I was absolutely euphoric, of course, when the bandages came off and I saw my mouth no longer looked like it belonged to a shark."

He slipped his arm comfortably about her shoulders as they went into the house and she explained that Dirk was away on sheep-selling business.

Over a pot of tea in the kitchen Lysander went on, "Apart from the aesthetic consideration, having two lips more or less in harmony has made my life so much easier. Of course, I went through a phase of imagining the improvement was far greater than it actually is."

He gave a short depreciative laugh as Chavi poured the tea. "Not for the first time, I might add. Strange how the human mind can take reality and distort it to fit deep-felt needs, isn't it?"

"How do you mean?" Chavi asked, sitting across the table from him and leaning forward, head on her hands.

"Would you believe there were times when I pretended to

myself that my scars weren't so bad, after all? That instead of a monster's face I had perhaps some slight imperfection, nothing more than a blemish really. Then I'd venture out into a social gathering, hoping my appearance would elicit only a small sigh of sympathy. Certainly nothing as demoralizing as outright pity."

Chavi held her breath. "What would happen—when you went out like that?"

"I'd stand with my back to the door. Sometimes I'd overhear women talking behind me. Ah, they'd whisper to one another, a new male in our midst. Look at those shoulders, what a body he has! Look how his thighs strain the material of his breeches. I'd start to turn around and face them, and the reality of what I am would come to me in a flash of indescribable horror. I'd stand there, frozen to the spot, knowing that if I turned and showed them my face the ladies who admired my shoulders would either faint in shock, hate me for destroying their illusions, or, at the very least, refuse to forgive me for being hideous."

"Oh, Lysander!" Chavi said softly, feeling a tear well up on the fringe of her eyelashes and go sliding down her cheek.

He pretended not to notice and began to tell her of his travels and adventures.

She hadn't realized how much she'd missed him, or how deadly dull his brother was by comparison. Dirk preferred to talk to the men rather than to her, and when they were alone he lived in some private world of religious meditation that she was forbidden to enter. Lysander, despite his caustic wit, was interested in everything and everyone around him, and took an almost mystic pleasure in nature. When he announced he was leaving again, only scant weeks later, Chavi was crestfallen.

He looked at her sharply, then reached out and tipped her chin upward with his forefinger. "Your husband is treating you well?" She nodded. His eyes searched her face. "What's wrong then?"

"Nothing. I—get so sick of sheep, that's all."

He laughed. "I can understand that. You should suggest to Dirk that you'd like to travel."

"Where are you going, Lysander?" she asked wistfully.

"I believe I'll join the gold rush to Western Australia. Rich new fields have opened up and men are making fortunes, I hear. I only came back to persuade Dirk to finance my expedition."

"I see," Chavi said. "Well, I wish you luck."

As she watched Lysander ride off, Chavi wished passionately that she could be as free as he. Perhaps she'd even wear that gargoyle face in return for such freedom. But, of course, she knew that would be too dear a price to pay.

Two years went by before he returned again, and it was clear that his fortunes had indeed changed. He was splendidly dressed, riding a magnificent horse and leading a pack animal loaded with gifts for Brenna and Chavi.

Lysander stayed with them for six months that time, before boredom drove him off again. Chavi was too proud to tell him that she felt like an unattractive old woman whose life was over. She pretended that being Mrs. Dirk Chambers was the answer to every dream she'd had. The expectant look Dirk wore before their marriage was gradually replaced by one of disappointment. He never told her what he found lacking, but she noticed he spent more and more time reading the Bible, and dragged them miles to the nearest church on Sundays.

At least Lysander continued to come back and visit. Sometimes for days, or weeks; always long enough to recapture Brenna's heart. He didn't seem to notice that Chavi was shriveling up and dying with loneliness.

But she noticed the changes in Lysander. Not physical ones, but subtle differences in his attitude and manner, especially when Brenna was present. The old abrasive growl disappeared and was replaced by a patient eagerness to answer the child's every question, to make her laugh or dry her tears. With Brenna, Lysander showed a tenderness and warmth that transformed him, making Chavi forget his ugly scars. Once Chavi said, only half jokingly, "She loves you better than me, I think."

He replied softly, "Her regard for me is so unconditional that she gave me a reason to live."

When Brenna was six, Lysander insisted that it was time she went away to school. Dirk immediately agreed. Brenna was a lively child whose very presence he found an irritant. Chavi was secretly glad that her husband's hurried probing of her thighs in the dark had not produced another baby. Dirk had so little patience with Brenna, although he lavished attention on the sons of visiting shearers who traveled with their fathers to learn the trade, and often remarked what a blessing a son would be.

"We'll send Brenna to school in England," Dirk said at once.

"No," Lysander said. "Sydney. So we can visit her."

Dirk's eyes met his in one of those innuendo-filled glances they exchanged but never explained to Chavi. Once, in desperate curiosity, she'd asked Dirk what had happened to Lysander's face. Avoiding her eyes, he'd replied, "An act of vengeance. The scars are the result of a hot poker and a knife—the man who did it wanted to turn him into a monster."

Sickened, Chavi whispered, "But why? *Why*?" She still didn't know why.

Lysander found a family in Sydney willing to board Brenna, and Chavi was able to visit her daughter at least once during the school year. Lysander, she learned, visited Brenna even more often, which probably explained why they saw less of him at Twelve Mile after that.

Then, six months ago, he'd arrived unexpectedly and had seemed more thoughtful than usual. Instead of regaling them with stories of his travels and adventures, he'd been quiet, watchful, and on his last evening he'd stayed up with Chavi after Dirk took his Bible to bed.

They sat in the flickering firelight as night turned into a new day, and for a while shared a companionable silence. At length Chavi said, "You've been watching me like a hawk. And Dirk too. Like you're seeing us together for the first time."

"Perhaps I'm trying to rejoin the human race?" Lysander suggested. "Becoming more aware of others than myself. You know, total isolation from other people is a torture that's indescribable. I was a poor candidate for solitary confinement in prison."

"It must have been terrible for you."

"All of my thoughts and perceptions turned inward. Did I miss the stars more than the sun? Did I view death as an escape, or as an even worse form of isolation? Parts of my mind were destroyed, and the frightening thing was that I knew they were gone forever. But what I failed to see then was that, although the damage was permanent, the sheer resiliency of the human spirit demands regeneration."

"There are many kinds of isolation, Lysander. You can be with other people and still be so alone."

He leaned forward in his chair, watching her with eyes that seemed to burn into her soul, then he struck at the heart of her misery. "Dirk is like many men, Chavi; he offers a cool attachment and expects little in return. Some wives are glad of such husbands, they're easy to deal with."

Chavi looked away, into the leaping flames in the fireplace, and Lysander added softly, "I would be a much more demanding partner."

Before she could speak he added quickly, "That is, if I were still a member of the human race."

Chavi said, "Please stop thinking of yourself as being a monster. You're not."

He was silent for a time, then said, "Perhaps Dirk is preoccupied with the station's financial situation. He's talked to you about the faltering world market for wool?"

Dirk never talked to her about anything, but Chavi didn't want Lysander to know that.

He went on, "The droughts of the past few years have wiped out many sheepmen."

Dirk would never let Twelve Mile be wiped out, Chavi thought, he would simply send to England for money from his estate in order to keep going.

Lysander glanced in the direction of a new addition to the room, a well-filled bookcase. "Since I've never seen Dirk read anything other than his Bible, prayer book, or some religious tract, I assume you ordered the books."

"They saved my life," Chavi said fervently. "When you left for the gold fields, I ordered one about prospecting, so I'd know what you were doing. And when you visited us last time you mentioned the rich gold strikes in South Africa, so I got one about that country."

Lysander stared at her for a moment. "I've just realized what it is about you that makes you different from most other people, Chavi. You listen, really listen to what I say. And you never forget anything you've been told."

She regarded him with surprise. "How else am I going to learn anything?"

"What a thirst for knowledge you have," he said wonderingly. "I'd like to think I inspired it in you, but I believe it was probably Lord Moreland."

Chavi considered this silently. Lord Moreland had indeed given her more than her beautiful raven-haired daughter, he had given her her very first book. The slim volume of Keats she had caressed with loving fingers long before she was able to read the words. But ah, the words! How could a mere twenty-six letters conjure so many bright and shiny images, such vivid pictures in her mind? How could a man seduce, betray, and at the same time, inspire? Not wishing Lysander to know what she was thinking, Chavi said, "Oh, I was always curious about everything. And as far as knowledge is concerned, why, around here I learn more about damned sheep than I care to know. The endless constant discussion of sheep diseases and ticks and branding and sheep dip and how to protect them from the dingoes—do you know, the men rush out to kill dingoes at night and completely forget Brenna and I are alone in the house? Some of the wild dogs have come scratching around the porch."

Lysander muttered something under his breath and she recognized the angry flash in his eyes as concern for Brenna. He said, "First thing in the morning, I'm going to teach you how to use a rifle."

"Good," Chavi said. "That will be one more thing I can do for myself."

When they went up the stairs to bed, Lysander slipped her arm through his and they walked side by side, like a loving married couple. At her bedroom door he looked at her for a long moment and she was puzzled by what she saw in his eyes. But before she could question him he touched her cheek lightly with one finger and said, "Sleep well, Chavi."

As she went into the darkened room she shared with Dirk, she realized that Lysander had at last begun to call her by her given name, rather than gypsy.

Lying in her bed this Christmas Eve, Chavi waited with even more nervous anticipation for Lysander's promised visit than her daughter did. A vague plan that had been hatching in her mind depended upon him. When Dirk crept into their room, long after midnight, she turned over and feigned sleep. The act of making love with her husband seemed pointless, since it never brought them closer, gave them pleasure, or produced a child.

Sometimes, after a long and particularly vicious drought, when the bleak landscape of the Outback withered and dried

to a lifeless brown, Chavi seemed to experience the emptiness
and hopelessness of the earth itself, for she was just as barren.

In two short years a new century would be born and
Chavi had promised herself that by then she would have a
new life. Tomorrow Lysander would arrive and she would
discuss her plans with him. She believed she could count on
him for unconditional support. It was a comforting thought
as she fell asleep.

Before the sun rose into a cloudless sky on Christmas
morning the heat was already stifling. Nothing stirred in the
dry air. Baked earth and seared rocks still reflected the heat
of the previous day. The leaves of the gums had stopped their
incessant whispering and out in the paddocks even the sheep
were strangely quiet.

As Chavi rose and dressed she found she was taking many
shallow breaths, sucking in the arid air as though each gasp
might be her last. There was an indefinable sense of tension
abroad, as though the earth were braced, waiting for some
threat to materialize.

Boomer was already up and slicing ham for breakfast.
Chavi snapped at him, "Why don't you wash and shave
before you start handling the food?"

"Happy Christmas to you, too," the old man said, shuf-
fling out of the room. Chavi felt ashamed, but no less irritated. She went into the dining room to start setting the table
for the traditional festive breakfast, and catching sight of the
undecorated tree, gave a sigh of exasperation. Usually after
Christmas breakfast the presents were opened, but no doubt
Brenna wouldn't hear of it this year until Lysander had
arrived. Not that it mattered. Chavi had never felt less like
celebrating the season of peace; the terrible energy-sapping
heat sucked the life out of everything and all joy from the
day.

Having stayed up so late, Brenna still slept, and Chavi
decided not to wake her, since there was still no sign of
Lysander.

Dirk appeared as Chavi was drinking her second cup of
tea. He kissed her cheek and said, "Happy Christmas." He
didn't appear to notice that Brenna wasn't present.

The window frame shook suddenly and a moment later a

shower of dried leaves rattled against the glass. Dirk glanced up. "Wind's getting up."

"I can't understand what happened to Lysander," Chavi said. "He wrote that he'd be here. And he always keeps his word. You don't think something happened to him, do you?"

"Nothing happened!" Brenna's voice came from the doorway. "Lysander will come. He promised."

"Some children wait for Father Christmas," Dirk said dryly, "But our Brenna waits for her adopted uncle."

"I'm too old to believe in Father Christmas," Brenna said.

By the time they'd finished breakfast the rising wind was howling in the chimney and they felt its dragon breath throughout the house. Dust was driven in through every crack and soon covered everything in a reddish brown film. Brenna refused to open her presents until Lysander arrived.

Dirk reluctantly decided to postpone going to church until the evening service, in the hope the wind would have dropped by then. He settled in his easy chair with his prayer book and Chavi went to the kitchen to discuss dinner with Boomer. Brenna went to her room to watch the dirt road snaking over the hill for any sign of Lysander.

In the late morning the violence of the wind drove Dirk and Boomer and the other stationhands out into the paddocks to check on fences and gates, then ride out to see how the range sheep were faring.

Chavi was in the kitchen, unwrapping a Christmas pudding she'd made a month earlier and left to ripen, when she heard Brenna's excited shriek. "He's coming! Lysander's riding down the road!"

It was more likely that the approaching rider was just some swaggie escaping the windstorm, or looking for a free Christmas dinner, but Chavi went with Brenna to greet him.

They wrenched open the front door and were met by a fierce gust of wind. Great clouds of billowing dust almost obscured the approaching figure, who rode like a madman toward the house. He yelled something as he approached that was lost in the roar of the wind.

Clutching Brenna to keep her on her feet, Chavi clung with one hand to the porch rail as Lysander leapt from his horse and ran up the steps. "Where are the men?" A coating of dust on his face cracked as he spoke.

"They rode out—"

"Which direction?"

"North."

Seizing Chavi by one arm and Brenna by the other, Lysander dragged them back into the house and slammed the door on the wind. "I stopped at a station east of here two days ago. There's a huge bush fire burning. With this wind it will be upon us in a matter of hours."

22

Andrew McGreal placed his black bag on the overhead rack of the second-class compartment and settled into his seat as the conductor slammed the door. A burst of steam obscured the platform when the train began to move slowly through Euston Station.

The compartment was crowded, and wedged between a perspiring woman of considerable girth and a burly man in an overcoat, Andrew regretted not retrieving the book from his bag before taking his seat. To rise and get it now would cause a disturbance of major proportions. Perhaps some of the passengers would leave as the train headed north. No matter, he'd read and reread the book. It just seemed appropriate to read it again at the start of this journey.

To be returning to Merrin Quarry again after all these years seemed in itself a dream. His purpose in going there probably bordered on the realm of fantasy. Was he doing it for her, as he told himself, or was it for himself?

The years had blunted the sharp edge of his anger, but could not obscure that raging sense of injustice that overcame him when he considered that the perpetrator of so much evil still lived in luxurious idleness and probably still took his pleasures where he found them, giving no thought to the human misery he left in his wake. Andrew had considered returning to confront Lord Moreland so many times in the past. At the very beginning, in fact.

Andrew had left Merrin Quarry the day after the inquest on Sir Randolph Leighton. The jury brought in a verdict of death by misadventure at the hands of person or persons unknown.

The body, stabbed several times, had been found partly submerged in a bog on a particularly bleak stretch of moors. No doubt the murderer had hoped the bog would swallow the evidence of his crime. Decomposition had already begun, making it difficult to say exactly how long Leighton had been dead, especially since he had not been reported missing, as he was believed to be living in Lancashire.

Someone else had also disappeared, less than a week earlier. James, son of Lord Moreland, had abruptly departed following a party at the Dunstans' where apparently he'd been hazed mercilessly by Gilbert and his friends. The Merrins put out the story that James was going away to school, and the tight ranks of the local aristocrats closed against village gossip. The Merrins didn't elaborate, and neither did the Dunstans or Pettigrews.

Andrew paid a final house call to check on young Robbie Merrin before leaving on his quest to find Jean.

Sarah looked lifeless; her eyes had a bruised look as though she'd spend several sleepless nights.

"You're deeply troubled, aren't you?" Andrew asked. "Robbie seems well enough, so I assume it's your own son you're worried about."

"It was a difficult decision," she said, her voice so devoid of emotion that he knew she had rehearsed the words. "But we thought—a boarding school for a time might better prepare James to live in our society."

"Capital idea," Andrew murmured. "And of course he'll be home during the holidays."

She made a small sound and turned away from him. "What is it?" he asked.

She answered, "He won't be coming back to Merrinswood. I don't think he ever will. He hated his life here."

"I see. What about you? Are you staying?"

"Yes. I feel responsible for Robbie and Emily, for one thing. And then there's Danior."

The gypsy child had appeared on Andrew's doorstep the

same day that James had left Merrinswood. Danior had said only that he was to wait with the doctor until someone came for him. Sarah herself had come to collect the boy, who, Andrew was distressed to learn, had no idea where his sister Chavi and her baby had gone. Andrew asked, "What did you decide to do about the gypsy boy?"

"I'm going to bring him up—in the nursery alongside Robbie and Emily. They're about the same age, you know, and Danior has been abandoned by his people."

Hiding his astonishment, Andrew asked, "Lord Moreland has agreed to this?"

"Oh, yes," Sarah replied. "I think it's his way of compensating me for the loss of Hakan . . . James."

Perhaps if Andrew hadn't so singlemindedly pursued the mystery of what had happened to Jean Leighton, the other pieces of the puzzle would have formed some sort of a pattern in his mind rather than appearing to be isolated bits of unrelated events. Looking back later, Andrew wondered if the almost simultaneous occurrences of Sir Randolph's death, James's abrupt departure, and Danior's arrival, were something more than coincidences.

But immediately after giving medical testimony at the inquest, Andrew had left the village and begun his search for Jean Leighton. He went first to the inn at Carisbrook and took a room. He spent several evenings sitting in the saloon bar alone before a pretty young barmaid took pity on him and began to engage him in conversation. Walking her home one evening, he confided that he was searching for his missing sister, and described Jean. The barmaid gazed at him blankly until he added, "I believe she may have run off with a man. Very tall, bright gold hair, piercingly blue eyes—"

"Mr. Tomlinson," she said at once. "One of our regulars. Wait a bit—now I remember! He usually came on his own, looking for a bit of stuff, you know, but he did bring someone one night. But . . . the woman with him couldn't of been your sister. Why, she looked more like a gypsy."

Under patient questioning she also recalled that when she went home that night the local carriage company had been delivering a hired carriage to the inn's courtyard. She also noticed that Mr. Tomlinson's carriage remained at the inn for at least two days before he returned for it.

There was only one company in Carisbrook that offered

carriages for hire. They were furnished, Andrew was relieved to find, complete with driver. The owner allowed him to question the drivers, but they all claimed they had not driven anyone remotely resembling the man and woman he was seeking.

Disheartened, Andrew returned to his room at the inn. Late that night he packed his bag and tried to decide what to do next. At first the hesitant tap on his door sounded like just the creaking of ancient timbers, but when it was repeated Andrew opened the door and looked into the face of one of the carriage drivers he'd spoken to that morning. "Listen, guv', it'll cost me job if I'm caught—but I'm the driver who took Tomlinson and the woman that night."

Andrew drew the man into his room and closed the door.

"I knew somethin' was wrong when he carried her out. Unconscious she was, not sleeping like he said." He paused, his eyes greedy, speculative.

Andrew reached into his pocket. "Where did you take them?"

"Listen, if I tell you . . ."

"No one will know." The two half crowns changed hands and the man looked a little disappointed at the amount.

"All right, guv'—only I don't know 'ow much help it'll be to yer, 'cos I left 'em out in the back of beyond. He was met by a carriage what was waiting for us. Wild country out there, you know, not much in the way of towns or villages. Mountains and woods, that's all. But that there carriage—all closed up like a bleedin' hearse, curtains on the windows and all—was waiting for him, to take 'em somewhere."

"Where? Where did you rendezvous with the other carriage?"

"I'm trying to tell yer. In North Wales, that's where."

The Welsh village consisted of a chapel, a combination post office and general shop, and a few stone cottages. There was little evidence of farming in the surrounding valleys, no doubt due to the rocky inhospitality of the ground, and the rugged Welsh mountains towered over all like silent guardians of some forgotten planet. There seemed to be no reason, in fact, for the existence of the village at all.

At the post office Andrew was met with a suspicious resentment of outsiders that bordered on rudeness. A bleak-faced post mistress answered his questions tersely in English, then turned her back on him to address another customer in Welsh.

No, there was no inn or place for him to take lodgings. No, they knew nothing of the man and woman he described. The post mistress grudgingly left her wire cage to go to the grocery counter of the shop to sell him a loaf of bread and a wedge of cheese, and then he went outside to explore.

The village nestled between three mountains, and only one road went through. According to the map he studied before coming here, there were no towns or villages on that road between here and the coast, just the mountain range and several miles of woods. Where could Merrin possibly have taken Jean? Where could he have left her?

Leaving the village, Andrew climbed to the top of the smallest of the three mountains. The forest to the south seemed to stretch to infinity. In the rocky valley to the west he could see a man, gun tucked under his arm, a dog prancing ahead of him. Andrew scrambled down the steep slope of the hill to intercept the hunter.

"Excuse me, sir," he called as he approached. "I wondered if perhaps you live nearby. I'm looking for a boarding house, or somewhere to stay."

The hunter's dog stopped, baring his teeth. The man's hand tightened on the barrel of his rifle. "There's no such place."

"Would your wife put me up then—just for the night?"

The man muttered he had no wife and walked briskly away, the dog at his heels. Andrew spent the night sleeping under a tree in the woods.

The following day he went back to the village, determined that someone was going to answer his questions. As he approached the post office he saw a trio of young women walking up the street. They were dressed in identical navy blue serge dresses, with short matching capes and white caps on their heads. Nurses! With his heart hammering, he approached them and said, "Good morning. My name is Doctor McGreal and I believe you ladies might be able to direct me where I need to go."

One of the nurses gave him an impudent grin. "They wouldn't tell you where it was, eh, Doctor? The villagers here don't like to talk about the place, you know. Pretend it's not even there. Well, let me tell you, there'd not be much work for them and no need of a post office or a shop or anything if it weren't for us. You can come along with us. We've done our shopping, and there's a carriage waiting for us down by the bridge. It's too far to walk."

"Why do you think the people are so reluctant to talk about the nursing home?" Andrew asked, falling into step beside them. The possibility of some sort of convalescent home seemed more likely in this remote spot than a hospital.

The young women exchanged glances. "Nursing home? Go on! Did Doctor Voigt get you out here on false pretenses? It's no nursing home, Doctor. It's an asylum."

An uncomfortable silence fell and persisted until they reached a grim, barrackslike building set in pleasant grounds but surrounded by high walls.

The administrator and resident physician, Doctor Voigt, a colorless man with a fishy stare, was adamant that he had no patient named Jean Leighton.

"As her personal physician," Andrew said, "I must insist that you allow me to see her. I know she's here. Shall I return with a writ of habeas corpus?"

"That won't be necessary," Voigt said. "I'm perfectly willing to allow you to look at our record of incoming patients—for as far back as you wish. You'll see there is no Jean Leighton."

Andrew considered for a moment. There was no point in taking Voigt up on the offer, as obviously there would be no Jean Leighton registered. She must therefore be there under an assumed name. But what? He decided to try a different approach. "She was brought here by a man named Tomlinson. Perhaps she was admitted under his name?"

Voight's relieved smile told Andrew there would be no Tomlinsons either. Andrew was ushered from the building by a pair of burly attendants. The sturdy walls of the asylum muffled, but didn't obliterate the anguished shrieking of the patients. Andrew felt a cold hand clamp around his heart. If Jean were here, how could she remain sane under these conditions?

He would have to find a way to get into the grounds, wander about the wards; there was no other way to find her. But the grounds were enclosed by ten-foot stone walls, the tops of which were covered with broken glass imbedded in cement. There was only one set of gates, manned day and night by gatekeepers.

All right, it would be impossible for him to get inside undetected. But the staff went into the village, to the post office and general shop. Everyday, Andrew waited on the bridge leading to the village and spoke to any nurse or attendant who happened by. He described Jean and Lord Moreland and in response was either told they hadn't seen either of them, or advised that they didn't talk to strangers about their patients.

He was about to give up when one day a nurse came into the village alone. He recognized her as one he had already questioned and merely gave her a hopeful smile as she alighted from the carriage that belonged to Voigt. But on her return later that day, she suddenly came to him and whispered, "Listen, if you've got a photograph of the lady you're looking for, I'll help you." The young nurse had wavy auburn hair and a soft Irish brogue.

"I don't have a photograph," Andrew said. "But please, could we talk?"

She glanced in the direction of the waiting carriage. "For just a minute then. Come on." She led him down under the bridge where a shallow stream ran over smooth pebbles, the sound of it muffling their voices. She said, "A photo mightn't help much anyway. The patients change so . . . poor souls. Are you sure she's here?"

"Yes. Do the patients talk to you? I feel Jean would have given some indication to someone of who she is."

"Most of them babble and scream. A few you'd swear are as sane as you or me and talk quite rationallike. But some don't talk at all. What does she look like, your Jean Leighton?"

"I suppose," Andrew said slowly, "her eyes are her most striking feature. They're very large, dark blue with a velvet sheen, and seem to express a great compassion—"

"Oh, dear God in heaven!" Brigid O'Connell exclaimed.

Andrew had no legal recourse, since he was not a relative; nor could he have her brother sign a release, since Randolph was dead. Jean was alone in the world, and according to Brigid, she was catatonic, so there would be little she could do for herself. Andrew felt white-hot rage at what Merrin had done, and the crowning insult had been to pass Jean off as his gypsy mistress. But justice would have to wait for now. First Jean must be taken from this terrible place. The only possible way to get Jean out of there was to smuggle her out dressed as a nurse.

"I'll be out of a job when they discover she's gone," Brigid said. "They'll know it was me what done it, because they know how I feel about her. But no matter."

"You'll come with us, then," Andrew said. "I'll need you to help me look after her, anyway, since I'll have to work to support us."

The arrangements were made. Andrew would ride the coach that made a once-weekly trip from the village back to the nearest town. There, he would hire a private carriage and return, hiding it in the woods near the asylum. Brigid would dress "Chavi"—she still had trouble referring to her as Miss Leighton—in one of her own uniforms. She would select a day when no other nurses were going into the village and hope the driver of the asylum carriage wouldn't look too closely at her companion. Andrew wished he had enough money to bribe the driver, but his funds were barely enough to pay for a carriage and then get the three of them aboard a train to return to England.

Andrew waited for several days until the closed carriage rattled to its customary stop beside the bridge and only two women alighted. His breath stopped somewhere between his heart and his throat when he saw Jean. She moved with the stiff movements of a puppet, her head slumped forward as she stared at the ground. Brigid linked her arm through Jean's and propelled her forward. Fortunately, the driver's attention had been caught by one of the younger village women, who was riding a bicycle along the street, her skirts billowing in the wind.

Moving quickly to the other side of Jean, Andrew slipped his arm around her waist to help her. He was shocked at her thinness under the rough serge dress. She'd always been slender, but now there was a skeletal fragility to her body that made him worry he would crush that delicate ribcage merely by touching her. She didn't even look in his direction, but simply allowed him to lead her where he would.

He had never seen anyone in a completely catatonic state before. Despite his medical training, he felt utterly helpless. Oh God, what could he do for her? What could anyone do?

*   *   *

Andrew took Jean and Brigid to London, feeling perhaps there might be a Harley Street specialist who could help her. The doctors he approached told him it was hopeless. Nothing could be done. There was simply no way to reach her. She'd retreated into some dark corner of her mind that no one could penetrate. She was incurably insane, they told him; commit her.

He rented two rooms in a dismal tenement in the East End, then made the rounds of the hospitals, looking for a position. Most of the resident physicians expressed astonishment that he'd given up private practice to come to the teeming slums of the city. Eventually he was forced to take a job as a hospital orderly in order to feed the three of them.

Then one day a drunken patient with a spurting stab wound went berserk in the emergency room. Pulling a knife from beneath his coat, he slashed wildly at the doctor trying to help him. In the resulting melee it was Andrew who managed to subdue the man, and then treat both the patient and his physician.

The wounded doctor was surprised to find that he was being stitched up by a qualified doctor. "But my God, what are you doing mopping floors and scrubbing bedpans?"

"I'm new in London. I haven't been able to find anything else. My savings are gone and I have . . . a wife who is ill and her nurse to provide for."

"What's wrong with your wife?"

"A mental disorder."

"For Christ's sake, I'm a doctor. Be specific."

"She's catatonic. It happened quite suddenly."

"No communication with her at all?"

"No."

The wounded doctor thought about this for a moment, then said, "I have a friend who runs a clinic in the East End. He won't be able to pay you much, but he'll at least provide food and shelter for you and your wife. Your wife's nurse would also be a useful addition to his clinic. And you could follow your profession until you get started in practice again." He paused, then added, "More importantly, my friend Noel has made a study of the mentally unbalanced."

A few days later, Andrew presented himself at the East End Clinic.

Noel Brannock, M.D., had given up a prosperous Harley Street orthopædic practice after his unmarried daughter had been arrested, tried, and convicted of murdering her infant son shortly after giving birth. She was now serving a life sentence in an asylum for the criminally insane.

A man of gaunt height, with stringy brown hair and sunken features that resembled a potato that had shriveled in some dark cellar, Dr. Noel Brannock's only redeeming feature was a pair of probing gray eyes that seemed to reach inside his patients' minds to find the source of their pain.

He provided Andrew with two attic rooms, grumbling that no doubt Andrew, like several predecessors, would move on as soon as he got his bearings. He then requested permission to spend some time with Jean.

"Yes, of course," Andrew said. "But I'm afraid she appears oblivious to the presence of anyone."

"Even her husband?"

"Her husband?" Andrew repeated blankly.

The metallic gray eyes probed him unmercifully. "She isn't your wife, is she? Don't beat around the bush with me. I want the whole story."

"I did intend for her to share a room with Brigid—" Andrew began, feeling color flood over his face.

"Your sleeping arrangements are of no concern to me. Tell me about Jean." Andrew told him everything.

Noel paced about the shabby cubicle he used as an office. His patients were drunken laborers, diseased street tarts, and undernourished children. Their worn-out mothers simply gave up the ghost without seeking medical aid. He badgered various charitable organizations for financial aid when he had time, and the street women were generous when they could afford to be, but for the most part Noel's life was as austere as any of his patients. Later, Andrew would wonder if Noel lived as he did as some sort of penance for what had happened to his only daughter.

"I see," Noel said when Andrew had finished telling him about Jean. "I'd like to sit with her when I have time and observe her. Perhaps I can think of a way to break through to her."

"I'll have none of the horrors inflicted on her that Brigid told me were perpetrated at the private asylum," Andrew said in alarm.

"Don't worry. I shan't try any of those frightful shock treatments. What I have in mind is much more simple and has been effective with a couple of other patients of mine."

"Your daughter?" Andrew asked.

Noel's eyes expressed such anguish that Andrew was sorry he had mentioned her. Noel said, "Alas, my daughter isn't the quiet catatonic your Jean is. My Bess is a screaming, clawing madwoman. My former wealth and position saved her from the gallows, but I confess that sometimes I wonder if she'd be better off dead."

"I'm so sorry," Andrew said.

"She wasn't always this bad. Her condition has worsened over the years, due in a large part, I'm convinced, to her surroundings and treatment. I have a theory that many women go through varying degrees of depression after childbirth. My Bess was distraught that she'd had an illegitimate child whose father abandoned her. In that postpartum depression, something in her mind snapped. . . . I've spent many hours at various asylums and prisons. I've talked to men and women who have been declared insane and I'm convinced that mental illness can happen to anyone. Our profession turns its back on any disease that can't be treated with a scalpel or a dose of some vile brew."

Andrew said, "I'd be grateful for any suggestions you have regarding Jean's condition."

Andrew worked alongside Noel, often putting in eighteen-hour days, but slipped away every minute he could spare to be with Jean. He would simply sit beside her, holding her hand or reading to her, even though she gave no indication she knew he was there. Noel approved of this treatment and he too spent as much time as he could in the cramped but sun-filled attic room with Jean. Andrew took her to Hyde Park on fine afternoons, and Brigid washed and dressed her patient and brushed her hair until it shone.

Then one day, when Andrew was called to the docks to treat the mangled arm of a laborer who had fallen down a ship's hatch, Noel tiptoed up to the attic and said to Brigid, "Go on downstairs—go for a walk, do anything you like. I need to spend a couple of hours alone with her." At the door he whispered, "Don't come back, no matter what you hear, do you understand? I'll call you when I need you. Andrew probably won't be back for hours, but if he comes, send him to the chemist for laudanum. Tell him we haven't any and I need it immediately."

Brigid had grown to trust him, but she hesitated, glancing at Jean. "Go on, woman," Noel said. "I shan't hurt her, I give you my word. But we've got to treat her and we can't while she's like this."

After Brigid departed, he placed his chair at right angles to the one in which Jean sat, her eyes wide and staring, her hands folded limply on her lap. Leaning one elbow on the arm of his chair, Noel propped his chin on his hand and stared at the opposite wall.

For two hours he sat immobile, silent. The only sound in the room was the ticking of a clock on the chest of drawers beside the bed. The sunlight slanted in through the dusty dormer window, moved slowly across the bare wood floor. They were like two statues cast in stone; neither blinked, breathed audibly, or moved.

Then suddenly Noel leapt to his feet, shouting at the top of his lungs, "God in heaven! I can't stand this! I hate this! I'm in a prison here! Let me out!" He bellowed and shrieked and stamped his feet, then picked up his chair and beat the wooden floor with it.

Jean jumped, then rose shakily from her chair, staring at him as though seeing him for the first time. "Oh!" she said in a small tremulous voice. "You frightened me!"

Andrew's joy in the change in Jean's condition was short-lived. Although she would feed herself and answer questions and even take an interest in her surroundings, it was quickly evident that she didn't remember Andrew, or any part of her life before she was locked away in the asylum.

She did remember Brigid, and it distressed Andrew that Jean would allow Brigid to touch her, but screamed in terror if he or Noel even accidentally brushed her hand or body. Even when Jean awakened from a nightmare, crying and terrified, only Brigid could calm her. Loving Jean as he did, Andrew wanted to comfort her and it hurt terribly to have her so afraid of him.

One day, in desperation he said to Noel, "Perhaps if I took her back to Merrinswood—if she were to see her children again, it might restore her memory."

"And at that time you'd tell her that her twin brother,

whom you say she idolized, is dead. Murdered, his body dropped into a bog, his assassin uncaught, unpunished. What do you think that would do to her fragile hold on reality? Have patience, man. You wouldn't expect a victim of pneumonia to recover overnight—this will take time, too. We may already have accomplished all we shall ever be able to. Lord, we know so little about the workings of the human mind."

Andrew told himself that it was enough that Jean smiled at him occasionally, listened attentively when he spoke, and daily grew physically stronger. She soon joined Brigid in helping to care for the patients, particularly the children, and all four of them were usually so busy that time sped by. But Andrew's love for Jean was a man's love for a woman, needing physical expression. He wondered how long he could continue his chaste worship of a woman he wanted so desperately.

With his usual perception, Noel said to him one day, "You might have to face the fact that she'll never be able to have a physical relationship with you. Have you considered that?"

"Yes. I've wanted to ask her to marry me ever since you brought her back to us—but I've been afraid to, in case I push her back into that dark cage again."

"Several of our ladies of the evening have been quite open with their inviting glances in your direction," Noel pointed out.

"No," Andrew said quickly. "I find that idea distasteful."

"Quite so. But take it from me, it's a lonely life without a wife to share it. Bess's mother died when she was a little girl and I let the years slip away without trying to find someone else. Look at me now—would any woman have me?"

"Brigid admires you tremendously. She told me so," Andrew replied.

Noel's expression was incredulous, but after that Andrew noticed that he paid a great deal more attention to the young Irish nurse. Andrew wasn't surprised when eventually Noel said, "I've been thinking of asking Brigid to be my wife. Do you think she'll have me?"

They were married one rainy Friday afternoon in a registry office, and throughout the brief impersonal ceremony

Andrew watched Jean's reactions. She hugged Brigid and shook Noel's hand. Then she gave Andrew a radiant smile.

Noel took his bride down to Brighton for a couple of days' honeymoon at the seaside, leaving Andrew and Jean alone for the first time. The first evening they sat on either side of a hissing coke fire in the L-shaped surgery of the clinic. Jean gazed at him with trusting eyes. "They looked happy," she said.

"Yes. He's considerably older than Brigid, but they share a dedication to healing. I believe they'll make a good match."

"Marriage is essential to a woman, isn't it?"

Andrew answered carefully. "I believe it's the preferred state for both men and women."

She looked down at her folded hands and, as always when he lost contact with her eyes, Andrew felt deprived of those great luminous windows to her soul. He always felt he could sink into the depths of her eyes and lose himself there forever.

He had told her that he had been her personal physician once, but she had shied away in fright when he attempted to tell her anything about the life she had lived before. Noel had advised him against forcing the information upon her.

Sitting with her in the twilight-lit room, Andrew thought of Noel and Brigid on their honeymoon, and was overwhelmed with love and need. Before he could stop himself, he whispered, "I've loved you for a long time, Jean."

For an instant he was sure she would run from the room. Instead, she sat perfectly still in that way she'd learned. Rather like a fawn in the forest, rooted to the spot to escape detection. If I don't speak or move, then you'll go away, her attitude seemed to say.

Andrew went on hurriedly. "I know this must be a shock to you, but you must have wondered why I brought you here—why there is no other woman in my life."

She turned very pale. "You've been very kind to me."

"I want to marry you. To take care of you and protect you, forever. Say you'll be my wife, please. Then you'll never be taken away from me."

She looked up, her eyes wide with fear. "Someone could take me away?"

He leaned forward and took her hands in his. She didn't

pull away, but he felt her tremble. "If I were your husband you'd be safe."

"But I couldn't . . . I can't. . . ."

"You're afraid of the . . . intimate side of marriage. I wouldn't press you for that, Jean. Not until you're ready. We would have a marriage in name only until you're quite well again."

"But—there is the question of my past."

"I know most of what there is to be known about it. If you'll permit me, I'll be glad to tell you everything I know. There are people you should return to see—"

She wrenched free of his grasp and jumped to her feet. "No! No, I don't want to know what happened. I don't want to know who put me in that dreadful place. I don't ever want to remember anyone I knew before—"

Hardly aware of what he was doing, Andrew jumped to his feet and caught her in his arms, holding her tightly. Her violent trembling eased after a moment. "Jean, my dearest, there are people who love you, who must be terribly concerned about what happened to you."

She struggled again and he held her close to his chest. "No, Andrew! I can't go back to whatever life I had before. Please don't force me! I shall die if you make me go back. I want to stay here with you and Brigid and Noel."

He pressed his lips to her hair and murmured, "Will you marry me? I'll never ask more of you than what you're giving me now, at this moment. I swear it, Jean."

They were married in the same registry office as Noel and Brigid, and if Noel wondered why the newlyweds still slept in separate rooms, he didn't mention it.

Noel ran into a friend from his student days who had married into a wealthy family and who invited him and Brigid to spend a holiday at their villa in the south of France. When they returned from the Continent, Noel seized Andrew's arm and drew him into the tiny office of the London clinic. Noel's gray eyes were glittering with excitement. "Tell me, have you ever heard of Sigmund Freud?"

Andrew confessed he had not.

"A neurologist in Vienna—he studied under Jean Martin Charcot in Paris. Charcot was studying hysteria and apparently inspired Freud to do the same. On his return to Vienna, Freud reported to the medical society on what he'd seen, but was met with cold silence. Still, he switched from the brain to the mind. Now, Freud had a friend and colleague named Josef Breuer who treated a patient he called Anna O, using a method of reviving painful memories under hypnosis."

Noel had been rummaging in his bag and now produced a book. He handed it to Andrew who read the title, *Studies in Hysteria.*

"By the time Freud and Breuer published that," Noel went on, "Freud had abandoned hypnosis in favor of what he calls 'free association.' He's read several papers before medical societies, but it seems he's been ostracized as a crank."

"Why is everyone so hostile toward him?" Andrew asked, turning the book over in his hand.

"Because, my dear fellow, Freud came to the startling conclusion that various psychoneuroses are caused by unconscious sexual conflicts."

Noel turned to his littered desk and grabbed a pen. Dipping it into the inkwell, he drew a diagram on a sheet of paper. The diagram resembled an iceberg, with only the tip showing above the water, and the vast bulk below the surface. "According to Freud, this"—Noel indicated the tip above water—"is the conscious mind. And all the rest, below the surface, is our unconscious. If a doctor is able to reach down there and resolve those unconscious conflicts . . ."

The two doctors surveyed each other silently for a moment. Noel said, "Forgive me, but you know that I'm aware that Jean won't let you touch her. That in fact you've never consummated your marriage to her."

Andrew stared at the iceberg drawing. "Even if this Dr. Freud could help her," he said slowly, "how could I ever raise enough money to take us to Vienna?"

"You could go to the man who did this to her," Noel said, his eyes like rapiers, "and demand that he pay your way."

As Andrew sat on the train hurtling north to Yorkshire, he decided that at the next stop he would get his bag down from the overhead rack and again read *Studies in Hysteria.* It would perhaps take his mind off the coming ordeal at Merrinswood.

23

A fragile winter sun gilded the walls of Merrinswood but didn't warm the air. Sarah shivered as she alighted
from the carriage and hurried up the terrace steps. She always
felt bereft after putting the children aboard a train for departure to their boarding schools, but this year with Robbie and
Danior off to Cambridge it seemed that yet another phase in
her life was ending.

A vision of the three waving good-bye to her flitted
through her mind. Robbie so tall and golden, like his father
. . . like Hakan. Sarah had long ago stopped thinking of her
son as James. James was that bewildered youth who had left
under a cloud, while Hakan was still, in her mind, free,
untrammeled, an Apache brave.

Danior had hugged her fiercely, his emotions always more
visible than those of either of the twins. He was shorter, of
stocky build, his black hair always an unkempt tangle, his
lively dark eyes and quick laughter creating a bright place
wherever he went. Dear sensitive Robbie, with his shy smile
and hesitant speech, was by far the most thoughtful of Sarah's adopted children. His poor health as a child had left him
a little thin and slightly round-shouldered, but there was the
unmistakable family likeness to Hakan in his coloring and
features that tugged at Sarah's heartstrings.

Emily had turned from a plain, sharp-tempered child into
a drab, self-centered young woman with a lethal envy of
anyone she perceived as having anything she did not possess.

While Hakan had been at school, Sarah had traveled
south frequently to visit him, but even when Richard deemed
it safe for Hakan to come home for holidays, he had refused
to do so. These past few years she had seen her son less and
less, which was a constant source of anxiety and yearning.

Barlow, moving with the arthritic stiffness of age, came to take Sarah's coat and hat. He never said or did anything that could have been construed as hostile, yet Sarah felt the man's dislike. She would have dismissed him years ago had it not been for the fact that he had seen Hakan return, covered with blood, the day Randolph Leighton was killed. Once she had entered Robbie's room unexpectedly and found Barlow reverently holding a silver-framed photograph of Jean Leighton. The butler had not heard Sarah's approach, and for an instant she observed him as he gazed at the likeness of his former mistress with adoration and tears in his eyes. It had been a revealing moment.

Without meeting her eye, the butler said, "The post is here, milady. I put it in your study."

"Thank you, Barlow." Sarah resisted the urge to run into her study, not wanting the butler to see how desperately she hoped there would be a letter from Hakan. There had been so little communication with her son for the past year or so, although he'd visited Danior and Robbie at school.

Riffling through the bills and social invitations, Sarah pounced upon the envelope bearing the foreign stamp. She was about to tear it open when she realized that it was addressed to her in an unfamiliar handwriting and bore a United States stamp.

The letter was brief, written in a bold script.

Dear Lady Moreland:

I'm not sure that you'll remember me after all these years, but I couldn't come to England without at least letting you know. I'll be there in the spring, appearing with a wild West show that is touring the country.

Oh, yes—to jog your memory, I'm the same Sam Rutherford who was an Indian agent at the time you and your son were reunited with your husband's family. I've thought about you and Hakan many times over the years, and wondered how you were faring. I'd like to send you tickets for the show, if you'd be interested in seeing it. I thought it might remind Hakan of his boyhood with the Apache.

Sam Rutherford . . . The years fell away and Sarah was again riding with Hakan and Sam toward that ill-advised meeting with Philip and Randolph. She read the letter again, wondering how or why a man like Sam had become part of a wild West show. She hadn't actually seen one, but had read newspaper and magazine accounts that indicated the shows portrayed the Indians as bloodthirsty butchers rather than men forced to defend their homes against invaders. She was quite sure she would hate it. But Sam had been kind and it had been so long since she'd shared memories with anyone who knew anything about her life with the Apache.

It was possible that Hakan would be back in England by spring. He was due for a long leave, but she didn't expect him to spend any part of it in his ancestral home. Perhaps they could meet Sam somewhere, maybe even see his wild West show.

The last time Richard had seen his son was when they had traveled to Sandhurst to see Hakan, using the name James Oliver, commissioned as a second lieutenant in the Queen's Own Fourteenth Hussars.

At the pass-in-review, Sarah watched with tears of pride at the sheer pageantry and drama of the occasion as the handsome young mounted officers, sabers glinting in the sun, rode by. But later she saw that her son had already changed. It was in his eyes, in the wall of reserve he'd acquired, in the studied deliberation of his speech. That wonderful joyous naturalness was gone. We stamped it out of him, Sarah thought sadly, we, his family, and his school, and the academy. She hardly knew him and didn't know how to bridge the chasm between them.

Even Richard was dismayed by the change. "Lord, I hope they haven't killed all of his spirit," he commented after the visit was over. "He'll need at least some of his old aggressive nature in order to advance through the ranks."

"He still has his courage," Sarah said. "He'll no doubt be called upon to display it in the service of Her Majesty. I just hope it doesn't get him killed. Oh, how I wish we'd never sent him away. We should have told the police everything and let him stand trial."

"Are you forgetting?" Richard asked in an ice-cold voice, "Randolph was stabbed *in the back*. Your son could hardly plead self-defense."

Despite his father's concern, Hakan had quickly advanced to the rank of captain and had served with distinction in the far-flung outposts of the Empire. But he had never returned to Merrinswood. Sarah had met him in London on several of his leaves, and since Danior always begged to go along, she took the boy. But Richard usually made some excuse not to go. The last time she suggested it, he said, "It's been long enough now, since the Randolph Leighton mess, that James could safely return. It's sheer stubbornness that keeps him away."

"He stays away because he believes he'll bring disgrace to his family. I haven't been able to convince him otherwise," Sarah responded. "It would help if you would talk to him."

"Glad to, old girl—when he comes to Merrinswood. I'm damned if I'll go traipsing off to some dreary barracks to see him."

Sarah silently recalled exactly what Hakan had said. "I'd prefer not to return to Merrinswood until it is mine. When I inherit my father's title and estate, I'll be as powerful as he is. Until then, I'd prefer to stay away."

So she had to remain, Sarah thought despairingly, in order to be caretaker of his inheritance. She'd play her role as Countess and close her eyes to her husband's assorted vices.

When Hakan received his first promotion, Sarah took Danior and Robbie with her to the army base in the south. She also took a note from Nelia Dunstan, inviting Hakan to her coming-out party.

"Give her my regrets, will you?" Hakan said.

Robbie said incredulously, "Y-you wouldn't even c-consider coming home to see *N-Nelia*?"

Hakan glanced at him, amused. "What's this? Do I hear a note of interest in your voice, Rob? Bit young for that, aren't you?"

Robbie blushed furiously. "She asked if y-you'd write to her."

Hakan's vivid blue eyes showed elaborate, and perhaps contrived, disinterest. Probably for Robbie's benefit, Sarah thought. Hakan said, "Pretty young women are always in overabundance at officers' balls, Rob. I don't want to start a correspondence with one who will probably be married by the time I return to Merrinswood."

"No d-doubt to Charles Pettigrew," Robbie said gloomily, "If you d-don't g-get there f-first; no one else s-stands a chance."

Turning to Danior, Hakan expressed interest in Pas, the organ-grinder. Did his arm heal all right? Did he get his organ repaired? Where was he now?

"He's traveling in the Scarborough area—" Sarah began, but realized that Hakan wanted to hear it from Danior.

The boy obviously worshipped Hakan like a hero. He gazed at him with wide dark eyes as though beholding a god newly descended to earth. Sarah knew that Hakan had reset Pas's arm, but felt there was more to the gypsy boy's adoration than mere gratitude. There seemed to be a bond between the two that reached further than the casual encounter that had brought them together.

"Pas comes back to Merrin Quarry every couple of months," Danior said. "He sends word to us and your mother takes me to the village to see him." He paused and added wonderingly, "We have tea in a tea shop."

Sarah smiled, but felt sad. Sometimes she felt that Danior's wonderment at the little pleasures of life could so easily have been Hakan's, if only she hadn't waited too long to bring him home. A boy could have been molded, but Hakan had been on the threshold of manhood, and the Life-way too indelibly impressed. She said, "We also walk and talk and your father is aghast at the company I keep. But I find Pas a very intelligent, warmhearted man. Did you know that he had sung in the chorus of an opera company in Italy? I think some tragedy forced him to leave and come here."

"His throat," Danior said. "He had something wrong with his throat and now he can only sing very softly."

Sarah said, "I was astonished to hear Danior singing an aria in Italian one day—more amazed that Pas had taught him so much about opera."

Danior's eyes brightened. "I like to sing. But perhaps I won't find the notes when my voice changes."

Hakan placed his hand on the boy's shoulder. "Perhaps your voice will be even better when it changes."

As time passed, Sarah found herself striving to protect Danior from all she felt had disillusioned Hakan. The gypsy boy slowly became one of her adopted sons, and sweet, gentle Robbie the other.

Some stray gene had afflicted Robbie's blue eyes with a severe case of myopia and he peered nearsightedly at the world through thick spectacles, further alienating himself from his father, who felt the glasses were a symbol of too great an interest in books and made his son look weak and unmanly. But Sarah wouldn't allow Richard to bully Robbie in her presence. "The boy is intelligent and his glasses give him a thoughtful look. He's a fine young man and you should be proud of him."

Richard raised an eyebrow. "I believe the boy is still a virgin. What does that indicate to you?"

That poor Robbie was madly in love with Nelia Dunstan, Sarah thought, and didn't want anyone else. But she didn't say so.

On the day that Sam Rutherford's letter arrived from America, Sarah found her husband at the stables. Richard had purchased one of the new gasoline-engine-powered horseless carriages. The Red Flag Act of 1865 had at last been repealed and it was no longer necessary for a motor vehicle on the highway to be preceded by a man on foot carrying a red flag.

Sarah couldn't understand why he'd want one of the noisy, smoky motorcars, but perhaps it would be less dangerous for a man his age than galloping wildly across the moors on horseback. She didn't consider that she rode equally wildly with him.

"Come on, Sarah," Richard said, catching sight of her. "I'll take you for a drive."

"I don't have protective clothing," she began, but decided a ride even in this smelly contraption might be a good prelude for the discussion she wanted to have with Richard.

The engine had to be coaxed to life by means of a handle that was inserted into the front and turned. At last the motorcar began to vibrate, inched forward, hesitated, then lurched off down the driveway.

They drove through the vast open dales of the North Riding, and fat woolly sheep ran in fright as the motor sputtered and roared their approach. Sarah remembered riding horseback with Hakan when the heather had been waist high and no village or hamlet or any sign of man's existence had marred the rolling vistas of moors. They had stopped to gather bilberries and the song of the larks had filled the air with joy. She'd hoped that Hakan could one day grow to love this country, because it offered the space he needed. It was one of the few areas of England not cluttered with towns and villages within sight of one another. The moors were different in color and texture from the American southwestern desert where he'd grown up, yet were as open and unspoiled by man. He'd spent some happy days here, perhaps not as wildly free as his boyhood, Sarah thought, but surely when he finally came home to Merrinswood he would find a measure of peace and contentment.

Richard stopped the motorcar at the top of a hill, and spread out before them, the moors formed a rugged counterpane of greens and browns.

Sarah drew a deep breath of the fragrant air, feasted her eyes on the panorama of unspoiled nature, and thought how much she loved this part of England. In sudden surprise it occurred to her that she no longer missed the deserts of Apacheria and perhaps they had been merely the setting for her deep love of Lone Wolf. England had been her first home, and like a first love, had never really lost its power to enchant. Enjoying the countryside and appreciating a gracious way of life surely compensated—at least in part—for what could never again be hers. If she sometimes felt there was something lacking in her life, she recaptured in her memory the love and passion she had shared with Lone Wolf, reminding herself that she'd had her share of happiness and now must think of her son's future. Usually it was enough to still those vague unnamed yearnings. But not today. Why was she all at once so acutely aware that her life was slipping away?

"Are they worth a penny?" Richard asked.

"Oh . . . I was just thinking you shouldn't have shut off the motor. You don't have a groom to start it again." There was no chastisement in her voice.

"Have faith, old girl," Richard said.

Their relationship over the years had mellowed slightly, and while not without conflict, they had at least learned to live with each other the way they were, not expecting any compromise in the other each was not also prepared to make. They simply avoided discussing the matters that would bring about violent disagreements.

Richard still liked to taunt her occasionally with invitations to his bedchamber, but it had become more of a conversational ritual than anything else. Surprisingly, there were even matters upon which they were allied, since both were passionately interested in everything about the estate, although for different reasons. Richard often sought her advice and liked to discuss his decisions with her. They both loved horses and often rode together, becoming companions in a way they perhaps could not have had there been a sexual bond.

Then too, human memory being notoriously short, crisis-producing events slipped into obscurity. With the passage of time, the disappearance of Jean, the death of her twin, Doctor McGreal's departure, all faded in memory. Even Danior no longer seemed to pine for his long-lost sister.

Everyone in his or her own way rationalized the events and losses and came up with an explanation that eased the hurt. Robbie convinced himself that his mother had died of her illness, otherwise she would have written. Danior decided that Chavi was on the road somewhere, and besides, she didn't know how to write. Emily expressed only cold rage at her mother's abandonment.

Sitting beside Richard in the motorcar, Sarah felt a sudden wave of disorientation, like that of a person awaking from a deep sleep in a strange bed. For so long she had subjugated all of her own needs to those of the people around her, while assuring herself that everything she did, she did to insure Hakan's inheritance, that she had forgotten how to want something for herself. She wondered idly what had precipitated this unexpected yearning for something to which she couldn't give a name. Then she remembered the letter that had arrived from Sam Rutherford.

She had met Sam at a time when she was numb with grief, but in retrospect, saw that he had been a man who was unabashedly masculine, yet gentle and protective too, and had she encountered him at any other time in her life, he would have made her acutely aware that she was a woman. She felt a stirring of excitement at the prospect of seeing him again that surely didn't belong in the mind of a respectable matron.

Richard turned to look at her. "Did you get your brood safely on the train for school?"

"*My* brood?"

Richard laughed. "They're certainly more yours than mine. Especially your black-eyed little gypsy. If I hadn't put my foot down, you'd no doubt be inviting his organ-grinder friend to Merrinswood, too."

"You miss a great deal in life with your snobbery—that need you have to set yourself apart by excluding others."

"I daresay I do. And most of what I miss is ragged, inarticulate, and has a disagreeable smell."

"Pas is more of a gentleman than you'll ever be. I'm constantly amazed when Danior utters some profound gem of wisdom that he learned from his friend. You know, Pas feels that Danior shows a great love of music that should be encouraged. I thought perhaps piano and singing lessons."

Richard rolled his eyes. "I've indulged you this far, so go ahead. It will be on your head if you turn him into another sissy like Robert."

"Robbie isn't a sissy. He's sensitive, clever, and doesn't have a lazy bone in his body. As you very well know, during the school holidays he's happy to work for the estate in any way you allow. And one could hardly say I left a feminine imprint on Hakan."

Richard frowned. "When will you give up that ridiculous Indian nickname?"

Sarah said quickly, "I had a letter today from America." She told him of Sam Rutherford's impending visit to England.

"A wild West show? Sounds absolutely frightful."

"Perhaps. Still, I believe I'll go."

Richard gave her a long hard look. "You've never really let go of those years, have you?"

"Sixteen years is a long time to put out of one's mind."

"That wasn't what I meant. You know, I've always wondered what you looked like dressed in your squaw's clothes."

"I burned those clothes years ago. Richard, we made a bargain, you and I. Perhaps not an expressly stated one, but a bargain nevertheless. There were several unspoken clauses. I would be your wife in the eyes of the world, and you would name Hakan your heir. I would close my eyes to your affairs, and you would indulge my desire to bring up the twins and Danior at Merrinswood. It was never part of our bargain that we invade the privacy of one another's thoughts."

His hand slid from the steering wheel to her shoulder, then circled around her neck, turning her face toward him. A small mocking smile plucked at the corners of his mouth. "Nor invade the privacy of one another's bodies. What a dreadful waste that is, Sarah. You know, it astonishes me sometimes that I still find you so desirable after all these years. In fact, the mere idea that I want to make love to a forty-six-year-old woman is in itself something of a mystery. But I have to admit the years have been kind to you."

She said lightly, "You merely want what you know you can't have. Let's go back now, it will be dark soon."

Sighing, he removed his hand. "Have I ever told you that in addition to wanting you, Sarah, I admire you? You have an absolutely ferocious singlemindedness of purpose. You've endured me these past years because of your obsession with acquiring all I possess for your son. Tell me, what were you afraid of? That I'd dissipate everything of value and leave him only a title, and all your sacrifice would have been for nothing?"

Sarah stared straight ahead. He chuckled softly. "It's all right, love. It's been a good bargain for me, too. Believe it or not, I enjoy your companionship."

He got out to start the car, then they roared back the way they'd come. Long shadows crept across the ribbon of road and night clouds claimed the sky. They shouldn't have gone so far, Sarah thought, they should have made allowance for the return journey. They left the moors behind and were passing the dark stretch of Coombe's Woods when something collided with the windscreen. A moment later, Sarah cried out as feathers whirled in her face and the lifeless body of a large bird landed on her lap. The dead bird was a white owl.

It was several minutes after Richard flung the dead bird from the car before Sarah's heart stopped thudding and her sense of impending doom began to fade. Her immediate reaction had been that of an Apache. She was astonished to realize how in a single instant she had reverted back to such primitive emotions. Yet even while her logical mind pointed out that an owl did not represent an evil spirit bringing bad fortune, on a deeper level of consciousness she recognized that when she lived as an Apache she had learned to listen to her intuition, as they did. More than once it had saved them from danger. If that inner warning were triggered by an external event—the appearance of an owl—did it make it any less valid?

Richard was watching her out of the corner of his eye.

"The owl flew right into the windscreen. I couldn't avoid it, you know."

She nodded, wondering what he'd think if he knew she was contemplating what might happen if she were to ever impulsively react with deed rather than thought to her Apache conditioning.

Entering the officers' mess at Aldershot, Hakan overheard a young subaltern at the bar whisper to his companion, "There he is now. See how he walks on the balls of his feet, rolling side to side so that he doesn't make a sound? His regiment recently returned from putting down the rebellion in Zululand. I heard all sorts of stories about him. Brave, but a bit too reckless. They say he's up for another medal. I heard he can read signs and track the enemy better than any native scout. Bit of a mystic, y'know. A strange one, I can tell you. Doesn't make friends among his fellow officers, but attracts women like flies, and they say his men would die for him. Let's buy him a drink."

Giving no indication that he had heard every word, Hakan went to the far end of the bar and ordered cognac. Extremely sensitive hearing, he decided, was both a blessing and a curse. He turned his back on the two subalterns and drained his glass. It had taken a year or so in the army and a couple of brutal campaigns before he learned to tolerate the taste of spirits. Tonight some old wounds had been opened again by the letter from his mother which had been awaiting his return, and he felt the need to numb his mind with brandy.

"Captain Oliver, isn't it?" a voice at his side said.

Turning, he saw the subaltern who had been talking about him. "Excuse me," Hakan said. "I was just leaving."

He walked through a misty drizzle of rain, feeling isolated, angry, impatient to be doing something, anything, that would stop his thoughts from pulling him in a direction he didn't want to go.

It didn't seem possible that the man he was today had any connection with the youth who had left Merrinswood in disgrace. Everything that had happened to him, he decided, was for a purpose. One day he would be the seventh Earl of Moreland and as wealthy and powerful as any man on earth. Then he would be able to forget those other rites of passage he'd gone through in order to be an Apache brave. He would be happy, and somewhere the ghost of Lone Wolf would look upon him and smile, because Hakan would be an even more powerful chief than his Apache father had been. But Hakan vowed to be a very different chief than his English father. When his schoolmasters had emphasized the code of honor by which an English officer and gentleman must live, no one listened more intently than Hakan.

Hakan had gone first to a "cramming establishment" for young gentlemen who wished to be admitted to the Royal Military Academy of Sandhurst. The school was run by an ex-army colonel who believed the only way to instill knowledge into would-be army officers was to pound it in with cane and ruler. The older boys were allowed to bully the younger ones unmercifully, while the instructors were as skilled in martial arts, which they practiced on their pupils, as in any of the subjects they taught. It seemed to incense them that Hakan would not flinch when a bamboo cane whistled through the air and raised a red welt across his palm, so he would be rewarded by twice as many strokes as anyone else.

Hakan had to be proficient in five subjects in order to pass the Sandhurst entry examination. Three were obligatory, Latin, mathematics, and English. He had no great difficulty with these, but regretted selecting chemistry and history as the other two.

When it came to physical activities, he had no peer, and his riding and running prowess quickly inspired awe in his fellow students and the respect of his instructors, these skills probably kept him from being expelled when the pressures built to the point that he rebelled against the often unjust discipline of the school, especially when it was directed at the more timid boys. Before long he was the object of both admiration and envy among his classmates, but because he was "James Oliver," whose family lived abroad, he dared not make close friends who would expect to share confidences.

He passed into Sandhurst with a cavalry cadetship just before his nineteenth birthday, and astonished the riding masters the first time they saw him astride a horse. He learned to run up bills at the local livery stable on the strength of his future commission, won a cadet-arranged steeplechase, and was invited to join a polo team. He easily won the three-mile footrace, but did badly at fencing, which he found too structured and not feasible as either a method of attack or defense.

He hated the drills and was put in an "awkward squad." He learned tactics and field fortification, dug trenches, cut railway lines, learned to blow up bridges and make pontoons. He drew maps and made road reconnaissances, the latter arousing suspicion due to his almost supernatural skills in plotting terrain.

Throughout his Sandhurst training he was respected by the other cadets, but still he made no close friends, feeling duty-bound not to discuss his family or previous history, and this caused him to be regarded as cold and distant.

Eventually he passed out of the College, and during the next few years served in the Sudan and Malakaland and India. He rode in two cavalry charges and was mentioned in dispatches.

At first there had been excitement and strange places and people and the sheer challenge of staying alive. There had also been loneliness. But the worst enemy was within himself. He thought perhaps it was called disillusionment. That so much of life had to be spent in pursuit of a goal, that striving for it couldn't be a source of contentment in itself.

When longings for the Apache country of his boyhood surfaced occasionally, he reminded himself he could never go back. He was no longer the boy who had left Arizona, who believed in White Painted Woman and Coyote and the Spirits of the mountain. The man he was today would be as out of place there as the Apache boy had been when he first came to England. Besides, there were no longer any free Apaches roaming the American Southwest. They were all prisoners-of-war in a stinking Florida swamp that was as different from their desert home as an army barracks was from Merrinswood. Someday he would return to Merrinswood and take his English father's place, then set about rebuilding the good name of the family. In the meantime, he'd be the best soldier he could be.

As he walked the rain-blurred street, he thought of his mother's letter and felt the disappointment that she would consider he'd want to see Sam Rutherford make a spectacle of himself in some inane parody of life in the "wild West." That gave way to curiosity as to why Sam was part of such a troupe.

A shadow detached itself from a doorway and a small hand clutched his arm. "Would you like a bit of fun? Anything you want, ducks. I stop at nothing, I don't."

She was thin and pasty-pale in the yellow orb of light that came from a gaslamp at the corner of the street. Her body odor wasn't appealing, but there was a certain gamine attractiveness to her pinched features. Hakan said, "I'd like a drink. I'll buy you one, and pay for your time if you'll sit with me."

Unable to believe her luck, the streetwalker accompanied him into the saloon bar. He bought ale to wash down their brandies. She said her name was Polly and she looked very young to have such ancient eyes.

Feeling the warmth of the brandy begin to seep into his bones, Hakan said, "Has it occurred to you, Polly, that we live in a time of breathtaking advances in technology? Everything from wireless telegraphy to motorcars. Soon we'll say good-bye to all this murky gaslight and use that modern marvel electricity. And amid all these wonders, we still have girls like you selling their bodies on the streets."

Polly's eyes widened above her glass of ale and when she put it down a rim of froth remained on her upper lip. "Oh, stone the ruddy crows! Are you one of *them*? Crikey, and you a soldier too."

Hakan wasn't listening to her. She was there simply to keep others at bay. "We use troops to put down unemployment riots at home and to impose our government's will on other countries. Do you think any well-bred young woman wants to hear about the business I'm in, Polly? Cavalry business? Lord, no! She wants me to tell her how pretty she is and how my heart beats faster when she's near."

Polly slurped another mouthful of ale and gave him an encouraging leer. She had a range of expressions, from pretty pouts and cheeky grins to lowered-lidded invitations with her ancient eyes.

Hakan regarded her sadly. "Our society is obsessed with the stock market, the expansion of trade and industry. Whenever there's a lag in wages, or trade sags, or any other economic ailment afflicts us, the cause is traced to a shortage of gold."

"Wot the 'ell has this got to do with me, guv?" Polly asked cheerfully, finishing off her ale and wiping her mouth with the back of her hand. "Listen, are we going somewhere to do it, or wot? I can do yer outside in a doorway if yer like and we won't need no room or even to take off our clothes. Bloomin' freezing it is, for getting undressed."

He blinked her back into focus. "If I wanted to make love to a woman I wouldn't have invited you in here for a drink, Polly. Women willing to sleep with me are extremely easy for me to find. A woman to talk to—who will listen to me—is much more valuable."

Polly pouted. "Don't you want me then? Cor, you dunno wot you're missing." She ran a pink tongue around her lips provocatively, suddenly challenged by his lack of interest in her undernourished body.

He went on. "So, where was I? Gold . . . that's our problem. Or rather, the shortage of it. Production has increased more than there is gold to pay for it. Now, isn't it providential that at this point in time there has been the greatest discovery of gold that ever was? Gold in quantities that dwarfs all that has ever been found in the history of man.

"They've discovered gold in the Transvaal—in a long ridge of high ground called the Witwatersrand. Do you know what that means, Polly? That means that inevitably we'll have a war over it. Whites have been trekking from the Cape into the hinterland after gold in increasing numbers. The trekkers—frontiersmen—are British subjects, but they're of Dutch, German, and French descent. They're called Boers. Anyway, there's a big war coming, Polly. Next year, the year after at latest."

"Cor," Polly said. "A war? Where?"

"I just told you," he said patiently. "In South Africa. Against the Boers. And when it happens, my life will have completed its circle. Perhaps now is the time for me to return to Merrinswood and remind myself of what I'm fighting for. While there's still time."

Perhaps some premonition had produced the thought, because the following morning he was summoned to the officers' mess to see a visitor.

"I thought you were at Cambridge," he said as Danior, in his usual uninhibited way, clasped Hakan in a welcoming embrace.

As they pulled apart, Hakan saw that Danior's dark eyes

were deeply troubled, his usually animated expression grave. "Hakan, we've had bad news from home. Can you get compassionate leave right away? Robbie's on his way to Merrinswood and I came here to ask you to go too. Your mother needs you."

A chill crept along Hakan's veins. "My mother—is she ill?"

Danior shook his head. "It's your father. He's had a stroke. He's paralyzed, can't talk . . . he may be dying."

24

TWELVE MILE STATION, AUSTRALIA

By the time Lysander returned for them, great clouds of black smoke lit with bronze sparks were billowing along the horizon, and they could almost hear the crackle of the flames as the bush fire roared toward them, borne on the gusting winds.

Chavi had already packed bags for herself and Brenna. Boomer had loaded some of their valuables on a wagon and harnessed the horses. There had been many other fires, but none of this magnitude. A disaster was in the making, Chavi knew. If they lost the house and shearing sheds and paddocks . . . if they lost the stock and the sheep, what then? Lysander had said the constant droughts and sagging world market of the last few years had wiped out many sheepmen. Could even Dirk hold on if he lost everything to fire? She'd seen bush fires devour every blade of grass and bit of scrub, leaving nothing for surviving sheep to eat.

"Did you find them?" she asked as Lysander came into the house and Brenna hurled herself into his arms.

The film of dust on his face seemed to etch the livid scars in even deeper relief as he regarded her over Brenna's burnished hair. "Dirk and the men are driving the sheep west, away from the fire. Chavi, with this wind there's no way we can save the house."

"I know. We're packed and ready to leave." Chavi tied the ribbons of her bonnet. She cast one last glance about the room, thinking of the months she'd waited for odd pieces of furniture and rugs to arrive from England. Strange how little she cared about losing any of it. She followed Lysander out into the searing wind without a backward glance.

He placed Brenna in the back of the wagon and covered her with a blanket. To Boomer he said, "Go and fill some containers with water."

"Done it already," the old man growled. "Come on, let's be off."

Lysander placed his hands on Chavi's waist and lifted her into the wagon beside her daughter. "If we run into any hot spots, or the smoke starts to choke you, douse the blanket with water and pull it over your heads."

He hitched his horse to the back of the wagon and then swung himself up into the driver's seat.

They were twenty minutes away from the house when Chavi realized she hadn't questioned the fact that it was Lysander who had come back for them rather than her husband. But by then the wind-driven fire was a terrifying sheet of orange flame, racing after them and consuming everything in its path.

Lysander used the whip on the horses, although the frightened beasts needed little urging. Ears laid back and manes flying, they bolted. Behind them the wagon swayed alarmingly. Birds and animals joined them on the rutted path, kangaroo and emu and wild pigs and rabbits, oblivious to one another in the common terror of the fire. Brightly colored parrots flew out of the trees and were picked up on the wind and rushed away, along with kookaburras, their jackass cry stilled, or perhaps lost in the roar of the wind.

Chavi kept one arm around Brenna and with the other held the blanket up to their chins, ready to pull it up over their faces if smoke or flying cinders caught up with them.

"Don't worry, Mummy," Brenna shouted, "Lysander will save us."

Chavi didn't answer as they had reached a vast open plain and on the horizon to their right she saw another plume of smoke. *Oh, God no!* A second fire had broken out. Lysander saw it too, and pulled on the reins to wheel to the left.

Even as she watched, the smoke divided and spread, a black coil circling with incredible speed. Within minutes Chavi, up on her knees now, could see flames leaping into the air. A great ring of fire was closing in on them, leaving only a narrow pathway to safety. But even if they got through that break in the circle, how many other fires had been spawned by wind-carried embers? Perhaps even now they were racing toward incineration.

Chavi supposed she should be praying for deliverance, but her only thought at that moment was regret for all she hadn't done with her life.

Brenna clung to her, frightened but trying not to show it, and Chavi felt anger that her daughter might not experience any more of life than she'd already known. They were going to die, she thought, the horses couldn't keep going at this pace in this heat. The fire would engulf them.

A glowing cinder flew overhead, landed beside the wagon, and ignited the tinder-dry grass. The wind caught the flame and whipped it toward a clump of saltbush, which exploded with a hissing roar, sending sparks in every direction.

Glancing over his shoulder, Lysander yelled, "Get down— wet the blanket and get under it."

Pouring water onto the blanket, Chavi looked up at Lysander's broad back. He was on his feet, snapping the reins, shouting to the horses, somehow keeping the wagon moving. It was a miracle they hadn't overturned.

Smoke now swirled about the wagon in choking clouds. The last thing Chavi saw before pulling the wet blanket over her head was a shower of sparks descending on the heads of Lysander and Boomer.

It was suffocating under the blanket. Chavi sucked in the limited air with shallow breaths, cradled Brenna close, and became even more aware of the bumping of the wagon over rough ground. The heat and acrid stench of smoke was unbearable, but not being able to see what was happening or where they were going was worse.

Seconds ticked into minutes, measured by her thumping heartbeat. At any moment she expected the wagon to burst into flames around them like a funeral pyre.

She lost track of time. Every bone in her body ached from the bouncing of the wagon, and her throat and nostrils were so parched it hurt to breathe.

Fumbling under the dark canopy of the blanket, she found a water bottle still partially filled and wrenched off the cork to offer it to Brenna, who gulped thirstily. When Chavi tipped the bottle to her own lips she found it was empty.

How long had they been traveling? Was it day or night? Impossible to tell in the pall of smoke. Turning back a corner of the blanket, she saw a tree on fire and quickly pulled the cover over her head again.

They could hear the crackle of flames and they gasped for breath. Brenna began to cry. "Shut up," Chavi said savagely, her voice a hoarse croak filled with her own fear. Brenna's chest heaved, but she stopped sobbing.

Suddenly the wagon lurched to a halt. Chavi flung aside the blanket and sat up. On either side of them the ground was blackened, charred remnants of trees and brush testifying to the long-ago bush fire that had devastated the area. A few hardy shrubs pushed through the burned earth, and a few patches of wilted grass struggled to survive. But Chavi's gaze swept to a more wondrous sight.

Stretched in front of them like a silver ribbon, a smoothly flowing river offered protection from the advancing flames. The opposite bank was a blessed green sanctuary. Lysander had brought them to the only place where they would be safe.

The river was wide but fairly shallow, and the horses plunged eagerly into the cool water. In the center the wagon began to float and Lysander slipped over the side to guide its progress, but the horses swam only a short distance before their hooves hit the bottom again. Chavi and Brenna remained dry, as did the contents of the wagon.

On the other side of the river they found a small farmhouse, almost hidden in a copse of silvery gums. There was no sign of the owner.

Lysander stopped only long enough to unload his passengers. "I'm going back across the river to clear the odd bits of brush," he announced. "The burned area should be wide enough to stop the fire, but I don't want to take any chances."

"No!" Brenna cried. "Don't leave us!"

He bent to hug the child and Chavi saw that the flying sparks had burned holes in his shirt. A portion of his hair was scorched. Before she could say a word, he spoke to Brenna. "Listen, princess, the only way to put out that fire, short of a cloudburst, is to get rid of every scrap of fuel for it. Boomer and I will chop down the new scrub, bury the grass patches with dirt, and then there will be nothing for it to burn. Now you be brave and go help your mother make a meal for us."

Straightening up, he fished in his pocket and produced two small smoke-grimed packages. "I almost forgot—Happy Christmas." He handed one to each of them and then grabbed a shovel and scythe from the back of the wagon. "Come on, Boomer, we've work to do."

Grumbling, the old man followed. Chavi turned wearily to go into the house, wondering how Lysander found the strength to do another thing. But to the east the sky was like a vision of hell, an inferno of black clouds of smoke and shooting flames, sparks exploding in the air like the Devil's fireworks. He was right, in this wind one bit of scrub in the previously scorched area could catch a stray spark and relay it across the river.

"Oh, look, Mummy!" Brenna exclaimed. She had opened her present and was holding up a gold locket on a slender chain. "There's a place inside to put pictures," she said. "I'll put Lysander in there."

The idea of Lysander allowing anyone to have a picture of his ravaged face was ridiculous, of course, but Chavi knew better than to mention this. "I think he meant for you to put a picture of Daddy and me in there."

Brenna scowled. "He isn't my daddy. He doesn't like me."

Too tired to argue, Chavi said, "Come on. Let's go and find the kitchen. We've a Christmas dinner to make." On the way into the house she opened Lysander's present to her. It was a beautiful cameo brooch. Dirk had given her a gilt-edged prayer book.

The wind dropped slightly during the evening and men began to straggle into the farmhouse. They drank thirstily, then went to help Lysander clear the brush. Some of them carried flasks and reminded Chavi it was Christmas and insisted she take a drink. After several sips of whiskey, brandy, and gin, she began to feel lightheaded. She and Brenna made sandwiches from the bread and corned beef Boomer had packed on their wagon, but no one had time to eat.

Some of the men who arrived were from Twelve Mile. They brought grim news. The house, shearing sheds, everything was gone. They'd lost most of the sheep when the second fire erupted and the terrified animals bolted right into it.

"Where's Dirk?" Chavi asked. "Have you seen him?"

"He went after some of the horses," one man told her. "No worry, he'll be along directly."

Relieved, Chavi accepted yet another Christmas drink and promised herself she'd eat something soon.

Brenna fell asleep on a couch, oblivious to the thumping feet and conversation of men coming and going. Chavi asked one of the men to carry her daughter into a small spare bedroom that appeared to be unused, then stole a moment to go down to the river to wash her hands and face.

The owner of the farm, an older man, wiry and sun-ravaged, came riding in, not at all surprised to find his place full of strangers. "Been out rounding up my stock. They could smell the fire and were getting jumpy. Didn't want 'em wandering too far," he told Chavi as he stopped to let his horse drink. He insisted that Chavi take his bedroom. "Go on, you're ready to drop in your tracks."

"There's something I want to do first," Chavi said. She walked away from him, following the bend of the river until she came to a secluded spot, then slipped off her clothes and slid into the cool water, hoping the effects of too much alcohol might wash away. But when she emerged from the water she still floated rather than walked, unconcerned, although shaking all over with fatigue.

By the time she returned to the house men had fallen asleep on almost every inch of floor space, but the owner of the house stood guard at his bedroom door. "You sleep in there, no arguments. And here, drink this, looks like you could use it."

Before she realized what she was doing, she had swallowed a generous glass of sherry. He motioned for her to go into his bedroom. Too tired to argue, Chavi did so, staggering slightly.

When she turned out the lamp the room was plunged into deep darkness. Heavy shutters covered the windows and smoke still blotted out the stars, so no glimmer of light entered the room. She undressed and, not having a nightgown, slid naked into bed. The heavy darkness pressed down upon her and almost instantly she fell into a deep sleep.

The dream began with whirling clouds of smoke that obscured the man walking toward her. A tall man, a Greek god of a man, whose silhouette grew larger than life. Chavi tried to move toward him, but her feet were mired in mud. Had she been foolish enough to slip into a bog? This part of the moors was treacherous, she should have been more careful.

The man in the dream beckoned her, and although she tried to follow, she couldn't free herself. He turned and looked back over his shoulder and called something to her, but she couldn't understand what he said.

Then all at once the smoke swirled even thicker and she could no longer see him. She began to cry, because she thought she'd lost him forever and couldn't bear it.

Sinking to the ground, she found she was lying on a soft bank. The heather smelled so sweet. His hand touched her arm. She sighed, grateful that he'd returned.

Gently, so gently, his fingers slid across her belly, upward to find her breasts, lingering first with one and then the other. She could feel her nipples harden and thrust toward the caressing hand. The powerful length of the man lay beside her, his body radiating strength, filled with promise.

Her eyelids were too heavy to raise, and when she tried to move her arms they felt limp, useless in the mindless manner of one's limbs in a dream. But her reaching hand found the back of his head and felt the brisk waves of abundant hair. She guided his head toward her and his lips touched hers, tentatively at first, then growing bolder, more demanding, his tongue wanting all of her mouth, eagerly seeking every part of it as if he'd never known it before and was exploring delights he'd only imagined.

She slid her arms around him and her hands moved lightly down his back, marveling at the life-force that surged in the muscled flesh, and knowing no shame, she allowed her wanton hands to seize his firm buttocks and bring him close to her.

But he held back, released her lips and allowed his mouth to travel down her throat, pause for a moment to savor her breasts, then press a warm pathway downward to her inner thighs.

Chavi sighed and squirmed in semiconscious anticipation. She'd had this dream before, especially on the nights she'd helped herself to a large glass of wine before retiring. The dream had begun long ago, one night when her husband had left her unsatisfied yet again. She'd been surprised to awaken at the moment of release, unaware that a mere dream-lover could fulfill her when her handsomely endowed husband could not.

Willingly, she parted her thighs for her dream-lover's probing tongue. When her passion spiraled out of control, she wanted to push him away and caress his body with feverish need, but she seemed unable to move. It was as though in this particular dream she must receive rather than give. In the enclosing darkness his erect manhood touched her. She wanted to tease it with lips and tongue, until it pulsed and throbbed with a life-force of its own. In the dream she could do anything she wanted to do, without fear of censure. And the wish became the act, although she still had no sensation of being able to move body or limbs.

Her lover laughed softly, tantalizing her as he waited for exactly the right moment to enter her. Now his kisses and caresses elicited a soft moaning and she knew the best was about to begin.

He whispered her name as they came together and began to move in a wondrous ballet of the senses that was as old as time. She rose and fell with him, and although in the dream they spoke, there was no sound, so perhaps the words of love were inside their heads. They were the only two left on earth, enclosed in the densest darkness, protected by whirling clouds of black smoke, as if they'd returned to the womb itself, and perhaps were entombed together for all eternity; their beginning and ending coming together to form the mysterious circle of life.

At the instant of her climax, Chavi awakened from the dream to realize that tonight no phantom lover worked his magic inside her. This was a flesh and blood man whose seed scalded her at the very same second she reached her zenith and cried out her ecstasy.

She sagged in his arms, bathed in perspiration, panting in the hot darkness of the room, unsure if she were awake or asleep, unwilling to let go of the feeling of utmost contentment, the sublime peacefulness. Nestling closer to her husband, she didn't speak for fear of breaking the spell. He held her to his chest and she listened to his heartbeat and let sweet lethargy claim her. Perhaps it was thankfulness at their deliverance from the fire, the knowledge that they could have perished but were still alive that had brought them this wonderful gift. Chavi was too exhausted and too sated to question what had happened. Time enough to wonder in the morning about the miracle that had taken place tonight. Besides, in her half-awake, half-asleep state, she was still unsure whether it was all a dream.

Bright sunlight flooded the room as the heavy shutters were folded back from the window with a jolting crash. Chavi blinked open her eyes, startled because she didn't recognize her surroundings.

At the window Dirk said, "Come on, get up. We need breakfast out here."

He walked to the door and she saw he was unshaven and fully dressed in the same clothes he'd worn the previous day. Turning to look at her he added, "I don't think it was a good idea for you to sleep naked in a stranger's house."

She stared disbelievingly at the closed door. How could he have diminished their lovemaking by not even mentioning what had happened between them last night? Surely he must have known it was the first and only time she'd climaxed with him? Bewildered, she pressed her fingers to the dull throb in her temples. How much had she had to drink last night?

Sitting up, she pushed her hair back over her shoulder, feeling disoriented, queasy from too much imbibing, and at the same time filled with a sense of loss, of wanting something too much for it to ever come true. Had she been dreaming? Had it been part of the dream that she woke up with him inside her? Judging by Dirk's attitude this morning, it must have been a dream. Certainly she'd been alone in the bed upon waking.

By the time she'd dressed and fastened up her hair, Boomer had started cooking breakfast. Chavi went to help him serve it. The men were silent, grim-faced, and no one spoke. There was no sign of Lysander, or of Brenna, but Chavi didn't worry about her daughter because she knew wherever Lysander was, Brenna wouldn't be far away.

When at last Chavi herself sat down with a cup of tea, she looked across the table at her husband, who stared morosely into space. She said, "Cheer up, at least we're all alive."

He dismissed her with a glance that chilled her soul. "We lost everything. *Everything*, don't you understand? There's nothing left."

She stammered, "Well then, it's lucky you still have a place in England, isn't it? Maybe this is a sign you should go home and take over your parents' estate."

Dirk's eyes hardened and his lips curled in an expression of such disgust that Chavi was startled by the intensity of it. He pushed back his chair, stood up, and strode outside without another word.

Jumping to her feet, Chavi followed. But he was already mounting his horse. He rode away, ignoring her plea that he come back and talk to her.

She stamped her foot in frustration and had to bite her lip to keep from screaming after him like a fishwife. Lysander, with Brenna at his side, appeared around the corner of the house. The two of them had evidently bathed in the river, as they were both clean and their hair damp. Lysander's eyes flickered over Chavi in their usual knowing way.

"Good morning, Chavi. Isn't it a grand day?" He smiled at her as they approached.

"Lysander and I had breakfast hours ago and we went swimming," Brenna said. "Look Mummy, the fire's burned itself out."

"Brenna, you go and help Boomer now. I want to talk to your mother," Lysander said, ruffling the little girl's hair.

As usual, Brenna obeyed him without argument. Lysander looked at Chavi and she was puzzled by what she saw in his eyes. Too many emotions for her to single out one and define it. He picked up her hand and slipped her arm through his. "I believe we need to have one of our famous heart-to-heart talks. Come on, let's walk by the river."

"Dirk won't tell me what he plans to do now and he got very angry when I suggested we go back to England."

"There's nothing left for him back in England either," Lysander said flatly.

"But—your parents' estate—" Chavi began.

"Remember when he went back and spent eight months there, just before you were married? He disposed of everything then."

"Disposed?"

"Gave it away. To the church, as a matter of fact. An act of penance, he said."

"But why?" Chavi asked, aghast.

"You have to remember how well he was doing here then—before the endless droughts and small disasters began, before the price of wool dropped. How could he have known how bad things would get? You know how severe his financial losses have been these past few years."

"He never talked to me about such matters," Chavi answered dully. "Why did he give away what you had in England? How could he do that? It was half yours."

Lysander stopped and gripped her hands. "No, Chavi, it was his to do with as he wished. I was grateful he financed my expedition to the gold fields. He wasn't obligated to, under the terms of my father's will."

"You said giving away his inheritance was penance. For what?"

He drew her down on the riverbank and sat staring across the water. She could almost feel him doing battle with himself and hear his unspoken question . . . *Shall I tell her everything, or not?*

At length he spoke quickly, as though afraid if he paused he'd think better of it. "Believe it or not, we were a church family, and our father, the younger son of well-connected landowners, rose in the hierarchy of the church to . . . well, never mind. We, his sons, were supposed to live lives beyond reproach. But I suppose like most young men we were both a little too fond of the pleasures of the flesh—drink and women. The daughter of a very fine old family was impregnated. When she learned she was not to be offered marriage, she attempted to get rid of the baby, and killed herself in the process. Her father, in a blind rage of grief, hired some men to hold down the man he believed to be the seducer while he took a hot poker and a knife and disfigured him."

"Dear God!" Chavi breathed. Lysander was silent for so long that she clutched his arm. "Go on—please."

"He wanted to make sure that I'd go through life hated by every woman who laid eyes on me, and, of course, he succeeded. Better to have killed me. Perhaps better even to have castrated me so that I'd no longer want a woman. As it was, I was cursed with this parody of a face and a man's longing for a woman."

"But you married—you had a son."

"My wife was blind. She lost her sight in an accident shortly before I met her. She never saw my face, or the reactions of others who looked at me. Looking back, I think our marriage was some sort of compromise, a bargain. Her blindness in exchange for my disfigured face. We both poured all of our love into our son because at that time in our lives we were too damaged to love one another. We came to Australia, away from everyone, and started Twelve Mile. After a time Dirk joined us. Then, when our son died and she left me, I went back to England. I wanted to die, but I wanted revenge on the man who'd disfigured me. I hunted him down like an animal and killed him. I was sentenced to hang, but my father used his position in the church and family wealth to have the sentence commuted to life in prison. It was his last act of misguided charity toward me. He cut me out of his will and never saw me again. I was left to languish in solitary confinement in prison. I escaped—by killing a brutal guard and thereby compounding my felony—shortly before my encounter with Lord Moreland."

Chavi digested this grim story in silence for several minutes, then asked, "The sheep station was yours?"

"No, it was Dirk's. He put up the money to start it. When our parents were killed in a train accident, Dirk was at last overcome with guilt and remorse. He followed me here, wanting to make amends."

"Amends? Wait a minute . . . you said," Chavi's mind raced back over the details he'd given her. "The man who disfigured you *believed* he had the seducer—"

When Lysander spoke his voice was devoid of any emotion. "Dirk was the seducer, the father of the child, not me."

Chavi's hands flew to her mouth, formed fists to ram against her teeth and hold back her cry of anguish.

Lysander said, "After he came to Twelve Mile and fell in love with Australia, he changed—from the wild young man he'd been, to a man very much like our father, somewhat somberly religious. I knew he desperately wanted to have a son, yet was afraid he wouldn't find a woman willing to share the loneliness of the Outback. That's why I knew he'd want to marry you. Yet you haven't conceived a child with him. It almost seems like divine retribution, yet logic tells me that life doesn't happen like that."

"You never told anyone—you let everyone think it was you? Your father disinherited you . . . the girl's father carved your face into a gargoyle . . . dear God, Lysander!"

"I believe when Dirk gave everything to the church it was the gesture of a man who felt real remorse and wanted to make amends. Yet he wasn't really to blame. How could he have foreseen that in refusing to marry the girl she'd die at the hands of a back-street abortionist? Or that her father would mistakenly believe I, not Dirk, was the culprit, and have his thugs knock me unconscious that night? I no longer bear my brother any ill will. Life is a great spinning-out of events, Chavi, the ripples of a pebble flung into a pool. None of us knows where some simple little act might lead us. There are complex consequences to every single thing we do."

"That's true," she agreed. "If Lord Moreland hadn't fallen off his horse that day when I was washing my clothes in the river . . . I wouldn't be here."

"Ah yes, Lord Moreland," Lysander said grimly. "I was getting to him. Chavi, the fact is, Dirk is bankrupt. He told me last night that he'll probably work as a shearer now. You know what that means. Endless travel. No home. Now, I made a little money in the gold fields. It's by no means a fortune, but it's enough to take you and Brenna back to England."

"And Dirk, too?"

"No. He'll never leave this country. Look, Chavi, I know you're not happy with him. If I'd have opened my eyes I'd have seen it years ago. Don't waste your life with a man who makes you miserable. Go back to England and demand that Lord Moreland makes financial provision for Brenna. She's his daughter and it's her birthright."

"But we weren't married—"

"When a man fathers a child he has a responsibility to that child no matter what his relationship to the mother. Merrin is one of the wealthiest men in England, and part of that wealth belongs to your daughter."

For an instant it was as if Lysander had opened the door to the future, just a crack, and shown her a glimpse of exciting events about to happen. She was eager to move on, but saddened too that her husband didn't want to go with her, especially now that they had at last found one another. Oh, how wonderful it would be to make love every night as they had last night in that stranger's bed. But perhaps Dirk had only given in to the pleasures of the flesh because he knew they were parting. It had been his way of saying good-bye. She saw all too clearly now that Dirk felt she'd failed him in not giving him sons. Hadn't Lysander as much as told her so?

"With Merrin's sponsorship, you could have a house in London—friends, theaters, parties. Riding in the park, holidays on the Continent—"

"Stop!" Chavi cried. "I'm convinced." She turned to him, her eyes shining. "Lysander, you must come with us. I can't do it by myself."

"Have you forgotten? I'm wanted for murder in England. I can't go back. I'll hang if I'm caught."

Chavi felt some of her excitement dissolve. He said, "But I'll keep in touch, and I'll tell you exactly what to do. Perhaps I'll go to Ireland. You and Brenna could visit me in Eire. It's a short voyage from Liverpool."

The thud of hooves interrupted their conversation, and looking up, they saw Dirk guiding his horse toward them. In a flash of intuition Chavi said, "He asked you to tell me he was leaving me, didn't he? He can't be bothered with Brenna and me while he goes traveling from one station to another with the shearers."

Lysander's silence told her the answer. In the instant before Dirk dismounted, Chavi remembered how tender his lovemaking had been in the enclosing darkness the night before, and how her own body and mind and soul had joined with his in one perfect moment of total union. That man— had he been real—would never leave her. It must, she decided with numbing regret, have been a dream, after all.

She paid scant attention to her husband's litany of woes. In her mind she was already back in England. No longer an ignorant gypsy wench. The woman she had become, with Lysander's help, would be more than a match for Lord Moreland.

25

It was evident the moment Andrew reached Merrinswood that he wasn't the only visitor. Several carriages and a couple of motorcars waited on the driveway. As he walked up the terrace steps the front doors opened and a man carrying a black medical bag came out. They stared at one another for a moment, then Andrew spoke. "I'm Andrew McGreal, Doctor Harkness—you took over my practice."

"Yes, of course, how are you?" They shook hands. Harkness looked at him curiously. "What brings you back after all these years?"

"Since I'm arriving unannounced, perhaps I should inquire as to the nature of your visit? Is someone ill?"

"You hadn't heard? Lord Moreland had a stroke."

Andrew waited to hear the extent of the affliction, but Harkness said, "You must stop in and see Mrs. Tremayne. She's spoken of you fondly for many years and was disappointed she never heard from you."

"Yes, of course," Andrew murmured, wishing he'd written to the Merrins instead of coming in person. He could hardly confront a sick man.

At that moment Sarah Merrin came hurrying out of the door calling for Doctor Harkness. She stopped as she caught sight of Andrew. He removed his hat and said, "Good afternoon, Lady Moreland. Please forgive the intrusion, I had no idea your husband was ill."

She was still a handsome woman, her golden hair only slightly silvered. "Andrew? Doctor McGreal? Please go into the house—I'll join you in a moment." She turned to Doctor Harkness. "You left your stethoscope. Here it is."

Handing him the leather case, she turned to Andrew

again, who still stood on the same spot. "I can't believe it. I never expected to see you again."

They walked into the great marble hall and Andrew saw through the open door of the drawing room that several visitors were gathered there in quiet conversation. Sarah said, "Let's go into my study to speak privately."

Andrew said uncomfortably, "My visit couldn't have been more ill-timed. I don't know what to say. I had no idea—"

"My husband came home from the hospital yesterday, that's the reason for all of the visitors."

"Ah," Andrew said, relieved. "Then it was only a mild stroke?"

She looked away. "He's almost completely paralyzed and unable to talk. I thought if I brought him home . . ."

"I'm so sorry. Have you asked Harkness for a second opinion? Sometimes—"

"Oh, yes. Everything that can be done for Richard is being done. Please, sit down. I'll ring for tea."

"No, no, please don't bother. I had tea on the train."

They sat down and Sarah asked, "Where have you been and what have you been doing? I always hoped to hear that you had found Jean."

"I did find Jean. We're married."

She stared at him. "But, we thought—you mean . . . oh, my God! Why has she never come to see her children? Not a word, all these years! How could she have been so cruel?"

"Please don't judge her until you have all the facts."

Sarah jumped to her feet, an icy glint in her eyes. "There are no facts to justify abandoning one's own children."

"Please," Andrew begged, "hear me out."

He began to tell her all that had taken place, and after a moment she sat down again, listening intently.

Even to his own ears the reasons he gave for never having returned for Robbie and Emily sounded hollow. Had he really been afraid that forcing Jean to remember both the joy and the pain of her past would sever her fragile hold on reality? Or were his reasons more selfish? Was it simply that he didn't want to share her with her children? He faltered, appalled at the possibility. If there was divine judgment, then no wonder his marriage to Jean had become an addiction to a hopeless need. His guilt and shame, which he'd believed were due to his recent patronage of prostitutes, perhaps had its origins in deeper sins that he'd refused to acknowledge, even to himself.

He became aware of the silence that had fallen. Sarah stared at him, her expression no longer angry, merely one of deep sorrow. "And now? You've come here alone. Why?"

"I came . . ." *To demand money to take Jean to Vienna to undergo a new and unproven method of treatment.* How could he possibly say that after almost ten years? He'd given up that right when he kept silent about the children, and when he married Jean, forcing her to share the spartan way of life he'd chosen. Jean was his responsibility, not theirs.

He brushed his hand across his eyes. How painful it was to suddenly look below the surface of the water and see the jagged mass of the iceberg of one's own unconscious motives. He had nurtured self-righteous anger and an insidious need to punish Richard for what he'd done to Jean while overlooking his own part in perpetuating her condition.

"Yes?" Sarah said.

"To find out . . ." he stammered, "if Jean might see her children." He hadn't known he was going to ask.

Sarah looked at him coldly.

He said in rising desperation, "Please don't blame Jean. She doesn't even remember that she has children."

"*You* knew, Doctor McGreal."

"All right, I knew. Don't judge me for what I did without considering what your husband did. He committed her to an asylum where she underwent frightful shock treatments."

"*If* he committed her, then she was mentally ill at the time. Since Richard is totally incapacitated and unable to give us his side of the story, we can only rely on what the doctor at the asylum told you, that Jean was suffering from hysteria and delusions. You yourself admit that it was a long time before she even spoke to you, and that she has no memory of what happened to her."

Andrew rose to his feet. He supposed even Richard's wife couldn't conceive of him doing such a monstrous thing to Jean to get her out of his life. "I won't detain you any longer," he said stiffly.

He started for the door, but Sarah asked quietly, "How and where would you like to arrange for Robbie and Emily to meet their mother?"

※   ※   ※

Sarah urged her horse forward at breakneck speed. The wind whistled in her ears and her hair escaped from her hat and flew behind her. At length, when rider and mount were both exhausted, she drew in the reins and leaned forward against the damp mane of the animal. Anger and revulsion still washed over her in clammy waves. She threw back her head and cried out, the high keening wail of a grieving Apache squaw. Her voice echoed about the lonely moors, fading away into the mists.

She had not cried out like that when Lone Wolf was killed, and in fact her cry was not one of grief, but letting out a rage that surely would poison her whole body if she kept it inside.

Despite what she had said to Doctor McGreal, Sarah didn't doubt for a second that Richard had indeed callously committed Jean simply to get her out of the way. But what right did Andrew McGreal have to burden her, Sarah, with that knowledge now? Richard was locked in a nonfunctioning shell of a body and could not be held accountable for past misdeeds.

But more importantly, she loved Robbie like a son and felt a maternal possessiveness. The idea of Jean suddenly reappearing to demand the rewards of motherhood she had scarcely earned embittered her. Besides, Sarah relied heavily upon Robbie to help run the estate. Jean would probably expect her son to move to London with her and her husband.

Was her savage cry of anguish, Sarah wondered, at the prospect of losing Robbie, just as she had lost Hakan? But surely Robbie loved Merrinswood too much to leave?

Another thought surfaced, growling through her mind like an angry bear. *Richard's will left everything to Hakan.* It was Hakan, who knew nothing about the estate, who would inherit Merrinswood; not Robbie. And she, Sarah, would have brought that about.

She swayed dizzily in her saddle. Be careful what you want, they had said, because you might get it.

Hakan stood beside the canopied four-poster bed and looked into his father's eyes. Hard cobalt eyes seemed to be all that was left alive in his sunken face. Those eyes expressed pain and rage, (and perhaps) panic.

Shocked by how old and shrunken his father looked, Hakan wondered why he didn't feel more pity. It had been years since they'd seen one another, so perhaps the decay and deterioration that had turned a robust handsome man into this pathetic parody of a human being had been a gradual one, not wholly caused by his illness.

His father's eyes were fixed on him in what seemed to be a silent plea, but for what? His mother had said his hearing wasn't impaired, so Hakan cleared his throat and spoke. "I'm sorry to see you like this."

He tried to think of something else to say, but they were strangers meeting in the alien territory that belonged to Death, where words were meaningless.

When the doctors told his mother that Richard was very weak and might have only days left to live, she had insisted—against their advice—on bringing him home to die. What a miserable business a slow death from a lingering illness was, Hakan thought. How much better to fall in battle, cut down quick and clean and still in full flower of manhood. Was that why he'd stayed in the army? To escape the fate that had befallen his father?

No, he'd never considered it. He'd agreed to go at first because he thought perhaps the Life-way of a British soldier might resemble the Live-way of an Apache brave. How wrong he'd been! In the army there were no summer months on the rancheria, peacefully harvesting nature's bounty, hunting game, singing and dancing, and playing the games, which balanced the exhilarating clash of opposing warriors and swift raids on enemy camps.

He missed the comradeship of the Apache braves, which he'd never been able to duplicate with Englishmen. In the beginning, they had kept their distance, regarding him as some strange beast they were forced to share quarters with. He remembered vividly a conversation he'd overheard between two of his superior officers after his first campaign. The colonel had said, "I never saw another untried young officer like Oliver. He kills like an animal—quick and clean and without remorse." The other officer had responded, "Is there a better way to kill?" Then the colonel said, "A purely physical specimen, that lad. I doubt he's got much upstairs. Not that it matters." They had chuckled about it. Hakan had pondered long and hard about that particular exchange, and later it was he who rebuffed any advances made in friendship.

Feeling his father's eyes boring into him, Hakan said, "I have seven days' leave. I'll be up to see you again. At the moment the drawing room is full of people who wish to welcome you home."

Hakan clasped his father's limp hand. The skin felt as dry as a dead leaf, ready to crumble under his touch. Richard's eyes sent angry messages that disturbed Hakan. To be so helpless, to be trapped inside a useless body . . . Hakan placed his father's hand back on the counterpane and was glad to escape from the claustrophobic room.

He met Danior halfway down the stairs. "Come on, let's go for a ride. You look as if you need to get into the fresh air," his friend told him.

Hakan glanced down the staircase, thinking he should be at his mother's side, but Danior added, "She's in the study with one of the visitors. Would you believe Doctor McGreal has come back after all these years?"

For a moment the name was meaningless. Then Hakan remembered a thin, sandy-haired man with a hint of a Scottish burr in his voice and a slightly secretive look in his eyes. It amazed Hakan that so many people had come to pay their respects to his father. There had been a parade of tenant farmers, villagers, and tradespeople, in addition to relatives and friends. Earlier that day Lord and Lady Dunstan had called. Gilbert, whom Hakan hadn't seen since that terrible weekend, was said to be abroad on holiday, and his stunning sister, Nelia, had married Charles Pettigrew, breaking Robbie's heart. They had gone to live in the south and were rumored to be experiencing financial difficulties.

As they reached the bottom of the stairs the drawing room door opened and Emily emerged, followed by Robbie. Looking at Emily's pointed features, discontented mouth, and mousy hair, it was difficult to believe that she and the golden-haired Robbie were twins. Even the thick-lensed glasses Robbie had to wear couldn't disguise his handsomely sculpted features, and the engaging smile that lit up his face.

Robbie asked, "Is f-father awake?"

"Yes," Hakan answered. "But you should ask his visitors to stay only a moment, I believe."

Emily pulled the drawing-room door shut, then asked in

a sharp whisper, "Well? What do you think? Will he last the night?"

Robbie gave her a reproachful look and Danior exclaimed, "You are the bloody limit, Emily."

She tossed her head and glared from one to the other. "Oh, don't pretend you don't resent this deathbed ritual he's putting us through. Or that you didn't wish he'd had the decency to die right away."

"Do you hate him so?" Hakan asked, genuinely surprised.

"*Everyone* hates him. Oh, it's all right for you, you went away and never came back. We're the ones who stayed and endured the old tyrant. And as for you, Danior, I wouldn't be surprised if you hadn't concocted some gypsy potion and caused his damn stroke. God knows he made your life a misery with his constant taunts and cuffs on the ear. Then there's Robbie—father had a different method of attack for him." She mimicked her father's most sarcastic tone: "My *other daughter*, Robert, don't you know, is *so feminine* . . . such a priceless little sissy."

"What about you, Emily?" Hakan asked. "What did he do to earn your hatred?"

"He reminded her everyday of her life how plain she is," Danior said. "He told her that a woman's only function is to be beautiful."

"Look, you chaps," Robbie said nervously, "this is n-neither the time nor place for such a conversation. Besides, Emily d-d-doesn't mean what she s-says."

"Don't I? James has been away a long time, he needs to have his eyes opened. Are you aware that your father has humiliated your mother for years with his affairs with other women? Everyone knew about them. The only reason she stayed was because she wanted to mother Robbie and Danior. And, of course, to keep the nest warm for you."

Hakan glanced at Danior, who didn't deny any of Emily's accusations. Hakan felt a spark of anger and knew now why he felt so little pity for his stricken father.

"If he's dying," Emily said in a low voice, "the question is . . . what becomes of the estate? Will it pass into the hands of a man hiding in the army under an assumed name? I think not. Therefore, I shall have to see to it that Robbie inherits."

"So," Hakan said, "the vultures are already circling." He turned to Danior. "You were right. I do need fresh air."

"I've got two horses saddled and waiting," Danior said.

They rode in silence through the wintry chill of the late afternoon until they came into sight of the trees of Coombe's Woods.

Hakan reined his mount so suddenly that the chestnut stallion reared on his hind legs and whinnied in alarm. Hakan stared at the stark winter-bare branches of the trees etched in charcoal against a pewter sky.

Danior, whose horse had cantered ahead, wheeled around and came back. His dark gaze followed the direction of Hakan's mesmerized stare. Guiding his horse alongside Hakan's, Danior clasped Hakan's arm. "We have to go there, sooner or later."

"I wasn't aware we were riding in this direction—I thought we were heading for the moors," Hakan said in a voice that seemed to be coming from far away.

"Tell your father what happened there," Danior urged. "Before it's too late."

"No! What purpose would it serve to pick at old bones at this late date? You know how that episode shamed me."

"For pity's sake—they got you drunk and tied you up. There's no shame in one man being tricked by three. Hakan, you heard Emily. You've got to fight for your birthright—now, while your father's still alive."

"Don't worry, nothing will stop me from inheriting. What happened in Coombe's Woods has nothing to do with it."

"It has *everything* to do with it. All right, your father's marriage to Jean Leighton wasn't valid so Robbie's a bastard—besides, your father couldn't stand him, so you'll be named heir. But Emily knows why you went into the army under an assumed name. She was up on the landing that day you came home and she listened at the door to your entire conversation with your father and mother. Robbie told me about it. The minute your father dies she'll bring charges against you. The police in this country never close the books on a murder, Hakan. You've got to clear yourself now."

"You want me to cross a bridge before I come to it. How can we foresee what might happen?"

"Hakan, listen to me, for God's sake. I was a little boy then, a terrified gypsy lad sure the whole world was out to hurt me. I'd seen Pas bullied and beaten by village louts, you bound and stripped naked, carried unconscious into the woods—"

"Danior, shut up! We've talked about this before and the answer is still no!"

Danior's grip tightened on his arm. "Your father may be dying. Tell him the truth."

"It doesn't matter to my father. It didn't matter ten years ago, it doesn't matter now. A scandal was avoided, the whole thing hushed up. That was my father's only concern."

"What about your mother? Do you know the pain we've caused her? Hakan, you made me swear to keep silent, but I can't any longer. If you won't tell them, then I will."

Hakan closed his eyes and allowed his mind to whirl him back to that night when he'd lain naked on the decayed leaves, wrists and ankles bound, while Sir Randolph Leighton stood over him and tossed a heavy branch back and forth from one hand to the other while his boot pressed down on Hakan's chest until it was difficult to breathe.

"I'm going to kill you, Indian," Leighton had said. "I want you to know that you're going to die. I'm going to smash your skull, and with each blow I'm going to remember that because of you my sister's children are bastards, motherless, and God only knows what's happened to her."

Hakan had twisted aside and the first blow had landed on his shoulder. The second smashed into his ribs. Cursing, Leighton lashed out with his foot, kicking Hakan in the groin, at the same time bringing the tree branch down on the side of his head.

Stars exploded in his eyes and he felt a trickle of warm blood run down his ear. Bracing himself for the next blow, he saw through dazed eyes that Leighton suddenly stiffened, the branch still held over his head. His mouth dropped open in surprise as his body jerked, chest flung out, spine arched. A faint gasp came from his lips as again a convulsive spasm passed through his body. The branch slipped from his hand.

He staggered, clutching the air, and it was then that Hakan saw the small boy who had crept up behind Leighton. In the predawn darkness Danior stood, transfixed with horror, as Leighton collapsed, the handle of the carving knife that Pas had sharpened to a fine edge protruding from his back.

Danior still held in his other hand the leather sheath that

had protected that most special of knives, the one Pas had made razor-sharp to demonstrate his skills.

Leighton wasn't dead. Glassy-eyed, unintelligible gurgles coming from his throat, he fell across Hakan, soaking him with blood, and fastened his hands around Hakan's throat.

Hakan felt himself slipping back to oblivion, and fought to stay conscious. But the choking fingers were doing their work and the darkness closed in. Distantly he heard a child sobbing and the sound was his last link to reality.

Danior had saved his life, of course. Even in the child's terror, he had grasped the handle of the knife again, pulled it free, and plunged it into the man's back over and over again, until Pas, still weak from his fever, staggered out of the hidden glade and stopped him.

Hakan was aware of what had happened, but dimly through the veil of fading senses. Pas had instructed Danior to go back to where they'd left their belongings and find a pair of trousers for Hakan to wear.

When the boy left, Pas crouched beside Hakan and cut his bonds. "We heard the others bring you here—heard this man say he would kill you. Danior ran and got the knife. The man is dead. Oh, Holy Mother, what will happen to the boy now?"

Still dazed from the blow to the head, Hakan sat up slowly. "Nothing will happen to the boy. I give you my word. He saved my life and no one will ever know it was he who used the knife. Take him to the village and leave him at the doctor's house. I'll send someone for him. Then you get away from here—don't tell anyone what happened."

"But—you would . . . *farsi a pezzi per qualcuno* . . . you would tear yourself to pieces for a boy you hardly know? You will be accused of this," Pas had said.

"I am James Merrin, son of Lord Moreland. Nothing will happen to me," Hakan had said.

Nothing will happen to me. . . . How wrong he'd been! He was more isolated from his fellowman now than he'd been then. He was a soldier, whose only purpose was to kill. Not in defense of his people or his own territory, as he would have done as an Apache brave, but in order to expand and maintain a distant empire.

The first time he and Danior were alone after Leighton's death, Hakan had asked how the body managed to travel from Coombe's Woods to a bog on the moors. "Pas and I put him on the cart and took him there," Danior answered. "Pas said it would look like a robbery. Besides, the other two who took you to the woods had to believe you *both* left—and Leighton was crossing the moors when he was accosted by a robber."

A cold wind came from the direction of the woods, ruffling the chestnut stallion's mane. "Hakan?" The memory pictures faded as Danior's insistent voice intruded. During the past ten years Danior had begged Hakan many times to let him tell what had happened in the woods that night, but Hakan had refused. Now Danior said, "Consider this: With your father's illness, and you coming back to Merrinswood again after all these years, the village gossip will begin again. It will hurt your mother. She at least should be told it was me, not you, who killed Leighton."

Hakan shook free of his hand. "You think it will hurt her less to know you killed him? Danior, she probably loves you as much, if not more, than she loves me. I'm a stranger to her now. You're much closer to her."

Danior stared in the direction of the woods as night shadows raced across the sky and the first star of the evening appeared. "That first time I saw Pas . . . months after it happened . . . when he found out you'd been sent away . . . he said, *tutti i nodi vengono al pettine*—literally, all knots come to the comb . . . one's deeds have to be accounted for, sooner or later. He told me I must tell your mother and father. But I was afraid to then. I was safe and warm and well-fed for the first time in my life, and I pretended to myself that you meant it when you said the army would be a fine life. Pas never mentioned it again, but I knew he was sad that you were being punished for what I'd done. Then when I got up my courage and told you that we had to tell the truth—"

Hakan sighed deeply. "We were both ignorant boys and Pas a foreigner in a strange land. All three of us expected to die for the crime, and none of us considered Leighton's part in his own death. But it's all past and done. I'm telling you now what I told you then: Forget about it."

"I can't! Everytime I see you, I feel your sorrow grow deeper."

"You think it's because I was sent away to be a soldier? Danior, I could be playing polo on the lawns at Merrinswood and be as miserable as I am sticking my saber in some poor unfortunate native. Don't you understand? I lost my sense of knowing who and what I am. But I'll regain it again, I swear to you. On the day I become the seventh Earl—Master of Merrinswood." He tugged on the reins, turning his mount to return to the great golden house and all that it promised for the future.

Andrew waited until Doctor Harkness's morning surgery was over, then walked up the path and rang the doorbell. Mrs. Tremayne, swathed in woolly cardigans and shawls, her face more lined and withered than Andrew remembered, answered the door.

Peering at him nearsightedly she said, "Afternoon surgery starts at three."

"Mrs. Tremayne, don't you remember me? Doctor McGreal. I came to see you, not Doctor Harkness."

"Oh—yes, the doctor said you were back. Come in." She gave him a reproachful smile. "You never sent so much as a card. Thought you'd forgotten all about me."

"I'm sorry. So much happened . . ." It was probably a mistake to visit her, Andrew thought, but it was too late now. She led him into the kitchen and offered him tea. He told her of his marriage, without telling her of Jean's mental problems.

Mrs. Tremayne pulled a long woolen muffler from a drawer and wrapped it around her neck. "Perishing cold today, isn't it? You know, if you'd seen fit to send me your address, I'd have forwarded your letters to you. Here, you drink your cup of tea and I'll go and get them."

She bustled off, leaving him to wonder why she'd kept letters for ten years and what possible value they'd be to him now.

He didn't open the yellowed bundle of envelopes until after he'd left. He tore open a couple of ancient unpaid bills, and then was surprised to see the envelope with the Australian stamp.

Chavi . . . the gypsy girl who had borne Lord Moreland's illegitimate daughter . . . so that was where she'd gone. She had written asking him to give her address to Danior and tell him that as soon as she had the money she'd send for him.

But that was ten years ago. Danior was now a university student with a doting adoptive mother. He probably wouldn't want to emigrate.

Missed opportunities, Andrew thought, how they changed the course of lives. Well, he'd see that Danior finally got his sister's letter. There was time to deliver it before he caught the London train.

Halfway back to Merrinswood, Andrew suddenly realized that if Richard Merrin were dying, it would be interesting to see which of his children, legitimate or otherwise, would inherit the vast estate and great golden house.

26

Jean twisted her gloves nervously as the hansom cab came to a halt in front of a tea shop near Hyde Park. She turned to Andrew and said again, "You know how I hate to meet strangers. Why did you insist we come here?"

Andrew picked up her ice-cold hand and massaged it gently, inwardly castigating himself for not having prepared Jean for the meeting with her children. The trouble was, she refused to discuss the possibility that anything good had happened to her before Andrew came into her life.

Her sleep was often disturbed by nightmares, and when he held her, calming her, she would whisper, "My shining knight, how could I live without you? You saved me from an existence that was worse than death and damnation. Sometimes I dream that I am standing before a closed door, and I'm filled with indescribable dread. The door starts to open and I know that behind it are concealed horrors too terrible to face. I know that dreadful things were done to me in the asylum, but I can't remember them. Thank God, I can't remember! I never want to remember anything before you came to rescue me, my beloved husband."

Upon his return from Yorkshire, he'd told her that he had visited her former home and she became hysterical. "Don't tell me about it! I don't want to know."

When he'd tried to explain, she fainted dead away, and after coming to her senses she had spent the rest of the day staring vacantly at a blank wall, in that way she had when he first took her from the asylum. Afraid she would slip away from him again, he gave up.

Andrew confided to Noel that he regretted telling the twins their mother was still alive. "Jean walks on such a delicate edge, balanced between the present and that void she was in, I'm afraid if I push too hard she'll fall back into it."

Noel replied bluntly, "Arrange a meeting on neutral ground. Surely coming face-to-face with her own children will accomplish what all your gentle pleading has failed to bring about. You have to make her face the past, Andrew, for your own sanity as well as hers."

As he helped his wife down from the hansom cab, Andrew felt that Noel's advice now seemed less sound. Fortunately, it would be at least an hour before Robbie and Emily arrived at the tea shop from their respective schools. By then he would have broken the news of their existence to Jean, and he hoped, prepared her for the reunion.

There were several other patrons in the small shop, which was dimly lit as the shutters were closed against the afternoon sun. Andrew ordered a pot of tea and Eccles cakes and selected a table as far from the door as he could find.

"Are you going to tell me who we are meeting?" Jean asked, ignoring her tea. "And why they are so important that we must leave Noel and Brigid to handle all of the patients without our help."

He reached across the table and clasped both of her hands in his. He was gambling on her natural reserve to keep her from either making a scene or leaving abruptly. In front of strangers she would surely listen quietly to what he had to say.

"We have come to meet a young lady and gentleman. They are twins, named Robert and Emily Leighton. Jean, my darling, they are your children."

All of the color drained from her face. She tried to pull her hands away from his, but he held them more tightly and went on rapidly, "You loved them, Jean, and they loved you. You were a wonderful mother."

Her lips were white and her eyes had grown enormous, like dark pools under storm clouds. She was trembling violently.

He was about to begin at the beginning, with her marriage to the Earl of Moreland, when the bell over the tea-shop door jingled and he looked up to see Robbie and Emily enter. Damn, they were too early! He wanted to shout to them that they must go away and come back when he'd finished telling Jean the whole story of their birth and lives together. But it was too late, they were crossing the room to their table. Andrew cursed his stupidity for not telling Jean about them before this late hour.

Robbie was so eager that he stumbled over his feet and, his gaze fixed nearsightedly on his mother, smiled happily at her. His twin, unsmiling, approached more slowly. Jean remained frozen in her chair and seemed to shrink backward when Robbie, his arms outstretched as though he might embrace her, stepped too close to her.

Hastily Andrew moved between them and shook Robbie's hand. Andrew murmured, "Let's all sit down, shall we? This is something of a shock to your mother. As I explained at Merrinswood, she suffers still from the amnesia that has afflicted her all these years."

As Andrew pulled out a chair for Emily, Robbie awkwardly took the seat next to his mother, still staring at her in wonderment. "Th-thank you for c-coming," he said, his voice cracking with emotion. "W-w-we're s-s-s-so h-happy—"

"Do shut up, Rob," Emily said rudely. "Your stutter is worse than ever. Let's hear what she has to say for herself."

Andrew felt his heart sink into his boots. Back at Merrinswood, Emily's lip had curled in scornful disbelief when he'd explained that their mother had had a nervous breakdown, and now it seemed clear that this sullen young woman would not easily forgive or forget what she considered to be Jean's abandonment.

Robbie leaned forward and said earnestly, "W-we w-want y-you t-t-to know th-that we understand. It m-m-must h-have b-b-been awful f-for you. P-p-ple . . ." He lost the word, struggled to go on and became more flustered. He was scarlet from the effort to speak, and it was excruciating to watch him.

Andrew silently willed the young man to find the words that would reach Jean, but Robbie shook his head in desperation, then spread his hands in resignation, indicating he was too overcome to continue.

Emily jumped vindictively into the gap. "It was also awful for us. Left without a mother, in the home of a man who took pleasure in constantly pointing out our shortcomings and reminding us of our dependence upon him. Whispered about . . . disinherited . . . shamed by the knowledge that we were illegitimate. Now we learn that we were abandoned and ignored by our mother for years, as she was intent upon making a new life for herself."

"I explained to you that I never told her about you," Andrew said. "I was afraid the shock would return her to the vegetative state I found her in at the . . . hospital. Please don't blame your mother. She only learned of your existence this very afternoon."

Jean, who had sat quietly throughout this exchange, now spoke directly to the twins, looking politely from one to the other. "I must apologize for the inconvenience my husband has caused you. Obviously this is a case of mistaken identity. You see, I was never married before, and have never had any children. Therefore I cannot possibly be your mother. I do hope you find her, however. Good afternoon."

To Andrew's astonishment, Jean rose and nodded a good-bye, as detached and impersonal as a stranger, then swept out of the tea shop. Robbie bit his lip, tears glistening behind the thick lenses of his glasses, while Emily merely shrugged and said, "I for one don't want her back. She's mad as a hatter. She'd be an embarrassment to us."

Andrew started to explain that Jean had been through hell and truly didn't remember them, but stopped short as he realized he couldn't leave Jean wandering the streets by herself, especially since he had no idea of her present state of mind. Muttering that he'd be in touch, he rushed after her.

She was walking past a row of small shops, glancing vacantly in the various windows. When he caught up with her, however, she wheeled around on him in tight-lipped anger. "Why did you torment me with such a fabrication? You deceived those young people, made up a story that I'm their long-lost mother simply to convince me that I once allowed a man to lie with me and do unspeakable things to me. Oh, Andrew, how could you?"

She spoke with more passion than he had ever seen her

exhibit, and her denial struck more fear into him than her withdrawal once had. "Jean, please—" he pleaded.

Her eyes narrowed. "Must I remind you of the promise you made before we were married? That you would never violate my body? If you made up this story about my mythical motherhood in order to demand conjugal rights, then the ploy has failed. I shall hold you to your promise or I shall leave you."

Andrew felt despair such as he'd never known before.

Chavi paced restlessly about the tiny sitting room of the boarding house in Carisbrook, one eye on the mantelpiece clock. Brenna was asleep upstairs and the landlady had said a gentleman caller could be received here, so long as he left before midnight.

The sky was still light this spring evening, although it was after nine, and Chavi wished Danior could be seeing her for the first time in disguising lamplight, despite the fact that her condition didn't really show yet. What a trick of fate that she'd been pregnant the last time her brother had seen her too. How would she explain to him why she'd left her husband at such a time?

Of course she hadn't realized for several weeks that she was carrying another child. By then she and Brenna had been aboard a steamer sailing for England. They'd said good-bye to Lysander in Sydney.

Brenna, who didn't know why he could never return to England, had clung to him, crying inconsolably, despite his assurances that he'd soon set sail for Ireland and would write to them from there. Chavi asked, "But why don't you come with us? You could get off at some foreign port before we reach England and take a ship from there."

"I have some investments here I want to dispose of first. Besides, I'll probably work my passage aboard as a merchantman. It will pass the time and shipmates will be less horrified by my face than fellow passengers."

Wishing passionately that she could think of something to say that wouldn't sound like contrived reassurance, Chavi said instead, "You're the best friend I have in the world, Lysander. Thank you for all you've done for Brenna and me."

As the moment of parting drew nearer, she was surprised when he took her into his arms and held her tightly. He didn't speak, but she could feel his breath whispering in her hair. After a moment he thrust her away from him and said, "Go on, they're getting ready to pull up the gangplank." When she and Brenna reached the deck they looked down at the quay, but Lysander was already striding away without a backward glance.

Those first days aboard the ship she'd thought she was seasick, despite calm southern seas, when every morning she lost her breakfast. But by the time the voyage was over she'd missed two monthly cycles, her breasts were excessively tender, and she knew another baby was on the way. Her first suspicions sent her mind racing back to that one perfect night of lovemaking, but that had been nothing but a dream, brought on by exhaustion and too much strong drink. Dirk had performed his usual perfunctory marital obligation a few nights earlier, and it was ironic that he should choose to end their marriage just when the purpose of it was about to be fulfilled.

Well, she wasn't going to write and tell Dirk his fondest wish was coming true, because she had no idea where in the vast Outback he was traveling. Besides, she was as relieved to be done with him as he was with her.

Sometimes when she remembered that night of transcendent love, she was disturbed by vague possibilities and strange, half-seen images that perhaps were best left unexamined. When she was a very small child there had been a wise old Romany woman named Mithuna who had tried to fill the void left by Chavi's dead mother. Chavi remembered Mithuna telling her how powerful the human mind was. That thoughts could become more real than what actually happened. She advised Chavi never to dwell on disturbing thoughts, because that breathed life into them. So it was better to tell herself that night had been nothing but a dream.

She had gone to Merrin Quarry and made discreet inquiries. Lysander had been right about life being a great spinning-out of events. The lady with the lovely dark blue velvet eyes who had brought Brenna into the world was no longer the Countess of Moreland. Richard Merrin's first wife had returned—she'd had a son too, but he'd left shortly after their arrival—and this Lady Moreland had raised the other lady's twins along with Danior, who had recently entered Cambridge. The idea of Danior at university was overwhelming to Chavi.

She'd promptly written to Danior and in due course received his excited response. He'd be home for Easter, which was only a couple of weeks away, and would come to see her before he went to Merrinswood.

But the most disturbing news was that Richard Merrin was a hopeless invalid, unable to speak or even to move. Chavi felt a little pity, but more anger that she'd be denied the pleasure of confronting him—she'd even brought the silver filigree necklace and earrings, the butterflies with sapphire eyes that he'd used to trick her into accompanying Lysander, with the intention of flinging them in his lordship's face.

A letter had arrived for her, *poste restante* at the Carisbrook post office, from one Lysander Smith of Dublin, Eire. She hadn't replied yet.

The doorbell rang and Chavi heard the landlady's heavy footsteps cross the hall. A moment later the sitting-room door opened and Danior stood on the threshold.

For an instant they stared, taking in every detail of the other's appearance. Danior was still her good-looking, swarthy-skinned, black-eyed brother, but he was dressed like a gentleman and carried himself with the air of confidence that only money and good schools truly achieved.

Wordlessly, they moved toward one another and embraced. For a long minute they were both too overcome with emotion to speak. Then Danior said, "You look marvelous, Chavi. I'd have known you anywhere, yet you're quite different from what I remember. Still beautiful—but, my God, you're a lady now!"

He spoke in the same cultured tones used by the Merrins and Lysander and Dirk. Chavi supposed that to acquire that perfectly polished English one had to use it from childhood. She said, "I'm not sure I'd have known you—you've grown so, and look at your fine clothes."

He glanced around the small room. "Brenna is in bed, I suppose? I'm sorry I couldn't get here earlier. The trains were packed and I couldn't get on the earlier one."

"You'll meet your niece tomorrow. Come on, sit down. I want to hear every single thing you've done."

"Australia! I still can't get over you going to Australia. . . . You said in your letter you were married, but your husband didn't come with you."

"Well, you see, there was a terrible bush fire—we lost everything. When Dirk gets back on his feet . . ."

They talked in rapid bursts, sometimes simultaneously, gulping down information and offering it in huge slabs, and each knew there was much the other was not yet ready to divulge.

She learned that Richard Merrin had been incapacitated for months now, and that Doctor McGreal had married Jean Leighton. "It's all very mysterious what became of her. Apparently she had some sort of nervous breakdown, lost her memory and doesn't even recall her own children. Poor Robbie was undone when he met her. Anyway, Doctor McGreal wrote and asked Sarah if he could bring her to Merrinswood."

Another of Richard Merrin's victims, Chavi thought grimly. How many lives had that man ruined? She'd have expected him to come to a more violent end than the slow deterioration from his illness. She noted that Danior called the Countess "Sarah," but referred to her husband as "Lord Moreland."

Chavi asked, "Do you like it at Cambridge?"

He gave a slight grimace. "My studies don't come as easily to me as Robbie's do—I doubt I'd have got through Eton without his help. I love music. I learned to play the piano, had some voice lessons, but had to give them up when I went to Cambridge. Lord Moreland reminded me that I shan't be able to make a living singing. But oh, how I wish I could."

"I'd love to hear you sing."

"Then you shall. In fact, we're to have a party for Lord Moreland's birthday—just family and close friends—and I know Sarah will want you to come when I tell her you're here."

Chavi was too taken aback by this suggestion to respond, but Danior didn't notice as he went on to tell her about his friend Pasquale, who had taught him so many wonderful songs and entranced him with the stories of the operas. "I don't see him much these days, I'm afraid. He's a wanderer—like we used to be."

"Do you ever think of our traveling days? Do you miss being on the road with all your belongings in a painted caravan?"

His dark eyes met hers and there was no need for him to answer, or for her to tell him of the lonely prison of her life at Twelve Mile. Besides, they both knew they could never go back to being Romany children again.

At length Danior said, "What are your plans now?"

"I have a little money. I'll find a cottage to rent and then a job. Eventually I hope to go and live in London, but not until—" She stopped herself from saying *after the baby is born.*

"What sort of a job?"

"I don't know yet. Luckily Brenna's old enough to look after herself when she comes home from school."

"You must let me help you. Sarah gives me a generous allowance."

She looked at the empty grate in the fireplace, thinking that she didn't want Merrin money filtered through Danior. Brenna had a right to her own allowance.

"What is it?" Danior asked. "There's something you're not telling me."

"Do you remember when I asked you to go to Merrinswood and fetch Lady Moreland to help me—when Brenna was being born?"

"Of course. Why?"

"Did you ever wonder how I'd met her in the first place?"

"How did you?"

"I'd gone to Merrinswood to try to see Lord Moreland—to tell him I was having his baby."

Danior's face darkened. "Oh, God! Brenna is . . ."

"His daughter. He paid a man to get us out of his life, out of the country. That's how I ended up in Australia."

A small cry escaped from Danior's lips. He leapt to his feet and raged about the small room. "That bloody swine! I'll kill him."

Chavi jumped up and caught him in her arms. "Hush— someone will hear you. Sit down. There's something else I must tell you."

The Dublin steamer nudged the Liverpool landing stage and from the deserted stern Lysander scanned the waterfront. Atop the Liver Building the great wings of the mythical bird were lost in a thickening fog that eddied in patches, dancing ghostlike upon the river and drifting in small gray veils about the Pier Head.

A misty landfall was more than he'd hoped for, but he could hardly expect to hide in the fog for this whole foolhardy visit. He stroked his beard. The thick growth of brown hair still felt as though it belonged to someone else. His mirror told him that the full beard, mustache, and side whiskers, grown as a disguise, also hid a number of ugly scars. Of course, there were still deep scars on both cheeks, and one side of his nose still bore the angry purple legacy of the worst of the burns, but he'd noticed lately that people didn't react quite so violently to his appearance, so perhaps the whiskers helped.

The other passengers were lining up at the rail, impatient for the gangway to go down. Lysander waited in the shadows, wondering what Chavi would think of his beard.

Chambers, you're a fool to even wonder if it would make a difference to her. There had been times when he'd cursed the sadistic fates that had caused their paths to cross, and times when just watching her, being with her, had been enough to give him a measure of peace, if not satisfaction. She'd forced him to live again and he was still unsure how he felt about his resurrection.

At first he'd felt only a protectiveness toward her baby. The infant Brenna had reminded him a little of his own doomed son, and Lord Moreland's casual impregnation of the young and innocent Chavi had recalled Dirk's careless sowing of wild oats.

When had it begun to change? When had concern for the welfare of the child blurred with regard for the mother? When had his own unbearable tensions driven him away from both of them? At what point in time had he realized that he loved them, wholly, unconditionally, irrevocably? Brenna with a fierce protectiveness he'd thought never to feel again, and Chavi with a hungry yearning that raged in his loins as well as his mind and soul.

Enough to consider a desperate masquerade. Yet even as he castigated himself for his trickery, he reveled in the memory of its reward. A man could perhaps exist the rest of his life on such a memory.

And now his love drove him back to England, risking his neck to find out how she was faring.

The passengers were disembarking now. He wished Chavi and Brenna were waiting for him on the dock, but they had no idea he was coming, and Chavi would have been aghast at the risk he was taking. But he couldn't stand being away from them any longer. Each parting, no matter how brief, had been like excising a part of himself. But this time, not knowing how they were faring since Chavi had written only one brief letter that told him nothing, had been the worst period of all.

How he'd missed Brenna's sweetness and loving ways, but it was Chavi who filled him with a longing that surpassed any he'd ever known. Chavi, so beautiful, so bright and eager to devour every scrap of knowledge he could offer. So spirited and courageous. She had been the only one—man or woman—who'd ever stood up to him. How he loved and desired her! What superhuman restraint he'd had to exhibit! He'd showered all of his love and affection upon the child, hoping that Chavi might notice that a large part of it belonged to her.

But why should she? She saw him as a deformed monster incapable of a man's feelings for a woman. As if the scar tissue covering his face had also choked off his physical and emotional needs. Oh, why did life have to be so damned physical? Why did people see only the outer façades of one another? If only they had the power to see the beauty or ugliness, the selfishness or the compassion that lay within. If people could be turned inside out, wouldn't they then know the truth of one another? But that was a foolish wish, because there'd been a time when he'd been as ugly inside as out and he was glad neither Brenna nor Chavi had known it.

Chavi's only letter indicated that she'd rented a cottage on the outskirts of Carisbrook and had met her brother again. She didn't mention the Merrins, which was maddening, because Lysander was afraid she had given up the quest to demand Brenna's rights.

Lysander, who had long ago stopped calling himself by his given name and had come to think of the name of the Spartan general of unscrupulous character as his own, decided he'd been a fool to think that Chavi would be able to confront Merrin alone. Years ago when they'd met, he'd despised the man on sight, but recognized the power he wielded.

Descending the gangway to set foot on English soil again after so many years, Lysander allowed himself to wonder if perhaps as soon as Merrin's will made provisions for Brenna, he should simply kill the man.

27

Noel Brannock continued to scrape the remnants of the fetus from the woman's womb as he railed at Andrew. "Your wife refuses to go to Vienna for treatment. The brief encounter with her children was disastrous. How long are you going to permit this stalemate to continue? Dammit, Andrew, Jean's not going to make any changes unless you insist on it. She's happy the way things are, so why should she?"

Andrew concentrated on looking at the patient's face, keeping his eyes averted from the curly triangle of pubic hair, bloodstained now as Noel worked quickly to undo the damage the woman had inflicted upon herself. The instrument she'd used—a knitting needle in all probability—had perforated the wall of the uterus. Could Noel be aware, Andrew wondered, that this particular young prostitute was one whose services he'd used himself? Oh, God—could that fetus have been his?

The woman on the table groaned and stirred. "Give her a little more ether, will you?" Noel said.

Placing the ether cone over the woman's face, Andrew told himself that at least nowadays a few doctors like themselves were beginning to be a little more concerned with "women's problems," which in the early days of his profession had been all but ignored. Would the day come, he wondered, when they also learned to give serious attention to the problems of the mind?

"Well?" Noel demanded. "What are you going to do?"

"As a matter of fact," Andrew said, "I've already bought tickets on next Monday's train to Yorkshire. I think perhaps seeing Merrinswood again might restore Jean's memory."

Noel's silvery gray eyes looked up briefly. "Does Jean know what you have in mind?"

Andrew dribbled ether onto the cone until the patient's

eyelids fluttered and closed. "Not yet. I intend to tell her this afternoon when we walk in the park."

"See that you do," Noel snapped. "I'm as concerned about you as I am about Jean. You can't live indefinitely in the vacuum you've created for yourself."

Andrew was grateful that at that moment the clinic's outer door opened and a moment later Brigid came into the cramped space of their operating room. "Sorry it took so long. Sure, and the pharmacist got a wee bit chatty when he found I wanted to pay the entire bill. I should've just picked up what we needed." She stroked the patient's hair back from her brow. "How is the poor thing? Are you ready for me to pack her vagina yet?"

"Uterus is perforated," Noel said. "Andrew, I won't need you now Brigid's back. You can take Jean for her walk—and don't come back until you've told her."

"Told her what?" Andrew heard Brigid ask with concern as he slipped out of his apron and left. Brigid still regarded her husband with the awe of a student nurse, and Noel's word was usually law. Despite her youth, she didn't seem to mind that Noel had decreed there would be no children. He'd once confided to Andrew that he practiced anticonception because he wasn't fit to father another child after what had happened to his poor mad daughter Bess.

It had occurred to Andrew then that, if a miracle happened and Jean ever allowed him in her bed, the possibility of pregnancy would definitely have to be eliminated, since Jean could not have more children. But he'd face that situation after the unlikely miracle occurred.

Andrew went up the narrow uncarpeted staircase to the upstairs rooms that had been home for so long, dreading what he knew Jean's reaction to the proposed trip to Yorkshire would be.

Perhaps, he thought as he opened the door to their attic room, Noel was right. The only way to convince her was to take her back to Merrinswood and attempt to rekindle her memory of her life there with the familiar sights of the house and surrounding countryside. As a last resort, perhaps she should see Richard in his sickbed, and be made to understand that he could no longer hurt her.

Although Jean had refused to go to Vienna to undergo analysis with Doctor Freud, saying that she didn't want to know what had happened in her early life, Andrew had taken it upon himself to write to the doctor, at first to express his admiration for *Studies in Hysteria,* and then to thank him for publishing the astonishing work *The Interpretation of Dreams,* which dealt not only with dreams, but also the structure and functioning of the deeper layers of the mind, the unconscious. Andrew was particularly interested in Freud's theory of repression and devoured every paper Freud wrote. When the doctor sent a brief response to his letters, Andrew wrote back and told him about Jean. He hoped there'd be a reply before they went to Yorkshire.

He had begun to talk to Jean, late at night, when she was half asleep and relaxed, about her very early life. She had even relived her grief at the death of her father, whom she had adored. Andrew was carefully leading her toward the blank part of her memory, her life with Richard, and each childhood memory she shared brought them a step closer.

When he reached their room Jean was already dressed for their walk in the park. She sat waiting with her usual patience, a madonnalike serenity cloaking her like sunlight gilding a statue. She had changed little since he'd known her; no wrinkles had appeared on her smooth skin and her eyes were more lustrous than ever, liquid like the ocean at eventide. He'd never been able to define what it was about her that caused him to worship her so. Her gentleness, her deep compassion for all of humanity? Was it the way she inclined her graceful neck, so that her head appeared to be weighted down by the abundant coil of burnished hair as she listened to all the little lost cries for help from the world around her? She worked as hard as Brigid, caring for the children who crawled like beaten animals into the clinic, and he'd seen her take the shawl from her own back to give it to a shivering old woman whose only home was a litter-filled alley.

No, if that were all there was to his feelings, then he'd have been content to love her chastely. But he could look at her tiny waist and the gentle swell of her bosom and become so aroused he had to leave the room. It was her face he saw above the willing bodies of the prostitutes who lay under him and feigned the act of love.

He realized that he was standing at the door, adoring her with his eyes, and she was smiling at him. She asked softly, "Are you ready for our walk, dear?"

They took a hansom cab to Hyde Park and walked beneath trees bursting into new leaf. The daffodils were a nodding yellow carpet everywhere they looked and the air was heady with the explosion of spring. But with the sense of rebirth came a pressing urgency, an awareness Andrew felt that time was slipping away and could never be recaptured. Jean had to face her past so that she could go forward into the future with him, and it was his task to bring that about.

He hated to lie to her, but a subterfuge seemed to be the only way. "I've been thinking that it's time we had a little holiday," he said as they came to a bench and sat down.

"A holiday? Can we afford it?"

"Noel insists that I take a larger share of our fees, and of late we've had a number of paying patients, as you know."

Jean averted her eyes. She didn't like to discuss those particular patients. In a time when old-school doctors still didn't examine female patients and merely prescribed sugar pills or patent medicines heavily laced with alcohol for their "feminine complaints," when few doctors performed surgery of a gynecological nature, Noel and Andrew were gaining a reputation as physicians who treated female disorders seriously, and who advised women worn-out with childbearing how to avoid pregnancy. The word was passed from one woman patient to another, and in a remarkably short time the nature of their practice had changed. Noel decided that having Brigid present when examinations took place would help alleviate the problem of the patient's embarrassment, but Andrew knew that he could never ask Jean to talk to a woman while he or Noel disappeared under the sheets to palpate her abdomen or examine her cervix. Jean would grit her teeth and hold clamps and not faint when the most gruesome amputation was necessary, but she would not acknowledge that women had any reproductive parts to their bodies.

"Where shall we go?" Jean asked.

"I'd like to surprise you. But I'll tell you this—it will be out in the countryside, far from the city."

She clapped her hands delightedly and he felt a twinge of conscience. He hadn't shared with her the letter he'd received from Sarah Merrin in response to his request.

Jean gave no sign that the railway station at Carisbrook was familiar to her as Andrew helped her down from the train. It was a blustery day, colder here than it had been in the south, and the wind knifed through their clothes.

"This is a wonderful part of the country," he told her as he took her arm and led her along the platform. "A meeting place where the moors and farmland and woods all come together to display their absolute best. A short ride in one direction and you're surrounded by heather and gorse, and the rolling moors seem to stretch to infinity. Go the other way and there's fertile fields and fat cattle and woolly sheep—turn around and you're in the middle of dense woods."

Jean held the brim of her hat to keep it from blowing away and so didn't see the carriage and four sleek horses waiting for them. Andrew was surprised to see that Sarah had come to meet them herself. She stood beside the carriage, the wind whipping tendrils of silver-streaked wheat-colored hair from under her hat, and her slender frame leaning like a willow determined to weather the storm. He saw Sarah's gray eyes were fixed on Jean and his fingers tightened around Jean's small hand protectively, although he realized that Sarah's intent gaze merely indicated curiosity about the woman with whom her husband had gone through a form of marriage.

"We shall be staying at a grand house, Jean," he whispered hurriedly, "right on the edge of the moors. The lady of the house is an old friend of mine and she's come to meet us. Her husband is a helpless invalid."

Jean received the news calmly, taking it as just one more surprise unfolding in the succession of surprises Andrew had promised for their holiday.

They reached the carriage and Andrew made the introductions quickly, anxious to get out of the wind. He tried to read Sarah's expression, but it was inscrutable. Jean thanked her for the invitation and Sarah glanced at Andrew questioningly, no doubt wondering about Jean's detachment, in view of her recent meeting with the twins. This visit had been carefully timed so that Robbie and Emily would be home for the Easter holiday in a couple of days.

When the carriage was traveling down the lane toward Merrin Quarry, Jean said, "I was sorry to hear of your husband's illness, Lady Moreland."

"Thank you. But please, you must call me Sarah."

"How lovely it is here," Jean said, looking out of the window. Sarah's eyes met Andrew's and he knew she was

baffled by Jean's dreamy lack of recognition of her surroundings. The carriage went through the village and Jean looked
at the shops and cottages and church as if they were completely new to her. Then they passed Coombe's Woods,
traversed the farmland of Merrin tenants, and she still gave
each passing view the detached interest of a stranger.

He held his breath as the amber-tinted walls of Merrinswood
came into view, hundreds of daffodils spilling down the
rolling lawns adding to the golden aura of the house, but
Jean showed no flicker of recognition.

Barlow came to greet them and Andrew saw that the
stony countenance of the butler crumpled as he looked down
on Jean. He whispered, "Welcome home, milady," and the
greeting was addressed to Jean, not Sarah, but Jean was
staring in wonderment at the magnificent carved staircase and
upper gallery, and did not hear him.

Sarah said, "I'm sure you must be exhausted by your
journey, so I'll send trays up to your rooms tonight to spare
you the ordeal of dinner. Nowadays we always seem to have
guests who come to pay their respects to my husband and
linger for a meal." From the slight edge to her voice, Andrew
deduced that many of the guests were keeping a death vigil,
which Sarah found painfully distasteful. "As a matter of fact,
it's Richard's birthday in a couple of days and a celebration
of sorts has been planned."

Jean said, "I am a little tired."

A footman showed them to two rooms on the second
floor that were connected by a small sitting room with a
balcony overlooking the as yet unblooming rose garden. Jean
appeared enchanted by the view, but then turned and saw the
four-poster bed through the open door to one of the bed-
rooms and her smile was replaced by a look of sudden fright.

Seizing the moment, he went to her and drew her down
on a sofa. "Tell me what you're thinking—what you're
feeling."

She was trembling. "I feel . . . suffocated. Please, we
must leave. We can't stay here."

"Do you feel you've been here before?"

"Yes. No. I'm not sure—don't make me stay, please."

"It would be impolite to leave now. Has something come
back to you? Share the memory with me—talk to me, Jean.
Say whatever comes into your mind."

"I don't like strange beds. One never knows what has happened in them."

"Were you ever frightened in bed as a child?"

She turned away from him, but he grasped her shoulders firmly and turned her around to face him. "You remember something from your childhood, don't you? It has nothing to do with that bed, or this house."

He had to tread carefully, he knew. She still stared in hypnotic terror at the bed in the shadows of the other room. But was it terror, or was it fascination? He said, "When I was a little boy my grandfather gave me a rose-colored stone that he said was quite valuable and would bring me luck. I was so afraid I'd lose it that I buried it in the garden." He smiled at her. "When I tried to dig it up again, I couldn't find it."

"Oh, how sad. Did you ever find it again?"

"For a long time I was passionately interested in rock collecting. It didn't occur to me until comparatively recently that I was still searching for the stone lost in my childhood."

"And what made you realize that?"

"When I began to study the teachings of Sigmund Freud."

She drew back, her eyes narrowing. He went on quickly, "We all look for things lost in our childhood, Jean. What was lost to you that makes you want to run from that four-poster bed?"

Her eyes were drowning. She whispered, "My innocence."

He wrapped his arms around her as she began to cry softly. Her words came out in a feverish flood, as though a cork had popped, releasing them. She told of worshiping her father, of how he had devoted his life to caring for his motherless twins. Then one night she'd awakened from a nightmare, terrified, and had gone to his room.

Andrew knew what had happened before Jean's stumbling words filled in the details. She had found her father having intercourse with their housekeeper. The little girl had crouched in the shadows and been afraid her father was killing the woman, because she gasped and moaned. This occurred shortly before her father's death, from heart failure, and in the child's mind his death was punishment for his "crime." Andrew held his wife and they talked far into the night, and all the while he wondered if around them the walls of Merrinswood contained a secret more deadly than a little girl's loss of innocence.

✳   ✳   ✳

Sarah felt like a woman standing before a crumbling dam, unsure which hole to plug to keep the raging waters beyond from breaking through. She stood at the foot of the stairs, steeling herself to go up to her husband's room; wishing she hadn't agreed to Robbie's suggestion that they have a birthday party for his father as usual. "I th-think he'd like it, I really do. He knows what's g-g-going on around him. It would be a s-sort of . . . affirmation. A statement that we haven't b-buried him yet."

Could it be that Robbie, the son most abused by his father, showed him the most compassion? Could anyone be that altruistic? Was Robbie concealing his real feelings, even as his twin expressed hers so nastily?

But Robbie was right that his father's mind was as clear as ever, which made its entrapment in a useless body even more horrible. Sarah had devised a method of communication with Richard, having him blink his eyelids in response to questions to indicate a "yes" or a "no." Richard had blinked once, a "yes" to having his birthday party as usual.

There was no way then Sarah could have known that on this, the day before the party, Jean Leighton-McGreal would be ensconced in a guest room.

Sarah had been appalled by the horror story related by Andrew McGreal, even though she had welcomed him and Jean with outward calm. There was surely a point when the mind becomes impervious to further shocks.

She wondered what her reaction would have been if she had known years ago of Richard's vile acts. Even more troubling was the thought that it had been her decision to bring Hakan to England that had precipitated Richard's actions.

Then too, there was the disturbing possibility that the McGreals would try to exact some sort of payment, vengeance even, from Richard. Since he was a helpless invalid, with little time left to live, according to his doctors, would Hakan be in some way involved? The sins of the fathers . . . ?

Sarah's tension and worry, held rigidly inside her, manifested itself in severe headaches and sleeplessness. The only way she was able to sleep at all was to imagine herself back at Lone Wolf's side, the two of them riding with the wind at their backs and all of Apacheria spread before them in the sunlight.

Andrew was convinced that the only way to fully restore

Jean's memory was for her to see Richard, and Sarah saw no way to refuse the request, despite Richard's condition. He would simply have to face the woman he had come close to destroying.

Apparently Jean had not recognized her children when they were reunited in London. Emily had been furious about the encounter, but Robbie defended his mother's actions. Robbie was such a deeply kind and compassionate young man that Sarah wasn't surprised when he came to her and said haltingly, "I-I want you to know that I have loved you very much. You were the one who was there when I had pneumonia. You comforted me when I was s-so afraid of returning to school. I was only seven when my mother went away and I don't b-believe I'd have survived without you. B-but she *is* my mother. . . ." He looked at her imploringly with his dreamy blue eyes, silently begging her to fill in all that was missing from his painfully stammered declaration. He added, "And yet, s-sometimes I feel I have two mothers."

"I understand. I love you for being just as you are," Sarah said, and embraced him.

As she went slowly up the stairs to Richard's sickroom, she wished he had been kinder to Robbie. Her footfall was silent on the landing as she approached his room. The door was ajar, just a crack, and she heard the low, rasping voice before she reached the room.

"You rotten old swine—go on, lie there and glare at me all you like. Sod you, is what I say. You deserve this, you stinking bugger. You think anybody feels sorry for you? Everybody's laughing up their sleeve because you got what you've been asking for all your putrid life, you devil. It's judgment on you, that's what it is. It's better than you going to hell—because we can all sit back and watch your misery—"

Angrier than she'd ever felt before, Sarah flung open the door. Mrs. Braithwaite spun around to face her. An ingratiating smile appeared on the housekeeper's wrinkled features, but not quick enough to disguise the hateful sneer she'd worn a moment before as she bent over Richard.

"Oh, Lady Moreland! I was just looking to see if the maid had changed his bed linen—"

"Get out, Mrs. Braithwaite," Sarah said, her voice shaking with rage. "*Now.*" She moved to the side of the bed, picked up Richard's limp hand and held it, never taking her eyes off the housekeeper. "Go to your room, pack your belongings, and leave this house at once. You're dismissed."

The woman turned and fled.

Sarah looked into Richard's blazing eyes, and said, "I'd like to take a whip to her. Instead, why don't I read to you until you fall asleep? A nap will help you put the incident out of your mind."

She picked up one of the books that lay on the table beside his bed, hardly aware of what she was reading. Bringing Jean to see him would have to be postponed until later, his poor beleaguered mind had all it could cope with at present.

Sarah was surprised by the depth of the pity she felt for her husband. It was an emotion he had never aroused in her before. Theirs had been a love-hate relationship from the start, a battle of wills that perhaps had added zest to both of their lives. It had also been a business alliance. But what struck her as most strange now was how much she missed his companionship since he'd become ill. She hadn't realized how much time they spent together, riding their horses over the moors, taking trips to the city in the motorcar to attend the theater, entertaining family and friends. She even missed their constant verbal dueling, and the sharp pleasure she felt when she came out the victor. It surprised her to recognize that passion had not been lacking in their lives, it had simply taken a form other than physical contact.

Somehow they had built a life together, and it had not been totally unpleasant once they'd both accepted that it could never be a real marriage again. Of course, she had had to act as a buffer between Richard and the children and suspected he had been too harsh with them when she was absent. Richard had always been ruthless and arrogant and managed to earn the hatred of so many people. Sarah wondered if she'd become inured to the worst of his character flaws because he had treated her with a measure of respect not afforded anyone else in his life. Was that why she felt pity for him now? Or was it simply that she felt contempt for anyone who would take advantage of his helplessness? Was it really possible to overlook all of his cruelties, refuse to judge him, and adopt the impersonal attitude of a nurse for a disagreeable patient? Faced with the wreckage of such a formerly robust man, was she letting her compassion blind her to his sins?

After a while his eyes closed, although she wasn't sure if he was asleep or feigning slumber to free her from the chore of reading to him.

Looking at her husband, Sarah wondered how many of his other visitors had taken the opportunity to berate him. Had every footman and upstairs maid harboring some grievance slipped in here to vent their hatred as the housekeeper had? What about Richard's family and so-called friends?

Even without having his enemies remind him, perhaps now that he was paralyzed his mind had become more active, dwelling on his misdeeds and all the people he'd hurt. A slow death allowed time to reflect on one's life; perhaps it was a form of damnation. Did he feel remorse? Sarah found it difficult to believe Richard was solely responsible for all of which he was accused. Surely, she thought, we all participate to some degree in our own fate?

She turned away abruptly, assailed again by a primitive emotion that refused to let her be. Lately her thoughts had taken her back, time and time again, to her years of living with the Apache. How strange that the Life-way of the *Tin-ne-ah* made even more sense now than it had then.

Not that she had any desire to return to the American Southwest. Life there without her beloved Lone Wolf would be intolerable. Besides, creature comforts meant more to her now than they had then, and she knew she was no longer young enough or strong enough to endure the harshness of life in the wilderness. But so much about the Apache culture lingered in her mind, directing her thoughts and feelings.

But perhaps she was remembering the Apache Life-way because the wild West show in which Sam Rutherford was appearing would be opening in London shortly.

28

Jean was frightened. Her terror ran in icy rivulets along her veins, formed clammy pools on her skin, manifested itself in a painful thudding of her heart against her ribs. At her side Andrew smiled at her encouragingly, but led her inexorably along the corridor toward the sickroom.

They had spent two days strolling the house and grounds and talking endlessly, and Jean had at last admitted that yes, she had been here before. Perhaps she had even lived here. Barlow and some of the older servants addressed her as "milady" and seemed to know her. But Jean hadn't confided to Andrew that *everything* in the house was terrifyingly familiar, except for the composed and quietly watchful Sarah Merrin, who seemed to be waiting in the same way Andrew waited, for Jean to make some earth-shattering statement.

She slept little, and when she did was disturbed by confused dreams. The worst nightmare of all was one in which she confronted the closed door, trying desperately to keep it shut, knowing that something indescribably evil lay beyond. She would awaken screaming as the door began to open.

Andrew insisted she go into his room and relate her nightmares to him immediately upon waking, but usually it was he who came to her in response to her cries, although she would not talk to him until they left her bedroom.

The night before, the meaningless jumble of dream-images had led her to babble incoherently about her father, and how he'd forced the housekeeper to do something unspeakable, something more degrading even than sexual intercourse.

But Andrew had pounced on her and said, "No, Jean. That wasn't your father and the housekeeper. You told me that the moment you entered their bedroom they stopped what they were doing. You're remembering what *you* did, with the father of your children. *With Richard, Jean, who is in this house—but can no longer hurt you.* I want you to go to the sickroom tomorrow and see for yourself."

She didn't want to see Richard. Wasn't it enough that she remembered Merrinswood had been her home? Nor could she deny with conviction any longer that she'd borne children. Andrew had become angry and told her to examine her own abdomen and see the translucent marks caused by the stretching of her skin to accomodate twins.

The bits and pieces of memory floated, unconnected, through her mind. She couldn't tell what was real or imagined, or even if she wanted them to form a cohesive picture. She wanted to run away and hide, but at the same time she wanted to please Andrew.

They had reached the sickroom. The door was ajar. Inside Sarah was keeping a vigil at her husband's bedside. She said, "Come in," when Andrew knocked on the door.

Jean was sure that the sound of her beating heart filled the entire room. At first she felt relief that the shrunken, twisted features of the man lying in bed appeared to be unfamiliar, but then her eyes met his hard blue stare. She stumbled and would have fallen if Andrew hadn't caught her.

Sarah said in a strange flat voice, "Richard, you remember Jean, of course."

The closed door in Jean's mind opened fully as she gazed at Richard. Images came flying through with lightning rapidity. How he'd walked away from her, leaving her struggling in the arms of two nurses as Doctor Voigt's pale eyes regarded her disinterestedly and he said, "Delouse her immediately. Burn her gypsy rags."

Terror and confusion and slimy pond water, long strands of algae hanging on her face like a shroud, ghostly figures and loud noises all whirled through her mind. Pathetic sobbing women, frightening madwomen who tried to kill themselves and one another. The echo of her own screams fading in the void she'd created for herself so that she might hide from her tormentors.

Richard's malevolent stare, somehow intensified by the broken shell of his body, pinned her to the spot. She couldn't move. Andrew said, "Jean, are you all right?"

When the silence had lengthened unbearably, Sarah said,

"The picture on the nightstand is of Emily and Robbie when they were children."

Jean wrenched her eyes from the sick man to look at the two cherubs captured inside the silver frame. She felt a tear slide down her cheek. Her darlings, her precious twins. She felt faint as faces and places pressed into her mind, demanding recognition. Andrew pulled a chair out for her and she sank into it and he massaged her hands. She whispered, "Randolph?"

"I'm so sorry . . . he's dead. We'll talk about it later. But the twins will be here tomorrow."

She recalled the tea-shop visit with the young man who stuttered so badly and the young woman with the discontented frown. Oh, no, Jean thought in dismay, those two grownup people couldn't be her little darlings. . . . What happened to Robbie's golden curls? Why was he hiding his beautiful eyes behind thick glasses? How had Emily's rounded baby curves become so angular? When did she acquire that unattractive downward slant to her mouth? How would they ever be able to forgive her for committing the worst sin a mother was capable of?

Sarah addressed her husband. "Hilliard Stoughton will also be here tomorrow. I expect your solicitor will have some suggestions as to what should be done. Now, if you wish us to withdraw, please let me know." She spoke as if she expected an answer despite the fact that her husband was unable to speak. A moment later she turned to Andrew. "He's tired now. Please go."

Jean reclined on a chaise longue in the dimly lit room. Andrew stood behind her, his hands resting gently on her shoulders. "I want you to look back into your childhood again. Tell me what you see. Tell me whatever comes into your mind."

She was quiet for several minutes, then said, "I hated our housekeeper. She defiled something that should have been beautiful, made it coarse and ugly . . . I can still hear the animal sounds she made."

Andrew silently considered the possibilities. Could it be, as Freud suggested, that Jean had equated her own sexual impulses with what she perceived to be the defilement of love—the housekeeper's sex with her father? Or was it that when Jean married Richard, in her mind *he* had taken on the role of her father and the taboo of incest tainted their lovemaking? Freud insisted that most neuroses had their origin in infantile sexual impulses, but even if Andrew had been thoroughly familiar with all of Freud's theories and methods, they were unproven.

"She was bleeding so dreadfully," Jean said suddenly.

Andrew froze. "Who? The housekeeper?"

"The bed was soaked with blood. I'd never seen so much blood. I was so frightened. The room seemed to be filled with it. He was bending over her when I went into the room—quite by accident. I was looking for the room where I'd left my wrap. He looked up and saw me before I could withdraw."

Andrew was bewildered. Her wrap? He had pictured a little girl in her nightgown creeping into her father's bedroom.

Jean said, "He was young then. So handsome. But he looked frightened, too. He told me that she had tried to get rid of her baby and that it was too late to save her. He said that he would have to get her out of the house without anyone knowing."

Andrew's mind was reeling. Freud had been right about free association leading into the depths of the unconscious mind. But Andrew didn't have Freud's experience and didn't know what to do when Jean's revelations veered off into a new and even darker direction.

She spoke quickly, in a breathless hurry to get it out. "He made me see that a scandal would be avoided if I were to keep his secret. Nothing could be done for the girl. Besides, he'd already suffered so . . . his bride of just a few weeks had disappeared, and he'd had to endure the loneliness of the seven-year wait to have her declared legally dead. Then this new tragedy."

She wasn't talking about her father. *She was talking about Richard.*

"I don't know what possessed me!" Jean began to sob. "I was under his spell. I would have done anything for him. Anything at all. We wrapped her in a blanket and I went ahead of him, to be sure there was no one about. Everyone was still downstairs, we could hear the music and laughter. He said she must have gone into his bedroom when we were at dinner. I stayed with . . . her body . . . hidden in the kitchen garden . . . while he went for his horse. Then he took her away. . . ."

"Who?" Andrew asked. "Who was the girl?"

"A scullery maid. Here at Merrinswood. She had a family in the village and they never knew what happened because he told them she'd run away. But I knew. . . ."

"You never told anyone?"

"No. Not even Randolph. Richard was courting me then. He asked me to be his wife, offered Randolph the position of estate steward. Don't you see? I'd always have the two men I loved near me, we'd always be together. How could I betray him? It wouldn't have brought her back."

Andrew's thoughts raced back to his first meeting with Jean, shortly after the birth of the twins. She'd been in labor for two days and a night, had almost died at the hands of the midwife. It was a miracle the two undersized babies had survived. Jean must have suffered terribly. When he was called to see her she was hemorrhaging and close to death. All of Jean's experience with sex and reproduction had been terrifying—as a child seeing her father in the act with the housekeeper and thinking he was killing her, then the Merrinswood maid dying from a self-inflicted abortion, and finally her own ordeal of childbirth, which had almost ended in her own death. It was little wonder that the very thought of lovemaking terrified her.

She began to speak again, and this time referred to herself in the third person. "She loved him so, you know, and wanted him to touch her, to hold her tenderly. To kiss her lips softly and stroke her hair. But that always led to him wanting to . . . *do that*. She was so glad when the doctor said she mustn't have more babies. But he said there were other things that didn't make babies . . . she knew it was wrong, evil, perverted. Of course she refused—for a long time she *did* refuse, you know. The very idea disgusted her. But that last night . . . when Sarah was on her way to Merrinswood . . . you have to understand, she loved him, she would have done anything to stay with him . . . to be sure the twins and Randolph would be taken care of. But his real wife was coming back. That's why she permitted him to do unspeakable things, she did them herself. She hated herself, but . . . ."

Andrew couldn't fail to recognize the excited thrill in her voice. He straightened up, full realization hitting him like a blow. Jean's inner conflict hadn't been, as he supposed, a fear and dislike of sex. She felt guilt because she'd enjoyed the kind of sex that didn't lead to the "punishment" of pregnancy. Hadn't Freud pointed out that their era had honed prudishness to a fine art?

Her voice changed again suddenly. Now it was low, vicious. "Richard is an evil, wicked man. He left Sarah to be captured by Indians. The young housemaid died by his seed, if not by his hand. He let the gypsy girl have his child in the woods. Put me in an asylum. He should be punished. He deserves to die for his crimes."

29

Danior paused for a moment outside Sarah's study, then knocked on the door and entered.

She sat at her desk, writing in her leather-bound journal which she closed as she saw him. "Hello, Danior. You're up late."

He wanted to rush to her side and blurt out all that she must know before his courage failed him, but knew he must be more considerate than that. "I'd like to talk to you, if I may. I waited until now so we could be alone."

"Let's have a glass of sherry. It's been a long time since we had one of our private chats. I was afraid you felt too grownup and wordly for them nowadays."

"Don't ring for a servant . . ." he began.

She smiled. "I intended to pour the wine myself. You forget, I did not spend my entire life being waited on hand and foot."

He stirred the embers of the fire, shoveled coal from the bronze scuttle, and watched her take two glasses and a decanter from a cabinet beside her desk. The firelight played softly on her light hair and softened the lines of tension that had appeared on her face lately. He had always regarded Hakan's mother both as a beautiful angel to be worshiped and as an iron-willed woman of great courage and fortitude. She had put aside any personal desires she might have had in order to provide for Hakan and the twins and himself. Danior would gladly have died for her, which made his guilt even harder to bear.

When they were settled in front of the fire he drained his sherry quickly, wishing it were brandy, and said, "I have a confession to make . . . of an extremely serious nature."

She waited silently for him to go on.

He put down his glass and desperately searched for the right words. "I should have told someone years ago, but Hakan made me promise not to. I'm breaking my word to him now, but I know that even though Lord Moreland can't speak or move, he understands what we say . . . and I thought he should know the truth before it's too late. But I couldn't bring myself to go to him until I confessed to you. Oh, God, if I'd only had the courage to confess when it happened. Now I'm afraid you'll hate me—"

"I could never hate you, Danior. You're like a son to me."

"But if I'd told you the truth, you would have had your real son, Hakan, with you all these years. And I would have been where I belonged—in a reform school, or prison. Do they hang children who murder?"

Sarah gasped. She rose slowly to her feet, her hand flying to her throat. "You . . . oh, dear God, I should have guessed! *You* killed Sir Randolph Leighton. That was why Hakan wouldn't tell anyone what had happened that night." Her lovely features twisted in pain. "Tell me, was your friend Pasquale involved? Did my son keep silent to protect both of you? Had he realized, even then, that there was one law for the rich and another for the poor?"

Danior couldn't bear the hurt and anger in her eyes, nor the contempt in her voice. He said quickly, "Please, you must hear the whole story."

He told her everything, how Charles and Gilbert had humiliated and tricked Hakan, then carried him, bound and gagged, into the woods. He did not spare her the details of how Randolph had kicked and beaten her son, of his threats to kill him.

When he finished she sat down again, her face impassive as she stared into the fire. At times, he recalled, she was able to shut all emotion inside herself so that no one and nothing could penetrate that invisible shield. It was, he supposed, a form of protection.

When she spoke her voice was heavy. "Danior . . . we can't go back into the past, any of us. We can never undo what has been done. You saved Hakan's life. In return he protected you from any possible consequences. It's so easy to look back and say, I should have done this, or that. We can't see the whole picture at the time, so we all do the best we can on the basis of what we perceive our choices to be. We're human, so we're fallible. . . ."

She paused, and he wondered if she were still talking about Randolph Leighton's death, or if it was her own decision to bring Hakan to England that troubled her.

As if in response to his unspoken question, she went on, "You mustn't blame yourself that Hakan became a soldier. Long before Randolph's death my husband had threatened to send Hakan into the army. The adjustment and sudden transformation from Apache brave to English gentleman was overwhelming. The chances are his father would have insisted he go into the army even if you hadn't killed Leighton. As far as confessing now is concerned, I think it would be the worst thing you could do, especially for Hakan. Give him the satisfaction of knowing he acted out of love and honor, that he protected you from punishment. Don't take that away from him, Danior, because if you do, all he'll have left is the regret that his sacrifice was for nothing."

Danior buried his face in his hands, feeling great sobs wrack his body. Seconds later he felt Sarah's arms around him and she cradled his head, stroking his hair as if to soothe a child.

"You've suffered enough, my dear," she said softly. "Let go of the guilt now and hold on to the truth . . . that you saved Hakan's life."

"But . . . his father may be dying. I can't let him go to his grave believing Hakan murdered Randolph Leighton."

"My God, Danior," she exclaimed, her voice harsh. She seized his face in her hands and forced him to look up at her. "Have you ever seen Richard display one ounce of fatherly concern for Hakan? For the twins? Have you ever known him to think of anyone other than himself? Richard lies on what is undoubtedly his deathbed, raging inwardly that his body has let him down. He doesn't give a damn about anything else. Don't you understand? He's dying in exactly the same way he lived, oblivious to the wants and needs and suffering of anyone around him."

"All right, then what about Randolph's sister? Now that she recalls her past, I must confess to her—"

"And will you tell her also what her brother did to Hakan? Do you think that will make Randolph's death easier for her to bear than believing he was killed by an unknown robber? Let the dead rest, Danior. Let the past be."

Danior felt a long shuddering sigh escape him. She was right. Not only about Richard and Jean, but also about what his confession now would do to Hakan. Danior had been tormented by guilt for so long that all he wanted was to be rid of it, but now he saw that the price of easing his conscience was too high.

Impulsively, Danior took her hands in his and kissed them. "Bless you, Sarah. For your love, for your wisdom. I'll never speak of this again to anyone. I promise."

He left her and went slowly up the staircase to his room. Long ago a ragged gypsy boy had raced up these same stairs, seeking help for his sister. Had he known then that Lord Moreland had defiled Chavi, Danior thought he might well have found a knife to plunge into his black heart.

Danior had considered telling Sarah that her husband fathered Brenna, but that bit of news would have to wait. She had too much to deal with just now. Besides, Danior had yet to decide how to deal with the knowledge himself. Richard's stroke and paralysis didn't seem like punishment enough for his sins. Danior's blood boiled when he thought about Chavi and her baby being sent to the far side of the earth.

Until he dealt with his need for revenge, which must take into account the welfare of Chavi and her daughter, he thought it best not to discuss the matter with anyone, least of all Sarah.

As a liveried footman handed her down from the carriage and Danior offered her his arm, Chavi looked up at the great golden house and marveled that it was as grand and awe-inspiring as she had remembered.

"Are you all right?" Danior whispered as they followed the footman up the terrace steps.

She nodded. "Don't worry, I won't set about the old swine."

"I wish we'd brought Brenna. It might be her only chance to see her father."

"Danior! I don't want her to know. I told you, I've changed my mind. I'm not going to make any demands on the Merrins."

The footman opened the front doors for them and there was no chance for further conversation. Chavi allowed the butler to take her wrap, squared her shoulders, held her head high, and walked into the drawing room as her name was announced.

Lady Moreland, a strikingly beautiful woman with pale gold hair lit with silver, came forward to greet her. "I have been looking forward to meeting Danior's sister. How very sad that he did not receive your letter from Australia until recently. I'm sure you have a great deal to share with one another, but let me first introduce you to some of our other guests."

Before they could move further into the room, a quiet voice at Chavi's side said, "Hello, Chavi, how nice to see you again, and how very lovely you look."

Turning, Chavi looked into the dark blue eyes of Jean Leighton McGreal. For a moment the two women's eyes locked in silent acknowledgment of their shared ordeal and triumph of Brenna's birth, and the mutual sympathy they felt that each had had the misfortune to be drawn into the life of Richard Merrin. Then Doctor McGreal appeared and greeted Chavi, and Lady Moreland introduced the twins, Robbie and Emily.

Chavi had avoided looking directly at the figure in the bath chair, but she was very much aware of him. She saw guests approach, speak briefly, then move on. Despite his immobility, Lord Moreland dominated the room, like some remote god reclining on a throne to receive his subjects' homage.

Lady Moreland said, "Chavi, this is my son, James."

It took all of Chavi's control to keep an impersonal smile on her face and offer her gloved hand to the man who stood before her. As it was, she couldn't keep herself from darting a sideways glance across the room to the bath chair, to be sure its occupant was still there. James Merrin, or Hakan, as Danior called him, could have been his father, years ago. The physical likeness was uncanny. The same penetrating blue eyes, sculpted features, gold hair that seemed to burn with the fire of the sun, the imposing height, the air of command—for an instant Chavi was fifteen again and overwhelmed by a being who seemed more a god than a man.

She murmured a greeting and Hakan responded, then Lady Moreland led her over to Richard. "This is Danior's sister, Mrs. Dirk Chambers. She recently returned from Australia."

Chavi looked into Richard's eyes, eyes that glittered like shards of blue glass in his motionless features. She shivered as she wished him a happy birthday.

One of the other guests claimed Lady Moreland's attention, and she moved away. Chavi realized that Danior was still at her side when he said softly, "You remember my sister very well, don't you? Look at her, Lord Moreland, and remember. Sooner or later we all pay for our sins. Even you."

"Danior," Chavi warned, "you promised to stay out of this." She looked at Richard again. "The Romany people believe that whatever we wish on others returns to us, in one form or another. You banished me and your daughter to the far side of the earth. Well, I see you've been banished to an even worse place."

"Your daughter, Lord Moreland," Danior said. "Brenna. Remember?"

Afraid Sarah might overhear as she stood chatting with a group of guests nearby, Chavi seized Danior's arm and dragged him away. "You said you'd sing for me. Please, ask the lady playing the piano to accompany you."

While Danior was singing, Sarah slipped from the room and stood in the deserted hall. She could hear Danior's fine voice, filled with passion and vitality, but for once it did not move her. She was wracked with so many conflicting emotions she needed a moment alone to try to make sense out of her feelings.

Perhaps, she thought, it was seeing Richard for the helpless invalid he was, at the mercy of any careless remark from tonight's assembly of family and friends, that caused her to pity him so acutely. It was like seeing an old warrior stripped of his armor and left to be torn to pieces by the jackals while his former enemies looked on. Yet even while she pitied the man trapped in a useless body, she hated him. That was the paradox.

Hakan appeared soundlessly at her side. He raised his hand and touched the furrow between her eyes, then inclined his head toward the library. She nodded and they crossed the marble floor and went into the library and closed the door.

"This whole evening was a mistake, wasn't it?" Hakan asked. "It's too much of a strain on you. Taking care of him, watching him wither and die . . . that's too much of a strain on you, too. You don't owe him this loyalty. Don't do this for me, please. There is no need. I'll fight for my own inheritance, I swear to you."

"What would you have me do?" Sarah asked wearily. "Go away? Leave him? There is nowhere for me to go. This is where I belong. It's where I want to be." She gave a small, self-deprecating laugh. "At least I can be miserable in comfort here."

"Don't you ever long for our old hunting grounds? Don't you ever think about going back?"

"What would be the point? It wouldn't be the same, would it? I am not the same woman who lived as an Apache. Life moves forward, never backward."

"But he's draining you. He's dragging you into the grave with him, don't you see? He's turned from being one kind of tyrant to being another—perhaps even more deadly. I've watched you carefully since I came home. You've lost yourself. You spend all your time taking care of others, especially him. What do you ever do for yourself? No, don't answer, because I know. You allow your mind to escape into the past occasionally and pretend to yourself that the happiness you had with *Tonsaroyoo* is enough to last you for the rest of your life. Don't you see how dangerous that way of thinking is? It makes it all too easy to simply give up."

"No. No, you're wrong. You're reading too much into a little fatigue, that's all. That, and the upheaval of the McGreals coming back." Sarah looked away from his searching gaze, remembering Danior's confession. She had an uneasy feeling that there was much more that both Danior and Andrew

McGreal hadn't told her. Yet she wasn't sure she could deal with any further revelations, especially if they concerned Richard's misdeeds.

"Is this what he's done to you?" Hakan asked quietly. "Now that he's ill, have you taken all of his sins upon your own shoulders?"

Something in his voice tore at her heart, an echo of long-ago voices from a different place and time. She looked up at her son, suddenly more afraid than she had ever been before. "Hakan, don't hate him so," she pleaded.

Lysander waited until dark before approaching Chavi's lodgings. Pulling his hat low over his forehead, he lifted the door knocker and let it fall. A moment later the door was opened by a short, plump woman who squinted up at him as if awakening from a nap.

He stayed back in the shadows, away from the yellow pool of light cast by a lamp in the vestibule. Keeping his voice low, he said, "Good evening. I understand you have a Mrs. Chambers lodging with you. Would you be good enough to tell her an old friend from Australia would like to see her?"

The woman yawned. "She's out. Gone with her brother to his lordship's birthday party."

"His *lordship*? Lord Moreland?"

"He's the only lordship in these parts." She closed the door before Lysander could ask to see Brenna. Just as well perhaps; the child would be asleep by now.

He turned away, disappointed, and walked down the street. He'd sent Chavi to Lord Moreland in order to make provision for Brenna, but the fact that she was attending his birthday party surely indicated that far from being in an adversarial situation with the Merrins, Chavi and her brother had somehow become a part of their social circle. Very mysterious and disturbing—unless the gypsy brother and sister had decided to boldly beard the lion in his den, in front of his guests no less. It was a possibility. Lysander grinned to himself, wishing he could see the look on Merrin's face when he was confronted by the grownup Chavi. Well, why not? He could slip into the grounds of Merrinswood, peer in through a window, and see for himself.

The cabbie he hired grumbled that he didn't want to leave

the village because he wouldn't be able to find a return fare, but quickly agreed when Lysander told him he would not only be returning almost immediately, but promised to pay him double. The driver looked surprised when Lysander ordered him to wait on a rutted path leading to one of the tenant farms.

"Don't you want me to take you to the door then, sir?"

"No, wait here. I shan't be more than half an hour."

" 'Ere, 'ow do I know you'll come back?"

"And if I pay the return fare now, how do I know you'll wait?"

The man considered. "I might not. Seems a bit queer, you wanting to get out 'ere. It might be a mile or more up to t'house."

"But I've already paid you twice the fare here. What if I give you half the return fare now, will you wait?"

The man nodded. Lysander paid him and set off across the farmer's field to the row of poplars that marked the boundary of the Merrinswood estate. Ten minutes later he approached the house by way of the rose garden.

Lights blazed from the house and he could see a number of carriages in the driveway. A pair of liveried footmen stood on the terrace steps waiting for any late arrivals. Lysander slipped around the side of the house and climbed onto the terrace. There was a hint of late frost in the air, and the French doors leading from the drawing room to the terrace were closed. He moved quickly, sheltered by the great stone urns, to a position near one of the narrow windows flanking the French doors.

The first thing he saw within the room was a handsome dark-haired young man standing beside a grand piano, bowing to acknowledge the applause of the other guests. Danior, Chavi's brother. Lysander could see the likeness. Despite the applause, Danior was unsmiling and there was a fierce glint in his eyes as he looked at someone across the room. Lysander wasn't surprised to see the recipient of that hard stare was Lord Moreland, who slumped in a bath chair, wrapped in a plaid blanket.

Merrin's eyes, which were all that seemed alive in his shrunken face, were in turn fixed on Chavi.

Lysander caught his breath. The impact of her beauty sent a yearning racing through him. He wanted to rush to her side, to crush her in an embrace and never let go. At the same time he was filled with unbearable rage that Richard Merrin should be feasting his eyes on her.

At that moment the Merrin's granite-faced butler suddenly appeared at the window, his mouth agape as he looked Lysander full in the face.

Within the imprisoning shell of his body, Richard's mind worked feverishly. His eyes swept the crowded drawing room. They were all here. Sarah, and James, who still managed to look more like Hakan the Apache than the heir to an English title; Jean Leighton with her sandy-haired doctor-rescuer in tow, their hatred of him giving their pallid faces life; the twins, Emily—ugly girl—and bespectacled Robbie, who stammered and cringed and hovered and didn't seem to understand how his sympathy irritated his father. Probably thought he was still mentioned in the will. Brother Philip in deep conversation with Hilliard Stoughton. No need to wonder what those two were talking about. Lady Dunstan was at the piano, accompanying the gypsy, Danior, who sang in a passable baritone. An operatic aria—in Italian, no less. Did his black-mirror eyes reflect his passion for the music or his hatred of his benefactor?

Richard's gaze came to rest on the most beautiful woman he'd ever seen. Could that really be the scrawny gypsy girl, Chavi? She carried herself like a queen, and her bold dark eyes, challenging as a buccaneer's, met his in cool appraisal. Her body filled her emerald green dress with voluptuous curves and her dark hair was piled up on top of her head, corkscrew tendrils escaping here and there to give her a wild, untamed air. Oh, to be young and strong again and have a second chance with a woman like that!

James couldn't take his eyes off her either. Richard laughed inside his head. Like father, like son. It would be interesting to watch James's reaction when he learned the exotic dark-haired beauty was the mother of his half sister. The child Brenna wasn't present. Pity, he would have liked to have seen her.

Family and guests approached him in ones and twos to wish him happy birthday and go through the motions of drinking to his health. How droll! His health was gone forever. It was amusing to watch their eyes and know that practically everyone in the room at one time or another had harbored thoughts of killing him. *Bloody cowards—do it!* He dared them to . . . he'd welcome death. The state he was in was a thousand times worse.

He was getting tired. Sarah knew immediately and came to him. She laid her hand on his arm and asked if he'd had enough and he blinked once, *yes*. Looking up at her it occurred to him with a startling flash of realization that of all the women he'd lusted after, Sarah was the only one he'd ever come close to loving.

She motioned for two footmen to come and carry him back up to his bed. He fixed them with a baleful stare to let them know how much he resented their aid.

Strangely, in the instant before he fell asleep, he thought of none of the people present that night. The face that came back to haunt him was a hacked parody of a human being . . . the man he'd paid to take Chavi to Australia. The man had apparently done considerably more for the gypsy girl than he'd been paid for. Richard wondered idly if the pathetic creature had fallen in love with her. Pity that living monster was so far away—perhaps he'd have done what all the others were too civilized to do. . . .

Andrew awakened abruptly to find someone shaking his arm. "Doctor McGreal! Doctor, please wake up."

Blinking, still stupid from sleep, he saw Lord Moreland's nurse bending over his bed. The curtains had been drawn back from his window, letting in the first glimmer of dawn.

"You've got to come quickly, Doctor. It's an emergency."

He sat up. "Lord Moreland?" She nodded. "Go back to him—I'll be there right away."

She scurried off and he fumbled in the half-light for his dressing gown, then found his medical bag and followed.

Too much excitement from the birthday party? Another stroke? Heart failure? Andrew considered the possibilities as he hurried to the sickroom. Lord Moreland was Doctor Harkness's patient, but Andrew was here and available. Why did an emergency have to arise now?

Entering the sickroom, he hurried to the bed and looked down. Even before he pressed his fingers to Richard's neck to check for a pulse, or bent to listen for a faint breath of life, it was obvious the man was dead. But Andrew saw at once other signs that filled him with dread. The bruises on Richard's face, bulging eyes, the gaping mouth, blue lips . . .

Quickly he closed Richard's eyes and pulled the sheet over his face. The nurse stood at the foot of the bed, weeping. He said quietly, "Go and wake Lady Moreland."

If Sarah asked him to sign the death certificate, he would, Andrew thought. Why should anyone doubt that he died a natural death? He glanced at the spare pillow, wearing a fresh pillowcase still stiff with starch, lying innocently beside Richard's head. The rest of the bed linen looked crumpled and slept-in, but someone had changed that one pillowcase. To dispose of the telltale signs it had been used to smother Richard?

The words Jean had uttered hammered in his head. *He deserves to die for his crimes.*

BOOK III

30

SOUTH AFRICA,
MAY, 1900

Hakan had been ordered to lead a band of fifty scouts on the march to Pretoria. His own scouting abilities were by now legendary. He had taught his men to distinguish between a cloud of dust kicked up by moving troops and one caused by the elements. They could follow a trail unerringly or slip unnoticed behind enemy lines.

But he hadn't been able to instill in them that sixth sense that warned of danger when there were no obvious signs. So, before Hakan could stop him, a young Australian lieutenant had gallantly ridden to investigate a white flag flying over a farmhouse, only to be blown out of the saddle by a hail of riflefire. It was the only instance of treachery Hakan had witnessed on the part of the Boers, whom he respected for their tenacity and courage. It also brought back to him in vivid detail the death of his Apache father. Lone Wolf had died because he also believed the message of the white flag.

The young lieutenant was still alive. They could see him moving feebly, but no one came out of the farmhouse to aid him. Hakan ordered one of his men to ride at once to the approaching main column to deliver the intelligence they'd gathered, and then told the rest to take cover.

"Sir, you can't get to him, it would be suicide," somebody protested.

"Perhaps not. There's an old Apache trick . . ." He surveyed the terrain. There was a cluster of boulders a few yards from the fallen lieutenant. "I'll try to drag him to the cover of those rocks. When I get him into that ravine, two of you enter from the rear and carry the lieutenant out. I'll keep the Boers pinned down in the farmhouse."

He rode at full gallop, hanging over the side of his horse with only his fingers and the tip of his boot showing above the withers of his mount, so that in the farmhouse they saw an apparently riderless horse.

The Boers were taken by surprise, and Hakan pulled the wounded lieutenant to safety just before they shot his horse. Incredibly, the wounded animal staggered after them into the ravine, collapsing only a few feet away. Hakan ended the animal's suffering with a bullet in the head.

The lieutenant was carried to safety as Hakan kept up rapid fire on the farmhouse. Mauser rifles spat back, and he raised his head once too often above the shielding rocks. Something struck his right temple, scarcely registering pain, sending his pith helmet flying, and in the half second of consciousness left to him he thought, *I'm hit*. Then the earth and sky met and he was lost in the chaos.

When he came to his senses the Boers were swarming all over the rocks around him. There were too many to have been contained in the farmhouse. Reinforcements had arrived while he was unconscious, and he was their prisoner. They'd wiped the blood from his face, tied a bandage around his head, and rope around his wrists, then left him where he lay because they were under attack.

He lay imprisoned in the rocky ravine, listening to the snap of riflefire. The afternoon sun had dried the blood on the rag they'd tied around his head, but still the flies came in hungry swarms. Nearby the carcass of his horse had attracted another buzzing cloud of insects.

He could see the Boers moving from cover to cover in their natural fortress, but the British force was out of sight, somewhere out there on the veldt, the kopjes hiding them from view. He could hear their disciplined volleys, a rippling roar at regular intervals that was heralded by the Boers dropping out of sight. The Boers watched the British officers, and when the signal to fire was given, dropped behind cover. The hail of lead sprayed the rocks around him. Hakan inched closer to the protective hulk of the dead horse.

When the volley ended, the Boers returned the fire. Minutes later a new sound intruded, the savage snarl of approaching shells. The English gunners had located them, Hakan thought; they'd be torn to shreds.

A shell screamed into a group of about eight men, blowing some to pieces and maiming the rest with shrapnel. The remaining Boers held their position, as Hakan expected.

They were a motley crowd, dressed in all kinds of farming clothes, from young boys to old men. Settlers defending their land who reminded Hakan of the Yankee settlers the Apache had tried in vain to drive away. The land itself was a little like Apache country. Rocky boulders and low scrub, some of the kopjes not unlike the mesas of the American Southwest. He felt a curious sense of displacement, identifying with both the attackers and the attacked. Loss of blood, probably. Time to think about getting out of there before all of his senses blurred again.

Listening to the British fire, Hakan considered again their foolhardy notion that the enemy should don uniforms and battle on the open veldt rather than wearing what they pleased and hiding in the kopjes to fight. It had cost them the American colonies, and was taking a terrible toll in lives in South Africa.

Young Englishmen learned their attitudes about war on the playing fields of Eton and Harrow. They wouldn't shirk their duty, they would sacrifice themselves willingly for the "team." War, like cricket, was a game. They'd play it fairly, by the rules, and if necessary, die honorably.

But Hakan hadn't attended Eton or Harrow, and had grown weary of the bloodletting in this war. He was sickened by the endless piles of dead soldiers, by the unrelieved suffering of the wounded. And far away the men who never saw the look on a soldier's face as he died invented more deadly weapons, more sophisticated machines to impose their will on others, and planned costly campaigns. The whole world remained as fascinated as ever by war. He'd seen the biograph in action, that modern marvel the cinecamera, which took moving pictures. For the most part pictures were staged and heavily infested with propaganda. And he'd met several war correspondents, Rudyard Kipling, young Winston Churchill, a couple of boisterous, hard-drinking Australians whose names he'd forgotten. They were all sending home tales of glory that would perpetuate the myth of the noble warrior. There'd always be wars, he realized, for the simple reason that men *liked* wars. To his fellow officers war meant promotion and excitement and too bad about poor Tommie with his head blown off.

Would he also have tired of killing had he lived as an Apache brave? Or had this aversion come hand in hand with the other aspects of his "civilization" by the English? He recalled meeting his Uncle Philip at his London club a year after Hakan had graduated from Sandhurst. They'd had several drinks together and Philip had said suddenly, "It's been rather awful for you, hasn't it? You had to learn how to be an Englishman and how to be an army officer simultaneously. Lesser men would have gone under—I would have."

Hakan had laughed shortly. "I'm not sure what I am anymore."

Philip answered softly. "I'm afraid, old man, that you're still too much of an Apache for the English, but I fear you may have become too English for the Apache."

It was true, Hakan knew. He had, in fact, spent very little time in England, having been stationed for the most part in the colonies and protectorates. He had been fighting for a country he barely knew; yet everything about him, his looks, accent, and most especially his uniform, proclaimed him to be an Englishman.

Besides, how could one ever put aside the first crucial sixteen years of one's life? The Life-way of the *Tin-ne-ah* still called to his soul and there had been many times during his army service when he'd found a lonely spot and allowed his mind to take him back. A couple of times he'd been caught. "Oliver's communing with nature again," his fellow officers would say. "Bit of a strange one, isn't he?"

He felt like two men inside one skin, fighting one another constantly, with first one in control and then the other, and was still unsure which one would emerge when the final battle was over.

When his English father had died two years before, Hakan had expected to resign his commission and assume immediate control of the estate. Instead, he learned that it might be months before all of the details of his father's will were settled. Hilliard Stoughton, the family solicitor, had been blunt: "There are legal aspects of the situation to be worked out. Your birth, for instance, isn't recorded anywhere. But never fear, your father has left everything to you. I'll sort things out for you." Stoughton had cleared his throat and tactfully suggested that since Hakan knew nothing of the running of the estate, he should appoint his half brother, Robert, as estate steward in the meantime. He added, "This arrangement will also give Robbie and Emily time to . . .

adjust to the situation." Hakan wondered if the solicitor expected Emily to contest the will and wanted him out of the way while he dealt with her.

Stoughton concluded, "You have to return to your army post to resign your commission anyway, and Robbie has been taking care of things since your father became ill."

Hakan had gladly agreed. The sudden overwhelming responsibility, his own lack of knowledge about the estate, and a certain emptiness where a feeling of triumph, of having succeeded in the quest he and his mother had set for themselves should have been, all combined to depress him.

The South African war had started before Hakan had had a chance to resign his commission, making it impossible for him to leave his regiment. In a way, having the decision taken out of his hands had been a relief. Having had the fulfillment of his goal within his grasp, he no longer was sure that was what he wanted. He knew that the day would come when his future path would be clear to him, or he'd turn and look back because there was to be no future.

But not yet . . . no, not like this, not by the fire of his own men. That's too ignoble an end for the son of Lone Wolf.

He continued to inch closer to the horse, the rocky ground scraping his back through his tunic. No time to find a sharp stone with which to saw through the rope around his wrists, the shellfire was getting more accurate. There was a slight rise, and if he reached the top he could roll out of sight into a deep gully. At the crest he'd be completely exposed, not only to friendly fire, but to the Boers who would see a prisoner escaping. But either alternative was preferable to being blown to bits by a shell.

The exertion brought a wave of dizziness and he rested for a moment, too weak to raise his bound hands to bat flies away from his face. Another shell exploded, earsplittingly close, and he choked on smoke and dust, shards of flying rock peppering his body.

Strange, he'd thought yesterday would have been the end. The Boers had ambushed a group of Worcesters, who could neither advance nor retire. They were penned like sheep but refused to throw down their rifles to end the slaughter.

Hakan had ordered his scouts to dismount and rush the Boers on foot, knowing they would be exposed, knowing it was madness. They had bounded over the rocks, firing as they went, not wildly, but with a quick upward jerk to the shoulder, rapid sight, then the shot. Hakan had taught them not to fire as the British troops were taught, in regular volleys, but to pick out a man and shoot to kill. To keep up lightning fire, yet never waste lead. To charge like buffalo, but keep the cool head of an Apache.

The Boers lay behind boulders, picking them off as they came, and the scouts leaped upon them and fired at point blank range, or smashed their heads with clubbed rifles. The scouts fought like furies and the Worcesters rallied and joined them.

When it was all over half of his scouts were dead or wounded, but the Boers had been routed. The surviving officers of the Worcesters couldn't believe their rescuers had numbered only fifty. The colonel in charge, badly wounded, had muttered to Hakan that he intended to see a Victoria Cross awarded for the day's work.

Yesterday a hero, today a prisoner. Hakan shook his throbbing head to discourage the ravenous flies and began to move again under the cover of an approaching shell. When the smoke cleared he was at the crest of the rise, inches from the steep walls of a deep gully that would not only conceal him, but offer protection from the shelling.

In the instant before he flung himself over the edge a bullet slammed into his side, stinging like a million bees; another struck his leg like a red-hot nail driven into his flesh. He left a flying rooster tail of blood as he plummeted down the rocky slope.

"What's all the shouting in the street about?" Noel asked as Andrew entered the surgery.

"Mafeking has been relieved." The long and bloody siege of the South African town was over.

"Thank God. Have you finished packing?"

"Yes. Jean and Brigid are having a last cup of tea together. Weeping a bit, of course."

"We'll travel to Yorkshire to see you, you know."

"Yes, we know. Noel . . . you do understand. She needs to be near her children."

"I know. But I'll still miss you both. Two years ago I wouldn't have minded your leaving. Been damn glad to get shut of you, in fact, when you and Jean first came back from

Yorkshire and used to sit up all night arguing and sobbing. But things seem to have calmed down lately. Andrew . . . just in the interest of science, of course, but you and Jean, do you . . . you *do* share a bed now, don't you?"

"The interest of science be damned, Noel. I shan't cater to your prurient curiosity."

The audience rose as one, filling the hall with applause and cheers and cries of *bravo, bravo*.

Danior felt the other members of the cast shove him forward and the curtain come down behind him so that he stood alone. He bowed again, and the acclaim of the audience washed over him in a golden wave, its energy fusing with his own elation until he felt he could soar in the air above their heads.

Sweat beaded his brow and his heart beat a tattoo against his ribs. In the orchestra pit the conductor was bowing to him, smiling his approval. An evening that could have been disastrous had been saved and an understudy had been given the chance of a lifetime. Was it possible that only hours ago they'd come to him and told him that he was actually to go on stage and sing the part of Escamillo? He, a real gypsy, singing in the most famous gypsy opera of all, because a motorcar had collided with a carriage, tossing the real Escamillo out on his face.

The audience roared their accolades, not only for his performance, but because he was the understudy, the unknown and untried, who had distinguished himself. Behind that curtain the slightly past-her-prime Carmen and an obese Don José would be seething.

Somewhere down there in the blurred mass of faces of the audience Robbie would be beaming nearsightedly, thinking, didn't I tell you two years ago that you didn't belong in university? That your voice needed training, every single day, and why waste time on anything else? You're where you belong now, Danior.

Sarah would be standing quietly, pride shining from her face, and Emily would be telling everyone who would listen that the understudy was a protégé of her family.

Pas, dear old Pas, would be weeping unashamedly. *Canta vittoria*, Pas!

If only Hakan could have been here . . . Danior had

wanted to enlist in the army at the outbreak of the Boer War, but Hakan had dissuaded him. "The boys will be the first to die—the eighteen-, nineteen-year-olds. They always are. Robbie's right, get your voice training. You've more to give the world than your body as cannon fodder."

Had Chavi arrived? Please let Chavi and Brenna have arrived in time to hear him. He'd scanned the audience just before the lights were dimmed and the two places in the front row reserved for them were still vacant. As the houselights went on he looked for them again, but they weren't there. Perhaps they hadn't received the message in time? It had all come about so suddenly. If they'd known he was to go on, surely nothing would have kept them away.

Fourteen-month-old Garridan Chambers sobbed and pounded with small fists on the closed door. Why didn't Mummy come and let him in? What was happening in there? It was so quiet, hushed like the middle of the night. But the sun was shining and Garridan had never been left alone like this.

Garridan had awakened from his afternoon nap to hear voices, frightening, urgent voices, and feet marching up the stairs. He didn't understand why he was being neglected. All he ever had to do was whimper and Mummy or Brenna would come running to take care of him. His pants were wet and he was hungry and they'd left him alone for such a long time. He'd played quietly for awhile, and when they didn't come for him, he climbed out of his cot.

But they were inside Brenna's room with the doors closed and wouldn't come out. The house was so silent. Garridan was very, very frightened.

He crept downstairs to the kitchen and found old Maude sitting at the kitchen table, her face buried in her hands, crying softly. But he didn't want Maude, he wanted Mummy or Brenna. He scrambled back up the stairs and waited outside the closed bedroom door, calling softly to them. When they didn't respond he began to cry, but even old Maude ignored his wails.

Suddenly a scream of anguish filled the house. His mother's scream. It went on and on and he covered his ears with his hands to shut it out.

The bedroom door opened and a tall man carrying a black

bag came out. His shiny black boots almost trampled Garridan, but he stopped in time, looked down, and then scooped him up with his free arm. He said, "Come along, young man, your mother can't take care of you just now."

Garridan struggled, but he was hauled down the stairs to the kitchen, where prune-wrinkled old Maude who cooked and cleaned for them still sat crying into a dishcloth. Garridan was dumped on her lap. The man said, "Keep him in here until I send someone over to look after him."

"She's gone, isn't she?" Maude sobbed.

The man nodded. "There was nothing I could do. She never regained consciousness."

"I don't even know exactly what 'appened."

He sighed. "Apparently her mother had sent her to post a letter to Ireland. Brenna was dashing across the street because she didn't want to be late for her Uncle Danior's performance when the motorcar struck her."

31

Sarah looked up as Barlow entered her study.

"A . . . person to see you, milady," he announced.

She wasn't expecting anyone. "Did you bring a visiting card?"

"He didn't have one, milady. Gave his name as Mr. Rutherford."

Sam Rutherford. After all this time. She said, "Show him into the library and order a tea tray for us."

She received Barlow's usual disapproving look before he disappeared. Sarah rose and went to the oval mirror on the wall above the mantle. She smoothed her hair and straightened the lace jabot at her throat.

Two years ago when his wild West show had toured the southern counties she had dropped him a note explaining why she was unable to use the tickets he'd sent her. He had sent his condolences on her bereavement and asked her to please contact him if he could be of service. She hadn't responded. At that time it was necessary to withdraw into herself in order to deal with Richard's death.

Her mirror told her that she looked empty, used-up in some way. Her seamstress had pleaded with her to at least wear a white jabot on her black dress now, with perhaps a cameo or locket, but Sarah continued to wear deep mourning.

Sam stood in front of the library fireplace, his big frame and fringed buckskin jacket a startling contrast to his surroundings. He twisted the brim of a white Stetson he'd evidently been reluctant to hand over to Barlow. When she appeared, his tanned, craggy face broke into a wide smile, lighting up his eyes.

"Sarah! Good of you to receive me, with no notice and all. How are you?"

"I'm happy to see you, Sam. I'm quite well and there seems to be no need to ask how you are, you look very fit."

He glanced down at his clothing and said with a touch of embarrassment, "My working clothes. We did a show in Birmingham and I had to run to catch the train. I planned to change into a regular suit before I came to see you, but goldarn if the railroad didn't lose my luggage. Reckon it got put off down the line by mistake."

"You look splendid," Sarah assured him. "Please, sit down."

He lowered himself carefully into a leather armchair with the attitude of a man afraid he might break something. "Real sorry I was to hear about your husband, Sarah."

"Thank you."

"How's Hakan—well, I reckon I should call him Lord Moreland now, but to me he'll always be Hakan."

"To me too, Sam." She looked down at her hands folded on her lap. "He's in South Africa fighting the Boers, and we haven't heard from him . . . for what seems like ages."

"Oh, Christ, no! Oh, excuse me, ma'am. He's in the army? I should've figured."

"He's been in the army for a number of years." She was saddened to think how little time her son had spent in England but didn't mention this to Sam, nor the terrible gnawing fear for Hakan's safety that never left her. She added, "So many young men have been killed or wounded—" She broke off as she realized Sam didn't know Charles Pettigrew, killed at Pretoria, or Gilbert Dunstan, who had lost an arm at Ladysmith. To change the subject she said, "I read about your wild West show. You've been very successful."

He grinned. "It's about as true to life as I expect some of those biograph pictures are I've seen about your war in South Africa. But I guess folks want to see things the way they expect them to be, not the way they really are. We just give 'em what they want."

"Have you been back home recently?" There was a wistful note in her voice that she couldn't disguise. "I suppose it's all changed. People, towns, railroads . . ."

"Oh, it's still a big country, Sarah. Plenty of space out West. Not that I've been back for a while. I did visit Bly in New York—she's attending a university now. Wants to be an anthropologist, believe it or not."

Sarah remembered Sam's rather rudely outspoken little girl, who had taken great delight in telling Hakan off just before they'd left New York. "Did your daughter's meeting with us spark that interest?" Sarah asked, smiling.

He grinned. "She was an awful brat, wasn't she? Not much better now, either. Too smart for her own good. But no, I guess my folks were always so secretive about Bly's mother that it was inevitable when she started to grow up she'd want to know about her own Indian blood." He fell silent and a shadow crossed his eyes.

Sarah looked at him questioningly and he said, "Some of the Indian reservations have problems . . . well, I guess I might as well tell you that the Chiricahuas are the worst off of all. Died like flies in that Florida swamp—and not doing much better on the Oklahoma reservation. In a few years I doubt there'll be any left. It's a real tragedy. I guess that's one of the reasons I put this show together. It was a way to get a few of 'em off the reservation."

Sarah felt a deep sadness that momentarily eclipsed her sorrow over the accidental death of Danior's niece, Brenna. The death of the child was heartbreaking, and Sarah felt Danior's pain. The gods had been excessively cruel in providing Danior's opportunity to sing in grand opera by the same circumstances that killed his niece . . . a motorcar accident.

Sam went on, "Bly and some of her student friends have been badgering congressmen and senators to do something about the Indians. Not that anybody's likely to pay attention to some female who can't even vote. But she's written some pieces for the papers, too, had 'em published under a male pen name." There was pride in Sam's voice. " 'Course, she isn't crazy about my wild West show, but at least I'm keeping some Indians from rotting on reservations. And a percentage of the profits goes to Indian relief."

A parlor maid brought the tea tray and Sarah poured from a silver pot, while Sam smiled and said, "I just had a mind-picture of you cooking antelope meat over a campfire."

Putting sadness temporarily aside to enjoy their reunion, they talked about themselves, their lives, and their shared memories. Sarah studied the man opposite her and noted that he'd changed very little. A little heavier perhaps, and his hair was peppered with gray, but he lived a physical life. The constant riding and playacting of Indian battles had kept him vigorously youthful. It was like a breath of fresh air to talk to him. For so long she'd conversed only with Philip, whose lighthearted banter could be amusing but sometimes left her feeling unsatisfied, as if she'd skipped dinner and eaten only a fluffy dessert.

Sam watched her with a hungry intensity, listened to her every word, and when he spoke he was direct, not hesitating to say what was on his mind. After an hour or so in his company it was as though they'd spent years together and were comfortable expressing any thought or asking any question.

Sam said, "You know, Sarah, this house . . . it's the grandest place I've ever seen—and that includes Buckingham Palace, which looks a bit too much like a barracks for my taste. But Merrinswood . . . I guess what I'm driving at is that it's hard for me to reconcile the fact that you spent so many years with the Chiricahua, coming from a place like this."

She answered honestly. "I fell in love with a man, Sam, and then I grew to love the sheer simplicity and closeness to nature of his way of life. After a while I loved the country, too. The freedom of roaming the mountains and deserts of the Southwest with no ties to any one place. I did have to bury my head in the sand and not allow myself to think about what he and his braves did when they went raiding. I suppose I rationalized it by telling myself—truthfully—that they took only what they needed to survive. And the land was theirs long before the Spaniards or Mexicans or American settlers came. The Apache never killed if they could take a captive and always tried to integrate prisoners who were worthy into the Chiricahua clan."

Sam nodded. "Geronimo was a Mexican captive, wasn't he?"

"Taken as a boy and raised by the Chiricahua. I saw a young journalist who was captured with me gradually change until he was almost pure Apache."

She gazed into space, looking back in memory. "I still miss sleeping under the stars on summer nights. The sheer heart-pounding thrill of painted warriors dancing and chanting, silhouetted against the flames of a campfire. Of riding into the hills in the spring and coming across a carpet of wildflowers so thick they looked like a brightly colored cape tossed on the slopes. Or traveling into the lower desert in winter . . . moonrises over the badlands and silver sunrises spilling over the rim of the earth. The unexpected beauty of a cluster of sandstone boulders or a towering saguaro cactus . . . Oh, goodness Sam, look what you've done! You got me started and I can't stop."

"You're making me homesick," Sam said. "You think you'll ever go back, Sarah?"

"It wouldn't be the same, would it? When *Tonsaroyoo* was killed I had to leave. I couldn't have borne my grief if I'd stayed. Every hill and tree and stream would have reminded me of him. I thought for a long time my only reason for returning to England was to claim Hakan's birthright. But there were selfish reasons too. It was a way to take my mind off my grief over *Tonsaroyoo*'s death."

Sam was silent, reflective for a moment. "And now you're still grieving for your English husband, two years after he died. Maybe you need to get away from these surroundings too for a while? It's time for you to start living again, Sarah."

"No . . ." She answered slowly. "I have to stay here . . . for reasons other than grief, or obligation, or anything you'd understand, Sam." She was the custodian of her son's future. They called him Lord Moreland, but he was still Hakan, unequipped to defend himself against devious enemies. She had to stay until she was sure it was all really his, that it couldn't be taken from him. She couldn't be sure of that while he was in the army, so far from home. They had both endured too much to let it slip away from them now.

She steered the conversation to lighter matters and late in the afternoon asked him to stay for dinner. When he accepted she excused herself to go and speak with Barlow about setting an extra place. She also took the time to go upstairs and substitute a white-lace jabot for the black one, then pinned a pretty sapphire brooch, which made her eyes sparkle, to the jabot.

Philip and Robbie were obviously intrigued by their American visitor and bombarded him with questions, while Emily, looking like a skinny crow in her unrelieved mourning gown, her mousy hair scraped back from her gaunt features, compressed her thin lips and frowned disapprovingly at everyone.

Sam had to perform in another show the following day, and said he'd be glad to pass out tickets if anyone wanted to go—it was to take place in the north country, so wouldn't involve much traveling. Emily dropped her napkin and said angrily, "Mr. Rutherford, you must have overlooked the fact that we are still in mourning for my father."

Sarah's fingers curled into her palms under the table. Emily, who had expressed the least sorrow over her father's passing, presented to the outside world the greatest amount of grief. Not only that, but Emily had often remarked to Sarah that she felt they should have called in Doctor Harkness the night Richard died, and that perhaps a postmortem would have been in order. That surely allowing Andrew McGreal to sign the death certificate and then having a closed coffin was peculiar to say the least. Sarah had responded that it was her decision and she didn't wish to discuss it. Now, two years later, Sarah decided that she'd put up with enough from this sullen young woman.

"I would love to see your show, Sam," she said. "And never fear, I shan't come in dreary black. Two years of mourning is long enough."

Emily's mouth opened and closed like a fish, but Robbie and Philip immediately said they would go too. Emily excused herself and left the table.

Moments later Barlow appeared, carrying a yellow envelope on a silver tray. "A telegram just arrived, milady."

Sarah rose slowly from her chair, feeling like a drowning woman coming to the surface for the last time. A telegram could only mean one thing: Oh, please God no, not Hakan too! If he was dead . . . was that to be her punishment?

She reached for the telegram with shaking fingers, but Philip grabbed it first and tore it open. She waited, heart stopped, while he read it. He began, "It's Hakan."

The scrolled ceiling with its coldly glinting chandeliers seemed to rush toward Sarah. As she crumpled to the floor, the rest of what Philip said was obscured by approaching darkness.

"He's been seriously wounded and is on his way home." Philip dropped the telegram and lunged to catch his sister-in-law. Loosening the collar of her dress, he added in awe, "And he's to be awarded the Victoria Cross."

Danior knocked on the bedroom door, and not expecting a response, went inside. The heavy draperies were drawn and the gas mantle was turned down low. His sister was a barely distinguishable outline, sprawled on the bed in an attitude of utter despair. Her untouched lunch tray stood on the bedside table.

"Chavi? You awake?"

"Yes." Her voice was hoarse from crying. "What do you want?"

"We need to make the . . . arrangements. We can't delay any longer."

"Has Lysander arrived?"

"Not yet. But we can't wait, in case he can't come. You said yourself that it's dangerous for him to come to London. Would you like me to call in an undertaker?"

"No. I want to take her up north. Can you find out about a train?"

"Yes, but why—"

"She's going to be buried where she was born—on the moors. I want her to have a gypsy's funeral."

Danior digested this news silently, vague memories stirring of the corpse of an old gypsy being carried uncovered to his grave. They broke his little finger, then on a red ribbon a little money was fastened so that the dead man might pay his fare across the river of shades in the country of the dead. His dearest possessions, including his violin, were placed in the grave with him, and wine poured both into the open and the closed grave. Danior said, "I'll see about a train at once."

"Danior?"

"Yes?"

"Would you sing for her—when we put her into the ground? Would you sing something from the opera she never got to see or hear?"

"Yes, of course."

They were silent for a while and Danior wondered which of Escamillo's solos would be suitable for a funeral. Remembering Brenna, she wouldn't want anything sad. He'd had such a short time in which to get to know her, but had loved her liveliness and the sheer spirited confidence with which she faced life. Yes, he'd sing at her funeral. It would be appropriate, because it would be the last time he'd ever sing in public.

At length he said, "After the funeral I must visit Merrinswood. I've just heard that Hakan has been wounded. Sarah will need me."

He picked up Chavi's cold hand, holding it quietly for a moment, feeling her shake with suppressed tears. Life seemed to have a habit of piling one disaster on top of another. He didn't know just how badly off Hakan was, and prayed he wouldn't be horribly maimed. It seemed to be the ultimate irony that Hakan was to be awarded his country's highest honor, yet had never really lived in England. But at least he was still alive, whereas pretty, bright little Brenna was not. Danior's hurt was so great he couldn't imagine what Chavi's pain must be. He'd worry about Hakan later; for now he must help his sister through her painful ritual of death.

32

A face swam slowly into Hakan's view, faded momentarily, then returned. A dream perhaps? Too beautiful to belong to a human woman. Surely it couldn't be a nurse? The nursing profession, like the religious orders of nuns, seemed to him to attract plain-featured women.

A halo of palest blonde hair framed features delicately piquant, cool as some remote goddess in repose, yet smoldering under the surface in a way that would surely resurrect the dead. Large green eyes that flashed with amber fire regarded him with intense concern.

"There! See? He blinked! I know he did. He hears me, I'm sure of it. Honestly, Lady Moreland, I really do feel he's coming back to us. I'm going to read to him again." The voice was a controlled contralto and expressed stern determination. Whoever this young woman was, she was not to be deterred from her purpose.

"Very well, dear. I'll leave you alone."

That was his mother's voice. Hakan felt vaguely disappointed that he'd lived, after all. That dark dreamless sleep had been so peaceful.

He tried to raise his eyelids again, succeeded in getting them up a fraction of an inch. He was back at Merrinswood; he recognized the room. It had once been his father's retreat, on the ground floor, with a wall of French windows overlooking the rose garden. The roses were in full bloom under a summer sun, their fragrance drifting in through the open window, and in the distance the trees wore mantles of misty green against a sky of delicate blue.

He supposed he should be glad they'd brought his bed down here, since it seemed more a place to live than to die. He hadn't forgotten his father languishing in that upstairs room that reeked of death and decay.

There were gaps in Hakan's memory. He remembered everything clearly up until the moment the bullets slammed into him and he fell into the gully. He recalled fretting about whether a Boer or a British bullet had struck him. After that, only vague memories came back to him. The young corporal who found him had turned away, saying, "This officer is dead." Hakan had tried to call him back, but lost consciousness. Luckily, the burial detail must have detected a trace of life left in him, because he had a brief recollection of being in a field hospital with a bloodstained doctor bending over him.

"One bullet grazed your temple. The second narrowly missed your heart and punctured a lung, and you took a third just above your knee." The doctor's voice droned on and might have been reciting items on a dinner menu for all the interest it expressed. "You've lost a lot of blood. You're lucky to be alive."

You're lucky to be alive. How many times he'd heard that tired refrain.

Hakan remembered weakness and pain and the suffocating ether mask on his face. He recalled fumbling treatment, dressings that stuck to his wounds and had to be ripped loose. He'd wanted to tell them to take off their filthy rags and fetch a shaman to treat his wounds properly with herbs and leaves and mud so that his flesh could heal itself . . . but he slipped in and out of pain-wracked consciousness, then finally into blissful oblivion.

He thought there was a dream of the rolling movement of a ship and the clean tang of salt air. Evidently it was no dream, because here he was at Merrinswood. He wasn't sure he welcomed awareness, since it brought pain, not only in his body, but in his mind. Sharp stabs of regret that they'd brought him here rather than taking him to his real home.

Then he fell asleep again to the sound of the cool blonde angel's voice reading a lighthearted comedy of manners. She paused once and said, "Of course, Oscar Wilde is a perfectly dreadful man and deserved to go to prison for his perversions . . . but I think he'll cheer you up, James."

Cornelia Dunstan. Nelia, of course, was the icy blonde with the hidden fires. She had married Charles Pettigrew and gone to live in the south. She was his green-eyed angel of mercy, who stayed at his bedside and forced him back into the world with her endless reading of *The Importance of Being Earnest.*

Hakan lay still, his eyes almost closed, and slowly let his hand inch across the coverlet toward the book resting on the edge of the bed, held by slender fingers with perfect oval nails.

"Oh!" Nelia gasped as his hand suddenly reached up and captured her wrist. The book slipped to the floor.

"I think I've heard enough of old Oscar," he whispered.

"James! Oh, thank God! I must go and tell your mother—"

His hand tightened on her wrist. "No, don't go. Let me look at you." She smiled, her rather aloof features softening, becoming even more beautiful. He said, "I probably would have gone on floating in my comfortable void forever if you hadn't kept pulling me back with your infernal reading. Since

I'm not at all sure I wanted to come back, you owe me the pleasure of looking at you instead of listening to you."

She laughed, a tinkling sound like crystal bells. "Doctor Harkness told your mother you were in a coma and it might last indefinitely. But Doctor McGreal said it wasn't a true coma, because you drifted in and out of consciousness, although you gave no sign you recognized anyone. He said we shouldn't give up hope. To keep talking to you and moving your limbs and so on. Your mother sat at your bedside day and night, and we all came to relieve her. But I just had a feeling when I was here that you responded best to me." There was a note of triumph in her voice and she regarded him with pride.

"How could a man fail to respond to you? You're the loveliest creature this side of heaven."

She lowered lustrous golden lashes over her eyes in a gesture that was meant to indicate modesty, but was somewhat diminished by the satisfied curl of her full lips. Nelia Dunstan was a young lady well aware of her charms.

He felt frighteningly weak, as if his body no longer belonged to him. Nelia's wrist slid from his clasp, the effort to hold it too much for him. She continued to chatter with a forced gaiety that indicated that she was afraid if she stopped talking, or said anything of a serious nature, he might slip away from her again. He would have to interrupt to ask her to bring his mother, but out of politeness first asked, "How are Charles and Gilbert?"

Her lovely eyes filled with tears. "Charles was killed, that's why I came home. Gil lost his right arm at Ladysmith . . . he's awfully bitter about it. Mopes about the house all day."

Hakan murmured condolences. That disastrous weekend at the Dunstans so long ago . . . how foolish it all seemed now. He wondered if those two had ever been troubled by their consciences, knowing that their actions had led to the death of Sir Randolph.

So much had happened in the first year of the new century that Hakan felt like an awakening Rip Van Winkle. The Boers had been beaten, the war was over. Electricity had reached the industrial plants and a veritable explosion of mass production had begun. He learned of the Boxer Rebellion in

China, of the unrest in India. He carefully avoided reading news about America and wouldn't admit even to himself the reason for this.

But it was the personal lives of the people he knew that touched him most deeply, especially Danior, with whom Hakan shared a bond stronger than blood ties could ever produce. It saddened Hakan to see Danior's animated features frozen in a perpetual mask of guilt and grief.

Danior irrationally blamed himself for the death of Brenna. "If she hadn't been hurrying because she was coming to hear me sing she wouldn't have dashed into the street under the wheels of the motorcar."

"You might as well blame your sister's friend in Ireland," Hakan protested. "And say that if Chavi hadn't written a letter to him and sent Brenna to post it, she'd still be alive."

But Danior refused to be comforted. Worse, he refused to return to the opera company in London. He swore he'd never sing again.

Sarah explained to Hakan, "Danior and his sister brought the child back to Yorkshire for burial. It was strange, the gypsy caravans appeared as if by magic, and Brenna was given a gypsy funeral. I suggested to Danior that he bring Chavi here for a while, but she refused to come. I've no idea where she is now. Danior's very secretive about the whole situation."

Nor would Danior discuss his sister with Hakan, and would disappear for longer and longer periods, until one day he announced that he was leaving Merrinswood for good.

"You're going back to London to resume your singing career," Sarah said, relieved. They were seated beside Hakan's bed. Doctor McGreal had just left after his daily visit. Since his return to Merrin Quarry, Sarah had reinstated him as family physician.

"No. I'm just going away," Danior answered. "I don't know where. I shan't need you to continue my allowance." His dark brooding eyes refused contact with either of them.

Sarah said faintly, "But you'll let us know where you are? You'll keep in touch, Danior?"

"That might be tricky. I'll probably be traveling about."

Hakan could see the hurt in his mother's eyes and said, "I have a longing for some lemonade, the kind you make yourself, not that sour brew they cook up in the kitchen."

It was an excuse to get her out of the room before Hakan turned angrily on Danior. "Couldn't you have broken that a little more gently?"

Danior regarded him moodily. "She has you now. She doesn't need me. Besides, if I don't get away from here I'll go mad."

"What are you going to do, really?"

"I don't know. Travel."

"I don't understand you. Why are you giving up a career in opera? With your voice—"

Danior leapt to his feet. "I'm never going to sing again. Do you hear me? *Never*."

"But why? How can your refusing to use your God-given talent possibly help a dead child or your living sister? It doesn't make sense."

Danior gave a short hard laugh. "You think that's the only reason?" He fumbled in his inside pocket for his wallet and withdrew a folded sheet of newspaper. "Here. Read it for yourself."

The clipping was from a London newspaper and was a review of the opera *Carmen* in which Danior had appeared. Hakan skimmed through it rapidly.

". . . understudy took the place of renowned baritone injured in street accident . . . result a ruined Carmen . . . the young and inexperienced baritone, said to be a real-life gypsy, is fussy, unintentionally funny, mannered, self-indulgent, and silly. . . . He managed to turn a poignant musical drama into a noisy display of street musician's raucous sounds and acrobatic movement. Swaggering about the stage embarrassingly, his transitions were excruciating, and he held his low notes for tasteless eternities.

One can only hope for a speedy recovery of the real Escamillo so that this young gypsy "singer" may mercifully return to the oblivion from whence he came, sparing us all the sorry spectacle of a single cast member turning grand opera into music-hall comedy. . . ."

There was much more, all in the same vein. It was a shattering, devastating critique not only of Danior's voice, but everything about him, including his manhood. Hakan had never before seen such vitriol in print. The opera re-

viewer had not only been unable to find a single thing to
praise in Danior's performance, but apparently it had so
enraged him that he had to crucify Danior for even daring to
appear on stage.

Hakan raised his eyes to meet Danior's tormented gaze.
He shrugged, desperately trying to appear unconcerned. "You
see, I'm not a singer, I just thought I was."

"But . . . everyone said the audience rose to their feet,
wildly applauding you—that the other cast members insisted
you take curtain calls by yourself. Surely my mother and
Robbie and Uncle Philip and everyone didn't lie? They said
the audience loved your performance."

"I thought they did," Danior answered bitterly. "But
you see what the reviewer said—the audience was merely
applauding out of politeness because I'd had to go on at such
short notice. That if I hadn't been an understudy they'd have
laughed me off the stage."

"I can't believe you'd let one anonymous critic destroy
your career! Are you really going to listen to a critic's verdict
and disregard the opinions of all the people in the opera
house who gave you a standing ovation? Don't you realize
that in all probability the man who wrote that piece is a
frustrated performer who simply resents the fact that you
were given a chance he wanted for himself? How much easier
to tear apart what someone else has achieved than to do it
oneself!"

"His wasn't the only bad review," Danior said wearily.
"Besides, he was right. I was just too damn full of myself. It
was like that kind of self-confidence you get when you're
incredibly drunk. I strutted all over the stage."

"Next time you won't. Besides, the audience didn't care.
They recognized that you have a wonderful voice."

"For singing in music halls perhaps. Hakan, my mind's
made up. Please don't say any more, your mother will be
back in a moment."

Hakan missed Danior sorely when he left, but Nelia
spent so much time at Merrinswood that he didn't lack
companionship. He looked forward to her bright chatter and
tinkling laughter and as time passed felt a twinge of guilt that
he came to prefer Nelia's lighthearted company to Danior's
formerly brooding presence. When he mentioned this to his

mother, she said, "Your own mind and body needs to heal, Hakan. You were almost killed. You need someone to make you smile and laugh, not someone who will burden you with his pain. Danior will overcome his in time and decide what his future path must be."

Hakan had not told her about the devastating review. Surely in time Danior would get over it. In a way Danior was better off than he himself, since a dream unfulfilled was better than no dream at all. But perhaps it was merely weakness that produced this frightening lack of focus on the future.

Robbie tentatively approached Hakan about the affairs of the estate. "Now that you're h-h-home, James, I really sh-should get your approval f-for—"

"What do I know about running an estate? You're handling it better than I ever could. Why, even my father needed an estate steward to help him do what you do single-handedly."

Remembering the boyish crush Robbie had had on Nelia, Hakan wondered if now that she was widowed Rob might let her know how he felt. But Nelia made it clear her only purpose at Merrinswood was to visit Hakan.

Emily was obviously holding her opinions in check until she felt Hakan's wounds were sufficiently healed, but it was clear from her attitude that a confrontation was inevitable. His father's will had left virtually everything to him, with only small trust funds for the twins.

One afternoon in July when the weather was particularly warm, Hakan sat on a lawn chair catching his breath after a short walk about the grounds that had exhausted him. His continuing weakness worried him and he began to fear he'd never feel strong again. He forced himself to walk a little each day, even though he required a walking stick to support his wounded leg.

From where he sat he could see the winding drive that led to the house, and long before it passed through the gates he heard the gasoline-powered motorcar coming.

He leaned forward and caught a glimpse of the man at the wheel. A big man, broad-shouldered, his deeply tanned face and strong profile emphasized by the bright red kerchief knotted about his neck. That profile was both strange and familiar. Hakan searched his memory, but couldn't at first place the visitor.

Then the car stopped and the man uncoiled himself from the driver's seat, displaying a plaid shirt and riding breeches. He reached into the car for a fringed buckskin jacket and put it on.

Hakan stood up so suddenly that a familiar vise squeezed his brain, causing momentary blackness. As he waited for the wave of dizziness to pass, Sam Rutherford ran up the terrace steps and a minute later disappeared into the house.

Cursing his body for not responding to his brain's commands, Hakan followed more slowly. Before he reached the house a horse came cantering up the drive and he recognized the slender figure of Nelia Dunstan, cool, composed, and beautiful in a black riding habit that set off her platinum-blonde hair.

Nelia waved as she approached, and for a moment he envied her the ability to ride a horse. Sometimes he felt like a young man trapped inside an old man's worn-out body, and the feeling made him wish he'd had more pity for his father in his last months.

She reined her mount and looked down at him, smiling her cool smile that, combined with the fire in her green eyes, made Hakan feel even less steady on his legs. He was acutely aware of the walking stick he had to use to get about, and maneuvered it behind his back as he greeted her.

"Hello, James. You look tired. Are you sure you should be walking about so soon?"

"I'm not tired. Just bored. I was hoping you'd come today. And thank God I see you didn't bring old Oscar with you." They laughed at their private joke. Hakan often teased her, but he was grateful for her companionship, admired her beauty, and as she was a widow, felt less restrained with her than he would have with a single girl.

He extended his hand to help her down from her saddle, but she said, "Oh, I can manage. You know you don't have to be the gallant gentleman with me. I'm fully aware of how ill you've been."

He felt a flicker of unreasonable resentment that she continued to see him as an invalid, even though he was one, because he wanted so much to be her protector, not the other way around.

She led her horse and carefully matched his slow pace as they strolled across the lawn. The turf was springy beneath his feet and he was young, with a pretty girl at his side, and he should have felt pleasure in simply being alive; he didn't.

"Did the doctor come to see you this morning?" Nelia asked.

"Yes," he answered shortly, not wishing to discuss his medical problems.

"You did the right thing in having Doctor McGreal treat you instead of Doctor Harkness. McGreal seems much more modern in his approach, don't you think? What did he say?"

"That he expects my strength will come back slowly and I can't rush things."

"It's a miracle you're still alive. You know that, don't you?"

Of course he knew that. No one would let him forget it. They reminded him constantly how lucky he was to be alive. He'd been told that he nearly bled to death and probably would have had he not landed on his side and the weight of his body slowed the flow of blood.

Nelia added, "I don't think you're limping quite so badly today. But you must be very careful with your health."

Hakan stopped, jabbed his walking stick into the turf, and slid his other arm around her waist. He pulled her close to him, roughly, and kissed her full on the mouth. He felt her stiffen, then relax against him. Her lips were cool and peppermint fresh, and she kept them primly closed. A moment later she pulled away, laughing breathlessly. "James! Someone will see us!"

He released her and she asked, "Why did you do that?"

"I wanted to kiss you. The reason must be obvious." The reason was that he didn't want her to keep reminding him that he was weak and broken in body and spirit. He had closed her mouth to keep the words from spilling out.

They resumed walking and she glanced at him sideways, her mouth demure now, but a seductive gleam in her eye. "I want you to tell me."

He shrugged. "You're a beautiful woman and I'm not quite dead yet."

"Oh, James, that's the dreariest thing you've ever said to me. A man who steals a kiss on a summer's day ought to at least have the decency to say that he has some tender feelings for the lady in question."

"You saved my life," he answered lightly. "I'll be your devoted slave forever."

She laughed. "That's more like it. Now tell me, whose motorcar is that in front of the house? You know, I've been thinking, you should learn to drive your father's car. I don't think it would be too strenuous for you."

Ignoring the suggestion because he disliked everything about the internal combustion engine, he answered her first question. "An old friend of ours from America. Come on, let's go meet him."

Sam replaced the fragile china cup of tea on the saucer and wished it would turn into stiff whiskey. He tried to keep from staring at Sarah, who still had the power to bewitch him, even after all these years. Perhaps it was the sheer impossibility of having her that fed his obsession. Maybe he'd fantasized about her all this time simply because he knew she could never be his.

She wore a gown of dusty rose that brought a warm glow to her fine skin, and her eyes were a clear true gray that reminded him of the still surface of a deep lake. He made some stupid remark about the weather and cursed his inability to come right out and say, *Sarah, tomorrow we give our last show and we'll be on a steamer out of Liverpool two days later. But if you'd give me one ounce of encouragement I'd figure out a way to stay here and be with you. . . .*

How could he say such a thing? What had he to offer a woman who already owned half of England? He fabricated all sorts of notions to indicate that she was interested in him. Hadn't she discarded her widow's weeds since he arrived? Wasn't her step a little livelier, her expression more eager? Or was that only his imagination?

She said, "I'm so glad you came, Sam, and it's wonderful that your daughter accompanied you on this tour. You should have brought her with you today."

"Bly didn't exactly accompany me on the tour," Sam said. "She's in England studying at Oxford, some sort of advanced anthropology. I did get to see her when we were in the south—and she'll be coming north for our last show."

"Oxford! My goodness, I'm impressed."

Sam gave what he hoped was a proud smile. The truth was, Bly had begged to come with him to Yorkshire. But she was as outspoken as ever, and educated far beyond what a girl should be, and Sam had been afraid she might say or do the wrong thing. He had made the excuse that he might not even stop at Merrinswood, that he was investigating other bookings for the show.

Sarah said, "We were all disappointed we couldn't come to see your show when you were here last. It seems I'm fated never to see you perform. But now that Hakan's home perhaps we shall. He'll be coming back from his walk shortly."

"How's he doing?"

Her face clouded. "He's terribly weak and doesn't seem to be making progress toward recovery as quickly as we hoped. Doctor McGreal is worried about him. He feels Hakan has lost the will to heal himself. Hakan insists he isn't up to traveling to London to receive his Victoria Cross. He has to use a walking stick and limps quite badly. Try not to look too shocked at his appearance. He's got a nasty scar on his forehead and a worse one on his body, but Doctor McGreal says that there are scars we can't see."

She paused and looked a little embarrassed, then explained. "This particular doctor is one of Sigmund Freud's disciples, perhaps a little more concerned with feelings and thoughts than other medical men."

Sam didn't know who Freud was, but from the sound of Hakan's injuries he needed a doctor's help with his physical condition, not someone worried about how he felt about being shot up in a war. "Maybe you need to bring in another doctor?"

Sarah stared at her hands, folded in her lap. "Doctor McGreal is more than just a family physician. He's . . . a personal friend. The husband of Robbie and Emily's mother."

That was a surprise. The twins lived here at Merrinswood with Sarah. Why not with their mother? Sam had assumed she was dead. Besides, with England's rigid class system, doctors didn't mix with the aristocracy.

As if reading his unspoken question, she added, "I never told you the whole story. Perhaps I should." She filled in the details quickly, then concluded, "When the McGreals moved back here, I suppose Jean thought she could get close to her children again, and I do think Robbie and she have managed to bridge the lost years. But Emily ignores her mother for the most part."

"Miss Emily isn't exactly warm to anyone, is she?" Sam asked with a smile.

"Someone's coming," Sarah said, cocking her head to one side. "It's Hakan, I can hear his walking stick—not his footsteps. There's someone with him. Nelia probably."

Sam laughed. "And you didn't even press your ear to the ground!"

Sarah was right to assume that he'd be shocked by Hakan's appearance. The thin, drawn man who leaned heavily on his walking stick, a livid scar slashing across his temple, seemed to Sam to be only the ghost of the striking golden-haired Apache warrior he'd turned over to Philip Merrin twelve years before. Sam had to bite his tongue to keep from exclaiming, "Christ in heaven, what have they done to you?" as Hakan, accompanied by a stunningly pretty girl, came into the room.

As he shook hands with Hakan and responded to the introduction to Nelia, Sam noted the other changes. Speech, manners, everything. James Merrin, seventh Earl of Moreland, was as far removed from Hakan, son of *Tonsaroyoo* and *Sons-ee-ah-ray*, as Sam was from the Prince of Wales.

"Mother tells me you're appearing in a wild West show," Hakan said, awkwardly attempting to pull out a chair for Nelia and looking defeated when she smilingly did it for herself.

"Yes. Last show tomorrow. I'd be proud to have you come and see it, and the young lady, of course."

"Oh, James, how exciting!" Nelia exclaimed. "Let's!"

Hakan eased himself stiffly into a chair. "I'm not happy in crowds." There was an edge to his voice that indicated to Sam that Hakan disapproved of his present occupation.

"Oh, that won't be a problem," Sam said. "I'll arrange for a private box for you."

"Don't worry, Mr. Rutherford," Nelia said. "We'll get him there."

Sam didn't doubt that she would. There was an air of steely determination behind Nelia's fragile exterior.

The day was overcast, gray, and the grass of the arena too green, too smoothly manicured to even remotely suggest the rugged terrain of Apache Pass in the Chiricahua mountains. The covered wagons looked authentic enough, but the riders accompanying the wagon train wore woolly chaps and out-sized Stetsons and looked more like cowboys than overland immigrants.

Hakan tensed as bloodcurdling yells preceded the appearance of the attacking Apache. Stripped except for breech-clouts, daubed with vivid war paint from face to toe, all the braves wore full feathered war bonnets such as no chief ever possessed even for the most ceremonious occasions, and their ponies sagged under enormous brightly colored blankets.

To one side of the arena there was a gate over which hung a sign "Fort Bowie," through which no doubt the rescuing cavalry would appear. On the opposite side of the arena were several gaudy "tepees," constructed, Hakan noted in disbelief, of canvas, in front of which a few dispirited-looking Indians squatted beside their war drums, pounding a desultory beat. Even more incredibly, a couple of braves appeared to be doing the squaw's work of tannning hides.

Hakan heard his mother's sigh of dismay and at the same time his Uncle Philip murmured, "Your friend Sam did warn you not to expect realism."

Sam's daughter Bly turned her head and glared at them. She had arrived after they were seated and there'd been time only for brief introductions. Hakan decided that Bly Rutherford hadn't changed much from the insufferable little girl she'd been when he first met her in New York. Her clothes were wrinkled and carelessly assembled, suggesting she had traveled in them and not bothered to change. Her dark, Indian-straight hair was simply pushed behind her ears. He didn't look too closely at her face, but could hardly miss that stubborn, clefted chin. This young woman, he decided, probably wished she were a man. She'd certainly been educated like one.

Robbie said, "The b-b-braves look splendid, James. They all f-fired their arrows off with s-such precision."

Nelia leaned forward, her lips slightly parted, her eyes fixed on the bronze bodies of the Apache. "James! They're marvelous!"

Hakan said, "They also outnumber the whites by at least two to one. If we'd had odds like those we'd still be living in freedom. In fact, if my father had been able to put as many braves into the field as are presently in this arena, he'd have controlled the entire territory."

Sam Rutherford, as wagon master, was now circling his wagons. The women, in gingham gowns and pretty sunbonnets, prepared to reload the men's weapons. The Apaches whirled, screaming, about the wagons, sending hails of arrows into the air, all of which fell far short. Hakan admired the ability of the Apaches to ride reasonably well, considering the encumberment of heavy feathered war bonnets and ridiculously large pony blankets.

Positioning his walking stick on the wooden floor of their private box, Hakan rose stiffly to his feet. "Excuse me, but I think I've seen enough. Please . . . all of you, stay and see the rest of the show. I'll wait for you in the refreshment tent."

Nelia rose at once and said, "I'll go with you, James." He protested, but she wouldn't be deterred.

A thin drizzle of rain had started to fall, dampening his spirits even further. The smell of trampled grass and sweating horseflesh intensified in the humid air. He poked his walking stick in the ground, dragged himself along after it, and felt like a man who had outlived his time.

"It wasn't like that . . . nothing like that," he said.

Nelia smiled. "Of course not. This is just for fun."

"But if men like Sam Rutherford won't tell the real story, who will?"

"Darling, *nobody cares.* By tomorrow half of those spectators will have forgotten what they saw today. In a couple of weeks most of them won't be able to recall the details. And five years from now . . . they'll probably all deny they ever saw a wild West show."

They had reached the refreshment tent and Nelia raised the flap herself in order to enter, further irritating him. She said, "Go and sit down at one of the tables and I'll bring us some tea."

"Don't be so damn bossy. You sit down and let me get it," he growled. "I'm not helpless."

She gave him an unperturbed smile. "Don't be tiresome, James. You can hardly carry a tray and use your walking stick." She turned and walked quickly to the counter, leaving him staring after her in mounting frustration.

Bly Rutherford came into the tent and strode toward him, her face set in tight, angry lines. He struggled to his feet as she reached his table. She said, "Damn you for your bad manners. How dare you walk out before the show is over? Is that how you repay my father for all he did for you and your people?"

"That whole spectacle is a farce—a parody. An insult to any North American Indian and a gross distortion of their life and ways. As for *my* people, my dear Miss Rutherford, they are English. Had you forgotten?"

"You seem to have forgotten who prevented you from being shipped to a Florida swamp along with the rest of the Chiricahua. You weren't English when I saw you in New York. You were pure Apache—blonde hair notwithstanding. You had no manners then and you've none now."

"Sam will understand why I walked out."

"No, he won't! He'll be hurt. He was in an absolute sweat thinking about performing for you and your mother. You're turning your back on him—and he's one of the few people since Tom Jeffords who's given a damn about the Apache. You certainly haven't done much for them, have you? You were too busy living in luxury. Do you even care that the Chiricahua are still prisoners-of-war after all these years?"

"I say, what *is* going on?" Nelia's aristocratic drawl interrupted. She placed a tray containing a teapot and cups on the table and her amused cool green stare went from one to the other. Beside Nelia, Hakan decided, Bly looked, at best, like a scrawny child dressed up as a careless and crumpled college professor.

Bly looked Nelia up and down insolently and responded, "I came to give you both a lesson in manners. And to warn you that if you say one word to hurt my father, I'll probably smash your heads together." She turned on her heel and stalked away.

Nelia's pale eyebrows went up in surprise. "How extraordinary! Ought we gird on our armor or something?"

"I understand she's returning to Oxford today, thank heaven," Hakan answered. Damn Sam Rutherford for his wild West show and his brat of a daughter. And as for Nelia and her icy beauty, perhaps it was time to ignite those fires that smoldered under her self-possessed surface. A year of widowhood with its resulting frustration was beginning to fray her a little around the edges.

33

Hakan tapped the carriage driver's shoulder with his walking stick. "Stop here."

They were at the crest of a gently sloping hill cloaked in purple heather. In front of them the rolling moors lay beneath a misty shroud that was not quite rain, nor fog, and would disappear with the rising sun.

Hakan had begun to take early morning carriage rides beyond the grounds of Merrinswood, partly to escape his sense of confinement, despite the vastness of the estate, but mostly to be alone. The young groom who drove the carriage would never dare address him without invitation, but was there to help him in and out of the carriage. Besides, Hakan was still too weak to handle the reins himself.

He walked slowly along the top of the hill, thinking about the encounter he'd had with Emily the previous evening. She'd cornered him in the dining room after everyone else had left and said, "Don't you think it's time you called in Hilliard Stoughton and rectified all of the errors in father's will? It's simply not fair that Robbie has to do all of the work here for a mere pittance. He should legally share the estate with you."

"Is there anything you, personally, require Emily?" Hakan had asked pointedly.

"Yes. A great deal. Your mother has done precious little since your father died, floating around the house like a wraith. Now she's taken up with that awful Rutherford person and she's less help than ever. I've had to take over most of her duties. I don't think either of you ever realized that the Merrin holdings are the equivalent of an enormous corporation. There's not only the land and the tenant farms here, but the land in the south, as well as the London bank."

Hakan said, "I'll speak with Robbie and get his opinion. And Emily, if you ever criticize my mother again, I'll have to ask you to leave."

A dull flush suffused her sallow skin and her mouth twisted angrily. She whispered, *"Sir Randolph Leighton"*, then turned on her heel and left. The implied threat of blackmail was clear.

A finger of sunlight cut through the mist swirling over the moors and illuminated the figure of a woman outlined against the sky at the top of the next hillock. She stood with her back to him, gazing into the blue-green infinity in much the same manner as he did. She wore a long cape against the chill of the morning, and her black wavy hair spilled loosely about her shoulders, tumbling down her back almost to her waist.

He had seen her on previous morning jaunts, but never close enough to get a glimpse of her face. She had perhaps seen him, but each of them always hastened away in opposite directions. He wondered idly what private demons she sought to conquer on her solitary sunrise journeys.

"I've brought someone to see you, James," Nelia announced, sweeping into the morning room as he was finishing breakfast.

Hakan looked up to see that she was followed by her brother Gilbert, the empty right sleeve of his jacket tucked into a pocket. Hakan rose and offered his left hand for the handshake. Gilbert's eyes didn't connect with his.

"Been meaning to drop in," Gilbert muttered. "But . . ."

Hakan rang for a footman to bring fresh tea and another rack of toast and platter of crumpets. They sat down, making small talk about inconsequential matters and carefully avoiding mentioning war or their respective wounds.

The similarities and differences between Nelia and Gilbert were disconcerting. They were both fair, but her hair was a shining halo while his was the dun color of wet sand. Her sparkling eyes flashed with the fire of emeralds, full of unspoken promises, but Gilbert's were the dull green of moss in a dark forest, and just as impenetrable. There was as much a family resemblance in their features as is possible between different sexes, but her self-confident composure seemed only a mask to hide her greedy desire to enjoy all of life's pleasures, while his concealed an underhanded self-interest of a much darker nature.

"I drove Gil over here in Daddy's new motorcar," Nelia announced gleefully. "Such fun!"

"I didn't know you knew how," Hakan said.

"She doesn't. We lurched all over the lane. Father will have a fit when he knows. He just has it on trial."

"Nonsense. I'm a natural-born driver. Still, I did forego my morning ride, so I'm off to the stables to borrow a mount, James. You two can catch up on all your news."

She whirled out of the room, leaving them to regard one another awkwardly. Hakan asked, "Do you . . ."

"Ride? No. What would be the point? I can hardly resume my polo playing without a right arm to hold the mallet, can I? Besides, Father is selling off our horses. He's in a bit of financial trouble." His voice dripped with self-pity and Hakan thought in sudden shock, I hope I don't sound like that.

"You've been seeing quite a lot of Nelia," Gilbert said after a moment's silence.

It was probably the other way around, Hakan thought, since it was she who visited him, but he nodded. "I've been grateful for her companionship."

Gilbert stood up and walked to the window, staring out at the garden. "Tragic about Charles, of course. Especially since he left her with tremendous debts. He always was too fond of gambling." He paused. "A lot has happened since you first came here."

Suddenly wary, Hakan asked, "And where exactly is that remark leading us, Gil?"

He didn't turn around. "Oh, I was remembering that weekend you came to Dunstan Hall . . . the weekend Randolph was murdered on the moors."

Hakan waited. Charles Pettigrew was dead but no doubt he'd told his friend Gilbert that he'd handed Hakan over to Sir Randolph Leighton that night. Hakan was tempted to tell Gilbert that if he had blackmail in mind he'd have to queue up behind Emily.

Gilbert turned around. He was mouthing a frosty imitation of Nelia's cool smile. "I . . . just wanted you to know that your secret's safe with me. I mean, after all, chances are we're about to become brothers-in-law, aren't we?"

So that was it. Hakan said carefully, "There is no under-standing between Nelia and me."

"But you're seeing each other exclusively," Gilbert per-sisted. "And if it hadn't been for the Sir Randolph mess, chances are she'd have married you instead of Charles." Hakan felt the throbbing pain in his head begin again and was glad when Nelia came back, announcing that it had begun to rain.

The following day, Hakan had a groom bring him a gentle mare and help him into the saddle. Ignoring a wave of dizziness, he guided her across the cobblestoned stableyard toward the fields to the rear of the Merrinswood grounds.

An hour later he was deep into the moors, every bone and muscle in his body aching from the ride. The blackened skin covering the wound in his left side felt puckered and stretched, like shrunken fabric; the headache that plagued him almost constantly pounded against his temple; and his wounded leg was numb, but he doggedly urged the mare along a narrow trail through the heather. He wasn't aware of the direction he was taking, but was afraid to stop and rest in case he was unable to remount.

The rolling moors seemed alien, unfamiliar without the insulation of the carriage around him, but at least today he was completely alone. He knew he should be turning back toward Merrinswood before his strength gave out, but per-versely kept going.

All at once the mare hesitated, reluctant to go on, and Hakan saw a dusty expanse of brackish water dotted with algae. Tugging on the reins, he guided the mare around the bog and into a sunny hollow.

He heard the child's voice first, strident, demanding. Then a woman's voice, low and soothing. The sounds came from the other side of a rolling hillock covered with yellow gorse. Hakan felt annoyed that someone else had invaded his private domain, and his first instinct was to turn back. But before he could turn the mare a child came over the top of the hill, tottering on unsteady little legs. A very small boy, probably not more than two years old, black-haired and as dark-eyed as Danior. The child laughed and plunged into the gorse bushes, obviously trying to hide from a pursuer.

Almost immediately a woman appeared, calling, "Garridan!

Garridan—come back at once. You bad boy. Where are you?"

Hakan recognized her instantly. She was not only the solitary walker in the mists he'd observed on other mornings, but now he saw that she was also the exotically lovely Mrs. Chambers. Hakan had met Danior's sister Chavi at his father's birthday party, the night he had died, and had never forgotten her. There was a quality of the earth about her that reminded him of some of his mature Chiricahua aunts, but Chavi was young and vibrant and that quality was unexpected and alluring in her.

The little boy galloped through the gorse bushes, picking up speed as the slope became steeper, and Hakan realized the child was hurtling toward the bog, which might well conceal quicksand.

Without pausing to speak to Chavi, Hakan turned the mare back toward the bog. The animal reared, whinnying in fright, and Hakan slid from the saddle, wincing as his injured leg hit the ground. He skirted the edge of the bog, so anxious to place himself between the treacherous quicksand and the child that he was unaware that he was moving without the aid of his walking stick.

The little boy skidded to a stop, looked up at Hakan and said solemnly, "Horsie."

Chavi came panting down the slope after him and swooped him up into her arms. At the same moment Hakan felt the familiar vise-grip around his head and momentary blackness. He went down on one knee, then rolled into a sitting position. Chavi and the child receded into a haze and Hakan shook his head, trying to clear his vision. He said, "A bog . . . I was afraid there might be quicksand."

"Yes, thank you. I've warned him, but he's so little, and a bit too adventuresome for his own good."

She came back into focus and he saw that she wore a guarded, closed expression. He realized she resented his presence as much as he'd resented hers. They had both come here to be alone. He still sat on the ground, unsure if he would be able to stand, certain he'd never be able to get back onto the horse.

Chavi's full lips curved slightly, not quite into a smile. She said, "You look so much like your father did as a young man. Seeing you on the ground like that . . . reminds me of my first meeting with him. His horse balked at a stream and threw him."

She wore a full skirt of deep burgundy and a pale yellow blouse, against which her dark hair was a glorious mass of waves. Her skin was golden, indicating hours in the sun, and only her eyes betrayed her inner turmoil. Although the death of her daughter was reason enough for that unbearable pain in her eyes, he felt there was some other mystery concealed there. He recalled that Danior had been angry and uncommunicative after being reunited with Chavi, but had never explained why. In those hectic days following his father's death, there'd been no time for anything other than the pressing affairs of the estate.

"I wasn't aware that you knew my father," he said. "I mean, before Danior brought you to Merrinswood for the birthday party." He recalled when he'd first met Danior as a child that the boy had told him of the lady with the kind eyes—Jean Leighton—assisting Chavi give birth. But there had been no mention of his father knowing her.

Chavi looked away. "Oh, I knew your father before that." She placed her son down on his feet, took his hand, and started to lead him away.

Hakan called after her, "Have you heard from Danior?"

She stopped, looking back over her shoulder through the silken curtain of her hair. "No. Have you?"

He shook his head. "I thought perhaps he was with you."

"Danior would never return to the caravans."

"You're living with the gypsies?" Hakan wasn't really surprised, since she wore gypsy clothes, but wanted to keep her in conversation with him a little longer.

"The caravans are camped over by the river. Just as they were the summer before Brenna was born. I won't go with them when they leave in the autumn, however. I wouldn't want to be too far away from her grave." She paused. "My father's buried here, too. If he were still alive I wouldn't have been able to rejoin the tribe."

She started to walk away, the little boy tugging at her hand, and Hakan asked, "Would you . . . come back and help me to my feet?"

Wheeling around, she regarded him with suspicion. "I beg your pardon?"

"Help me up," he said irritably, feeling helpless and hating it.

"Oh, I think you can manage. I'm not going to make the same mistake again." Without explaining the remark, she set off up the hill, the child racing ahead of her.

Hakan wallowed about on the ground, sweating and cursing at the way his wounded leg refused to take his weight, as every time he got to his feet it would buckle and he'd collapse again. But eventually he was able to balance himself on his good leg and lurch back to the mare. Leaning against her while he caught his breath, he realized in sudden elation that he had walked without the stick. Then he thought, now how the hell do I get back into the saddle?

It took several falls, every Chiricahua and English swear word he knew, and all his remaining strength, but eventually he was able to ride back to Merrinswood, feeling alive again for the first time in ages.

At Nelia's suggestion, Sarah was planning a party at Merrinswood, a delayed celebration of Hakan's homecoming and an official announcement to friends and neighbors that the mourning period for his father was over.

Emily waylaid Hakan on the terrace on the morning of the party and hissed under her breath, "If you're planning to announce your engagement to Nelia tonight, you'd better make some provisions for Robbie and me before you move that conniving female in here."

"What makes you think I'm going to marry Nelia?"

She snorted indelicately. "Everyone knows she set her cap for you years ago. Charles was her second choice. She's determined to be your countess and you, poor fool, will have no say in the matter. It's common knowledge that her father is almost bankrupt, hanging on by a thread and trying to convince everybody all's well. He even put on a big show of solvency by buying a motorcar though he can barely afford to feed a horse. Gilbert's not going to be any help and Nelia still has Charles's debts to pay off. A rich husband will solve all of their problems."

"You're misinterpreting her interest in me," Hakan said, "and mine in her."

"Men!" Emily spat out the word with thin-lipped disgust. "You turn into blithering idiots at the sight of a pretty face. It took all my time to convince Rob how foolish he'd be to rush over to Dunstan Hall and propose to Nelia the minute she returned as a widow. She would have laughed in his face. She's never given him the time of day, and never will, since he's a penniless bastard, thanks to you."

"Rob is your twin, Emily, and he puts up with both your acid tongue and your meddling in his affairs," Hakan snapped. "Don't try it with me."

She tossed her head in a gesture of disdain. "You'll be like putty in Nelia's dainty little hands, too. She'll catch you and move herself and her good-for-nothing brother in here for you to support."

Just as Jean Leighton and her brother had moved in with his father, Hakan thought, disturbed by the sense of history repeating itself. He wondered if his father had also been obligated in some way to the Leightons. He recalled his father saying to him once, "Beware of the meek—and the weak, my boy. They inherit the earth by being crafty enough to get the strong to look after them." Had he been referring to the Leightons? And had Hakan now put himself into the same position with the Dunstans? But no, there was nothing meek, or weak, about Nelia.

He leaned against the rim of a marble urn holding a profusion of summer flowers, stately lupins, closed-mouth snapdragons, and pansies with velvet eyes. He still felt unsteady without the aid of the walking stick, but was determined not to use it again. Emily made no motion to leave, and wishing to end the conversation, he said, "I have no intention of marrying anyone just yet."

Emily's nose twitched slightly, but she made no comment and simply walked away. He immediately went to the stables and had a boy saddle the gentle mare.

As he expected, Chavi was walking on the moors. She was alone and when he reined his horse and inquired about her son she said, "Mithuna, an old friend, is taking care of him. I wanted to be alone and I still do. Go away, Lord Moreland. I don't want you near me. The moors are big enough for both of us."

He slid from the saddle, managed to hide a grimace of pain as his feet hit the ground, and began to walk beside her. "Danior told me that gypsies have the gift of second sight. Is that true?"

"If you want your fortune told, go to the caravans. There are plenty of fortune-tellers there."

"Why do you dislike me so?"

"I don't know you well enough to dislike you. Nor do I want to know you."

"Were you hurt by my father?"

She turned abruptly, her eyes narrowed. "Who have you been talking to?"

"Nobody. It was just a guess. It seems my father hurt many people. I had a feeling I was paying for his sins."

"You don't need a gypsy then, you've got second sight yourself."

"All of mankind was born with the same capability of intuition. Primitive people rely on it constantly, but we so-called civilized people neglected it to the point that we've almost lost it."

She stopped walking and placed her hands on her hips. In the soft light of the morning her beauty was breathtaking, her large dark eyes luminous, and her perfect oval face framed with silken waves of hair as shiny as obsidian. "What is it you want of me?"

"I don't know," he answered honestly. "I kept coming back, morning after morning, just to see you walking in the dawn mists. You seemed mysterious . . . self-contained in some way I couldn't fathom. I'm curious about you." And fascinated by your beauty, he thought, but knew she wouldn't want to hear that.

"Go on back to your great golden house. I want nothing to do with you, Lord Moreland."

"My name is Hakan."

"Mine is *Mrs*. Dirk Chambers. I have a husband living in Australia and it isn't proper for me to be alone with another man."

"For years I've regarded Danior as a brother. You're his sister. Can't we at least be friends?"

"No. We can't even be acquaintances." Picking up her skirts, she hurried away from him. He couldn't catch up, he knew, and watched her go, still unsure why he wanted so badly to talk to her. Perhaps it was merely that he missed Danior.

Hakan went out through the French windows to the

terrace. Behind him the musicians played a waltz and couples whirled around the floor, the women's dresses a glistening rainbow of colored silks and satins.

The late summer evening was warm, heady with the scent of roses, and he felt restless, trapped by the house and throngs of guests. He'd become aware too of the distance that had sprung up between his mother and himself and was unsure why it had happened. His mother seemed distant and unapproachable, living in some world of her own. She seemed removed from all but the concerns of the family. She expressed the hope that Robbie and Emily had reconciled with their mother, wondered aloud sometimes what had become of Danior, but Hakan had the feeling that Sarah wasn't really there. It was as if her ghost softly trod the stairs or lingered in the upstairs gallery, silently staring at the family portraits.

Of course, Sarah had been a devoted nurse to him also, but they no longer talked about important matters as they had in the old days. She repeated, almost daily it seemed, "As soon as you're strong again, you'll take your rightful place here," until it became a litany, perhaps to reassure herself as much as to remind him.

He was particularly aware of this tonight as Sam Rutherford attended the party and was never far from his mother's side, while she in turn seemed to light up in some way when Sam spoke to her. He hadn't returned to America with the rest of the troupe, giving some excuse about unfinished business in England and visiting his daughter at Oxford, but Hakan was well aware that Sam was courting his mother and felt a natural male territoriality about that.

"James! There you are. Why are you hiding out here?"

"I was waiting for you," he lied as Nelia came rustling across the terrace in her ice-blue satin gown. The moonlight turned her fair hair almost white, and her bare shoulders were as pale as lilies. He reached out and let his fingertips trail lightly down her arm. "Do you need your wrap?"

She caught his hand and pressed it to her flesh, then tilted her face upward toward his. The invitation was obvious, and he bent and kissed her. A moment later she was in his arms and he crushed her slender body close to his, feeling desire again for the first time since he'd been wounded.

Nelia allowed him to part her lips, but his tongue ran into the barrier of closed teeth. When he slipped one hand upward to try to cup the breast that pressed so tantalizingly against his chest she pushed him away. "Now, now, James, be good!"

His arms fell to his sides. "Why do you do this? You've flirted with me all evening, given me glances that could only be interpreted as invitations, followed me out here and offered me your lips—now you slam the door shut in my face."

She pouted. "You take liberties beyond what I offer. I require some declaration about your intentions before I give more of myself."

"Very well. My intentions were to attempt to seduce you."

She gasped, then gave him a stinging slap. He rubbed his cheek ruefully, but felt little remorse as she haughtily walked back into the house.

After a few minutes Hakan followed. Robbie stood at the French windows. "Y-you all right, Hakan? Not g-getting too tired?"

Hakan took his arm. "Let's go into the library and have a quiet drink."

Nodding, Robbie murmured, "Capital idea."

They departed as unobtrusively as they could, and amid the silent stacks of books Hakan asked abruptly, "Do you still have a crush on Nelia?"

"N-no, of course not. Is that why you're h-holding off?"

Hakan wished they'd lit a lamp so he could study Rob's expression. It was important to know exactly how he felt about her, because Hakan knew he wouldn't be able to maintain the status quo with Nelia much longer. "I just wanted you to know that I'm not seriously interested in Nelia, Rob. She's merely playing Florence Nightingale with me, perhaps because she wasn't able to do so with Charles."

"Enjoy it then. Nelia w-wouldn't l-look my way if I were the last man on earth." He paused. "Therefore I'd be a f-fool to pine for her, w-wouldn't I?"

In the dimly lit library Rob's hand found its way gently to Hakan's shoulder. "B-but I do think the least you c-can do is k-keep her in the family."

There was, Hakan thought, a particular poignancy to Rob's last remark.

❖   ❖   ❖

Chavi put Garridan to bed in Mithuna's caravan and then slipped away by herself. Tonight the music around the campfire seemed too poignant, too sad. The violins called to that deep vein of melancholy that ran through her very soul. Nor did she want to be with Mithuna, whose sharp old gypsy eyes would probe and pry and uncover all her secret thoughts.

The river was a silver ribbon in the moonlight as she walked along the bank away from the encampment, wanting to lose herself somewhere; to leave behind the numbing grief of the loss of her daughter that was with her in every waking moment and brought her back from sleep many times each night. Oh, God, was there any more terrible pain than the loss of a child? Her torment was a knife in her heart that would be there forever.

When the sound of violins had faded into the distance, she sat down and wrapped her arms about her knees, gazing at the changing patterns of light and shadow on the water as night clouds drifted across the sky. Paper crackled in the pocket of her skirt and she remembered that she carried Lysander's last letter there.

She pulled out the crumpled sheet of paper and smoothed it against her knee, straining to read the words by the pallid light of a half moon.

My dear Chavi,

I'm writing to apologize to you. I realize now I had no right to criticize you for the manner in which you laid Brenna to rest. She was your daughter, not mine. I'm sorry for what I said to you and can only offer the explanation that I had not felt grief so acutely since the loss of my son in Australia. I suppose, too, I was hurt by your ignoring all of my invitations to visit me in Ireland, and by your apparent indifference to the risk I took in coming to Yorkshire for the funeral. I should have recognized that you were too overwhelmed by your grief to be aware of my feelings. But perhaps what devasted me most of all was Garridan's reaction to me. . . .

The little boy had screamed in terror at Lysander's scarred face, and no amount of coaxing would persuade the child to go anywhere near him. Chavi hadn't been able to understand why Lysander didn't simply leave Garri alone, instead of persisting in trying to make friends with him. Especially in the somber circumstances of the funeral preparations.

Wracked with grief, she had felt a callous disregard for anyone else's pain, which couldn't possibly be as great as hers. She had, in fact, taken pleasure in inflicting small wounds on those around her, in some mistaken belief that it would ease her own agony. When Lysander had asked why she'd ignored all of his letters begging her to bring Garri to Ireland, Chavi had responded, "Because we were having too much fun in London."

She supposed she had been cruel to Lysander. Perhaps if he'd stayed more than a few days she could have explained that she was simply unable to part the suffocating curtain of grief even a crack so that she could acknowledge his presence.

Looking back, she saw that she might at least have told him that she had missed him, because she had. But how to explain the heady excitement of those days before the tragedy, when it seemed that all of London was at her feet and life was an intoxicating banquet laid out for her delight? The parties, the pleasures, the suitors . . . Danior brought his friends from the opera company, and handsome young men surrounded her wherever she went, always ready to take her off on an excursion, or escort her to the theater or a ball. A rumor had circulated, she wasn't sure by whom, that she was a widow, and she didn't deny it.

There had been times when she'd return to her pleasant mews house, eager to discuss some event with Lysander, only to remember he wasn't there. With the press of one social engagement after another, there was never any spare time to write him. The trouble was, she wanted the life she was leading as well as Lysander's friendship, and she couldn't have both. He was exiled to Ireland, to some tiny little village outside of Dublin, and Chavi had had enough of being buried in the backwoods of life. She wanted to make up for every moment she'd languished, lonely and bored, in the Australian Outback.

She looked down again at the letter on her lap, reading for the hundredth time the words of condolence that Lysander had written.

Nothing anyone says is going to help you now Chavi. You're going to have to suffer for a while. There will be days when you'll convince yourself it never happened, that Brenna is still alive and will come back to you, and there will be times when you'll feel such anger that you're sure you'll burst from it. You'll rage against God and heaven and the cruelty of fate and wish you'd never been born. After that will come the time when you realize that it did happen, she's dead, her physical being is gone from you forever, and although it's the worst time of all, welcome it, because it will be the beginning of the healing for you.

After that you'll be able to remember her life, not her death, and know that she will never really be dead while she exists in your memory. You won't believe me now, but it is true that time will close the wounds, leaving only scars that you'll learn to live with. And if anybody on earth knows about living with scars, you know it's me.

You were angry with me because I had to leave immediately after the funeral, and wouldn't let me explain. No, it wasn't because I disapproved of your gypsy mumbo jumbo as you thought. I was afraid someone might see me and recognize me. You see, this wasn't my first visit to England since our return from Australia. I was in Yorkshire at the time of Lord Moreland's death.

I arrived at your lodgings shortly after your brother came to pick you up to take you to Merrinswood for Merrin's birthday party. Foolishly, I decided to follow you, to slip into the grounds and perhaps catch a glimpse of you consorting with the aristocracy.

How can I explain my stupidity? The pride of a mentor, perhaps, who wishes to see his student's graduation. I did see you—you were breathtaking in a deep green dress, and the eyes of every man in the room were on you—but unfortunately I too was seen. My face at the window must have almost caused that old butler to suffer a stroke similar to his master's. Luckily for me he wasn't able to move fast enough, nor summon help in time to catch me.

To one who has never experienced the horror of prison it might perhaps seem cowardly of me to fear recapture so much. But I do fear it, far more than I fear death. You know the other events of that night. I felt it best not to see you, so before dawn I was on my way back to Ireland.

And lastly, I am enclosing another bank draft for you from Dirk. He's still traveling the Outback. Further drafts will arrive for you in care of *poste restante* at Carsibrook, since you indicated you intend to remain in Yorkshire. Please write and tell me how you are faring, and I beg you again, as soon as you are inclined, to please come and visit me here in Ireland.

Your friend,
Lysander

Chavi folded the letter and slipped it back into her pocket. She wasn't sure why Dirk continued to send her money, or why he sent it via his brother instead of directly to her. She'd asked Lysander not to tell Dirk that he had a son, and was sure he'd respected that wish since if Dirk had known about Garri he surely would have wanted him. So Dirk's financial support was doubly surprising.

She was troubled by Lysander's admission that he had been at Merrinswood the night Richard died. Just before Danior had summoned a carriage to take her back to her lodgings that night, she had suddenly experienced a wave of acute horror. In the midst of a laughing crowd of people she had felt utterly alone and helpless. She had choked on a piece of birthday cake, gasping for breath, and been overwhelmed by a sense of impending disaster. It was there in the house, a force older than time, and as inexorable. The feeling passed in an instant and was replaced by a sense of utmost peace. But she felt weak and shivered so much that someone asked if she were ill.

The incident had occurred after Richard had been taken back up to his room. Members of his immediate family had gone up to bid him good-night. Danior, too. He'd said, "I'd better go and say good-night, for Sarah's sake, although I'd as soon punch his jaw, the old lecher. Then I'll take you back to your lodgings if you're still sure you don't want to stay the night."

It was while Danior was gone that she'd experienced the premonition of death, although she didn't realize it until the following morning when she learned that Richard was dead. Natural causes, they'd said, but Chavi knew that someone had helped him on his journey across the river of shades.

And in this moment, alone beside the endlessly flowing river, she wondered about Lysander's face at the window, and asked herself why she had come back to where her odyssey had begun, and what it was she waited for here.

34

Nelia arrived on the morning after the party just as Hakan was crossing the hall on his way to the stables. He said, "Good morning. You're up early."

She gave him a proprietary kiss on his cheek. Nothing in her attitude suggested he'd offended her the previous evening. "I heard about your early morning rides. Why didn't you tell me you'd started riding again?"

"I'm not very good yet. I'd rather ride alone."

She pouted. "But I want to go with you."

"As a matter of fact, I'm a little tired today. I'd just decided not to go." He was annoyed that he found it necessary to lie to her.

Her gaze lingered on his riding clothes for a moment, then she cast a practiced eye about the hall and up to the open portrait gallery above. "The early morning light isn't too kind to the old place, is it?" She lowered her voice. "You know, James, your mother's neglected the house dreadfully since your father died. All of the oil paintings need cleaning and restoring, and some of the carpets are showing wear."

"Oh, I don't think Merrinswood is going to wrack and ruin yet," he answered lightly, resenting the criticism and the implication that Nelia felt she could do better as the lady of the house.

Robbie came out of the study and peered nearsightedly in their direction. "Oh, th-there you are, James. I was hoping to c-catch you . . . oh, hullo, Nelia, s-sorry, d-didn't mean to interrupt."

She didn't look in Robbie's direction as she gave him a muttered, "Morning."

"Nelia's going for a ride," Hakan said. "Let's go into the study, Rob. I want to talk to you, too."

"Sh-she didn't look too p-pleased about you walking away and l-leaving her," Robbie said when they were in the study. "She's s-so b-beautiful . . . even when she f-frowns." His myopic blue eyes peered enviously at Hakan. "Y-you're a l-lucky man."

"Am I?" He sat on the edge of the desk. "I'm beginning to feel the jaws of the trap closing, Rob, and don't know what to do about it."

Robbie gave a hollow laugh. "If th-there were a way for me to bait the t-trap instead of you . . . I'd j-jump at the ch-chance."

Hakan looked at a painting which hung over the mantlepiece. It depicted a horseman riding on the moors, a ghostly figure riding the waves of blue-tinted mist. "You know what I'm most afraid of, Rob? That I'll unwittingly slip into the same way of life as my father. Marriage to someone like Nelia . . . and then what? The same constant searching for antidotes to boredom?"

It was clear from Robbie's perplexed expression that he couldn't appreciate such a dilemma. "B-but I assure you, you won't be bored when you t-take over the r-running of the estate. It's a c-constant challenge. And I know you're joking about becoming b-bored with Nelia. Why, I could just s-sit and l-look at her all day and not need any more from l-life."

Hakan wasn't listening. He tapped a neat stack of estate correspondence with his forefinger. "I want to talk to you about the Merrin holdings. I think it's time I found out exactly what it is I inherited."

"Wait, dammit! Don't run away."

"I told you to stay away from me," Chavi flung over her shoulder.

Hakan yelled after her, "I know where Danior is."

She came back slowly, her large dark eyes wary. The moors were damp and chill this morning, hinting that summer would soon end. She clutched a black wool shawl around her and her cheeks were pink, her hair a wonderful wild tangle, dewdrops of moisture here and there among the dark strands like scattered jewels.

When she reached his side Hakan handed her the picture postcard—a sepia picture of the beach at Blackpool. On the reverse Danior had scrawled, *I'm traveling with Pas and*

Alphonso the Second. Singing again, too. After all, the critics did say I was a street singer, didn't they?

Chavi stared at the words for a full minute. "A beggar, that's what he is. No gypsy ever begs on the streets."

"You're too hard on him. He and Pas aren't begging. They play their music and entertain in order to draw a crowd, then sharpen knives and scissors. That isn't begging. It's honest work."

"What sort of a life is that for a man who's been to university? A man who sang grand opera?"

"It's the life he chooses to live right now. Perhaps in time he'll choose another."

She sighed. "Strange how we can see things so clearly when it comes to strangers, yet be so blind about people we love."

"I wish I were one of the strangers you see things clearly about," Hakan said.

Her eyes searched his face. "You're very unhappy, aren't you? You're a man fighting a battle with yourself. No one can help you with that, least of all me."

He smiled. "I was hoping for a glimpse into the future from you. Instead you sound like Doctor McGreal."

"Speaking of the doctor, I must go. Garridan hasn't been well and Mithuna's medicine doesn't seem to be helping. So I'm taking him to the doctor this morning. If I'm to be first to see him, I must leave now. Thank you for sharing Danior's postcard with me."

"I'm sorry your little boy is ill. I hope he'll soon be well. Chavi—"

"Yes?"

"If you'd give me half a chance, I think I could show you that I'm not my father."

"No," she said thoughtfully. "I see now that you're not. Nor am I the girl I once was. But there can be nothing between you and me, because we both feel a certain tension that tells us we couldn't only be friends."

He was surprised by her directness and knew she was right, although he hadn't admitted it even to himself. There was a warm earthiness about her that heated the blood in his veins. He had never felt the combined need to be with a woman in both friendship and lust before. It was a disturbing sensation.

*   *   *

Andrew said, "Chavi's bringing her little boy in again today. Would you like to see her?"

Jean put the teapot back onto the breakfast table. "I . . . I'm not sure. Isn't that ridiculous?"

"No. It just means that you would still prefer to avoid reminders of your life with Richard. The fact that Chavi bore him a child surely must have caused you a great deal of pain."

"A child who is now dead." Jean sighed. "How very sad life can be."

Andrew's hand slid across the snowy tablecloth and caught hers. He squeezed her fingers. "Some people have happy endings. We did."

Her smile was radiant, lighting up her exquisite eyes like moonlight flooding the dark ocean. For a moment he lost himself in her eyes, feeling the warmth of their love flow between them. He stroked the back of her hand, savoring these tender moments they shared. His own life was so happy, so fulfilled in every way. Yet he constantly worried about his love being strong enough to protect her from Emily's rejection, from her fear that Robbie loved Merrinswood too much and would one day have to leave and his heart would be broken.

"How is Chavi's little boy?" she asked.

"A bad case of the croup. I'm concerned about him."

"And what about Lord Moreland? Will you call on him today?"

Andrew frowned. "Frankly, I don't know what else I can do for him. I can't find any medical reason why his leg still troubles him, or for his constant headaches."

"Perhaps you should write to your pen friend?"

"Pen friend?"

"Dr. Freud, in Vienna."

Andrew sipped his tea. "Yes, I may do that. When I look at that young man and his mother and remember how they were when they first arrived, glowing with health and vitality, and now. . . ."

"Sarah is ill?"

"She seemed to go into a decline after Richard died. Nothing I can detect, either physically or mentally, but there's a terrible lethargy about her I can feel rather than see."

Jean bent over her plate and Andrew felt a pang of jealousy that perhaps in her memory she was seeing Richard again, and remembering how she too had once loved him.

A very old gypsy woman barred Hakan's way, standing with arms akimbo in front of her brightly painted caravan. "She doesn't want to see you. Her child is sick."

"I can help him," Hakan said. She pointed back down the lane in the direction he'd come, in a silent command for him to leave. He shouted, "Chavi! I've collected some herbs that we can boil to make steam to help him breathe."

Mithuna said, "I've done that. It didn't help."

"Then you picked the wrong ones. Get out of my way, old woman, before I have to throw you over my shoulder and move you."

Several of the Romany men moved closer, forming a threatening semicircle around them. Hakan glanced at them contemptuously. He continued to address the closed caravan. "If you don't come out, Chavi, not only am I going to have to manhandle this old woman, but I'm probably also going to have to take on most of your tribe."

The curtains behind the driver's seat parted and Chavi's head appeared. "I should let you fight them. Then you'd stop limping about like an invalid."

"I'm not limping today. This is one of my nonlimping days. May I see your son?"

She motioned for him to climb into the caravan.

Inside, their belongings were neatly stacked and the little boy lay on a makeshift pallet, sobbing hoarsely between coughs and gasps. Hakan knelt beside him, feeling his forehead, which was dangerously feverish. He handed Chavi a pouch. "The herbs should be put in a kettle, and we'll need a sheet to trap the steam."

"Mithuna tried that. It didn't help. Doctor McGreal says it's the croup and gave me cough medicine."

"If he doesn't breathe easier after trying my remedies, I'll go away and never come near you again."

"Done," Chavi said, taking the pouch of herbs from him.

An hour later they sat side by side on the driver's seat of Mithuna's caravan as Garridan slept peacefully in the back. Hakan had stayed with the child, talking to him and calming him, and Chavi wondered if his presence and the touch of his hand on Garri's fevered brow had been more healing than his herbs.

Hakan said, "He may have a worse attack during the night hours. Will you trust me to prepare something for him to drink? It will help clear the mucus from his air passages."

Her face was drawn, the dark circles under her eyes telling of sleepless nights. "All right. Danior told me that you have ways of helping sick people."

Chavi intercepted him before he reached the caravan. "He's still asleep. He was so much better last night. I'm grateful to you." The dark smudges were still under her eyes.

"Good. When are *you* going to sleep?"

She bit her lower lip. "Don't worry about me. Hakan, I said I was grateful and I am. But I don't want you to come back."

"Why not?"

"Because twice before in my life I allowed unsuitable men to . . . to put me in situations that were bad for me. Twice bitten, thrice shy. It's not going to happen again, not with you."

"You speak empty words, without meaning. You try to talk away what you feel."

She turned and ran from him.

After that, Hakan took toys and baskets of fruit to Garri and Chavi couldn't bring herself to send him away. He patiently told the boy stories, held him when the coughing wracked his body, and for a little while relieved Chavi of caring for a very ill child.

"Why do you do this?" she asked him.

"I do it for Garridan—for myself. Perhaps for my lost brother, Danior, because God knows Garri looks a great deal like him."

Gradually Chavi's resistance to Hakan diminished, because her son clearly adored him. She would often stay just outside the caravan and listen as he regaled the boy with the fascinating stories of White Painted Woman and her children, and, most entertaining of all, the trickster Coyote.

Hakan became a familiar figure to the gypsies camped along the river, and Mithuna's perceptive old eyes especially watched him closely. Mithuna drew Chavi away from the others singing around the campfire one night and said, "Your heart isn't here with us. I can see in your eyes you're think-ing about that blue-eyed son of his father. But is that wise? His father betrayed you. Your Hakan is of the same blood—and the same station in life."

"Hakan is able to take my mind off Brenna, at least for a little while," Chavi said. "And Garri seems to like him. But don't worry, I'm not the gullible girl I was with his father. And I haven't forgotten that Hakan and I are of two different worlds. Nothing can come of knowing him."

Mithuna sighed. "Perhaps your destiny was always inter-woven with his. Perhaps this is something that must be dealt with between you, so you can both go on. I don't want to see you hurt again, child. Don't look for more from him than he can give you."

"You know, Mithuna . . . he's different from us, but he's not one of them either. There's a . . . majesty in him somehow."

The old woman caught her breath. "Is it already too late to save you?" She seized Chavi's hand and turned it over, looked at her palm, and then dropped it to clutch her head, pressing bony old fingers into Chavi's temples as if to squeeze every secret thought right out of her skull. Chavi had pulled away in alarm and said, "Don't tell my future! I don't want to know it."

Hakan and Chavi walked together along the riverbank. It was a clear crisp autumn evening with a crescent moon like a silver comma punctuating the sky.

"The caravans are moving on tomorrow. They'll go south for the winter, down to Devon or Cornwall," Chavi said.

He caught her hand and held it. "You won't go with them? I can't lose your friendship now. It's meant more to me than you can know."

She gently pulled her hand away. They always carefully avoided physical contact and usually met only in the early mornings on the moors, with Garridan playing between them. Now, as she walked in the still night air at the side of this strange, compelling man, she wondered if she'd allowed their friendship to continue too long for her own good. She had begun to look forward to being with him, to miss him when she didn't see him. She was even a little jealous of the fair-haired Nelia, whose pursuit of him was an occasional topic of discussion between them. He had spoken briefly about his boyhood in the Chiricahua mountains and south-western deserts of America, but she had learned more from the myths and legends he'd shared with Garridan. She had told him some bare details about the Australian Outback, including the small white lie that her husband intended to send for her as soon as he was back on his feet. There were also quiet times, when it was enough just to be together without conversation.

But Chavi knew it had to end. The physical tension between them was growing unbearable. Even while she told herself their parting was inevitable, she felt an old familiar yearning and wondered if it would be so wrong to give in to it, just once, before she said good-bye.

"Hakan . . . I asked you to come to me tonight because I wanted to talk to you without Garri or anyone else distract-ing us. I shan't be leaving with the caravans, but that doesn't mean I can go on seeing you. Whatever there was between us—perhaps it was only a time for kindred souls to be together . . . I had a friend once who said more people are bound by mutual need than for any other reason. Maybe it was like that with us. We were both wounded and needed time to heal, to be with a sympathetic companion. But what-ever it was, it has to end—tonight."

He stopped walking, turned and grasped her shoulders, ignoring her struggle to pull away. "I won't give you up. You're too important to me."

"I'm not yours. I never was and I never will be. Hakan, for God's sake—*I'm not free.*"

"I love you."

"No!" Her voice rose to a scream. "Don't say it. It's not true."

"It's the greatest truth I've ever known. I've never touched you, yet if I never see you again the imprint of your flesh will forever be on mine. My eyes will never look upon beauty again because it won't be shared with you. My mind will never capture a new thought or a fresh idea because you won't be with me to hear it."

In the pale light of the new moon his face was shadowed, immobile. His voice was low, filled with passion. There was at once a simplicity and a complexity to the feelings he stated. It didn't matter to him whether or not she felt the same way. She looked up at him with both sadness and admiration. Would any other man on earth have dared say those things without first being sure the woman was ready to hear them? She shivered, knowing instinctively that this would be the only declaration he would make, and if she denied him now, she would never see him again. But the obstacles between them were insurmountable. They were separated by more than a rigidly enforced class system, by more even than her legal ties to another man. Between them lay the impenetrable barrier of the ghosts from the past.

"Chavi," Hakan said urgently, "your husband lost all right to you when he sent you away. You haven't seen him for over two years. He abandoned his marriage, you, his child. How can you continue to be loyal to such a man?"

"He sends me money—"

"What is money? I send money to my tailor. To you I want to give every part of myself, to be with you night and day in tears and laughter. Together we can be whole, complete. I know it and so do you. I want you to be my wife."

"No, Hakan," Chavi whispered, tears spilling over. "It can't be, ever." She took his hand and drew him down on the riverbank beside her, then put her arms around his neck and pulled his head down to her breast, cradling him there next to her heart.

He pressed his mouth to the hollow of her throat, and she kissed the livid scar on his temple, then slipped her blouse from her shoulders. His hands hovered for an instant above her breasts, then he took the warm flesh in a gentle grip and bent to kiss the taut nipples.

The night air was cool against her naked body after she discarded her skirt and petticoat. When he fumbled impatiently with his shirt buttons she helped him. His body was beginning to lose the gauntness it had acquired after he was wounded, but she gasped when the moonlight found the blackened evidence of the worst of his wounds, sprawling around his side and over his chest.

"Oh, Hakan," she said, and kissed the puckered skin tenderly, then let her lips find his flat nipples. She ran her hands over his strong pectoral muscles and murmured, "How smooth your skin is."

Picking up her hand, he kissed her palm. "When the Apache first saw white men, they were repulsed by the sparse hair on their heads and abundant hair on their bodies—which reminded the Apache of bears. As I started to mature I used to take a stone and rub away the hair that grew on my chest. Luckily it was very fair, so it didn't show and shame me."

"I wish I could have known you then. When we were both very young and not so separated by . . . circumstances."

"We're together now," he whispered, his lips closing with hers. His hands were in her hair, then they were everywhere. Their bodies strained to be so close there was nowhere that her flesh ended and his began, it had fused into one mantle that enclosed both of them.

For Chavi his lovemaking was beyond what she'd dreamed of or longed for during the lonely years. It was fierce and tender and fulfilling as nothing, no one, had ever been before or would be again. This moment was pure joy. There was a singing in her heart she'd heard only once before, and then it had been but a dream, long ago in Australia the night she'd escaped from the bush fire. The refrain told of finding the one man her restless spirit had always sought.

She held nothing back, giving all of herself and receiving in return a myriad of sensations, and most of all, the affirmation of life itself.

As he shuddered and called her name, in that instant she was able to let go of every pain and sorrow and lose herself in acute pleasure that transported her away from the ordinary world and into some mystic realm of the senses. Minds met as bodies were left behind on some earthly plain, knowing when they were reunited there would be a rejuvenation of both spirit and flesh.

Hakan seized her face in his hands and kissed her mouth again. His voice shook with emotion. "Chavi, making love to you is like making love to the earth itself . . . like going home, like being one with all of nature and whirling through the air and the sky and being on the mountaintop and lifted beyond time. . . ."

Breathless, he collapsed on her, laughing and tasting her skin and kissing her breasts and fondling her thighs in astonished delight that the fulfillment of desire could prove more exquisitely satisfying than its anticipation.

"Long ago," he said, "I lived in direct contact with my world and my life was happy. Now I see what the so-called civilizing of me has done—it had separated me from nature, insulated me from being close to the earth. Tonight, making love to you, everything is clear to me again."

At length they came together again, wrapped in each other's arms, to lie quietly under the stars and reflect. Hakan said, "Of course you will marry me. If necessary, I'll simply throw you over my horse and ride off with you, as my Apache father would have done."

Chavi didn't laugh, as he expected. "We can't meet again. I asked you to come to me tonight so that I could say good-bye. My husband is back in England. I'm going to him tomorrow."

Hakan's arms tightened around her. "We'll go to him together—"

"No! Oh, God forgive me, I should have told you sooner." She paused for so long that he had to whisper her name to bring her back. She said, "There's nothing I want from the Merrins now that she's gone, but I think you ought to know that my daughter . . . Brenna was your half sister. Your father was her father."

Hakan squeezed his eyes shut as everything crashed down around him.

"There, you see?" Chavi said gently. "It's not just that I'm married, or that you're an Earl of the realm and I'm a gypsy. It's much, much more, isn't it?"

He was silent, wishing he could tell her what in his heart he knew would be a lie.

Chavi caught his hands in hers. "Don't be sad, Hakan. Be glad, as I am, that we had a little time together. I think we were both wandering around in the dark when we met. Now we can start looking for the dawn. I want you to think about something . . . I believe many people make the mistake of thinking that happiness is something that comes to us later in life, like gout or rheumatic bones. It seems to me that you've been waiting for something for a long time that you may not even really want."

Or was it, she wondered, something she wanted him to give up? Even as she had spoken the brave words to open the door for him to leave her, had she been hoping he'd tell her that nothing mattered except the two of them together? That he'd give up title and lands and everything that was his birthright in order to be with her?

He was silent for a long time, then at last said bitterly,

"Even from beyond the grave . . . my father destroys everything I love."

"Yes," Sarah said. "I've known since the night your father died. When I presented Chavi to him, I felt the undercurrent between them, as well as Danior's anger toward him. I left them with him and moved to another group of guests, but I overheard enough to guess the truth. When I asked him later, Danior confirmed that Richard had fathered Brenna."

She sat in her favorite chair by the library fireplace and Hakan sat opposite her, his legs stiffly stretched across the sheepskin rug. The unbearable ache in his wounded leg foretold of an approaching rainstorm, while a different kind of ache in his chest threatened to stop him from breathing.

His mother added, "I saw no reason to tell you. I offered to provide for Brenna, but Chavi refused the offer." She paused. "I didn't know you'd been seeing her."

"My dear *Sons-ee-ah-ray*," Hakan said sadly, "we don't share much about ourselves or what we do and think and feel nowadays, do we? I've been wondering about Sam Rutherford."

Sarah flushed slightly. "He's an old friend, nothing more."

"He'd like to be though, wouldn't he?"

"That would be out of the question."

"Why? Why don't you just pack up and go back to America with him? There's nothing to keep you here now. You've achieved what you set out to do. I'm the seventh Earl of Moreland."

She turned very pale in the firelight. "How far apart we've drifted."

"I'm sorry if that sounded cruel. I'm still trying to make sense of the tangled mess my father made of so many lives."

"Why do we always condemn the user?" she asked with sudden spirit. "Don't those who allow themselves to be used bear some responsibility too? The powerful are only so because the weak allow them to be."

"It wasn't a fair contest between a wordly, wealthy man and an ignorant gypsy girl. I feel such rage when I think of it."

"All the more reason not to associate with her. The specter of your father's dead child would always haunt you."

Hakan stared into the fire, seeing the coals shift as they were consumed. Some fell into ashes while others flared with a brief brilliant flame and then turned the dull red of infinity. All the patterns of life were there, he thought.

"You didn't answer my question about Chavi. I'm concerned that you show so much interest in her. She's married, even if her husband apparently doesn't live with her."

"I know that."

"And what if Nelia finds out you've been seeing her?"

"For God's sake! Has everyone on earth already married me off to Nelia?"

"You've reached an age when you should be considering marriage. I thought you liked Nelia. She and her family certainly believe you have an understanding. Besides, she's perfect in every way. She would slip as easily into the position of Countess of Moreland as she does into one of her gowns. She's trained all of her life to marry someone like you. And she's the prettiest young woman in the county."

"If I marry her, I'll be trapped here for the rest of my life."

She stared at him. "You feel trapped?"

"Yes. Don't you?"

She was silent for a moment. "This is one of the loveliest spots on earth. This house is more beautiful than any palace. Our every need is met. We want for nothing."

"Yet we're miserable. Don't you see? It doesn't have anything to do with a place or a house. It has to do with *what we were*, what we still *are* under the layers of so-called sophistication. We are *Apache*, we are the *people*. It was merely a trick of fate that you were born here. You found your way to the place where you were meant to be and I was born there. Life made sense then. Do you know the one thing that I've learned as an Englishman that troubles me most? I learned to question everything I do and think and feel. I can no longer simply be. The mistake we made was in coming back here."

His mother leapt to her feet, her book falling to the floor. "We can never go back! The Apache are no more, don't you understand? The Life-way is gone forever. The few who are left exist like caged animals on reservations."

"But you can't deny that *we* remain free, and we're still Apache."

"How can I deny that? I had to face the truth of how I feel about life . . . and death, in a way you cannot imagine."

Before he could protest, she swept out of the room, leaving him feeling as though he had had the answer to a puzzle within his grasp, but had opened his hands and watched it fly away.

Sarah stood in the darkened hall outside the library, waiting for her heart to stop pounding. Hakan remained inside the room, and when he didn't come out after a moment, she went to the staircase, sat on the bottom step, and stared at the closed library door.

A parlor maid came out of the drawing room, glanced curiously at her, but went on her way without comment. Sarah supposed that over the years the staff had grown accustomed to her less-than-typical upper-class behavior.

The years she had lived as an Apache now represented a much shorter span of her life than those lived as an English aristocrat. Yet time and time again her mind would flash back to the Apache years and she would find herself speaking—even acting—as she had then. It was a phenomenon she did not understand, but had come to accept.

For a long time she had believed that Hakan was as torn into two parts as she, perhaps even more so. But then after he'd come back from the Boer War, so badly wounded, and had been decorated with England's highest honor, she hadn't been so sure. Perhaps the army had succeeded in stamping out the last vestiges of the Apache Life-way. But his conversation tonight indicated that he still longed for the old ways.

Sarah looked at the closed library door again and whirled back in memory to the days, hours, before Richard died. She remembered the chaos of her thoughts and emotions, tossing her first this way and then that. Intermingled with her revulsion over the revelations made by Andrew McGreal about Richard's treatment of Jean was the pity Sarah felt for the man who had been her companion for so many years, a man who was enduring a living death. She remembered Hakan begging her to leave Merrinswood, recalled her fear that he might act according to the dictates of the Life-way. Then too, there was Danior, raging at what had been done to his sister.

How easy it had been, then, to remind herself what the Life-way solution would be to all of their problems. Yet how difficult, later, to separate her own warring emotions and determine which of them had precipitated her actions.

Reaching a sudden decision, Sarah rose and walked purposefully back into the library.

Hakan looked up in surprise as his mother returned. She paced in front of the fire and he could see her hands were clenched in the folds of her skirt. She said in a strange faraway voice, "I came to realize that our way—the Apache way—of meeting death was more compassionate than theirs. All I'd ever thought or known about being an Englishwoman was lost in one single moment of decision when I acted as an Apache squaw."

A drum had started to pound in Hakan's head. He wanted to leap to his feet and run from the room, but the leather armchair held him prisoner. Visions of his boyhood flashed across his mind. The nomad Apache, constantly on the move; a physical, vigorous Life-way that demanded every member of the clan keep up. When an Apache grew too old and feeble, when the quality of life became a trial to him and his family, the old one was left alone to die. "We'll come back for you later," the others would say, but both knew that the time had come for the old and feeble one to cross into the other hunting ground. The old one had once done the same thing to his elders, and expected it, welcomed it when life became a burden. Hakan had once heard an old man say wearily, "Enough now. I've had enough. I'm tired." When the white-eyes came they were appalled at what they called this cruelty and tried to put a stop to it.

He looked deep into his mother's eyes and saw that she had changed far less than he'd imagined. She was still *Sons-ee-ah-ray*, and in her heart still believed in the Life-way. He tried to rise, but he was shaking. He wanted to say to her, don't go on! Don't tell me what I already suspect! I say I am Apache, but in reality I am two men, and one of them is an Englishman burdened by guilt and conscience.

"I have to stay here, Hakan," she said calmly. "And so do you. Otherwise nothing makes any sense."

If his walking stick had been handy he would have reached for it. His temple throbbed. Slowly he pushed himself out of the chair and stumbled toward the door.

Behind him his mother said quietly, "No matter what Richard had done . . . or how many people he'd hurt . . . he didn't deserve to be left in that state of limbo, neither dead nor alive. I saw it clearly the night of his birthday party. The room was filled with people who hated him . . . who no doubt wished him dead. I saw it in so many eyes. But no one was going to kill him out of hatred. Someone had to end his suffering out of pity . . . out of love. I thought of the Life-way. Hakan, *it was an act of mercy . . . an act of love.*"

35

"Mr. Dirk Chambers's room, please," Chavi said. "I'm his wife."

The hotel clerk said, "Ah, yes, Mrs. Chambers. I'll have a porter take you up. Do you have any luggage?"

Chavi hoisted Garridan into her arms. "Just the bag on the floor."

Following the elderly porter across the foyer of the poshest hotel in Liverpool, Chavi thought gloomily that Dirk's fortunes must have changed very much for the better to be able to afford to stay at a place this grand. He must have arrived in Liverpool aboard a ship, since there'd be no reason to come here otherwise, although she'd thought all of the Australian vessels entered southern ports.

Garridan was sleepy, a dead weight in her arms. She was tired from the journey, too, but felt she might as well get this unpleasant interview over and done with. The worst part of it was that the impersonally typewritten letter on hotel stationery had merely told her to bring Garridan and come here. That meant that Dirk knew he had a son. Well, he wasn't going to take Garri away from her and she wasn't going back to him as his wife. She wasn't sure just how this could be arranged, but she'd think of something.

The porter stopped in front of a third-floor room and knocked on the door. There was a muffled response from inside and the man opened the door for her to enter, placed her small bag on the floor, and left instantly, without waiting for a tip. As she moved into the room she understood why.

Lysander's beard concealed some of his scars, but he was still a frightening sight to behold. "You . . ." she whispered, too tired to react with other than bewilderment. "But . . . the letter was from Dirk."

The smile disappeared from Lysander's mouth, lingered hopefully for a moment in his eyes, then faded. "I'd hoped you'd be glad to see me. I'm very happy to see you."

"I was expecting Dirk. I got myself all worked up into a state thinking about how I was going to tell him—oh, God, Lysander, why must you always lie to me? That letter was from you, wasn't it?"

His eyes searched her face for a moment, looking for something he evidently didn't find. "I'll explain in a moment." He took Garridan from her arms, turned the little boy around to the light. "He's grown. He's going to be tall, and look at those shoulders. He needs a haircut, he looks like a gypsy."

Chavi made a face at him. She sat down on a satin upholstered chair and took the pins from her hat. She'd worn a matronly gray bombazine dress and a matching wool coat. "I'm quite well, thank you very much," she said sarcastically as Lysander placed the sleepy child on the bed and sat down beside him. She was glad that Garri's eyes were heavy-lidded with sleep, so he didn't cry in fright as he had when Lysander came to Brenna's funeral.

Lysander gently covered Garri with a blanket, tucking it carefully around his feet, then fixed one of his paralyzing, intense stares on Chavi. "You said you'd worked yourself up to tell Dirk something. What?"

"None of your business."

He leaned across the sleeping child and asked in a voice so soft she sensed the question rather than heard it. "That you no longer wish to be his wife?"

She was silent. Did she want her freedom merely because it was the one obstacle between Hakan and herself she could eliminate? As she thought of Hakan and the pain of parting from him the night before, she saw a flash of angry awareness appear in Lysander's eyes. "So. You came to ask Dirk for a divorce. Since your married state didn't bother you before, I assume once again you've met a man you want."

There was no need for her to reply. The expression on Lysander's face indicated she still couldn't keep secrets from him. She felt resentment about this, as well as the residue of the estrangement between them that had begun at Brenna's funeral. She drew a deep breath. "Will you please tell me what you're doing here? You couldn't wait to leave after Brenna's funeral in case someone recognized you and put you back in prison. It must be something important for you to risk coming to England again."

He stared at the sleeping child, various emotions registering briefly on his face and in the way his gaze traveled over the small body of the boy. When he spoke, some of the old acid was back in his tone, but she knew now that it was one of his defenses against the world. "You didn't respond to my letters. You never do."

"I sent a note thanking you for the money Dirk sent. Lysander, what about the letter signed by Dirk? Is he here?"

"Yes, he's here. You're looking at him."

"What do you mean?"

"I used his passport to enter the country. I'm here as Dirk Chambers. The customs officials were most sympathetic about the terrible bush fire in Australia that left me so scarred. They said I really should have a new passport photo taken, because although they could tell that the picture was of me, my . . . er . . ." he mimicked the official's embarrased tone, "ah . . . slight scars did tend to distort one's . . . ah . . . first impression. Oh, God, is there anything more comical than an Englishman's inborn tact? *They* apologized to *me* for the discrepancies between my picture and myself."

"But what about Dirk? Where is he? Does he know you're using his passport?"

"Dirk was killed six months ago in the Northern Territory. He became one of the rarest of statistics when he foolishly took shelter under a huge gum in a thunderstorm. He was struck by lightning."

Chavi pressed her fingers to the furrow between her eyes, trying to assimilate this. If Lysander felt grief over his brother's death, he wouldn't show it, she knew. His had been the only dry eye at Brenna's funeral. Chavi felt sorry that Dirk's life had ended so tragically, but she had said good-bye to him long ago, so felt no sudden loss. "Six months ago . . . *six months!* Why didn't you let me know before this?"

"I wanted to be with you when I told you. I had to wait for Dirk's possessions to arrive and come up with a plan to get back into England without fear of arrest. When the steamer trunk arrived I looked at my brother's clothes—all in my size—and at his photograph in his passport. I could have been looking at my own likeness before my . . . accident. That's when I decided to assume my brother's identity."

"Six months!" Chavi said angrily. "And all that time—"

"Keep your voice down, you'll wake the boy. I was afraid if you knew you were a widow you'd rush out and marry some unsuitable clod before I could stop you. Evidently my fears were well-founded." He raised a mocking eyebrow. "Tell me, who is the current love of your life?"

"Damn you, Lysander! What I do is no concern of yours and I—" she stopped, another thought surfacing. "Wait a minute. If he was killed six months ago—why, I got a draft from you last week."

"Dirk never sent you any money, Chavi. It was all from me."

She fumed silently for a moment. "I should have guessed. The allowance increased when I wanted to take that lady's-companion position in London. You never wanted me to be independent, did you? Does it give you some sort of perverse pleasure to dictate how I live?"

"In the name of independence you'd have taken on some soul-destroying job catering to a whining old dowager. Garridan would have been brought up belowstairs by some ignorant servant. I had better things in mind, for both of you. Besides, I never told you, but I made quite a handsome fortune in the Australian goldfields. With careful investment, I'm now a moderately wealthy man."

"My heartiest congratulations. But you're not rich enough to buy me. I'm not your slave, nor even your protégée any longer. I don't want any more of your damn money, nor your interference in my life."

With his forefinger he brushed one of Garridan's black curls away from his brow. "Do you remember the night Twelve Mile station burned to the ground? When I took you to the farm on the other side of the river?"

"Of course I remember."

"The owner put you in his bedroom, and you were a bit tipsy. Quite a bit tipsy, as I recall. The place was swarming with evacuees, and when Dirk arrived I suggested that instead of disturbing you he allow you to sleep it off."

Chavi felt her cheeks stain bright red. "No . . . He came to me that night. That was the night—" She stopped before she said, Garridan was conceived.

She thought for the thousandth time about the night of the fire. The bush fire that became a different kind of fire in the dark room of a stranger's house. Had Garri been conceived that night? Had Lysander slipped into her dream . . . into her bed . . . and made exquisite love to her? Was it possible? And if so, what then? Mithuna once said that a woman sexually satisfied by a man would be bonded to him forever, that it was the last act between a man and a woman who were destined to spend eternity together, and it must follow the steps of friendship and courtship, when they would learn to be companions and confidants. All of these preliminaries, Chavi now saw, had been accomplished with Lysander, slowly, gradually. If he were her dream lover . . .

No, she must never believe he was. She wasn't in love with him and she didn't want to be bonded to him through eternity. As long as she didn't admit the possibility—even to herself—she'd be safe.

Lysander's eyes burned like coals in the fires of hell. "It was very dark in that room—heavy shutters on the windows, no moon, the stars blocked off by the heavy pall of smoke from the fire. Pitch dark. After everyone was asleep it was easy for someone of the same height and build as Dirk to slip naked into your bed. . . ."

Chavi screamed, waking Garridan, who began to cry. She didn't know why she sobbed in rising hysteria. Was it because there was no way she could go back into the past and know what she would have done about the situation then? She was a different person now, changed by time and circumstances. In the present there was Hakan and her feelings for him. How could she know now how she would have reacted to Lysander's declaration then?

Lysander dragged her to her feet and held her in a suffocating grip. "For God's sake, don't get hysterical. I thought you knew it was me. I'm sorry . . . for deceiving you then, for thinking that we could have more together than friendship. Most of all I'm sorry I let you leave Australia without me. I wanted so very badly to tell you how I felt about you—but I was afraid." He sighed heavily. "Afraid you'd react with the same horror you're showing now. That night wasn't part of the reality, was it? The reality is that I'm a scarred monster who has no right to a woman's affection, let alone her love or acceptance."

He pushed her away from him and turned his back. "Pick up our son and comfort him."

She held her child and rocked him back and forth, staring at Lysander's bowed head and the way his thick dark hair curled over his collar. Along with pity for his misery, she felt anger. He should have revealed himself then, that night he masqueraded as her husband, or he should have kept silent forever. Yet hadn't she suspected what had happened and refused to face it? How very easy it was for the human mind to suppress that which it didn't want to admit. No! She must never allow herself to think like that. She said, "It isn't true. I would have known. It was Dirk who came to me. How can you say such things? It's vile, hateful."

He turned and gave her a mocking smile. "You didn't think so that night."

"No! No, it was Dirk who came to me."

"Had he ever made love to you with such tenderness? Was he able to give you a child in all your years of marriage to him? You know, it's damned ironic, but I think now that probably that long-ago young lady who said Dirk was the father of her child . . . and whose father avenged himself against the wrong brother . . . that young lady no doubt had another lover too. I don't believe my brother was capable of siring a child. Certainly not one like Garridan. Look at the boy's eyes—they're my eyes. Look at that brow—Dirk had a somewhat lower forehead. If I were to show you pictures of myself at Garridan's age, you'd think we were twins."

The child was asleep again and Chavi put him down on the bed. She turned to Lysander and hissed at him between clenched teeth, "You're a damn liar! You always were. You lied to me when I first knew you and God knows how many other times. You're lying now. You think I wouldn't have known who was making love to me? Oh, I'll grant that Dirk was more caring, more considerate that night—but it was because he knew we'd have to be apart, perhaps for years." In a desperate need to believe, she reminded herself, it was always more intense just before parting. He wanted to give her something to remember him by and so he gave all he had left—his body . . . in a way he had never given it before. But it was Dirk. It *was*! Aloud she cried, "Dirk came to me that night. You're a filthy monster to suggest it was you." Was she trying to convince him, she wondered, or herself?

Lysander shrugged. "Garridan is my son, that's all I care about. And you're my wife."

"Are you mad? I'm not your wife and never will be."

He leaned forward, his eyes gleaming. There was no way to tear free of his gaze until he released her. "You are Mrs. Dirk Chambers, are you not? And I am Dirk Chambers, your husband. I have a passport and marriage lines to prove it. Oh, yes, I had a copy of the marriage certificate sent from Australia."

Numb with disbelief, she sank down onto the bed beside Garri. Lysander's voice softened. "Don't look so stricken. All I want is to be allowed to care for you and the boy. To be with you both. It won't be so bad. We used to get along quite well, in the old days."

But she hadn't known Hakan then.

"I could tell the police who you are. You're an escaped murderer," Chavi said.

"Dirk's brother is the escaped murderer, but no one has seen hide nor hair of him for donkey's years. I would simply explain that my wife is telling this farfetched yarn out of pique, that we're having a domestic quarrel. English law is very sympathetic in such matters. You've no doubt heard that a wife cannot be forced to testify against her husband. You see, my dear Chavi, although I'm still insufferably ugly to you—there have been great changes in my appearance since I was sentenced for my crime. The police picture of that man shows a fiend with the mouth of a shark. You'll recall the doctor who so successfully used his scalpel to give me the mouth I now have. In addition, my neatly trimmed beard and moustache, my distinguished-looking side whiskers, and not least, the fact that I'm older than the man who was convicted. No, I bear no resemblance to him. I am a well-to-do sheep rancher from Down Under, and I dare you to try to prove otherwise."

Chavi couldn't look at him. "Lysander, I've fallen in love—truly in love, I think—for the first time."

He was across the room before she'd realized he'd moved.

His hand went under her chin and he tipped her face upward and examined it closely. "Who? Who is he?"

She paused, momentarily shocked by the stricken look in his eyes. "Do you really think I'm going to tell you? Let go of me."

"Does he love you? Does he want to marry you?"

She could sense the change in him, felt his deep concern for her welfare; it was in his touch and his voice, and most of all, his eyes. For the first time she felt the initiative pass into her hands. Hakan had asked her to be his wife, but that was before he knew she had given birth to his father's child. She had not seen him since and was unsure if she ever would again. Besides, marriage between an Earl of the realm and a gypsy was out of the question. But if she could lie to Lysander and tell him she was going to be married, would he withdraw all claim to Garri and herself? But she couldn't lie to him. She respected him too much to deceive him.

"He loves me," she whispered. "But we can never marry."

Lysander's expression froze. "If he won't marry you, then he doesn't love you."

"You think one always goes with the other? I was married to your brother, remember? I'll take love without marriage any day over marriage without love."

Lysander snatched his hand back from her face as though he had been burned. "Very well. Go to him. But leave my son with me."

"You know I won't do that."

"We're at an impasse then, because nothing is going to come between me and my son. While we settle it, we'd better decide where we're to live."

"I've found a cottage, on the Yorkshire moors. I'll be going back there with Garri tomorrow morning."

"And I, my dear wife, will be going with you."

Lysander took one look at the cottage and refused to live in it. Instead, he found a Georgian manor house on the outskirts of Carisbrook, hired a solicitor to buy it for him, and moved in there. Not knowing what else to do, Chavi went with him. For one thing he would no doubt immediately discontinue his financial support if she didn't, and she had no money of her own. Then, too, Hakan wouldn't know her whereabouts.

She was terrified of where a confrontation between Lysander and Hakan might lead. Apart from their present rivalry, she was sure all the ghosts from the past would rise up in avenging wrath. Lysander would want to kill Hakan not only because of what Lysander would perceive as Hakan's seduction of her, but because he was Richard's son. Hakan would want to kill Lysander for being the man his father paid to spirit her and Brenna off to the far side of the earth merely to save him embarrassment. Hakan's contempt for such a man would be formidable, yet no less than Lysander's for him. No, at all costs she must keep those two apart.

Not that she was even sure Hakan wanted to see her again, after her confession about the affair with his father. But that didn't stop her from longing for him, or worrying what Lysander might do to him.

Garridan missed his friend desperately and kept asking where he was. Fortunately, Garri's first fumblings with language were still frequently garbled, and he'd had difficulty saying Hakan. In one of Hakan's stories he had mentioned *Y'sun*—the Apache supreme being, the giver of life. Garridan immediately grabbed a handful of Hakan's gold hair and said "You Sun!" After that he called Hakan "Sun," so when he asked why Sun didn't come, Lysander thought he referred to the sun—which certainly hadn't shone since their last meeting with Hakan.

Gray days persisted, the clouds so low the sky seemed to press on their heads like a damp blanket. There was intermittent rain and biting winds, and Chavi's gypsy blood called to her that it was time to seek warmer climes, but she ignored the internal clamor because she had to keep her wits about her and find a way out of this new maze in which she was trapped.

The first night they spent in the house, which was named Staley Hall after its previous owners, Chavi had taken a sharp carving knife to bed with her and slept fitfully. But Lysander hadn't come to her room and after a few days passed she was less fearful that he would.

He made tentative attempts to revive their old camaraderie, which she rebuffed. She hated the feeling that he was in control and allowed her rage to obliterate everything else she felt for him.

He hired a couple to be housekeeper and gardener, a Mr.

and Mrs. Arkwright, whom Chavi disliked on sight. They were like a pair of weasels, with greasy brown hair, darting little eyes, and sharp faces. Chavi suspected that with Lysander's forbidding looks he hadn't had much choice in servants.

She prowled the house, shut in by the rain, avoiding Lysander when she could, making and discarding plans. She thought of going to Hakan, but didn't want to lead Lysander to him. Lysander was a man who had admitted killing twice, who very well might have also killed Hakan's father. If Lysander found out that she was in love with the son of the man who'd banished her to Australia, would he suspect Hakan of the same dishonorable intentions as his father? Over and over again the same thoughts hammered in her brain. Her blood chilled at the thought of what Lysander was capable of. The man who had been her friend, who had loved Brenna so much, and to whom Chavi owed all of her present knowledge and sophistication, had suddenly turned into a menacing villain, in her mind if not in fact.

She didn't stop to consider that Lysander was exhibiting a great deal of patience and self-control, and behaving kindly toward them in view of her coldness and Garri's terror of the strange man who had suddenly appeared in his life.

Despite the fact that Garri ran and hid from Lysander, one night when the child awakened, crying from a bad dream, Chavi went into his room to find Lysander already there, gently patting Garri's back and murmuring soothingly. In a moment, the little boy slept again. Chavi and Lysander stood side by side in the darkness, waiting to be sure all was well, then tiptoed from the room together.

There was a lamp burning low in a wall sconce outside the door. Lysander's face, illuminated by the gaslight, looked curiously vulnerable. "I only want to protect you both. Garri from his nightmares . . . you from the men who would use you and hurt you."

Chavi looked at him steadily. "You have to let me go, Lysander. I have to be allowed to find my own way now."

He said despairingly, "If I thought you'd find your way back to me . . . I would. But you'll destroy yourself by choosing the wrong man again. It seems to be your one weakness. I can't let you take my son into the same hell you took Brenna. You think a child doesn't know when love has gone?".

She turned and sped back into her own room, not wanting to confront his truths, nor her own.

A large room on the second floor had formerly been a nursery and schoolroom, and Chavi placed Garridan's bed and belongings in it and spent much of her time there. She had Mrs. Arkwright serve breakfast to them at a small table in the bay window. But one morning it was not Mrs. Arkwright who appeared with the breakfast tray, but Lysander.

Kicking the door shut behind him, he strode across the room and placed the tray on the table. Garridan immediately ran to Chavi's side and pressed himself close to her. She put her arm around her son.

"Can't either of you say good-morning?" Lysander snapped. "And why are you hiding behind your mother's skirts, boy?"

"Don't shout at him," Chavi said. "You're frightening the life out of him." Lysander was also frightening her. What had happened to cause his sudden change of mood? This wasn't the easy, familiar Lysander. He had reverted back to that terrifying monster he'd been when she first met him.

He sat down and extended his arms toward the child, saying gruffly, "Come here, Garridan. Come and give your father a hug."

The little boy shook his head and buried his face in Chavi's sleeve. Chavi glanced at Lysander. "Can't you leave us alone? You've got what you wanted."

He stood up so suddenly his chair crashed to the floor behind him. "You think this is what I wanted?"

Frightened and angry, Chavi cried, "We're living on your charity. How do you expect me to feel about that? You're our jailer."

Lysander stared at her. "Is that what you're telling our son? Are you poisoning the boy's mind against me?"

"He's too little to understand what's going on. He doesn't know you, that's all. And your glowering and shouting isn't going to make him like you."

"Be fair. This is the first and only time I've been impatient with him. I'm not a patient man, Chavi, but I believe I've exhibited remarkable restraint up to now. I've done everything I can to please you both, yet you won't even speak to me. How much of this silent treatment do you think I can stand?"

Chavi hugged her son closer. "You were never impatient with Brenna."

"Brenna was always warm and loving toward me. And your attitude was different then. We return what we receive, gypsy."

Ignoring the derisive "gypsy," Chavi replied, "You knew Brenna from the time she was a couple of weeks old, she was used to you. Garri isn't. As for me, you were my friend then—now you look at me like a hungry wolf. I feel naked every time you look at me."

He started to walk to the door, paused and turned to look at her. "By the way, speaking of being naked, a seamstress will be coming this morning to measure you for some clothes. I've taken all your gypsy rags and burned them."

Lysander stared at his reflection in the mirror of his dressing table, appalled by the way he'd acted. He had paced the floor all night long, trying desperately to convince himself that he should return to Ireland and leave Chavi in peace. He had, in fact, taken breakfast up to her with the intention of announcing that he would do just that, that he couldn't bear to see her so unhappy.

What a picture they had made, the two of them. Chavi had been leaning forward, smiling and talking to the boy, who regarded her with solemn loving eyes, cherishing every word she spoke. Oh, if only Garri could look at him like that! If only Chavi would stop looking at him as if he were her executioner. Chavi, who had never once allowed her eyes to even hint that he was scarred and ugly, now seemed to recoil in revulsion at his appearance.

As they looked up and saw him, their warm loving expressions vanishing, replaced by fear and resentment, something inside Lysander had exploded, obscuring every logical thought with a red haze of jealousy and longing. He remembered everytime Chavi had run joyously to greet him when he returned to Twelve Mile, how they talked for hours, how they laughed and rode and played and studied and learned . . . how sweet it had been to make love to her. All those years of forging a bond between them . . . was he now to throw it all away simply because she was again infatuated with some idiot besotted by her loveliness without ever knowing the true beauty of her soul? No, absolutely not.

She'd got over her infatuation for Lord Moreland and for Dirk. She'd get over this too, whoever the hell he was.

But who and where was her lover? Lysander resolved to find out.

Lysander insisted they eat dinner together in the drafty dining room. They sat one at each end of a long table, separated by a huge sinister candelabra, and by hostility that was almost palpable. Mrs. Arkwright brought in covered dishes of overdone beef, drooping Yorkshire pudding, and soggy vegetables.

The wind howled in the chimney and the soup was luke-warm. Chavi put her spoon down and sighed.

He looked up suspiciously. "Sighing for your lost love, my dear? Why don't you simply go to him?"

Chavi took some satisfaction from the knowledge that it was driving Lysander mad trying to find out who it was she had met and fallen in love with. She gave him a small secre-tive smile.

"I taught you too well, didn't I?" he asked. "The faraway look in your eye, the dreamy smile. You know only too well the power you wield. But I'm not Dirk, I'm not like any man you've known, so don't underestimate what my reaction to you is going to be."

"I know you fairly well, too, Lysander," she answered quietly. "We were adversaries once before, remember? Only now I'm better equipped to deal with you, thanks to your own tutoring."

"I'll find out who your lover is, in time."

She shrugged. "Time is all I need, too."

He broke his bread into uneatable crumbs and seemed unaware he was doing so. "Don't you know yet that falling in love is self-destructive? It's a hunt for an elusive prey that's destroyed as soon as you capture it."

"Only you would think in terms of hunter and prey."

"I'm telling you that mad passion never lasts. It can't. Romantic love consumes itself with its own intensity. The dizzying rapture has to fade into the commonplace."

"You're an authority on the subject, of course."

"I know that you've created a fantasy lover. All of his attributes—whoever the hell he is—are in *your mind*, not in the man. Sooner or later you'll see him as he really is and vice versa. And the chances are you'll both be disappointed. How much better to start out without the illusions. With someone who knows your every flaw and fault."

"You, for instance."

"Why not? Remember how we used to talk together for hours? We were good friends once, Chavi. We could be again. And you responded to me that night I came to you and we made love—"

She jumped to her feet and ran from the room, almost colliding with Mrs. Arkwright at the door, who was weighed down by one of her cannonball suet puddings.

The following morning the rain was heavier than ever and Chavi felt imprisoned by the schoolroom. "Let's go downstairs today," she said to Garridan.

Lysander was coming out of his room and they met on the upstairs landing. He was dressed in a fine worsted suit and carried a hat and overcoat. A leather valise stood at the top of the stairs. "I'm going away for a few days. I'd been handling all of my affairs from Dublin, but now I want to transfer everything here. There's an investment bank in London I want to investigate. Don't expect me back until the end of the week."

Chavi was afraid the joy must have shone from her eyes like a beacon and hurriedly lowered her head so he wouldn't see.

"No word of regret at my departure?" he asked mockingly.

She looked up. "Have a safe journey."

His eyes flickered over her face knowingly and he gave a small enigmatic smile, as though he'd seen what he wanted to see.

That smile worried her as she donned a coat, found an umbrella, and told Mrs. Arkwright to watch Garridan carefully while she went into the village. "It's raining hard," the woman said, her tiny eyes suspicious. "If there's something you need, Mrs. Chambers?"

"I'll be back shortly, Mrs. Arkwright," Chavi said and went out into the dismal morning, unfurling her umbrella.

She plodded down the lane in the direction of Carisbrook, not even sure where she was going. Every nerve in her body screamed for her to go to Hakan, but every instinct warned her how unwise that would be. Hadn't Lysander told her never to chase a man? Damn him, he still invaded her thoughts more than anyone else. It wasn't that she hated him, but she couldn't let him go on ruling her life.

The first thing she needed was a paying position. Carisbrook was a thriving community, it had grown into a prosperous market town these past few years, the railway carrying produce from the surrounding farmland to the cities. Perhaps there would be something for her there.

Staley Hall was situated two miles from Carisbrook, and she was halfway there when a small carriage pulled by a single horse caught up with her. The man pulled on the reins and said, "Whoa. Chavi, is that you under that umbrella? Can I give you a lift?"

"Doctor McGreal!" she exclaimed, glad to see him. "Oh, thank you, yes. Are you going into Carisbrook?"

He jumped down on the muddy road to help her up. "I am indeed. And where are you bound on such a miserable morning?"

She shook the water from the hem of her coat and folded her umbrella, although the rain still drove in through the open-sided carriage. "I'm going into Carisbrook, too," she answered, deliberately being vague.

"I have to meet the London train. A friend of my wife is coming to visit us. Mrs. Brannock. She's the wife of a former colleague of mine from London."

"How nice," Chavi commented absently.

"I'd heard your husband had arrived back in England. But no one seemed to know where you'd gone to live. I assume you have a place not far from here?"

"Yes, Staley Hall. But Doctor McGreal, I'd prefer you didn't mention that to anyone."

"Anyone?"

"Well, to anyone at Merrinswood."

"Ah, I see."

"No, you don't, but that doesn't matter. Of course, if Danior comes back and is looking for me . . ."

"I understand."

The doctor told her that he'd started a practice in Carisbrook, too, because Merrin Quarry was too small to support both himself and Doctor Harkness. "I spend my mornings in Carisbrook, I have a cottage on the edge of town, and afternoon surgery is in Merrin Quarry. As soon as I build my practice in Carisbrook my wife wants to move there. She loves the cottage. We have a rather dreary terrace house in Merrin Quarry, but more patients there at present."

They were silent until the houses on the outskirts of Carisbrook came into view and then, on sudden impulse, Chavi said, "You wouldn't know of anyone who could offer a few hours work a day, would you? Anything at all, so long as it's for pay."

He glanced sideways at her. "For yourself?"

"Yes."

"Let me see if I understand. You and your husband have moved into Staley Hall, but you are seeking part-time employment?"

"I know it sounds peculiar, but I want to earn some pin money of my own."

"Here's the railway station. Why don't you come in and I'll buy you a hot cup of tea and a sticky bun and we'll talk about it? You see, with Brigid—Mrs. Brannock's arrival and subsequent visit, I shall lose the services of my wife to assist me with my patients. The ladies will want to chat and go out on jaunts together and so on. At least for the next couple of weeks I could use some help keeping my appointments straight and sending out bills. It could be handled from Carisbrook, so wouldn't necessitate traveling to Merrin Quarry. Of course, it would only be temporary, but—"

"Oh, thank you, Doctor McGreal. I'll take it."

"Good. And you needn't worry too much about anyone at Merrinswood finding out, because I usually go to them and on the rare occasions they come to me they would go to my place in Merrin Quarry."

"How soon can I start?"

"Tomorrow morning?"

Chavi gave him a smile and nod of acceptance. She'd have a week before Lysander returned; perhaps she could earn enough in that time to buy a train ticket. South, as far as the money would take her. Eventually she should be able to reach Cornwall or Devon and find the caravans.

For an instant the memory of the old Lysander tugged at her conscience, but the one thing she had learned from recent events was that unless she achieved a measure of financial independence, she'd forever be forced to do what some man wanted. She wanted her own choices in life too badly for that.

36

Nelia's green eyes glittered ominously. "You've been avoiding me. I'm quite sure you were here yesterday when I called, yet you had Barlow say you weren't home."

Yesterday Hakan had been riding a sodden horse over the rain-drenched moors, trying to deal with his feelings about the unwelcome revelations of both Chavi and his mother. He said, "Perhaps you should let us know in advance when you intend to visit Merrinswood."

"I don't visit Merrinswood. I visit you."

"Nelia, I was grateful for that when I was flat on my back, but as you can see, I'm pretty well recovered from my wounds now, and no longer confined to the house and grounds."

"You know there's more to it than that. You led me to believe . . . Why, you even talked to Gil—"

"Please don't embarrass yourself by saying any more," Hakan interrupted. "And you'll have to excuse me, but I have estate business to discuss with Rob."

Her lips parted, but she bit back whatever she was about to say. Spinning on her heel, she marched out of the house. Hakan watched her go, wishing Chavi were the widow instead of Nelia, wishing Chavi hadn't borne his father's child. . . .

The minute Nelia disappeared, Hakan went up the stairs to his mother's room. She hadn't come down to dinner the night before, sending a message with Barlow that she wasn't feeling well. Hakan realized now that he should have gone up then, but had believed she was merely avoiding being with him while he accepted in his mind the true nature of his father's death. But she didn't come down to breakfast this morning either, and now he was worried. He must hasten to reassure her that he was still Apache enough to accept what she'd done.

An upstairs maid was coming out of his mother's room carrying a bundle of bed linen. "How is she?" Hakan asked.

"Very poorly, sir."

"Send someone for Doctor McGreal at once. No, on second thought, I'll go for him myself, he spends his mornings at Carisbrook now. And find Barlow. Tell him if anyone calls, they aren't to be told my mother is ill. I don't want her worn out by a stream of visitors."

"Yes, sir."

One look at his mother confirmed his worst fears. Telling her to rest, he quickly withdrew. On the way downstairs Hakan decided that it would be faster to ride into town, since he could take a shortcut across the moors, which would be inaccessible to either a carriage or the motorcar that Rob used frequently nowadays.

Riding into the wind-whipped rain, Hakan felt real fear about his mother's illness, which had come on so suddenly and worsened so rapidly. He was the best horseman on the estate, despite having so recently been incapacitated, and he would bring help more speedily than anyone else. But in addition to that fact, he needed to be doing something to drive away the vision of his mother's head falling back limply on the pillow, her face a strange grayish blue.

She'd not looked well for weeks, he realized now. He should have noticed her sudden weight loss and reluctance to eat, but Sarah had again begun spending much time alone in her room, writing in her journal. One evening he'd gone up to say good-night and he'd asked how her journal was progressing. She answered, "I'm writing a novel instead. The same material, but fictionalized."

He had been surprised. "But I thought you were writing of the Life-way. Why not write it as fact? A text for historians."

"Who in turn would use it as a single source for *their* texts? No, if I fictionalize our story it will be safe from interpretation—and, I hope, be read by more people. Of course, I'll publish it under a man's name. A woman writer is expected only to produce a romantic novel of manners."

"Then write a factual text as a woman. Surely your own

firsthand knowledge of the Life-way qualifies you. You are one of the few people on earth, man or woman, who can write the truth about the Apache, since they have no written language of their own."

"Hakan, novels distill meaning from life—they offer explanations, the why of things. In a novel we learn that a character did this *because*. In life it's simply, He did this. If I blend fact with fiction, I shall be able to reach, I hope, both the head and the heart of my readers. Rather than merely describing how we lived, I'm sure I can make our place and time come alive more intensely through the eyes of my imaginary people."

"But those who read your novel will believe it is merely a series of lies."

"But don't you see? Those lies, as you call them, will express a truth that is only slightly false. I will have transformed reality into a form and shape that will be more palatable than the chaos of real life."

As Hakan reined his mount in front of Doctor McGreal's cottage in Carisbrook, he wondered if Sarah had finished her novel.

Fortunately the doctor's morning surgery hours had not yet begun, so Hakan wouldn't have to drag him away from a patient. Hakan rang the doorbell and looked in astonishment at the woman who responded.

Chavi's mouth dropped open, too. She held the door wider for him to enter and in the tiny vestibule they faced one another in swift silent appraisal. Hakan was aware of the faint scent of lavender, of the sheen of her dark hair, pulled into a chignon but escaping everywhere so that lively strands curled about her face and throat. But most of all of the beauty of her features, the warmth in her eyes. He felt his throat constrict and fought the urge to take her in his arms.

"I'm helping Doctor McGreal for a few days, while his wife entertains a guest," Chavi explained. "He's an old friend."

"I came for him because my mother is ill."

"Come into the parlor. I'll fetch him."

Their eyes locked for an instant before she turned to lead the way.

Hakan paced around a tiny immaculate parlor that smelled of beeswax and potpourri. A room lovingly assembled, polished and treasured. A moment later Chavi returned. "Doctor McGreal's gone to harness the horse."

"I'd better get back to my mother."

"Hakan . . ."

"Yes?"

"You've had time to think about what I told you—about me and your father?"

"Yes, I have." He looked into her dark eyes pleading with him to understand and forgive, but a wall of ice had descended between them. He had loved this woman without really knowing her. A foolish mistake. He still loved her, and James the Englishman didn't know what to do about it. Nor would he listen to Hakan the Apache. Perhaps he feared losing her too much to give her such power over his life. His mother's illness was even now reminding him that the hold he had on those he loved was fragile.

He said quietly, "You were right. It's better that we don't see each other again."

She looked away, but not before he'd seen the pain in her eyes.

After they'd left, Chavi tried to concentrate on the appointment book in front of her, but the names kept blurring. How could she have been so stupid to allow Hakan to become so important in her life that she wanted him to remain? *Life is a great spinning-out of events, Chavi . . . there are complex consequences to every single thing we do.* Lysander had said that. How right he was.

Mrs. McGreal and her friend Mrs. Brannock had gone to York to visit York Minster and do some shopping, and Chavi was alone with a couple of waiting patients when the doctor returned.

Chavi ushered the first of his patients into the examining room, wondering what had transpired at Merrinswood but knowing she'd have to wait until the surgery hours ended before she'd have an opportunity to inquire. She hoped Hakan's mother wasn't seriously ill.

Watching the clock anxiously for the hands to reach twelve, when she could lock the front door, she gave a sigh of exasperation when at a minute to noon the vestibule door opened to admit another patient. Her dismay gave way to fright when she looked up and saw Lysander towering over her.

He stood for a moment regarding her with a vitriolic stare. He didn't remove his hat. His overcoat was tossed carelessly over his shoulders and hung like the wings of a bat. The waiting room was now empty, as the last patient was with Doctor McGreal.

Chavi looked up at Lysander defiantly, determined he would speak first. Only two days had passed since he left for his week in London, which indicated that he had returned early deliberately, in order to spy on her.

"What the hell do you think you're doing?" he demanded.

"I'm helping out an old friend. Mrs. McGreal usually does what I'm doing, but she has company."

"What about Garridan? He needs a mother."

"Mrs. Arkwright's looking after him. He can get along without me very well for three hours a day. I'm only here in the morning. And it's just for a couple of weeks." She met his gaze unwaveringly.

Lysander's features contorted into the hideous mask he'd worn constantly when she first knew him, and she realized that his scars, terrible though they were, only constituted part of his fearsome appearance. The expression of love he'd worn while Brenna was alive had done much to improve his looks, while his present rage accentuated his scars.

He said, "Tell the good doctor that he must find someone else to help him out."

"I can't simply walk out. I'll have to stay until he can get someone else."

"Be home by dinnertime. I'm going to see my solicitor and I'll be at the house by then." He opened the vestibule door. "And be sure the doctor understands you won't be back tomorrow." He slammed the door behind him.

Chavi's hands shook as she closed the ledger she'd been working on and went to lock the front door.

As soon as the last patient departed, she went into Doctor McGreal's office where he was making an entry in his case-book. "Ah, there you are, Chavi. I expect you're ready to go home and have lunch with that little fellow of yours?"

"Could I talk to you for a minute first, Doctor McGreal?"

"Of course."

"How was Hakan's—I mean, Lady Moreland?"

He frowned thoughtfully. "I think perhaps it's a recurrence of the flu she had about a month ago. But I'm sure she'll get over it soon."

"Oh, I'm glad to hear that."

"Run along home to your little boy, then."

She still stood in front of his desk, wondering how to tell him. He glanced up at her again. "Is something wrong, Chavi?"

"I can't come back tomorrow—my husband is home and he objects to me working."

"Oh, I'm so sorry to hear that, but of course, your first duty is to your husband. Don't worry, I'll manage."

"I was wondering . . . I know I've only worked for you a couple of days, but . . . could you pay me now? I mean, right this minute?"

His eyes probed her more deeply. "Yes, I can. But first why don't you tell me what you need the money for. I have a feeling you're in some kind of trouble."

"I need the price of a train ticket—to anywhere. I want to leave my husband and I'd like to go today. Please don't ask me to go into details, but I can't stay with Mr. Chambers any longer."

"You're running away? Is that wise? Where will you go, what will you do?"

"It's none of your business," Chavi said, close to tears. "Just pay me what you owe me and I'll go."

He got up and came around the desk to her, placed his arm about her shoulder. "I didn't mean to pry, but it's a hard world for a woman alone. Especially one with a small child. And a woman as lovely as you—"

"Don't lecture me, please. If I stay here something terrible will happen, I know it for certain. There are horrible secrets in Mr. Chambers's past. You thought I ran away from you, years ago after Brenna was born. But I didn't. He climbed up into my bedroom at your other house in the village and spirited me off to Australia. I'm afraid of him—of what he might do. I can't tell you any more than that, but please believe me. If I could get to the south coast I could perhaps find the Romany caravans again."

"Would they be able to protect you from him, if he wanted to find you?"

She felt her breath leave her body. "No, I suppose not. But I've nowhere else to go, and I can't stay here."

Andrew walked back to the other side of the desk and wrote something on a slip of paper. Then he took the cash-box out of his bottom drawer and withdrew several bank notes.

"That's too much. I haven't earned that much," Chavi protested.

He placed the money and the slip of paper in an envelope. "In order to elude a pursuer, Chavi, you can never go back to doing something he knows you did before. You need a new life."

"I don't understand."

"After I examined Lady Moreland, I talked with her son for a few minutes. He asked me about you and how long you'd be helping me. I recognized the look on his face when he spoke your name. It's one I'm sure I wore myself when all I could think of was Jean and how much I loved her and wanted to be with her."

Chavi stared at the floor. She knew the doctor had mis-read Hakan's expression and his question. He simply wanted to make sure he didn't run into her accidentally again.

Andrew went on gently. "The Merrins are well known in this part of the country, Chavi . . . people talk. It was rumored that the young Earl was spending a lot of time hanging around the gypsy caravans."

"Oh, God! If Ly—if Mr. Chambers hears talk about me and Lord Moreland . . ."

"You've been a great help to me these past two days. You have a pleasant manner with patients, your handwriting is neat, and you've a good head for figures—I was amazed at how you've straightened out Jean's account books. Now, in this envelope is enough money to take you and your son to London. My friend and former colleague, Doctor Noel Brannock, has recently opened a small hospital in the East End and could use a bright young woman like you."

"Oh, thank you! I'll pay you back, I promise."

"When will you leave?"

"Today. This afternoon, while Mr. Chambers is seeing his solicitor. I'll go home and get Garri and be on the two o'clock train."

"I'd better give you a letter of introduction to take to Doctor Brannock."

He quickly wrote the letter and handed it to her. "Come on, I'll drive you home."

At the gates to Staley Hall he shook her hand. "Good luck, Chavi. I'll keep track of you through the Brannocks."

He watched her walk up to the house, then tugged on the reins and set off down the lane. His thoughts remained with Chavi for a little while and then returned to the perplexing illness of Lady Moreland. He hadn't discussed his patient with Chavi, partly because it wasn't proper, but more because he simply didn't know what was wrong with Sarah.

She was terribly run-down, complained of muscle pain, difficulty in swallowing, and double vision. Her neck was so weak that she couldn't raise her head from the pillow. She obviously had trouble breathing. Her lower facial muscles seemed to be affected, causing her to speak in a nasal tone and possibly inhibiting her ability to chew—that and the problem in swallowing probably accounted for her rapid weight loss. Her legs were so weak she was now unable to get out of bed. He calculated the onset of her symptoms at about five weeks ago, becoming acute apparently within the last twenty-four hours. Andrew admitted to himself he was stumped and decided to call in Doctor Harkness for a second opinion.

That evening, when Jean and Brigid returned from York, they prepared an especially elegant tea for him, with cold boiled ham, watercress, crusty brown bread, and freshly churned butter, as well as an array of cream cakes from the best confectioner in town. They were dressed in pretty gowns and gave him welcoming smiles when he wearily returned from his rounds.

"Well . . . what's all this?" he asked, pleased.

They fussed over him, kept his teacup brimming, served him the leanest ham, and pointed out the most delicious cakes. When the meal was finished they pulled his armchair closer to the fire and had his carpet slippers ready.

"You're spoiling me!" he protested laughingly. "I really didn't mind you going off for the day you know, you don't have to make up for it."

"Andrew, dear," Jean said, settling down on the fireside stool at his feet as Brigid sat in the other armchair, "we have something rather serious to discuss with you."

"Ah," he said. "It must be very serious, judging by the preliminary preparations."

"Don't joke, Andrew," Jean said, her face suddenly very grave. "Oh, dear, I don't know where to begin." She turned to her friend in mute appeal.

Brigid's red hair was burnished to a fiery bronze in the light of the leaping flames. She was an attractive young woman, but he saw now that her pretty features were sorrowful and there were deep circles under her eyes. She said in a tremulous voice, "I've left Noel, Andrew. I'm not going back to him."

Jean said hastily, "She must stay here, mustn't she, Andrew? She could live in this house and we could move to the cottage at Carisbrook. That way you'd have a nurse here all the time. Brigid would be such a help. Why, she could even make some of your house calls for you if we got another carriage."

"Yes, of course, she's welcome to stay as long as she wishes," he answered. "But I'd like to know more about this separation, Brigid. Is it going to be permanent? Noel needs you too and I believed you were happy together. Is there no way to save your marriage?"

Brigid bit her lip, shaking her head. "I can't . . . condone what he's doing. It's against my religion—I can't be a party to it anymore. I told him that he'd have to choose between . . . what he's doing and me. He said he would have to choose his work."

"His work?" Andrew asked. "I suppose you're referring to his interest in psychoanalysis? It's true it's a new science, Brigid, but—"

"No, it's not that," she interrupted. She glanced at Jean, as if wondering how much she could say in front of a layperson, but when she began to speak he realized that part of her hesitancy was due to the identity of the woman of whom she spoke. "Do you remember . . . a certain patient who tried to abort her baby and perforated her uterus? It was the day Mafeking was relieved."

Andrew remembered the pathetic young prostitute very well. Noel had been unable to stop the hemorrhaging and she had died later that day.

Brigid went on, "I think that was when it started. At first he kept it from me, but I suspected, I think, after you and

Jean left, when he hired another nurse and only she was allowed to help him with certain patients. I wasn't sure until he opened the hospital. It's not a large building, it was a run-down hotel previously. All of the upstairs was set aside for his . . . special patients."

Andrew already suspected what she was about to say, but Jean put in, "It's not only that Brigid is a devout Roman Catholic, and life is sacred to her, including life in the womb, but Noel is breaking the law. He'll be arrested and sent to prison if he's caught. And we know he will be if he keeps on."

"He's performing abortions," Andrew said heavily. "Oh, God."

"It's no use you thinking you can talk him out of it," Brigid said. "If he wouldn't listen to me—if he'd let me leave him—he's adamant about it. He says the law is wrong. When I said it was God's law . . ." her voice trembled on the brink of tears. "He said then why didn't God care for the unwanted children?"

Andrew was listening to her, but he was thinking about Chavi, who by now would be knocking on Noel Brannock's door with a letter of introduction and a request to work for a doctor performing illegal operations.

37

Noel Brannock was a strange looking man, Chavi decided. He was ugly in an attractive sort of way, with penetrating intelligent eyes; at least fifty, but his movements were quick and sure and he missed nothing going on around him. He was the kind of man who never had to be told anything twice. She trusted him on sight. He made friends with Garridan by offering him an old wooden-handled stethoscope to play with and didn't mind when the child brought further chaos to his already untidy office.

After reading Doctor McGreal's letter of introduction,

Doctor Brannock gave a small smile that seemed born of irony rather than amusement. "So . . . my good friend Andrew has sent you to replace my wife."

"Your wife, sir? Oh, no—"

"You didn't know that my wife had left me?"

"No, I didn't, and I don't think Doctor McGreal did either. At least not when I left Yorkshire. Of course, Mrs. Brannock only arrived a couple of days ago. Perhaps she hadn't told him yet."

"I see. Well, before we go any further, young lady, I think you'd better know that my wife disapproved of a portion of my medical practice. I don't feel I should go into detail, but can hardly employ you without knowing your feelings on the matter, so we have a dilemma. What to do?" He ran his hand through his hair, leaving it standing on end.

"I don't have anywhere else to go," Chavi said. "I need a job desperately. I can't afford to disapprove of anything— least of all what a doctor does."

His gray eyes probed her unmercifully and at length, satisfied by what he saw, he said, "I'll put you and the boy up and you can spend as long as you like with me as my guests. If you were to sort out my files, or make any sense out of my accounts, I certainly wouldn't object—but there's no obligation to work for me. That way you wouldn't be participating in any way with . . . that segment of my practice of which my wife disapproved."

"Thank you. I'd like to stay."

He studied her again with unabashed interest. "Tell me . . . are you Catholic?"

"No, sir. I'm a gypsy."

"And therefore not likely to remain long in one place? So, why worry about what might not happen?" He smiled suddenly and his face was transformed. "You're quite possibly the most beautiful woman I've ever seen. I believe I could parade you through a male ward and have every man on his feet in an instant. Cadavers might even rise up from the slab." He chuckled, fished in his pocket to produce a small package of lemon drops, and offered one to her and one to Garridan.

Chavi hated the teeming dirty streets of the East End of London, the gray buildings, and gray-faced people. When she'd lived in the city before, she'd had a nice mews house across from the park, thanks, she now knew, to Lysander's financial support. Adding to her gloom were the unanswered questions in her mind about Lysander and Hakan, that had less to do with their feelings for her than hers for them. She decided to concentrate on putting Noel Brannock's office in order, and not to think beyond the task at hand.

Afraid to let Garri play with the tough Cockney street urchins, she kept him with her while she worked, and when the autumn weather permitted, took a hansom cab to the park so the child wouldn't forget completely what trees and grass looked like.

A letter came from Andrew McGreal, full of veiled hints. "*Was unaware of certain circumstances when I suggested you go to Dr. Brannock . . . please advise if you wish train fare to come back. . . .*"

No, as bad as London was, she didn't want to go back to Yorkshire. She wrote and told Andrew that she was quite happy where she was and reminded him of his promise to keep her whereabouts a secret.

It was quickly evident that most of Doctor Brannock's patients were women, of all ages and classes, from flamboyant actresses to dignified dowagers. He and an extremely handsome, though somewhat sullen-looking, foreign doctor named Ram Majumbdar, were the only two doctors, and with a rotating staff of nurses, a cook, and cleaning woman, they ran the hospital more on the lines of a private home.

Doctor Ram Majumbdar, Chavi decided, was more than handsome. He was almost sensually beautiful, but his glance dismissed Chavi and Garridan as some temporary annoyance to be tolerated, and he went to great pains to ignore them. It was obvious that he idolized the older doctor.

Although Noel—he insisted she call him by his given name—had joked about her curing male patients with her mere presence, the fact was there were no male patients beyond an occasional emergency-accident case. So the two doctors were constantly surrounded by an adoring, subservient collection of women, nurses, and patients. Perhaps that was why Doctor Majumbdar didn't care for her, Chavi thought, since she'd long ago stopped bowing and scraping to men.

The doctors evidently specialized in various "female complaints," and delivering babies—unusual for doctors, who usually left childbirth to midwives. The new mothers and babies stayed one or two weeks, and the others varying lengths of time. Then there were those women who came in for "minor operations" who left the same day.

Noel also saw patients occasionally who had no apparent medical problems, and these—usually women—he talked to in what he called his parlor, a bare room furnished only with a couple of battered chairs. When one day she saw him emerging from his parlor carrying a couple of bulky file folders, she inquired if she could put them away for him.

He responded, "No, not these. These are my psychoanalysis patients. My special few. I'm a disciple of Sigmund Freud, as is your friend Andrew. However, he merely reads the doctor's books and medical papers. I had the good fortune to spend last summer studying with him."

Chavi had no idea what he was talking about, but nodded as if she did. Later she went to the library and eventually found two books and several medical journals, with indexed articles, labeled "Sigmund Freud." Fascinated, she read that Freud believed that the mind could become as sick as the body.

Could this be the reason Noel's wife had left him? Had she disapproved of his listening to intimate details of his female patients' lives? Especially since Freud seemed to think most of what ailed people had sexual origins. Chavi privately thought the missing Brigid was a foolish woman, because it was certainly true that sexual feelings were a powerful force in human relationships.

Noel Brannock treated Chavi as an equal, didn't talk down to her, and seemed to assume she'd had a formal education. Since he never explained anything, she found herself often slipping down to the basement library to look into dictionaries and encyclopedias to make sense of what he'd said.

She thoroughly cleaned and tidied his office, put the files in alphabetic order, paid the bills, entered accounts due and balanced the ledgers, sent out invoices, and took an inventory of supplies. She enjoyed bringing organization to what had formerly been chaos, and at the end of the first week Noel presented her with a pound note, which he insisted was a gift for Garri and should in no way be construed a wages. It was a princely sum, but Chavi had earned it, whether or not it was wages, so she kept it. Since their needs for food and shelter were met, she retained only a few shillings to use for cabfare and treats for Garri, and put the rest into the bank. She began to feel in command of her life, independent, and was so busy she had little time to either think about the men in her life or dwell on her grief over the terrible loss of Brenna.

There were still times when she'd awaken in the night thinking she heard her daughter's footsteps, or when a little girl's laughter would bring tears to her eyes, but there was so much to do between caring for Garri and keeping Noel's office in order that the hours flew by.

Chavi had glanced at some of the files she kept, but for the most part the long medical terms were meaningless to her. There was no further word from Yorkshire, and Noel's wife did not return. There was sadness in Noel's eyes sometimes, but it was overshadowed by a fierce dedication to his patients. He didn't seem to let down his guard with any of the staff, or his colleague. But Chavi felt his loneliness and pretended not to notice that he talked only of medical matters. Whenever she could she would chat with him about less serious subjects. She arranged her work so that she could be free to take meals with him and tried in a small way to fill the terrible void left by his wife.

Her only qualm concerned the other doctor, Ram Majumbdar, who clearly disliked her. One morning when they were alone at breakfast she couldn't stand it any longer and asked, "Have I done something to offend you, Doctor Majumbdar?"

His amber eyes flickered over her. "It's so easy to catch a man on the rebound, isn't it? You don't belong here, you have no place among us, no medical skills. Why do you stay? Your small son is a nuisance and you are a distraction to Noel, keeping him from his work."

She jabbed her fork into the kipper on her plate and said, "I don't have any designs on Noel. Do you?"

A flush appeared under his coffee-toned complexion and he angrily left the room, leaving her feeling sorry she'd spoken so hastily.

One evening after she had put Garridan to bed she decided to go down to the library and read a little more of Freud's book about dreams, as hers had always been particu-

larly vivid. As she opened the library door she saw that a
lamp was lit and Noel Brannock sat alone, reading. She
started to turn away, but he saw her and called, "Come in,
Chavi. You won't disturb me, and I shan't interrupt your
reading."

He was such a lonely figure. Chavi watched him covertly,
while pretending to read, thinking that he must miss his
pretty young wife terribly.

Feeling her eyes on him, he looked up and smiled. "Are
you finding Freud a bit radical for your tastes?"

She looked down at *Interpretation of Dreams* and said,
"So many of his patients seem to be women, just as yours
are."

"So?"

"I was wondering how any man could possibly know
what was in a woman's heart."

"A psychoanalyst finds ways of having her tell him." He
studied her for a moment. "I've been curious about you,
Chavi—who you are and where you come from. Oh, I know
you were born a gypsy and that you're a widow, but there's
so much more I don't know."

Perhaps it was the lateness of the hour, or the hint of
intimacy in the closeness of their chairs, wedged among the
bookcases, or maybe it was simply that she already trusted
and admired this man with that inborn second sight that told
her he'd never harm her. Whatever the reason, she suddenly
found herself telling him her life story without excuse or
explanation. She did not identify by name any of the men
she'd known.

Noel leaned forward eagerly, lapping up very word like a
great bloodhound. When she paused, he prompted her to tell
more, so that soon she had divulged not only what had
happened, but her reactions, feelings, innermost emotions.
The overwhelming grief about Brenna, her disappointment
that Lysander had reverted from friend and mentor back to
villain and persecutor. Her ambivalent feelings about Hakan.

"This young man," Noel said, "the son of the man who
fathered your daughter . . . you say you don't know how
you feel about him, but you do."

She spread her hands on the bookcover and stared at
them. "I thought I was in love with him, but now I'm not
sure. Perhaps I was drawn to him because we're both pilgrim

souls, and we shared the journey for a little while." She looked up, and added quickly, "But I tried to stay away from him. I knew he'd find out about Brenna eventually—I knew my station in life was far below his. Besides, I've been married, widowed, had two children. . . . I couldn't have been more wrong for him. I knew we couldn't ever be together, not completely. I never counted on that, Noel. What makes me angry is that I tried so hard to drive him away, to make him leave me alone. But he persisted—he wouldn't stay away. Why didn't he leave me alone? Why did he stay until I didn't want him to leave?"

"You told him you'd had an affair with his father. That was the reason for his rejection of you."

"Yes. And I was just as foolish and impulsive with him as I was with his father. I let him make love to me—I made love to him. I suppose I've never had a lot of control over those feelings. The other man I told you about warned me that it was a mistake to sleep with a man before—" she broke off, embarrassed.

"Before marriage? But you said yourself that marriage was out of the question. You didn't even know you were a widow at that time. Has it occurred to you that perhaps the sheer unavailability of this man is what made him attractive to you? Just as the fifteen-year-old Chavi was bowled over by another man she could never have. You interest me greatly, Chavi. You seem to seek and find the most unsuitable men. If you were a man instead of a woman, I'd say that your problem is that you need to find *yourself* first, fulfill your own destiny, but you're not a man, and wifehood, motherhood, is the destiny of all women, dictated by your female biology."

She grimaced. "I've had wifehood and motherhood, and now widowhood. Isn't there any other hood for me?"

He laughed. "You might try sainthood, but I doubt you'd enjoy it. And you certainly don't look the part—you're more temptress than saint. You know, the other man you talked of is another fascinating case. Can he really be the deformed fiend and murderer you say he is? It sounds to me as if he befriended you and your daughter, and gave you both a great deal of love over the years. I'd guess that losing you both—knowing he couldn't come to England to see you, added to his grief not only over the death of Brenna, but also the loss of his brother—caused him to resurrect all of his old unresolved grief over the death of his own young son. He then convinced himself that Garridan is his son, not his brother's, and concocted a story to rationalize his belief. I wish I could have the opportunity of speaking with him. I'd like to know about his childhood, his rivalry with his brother, his feelings about his father. It might just be possible to restore his sanity."

Chavi decided not to discount his evaluation, because it seemed to please him so much. There was no doubt in her mind that Garri was Lysander's son, although she still refused to deal with that knowledge. She murmured, "You're so very wise."

"Ah, but you have a more endearing characteristic—the ability to be with another person in a magically companionable way that causes them to endow you with mystical powers. One feels that you could make everything right by simply waving your hands. There's a marvelous quality of understanding about you."

She smiled. "Funny, that's how I feel about you."

"Chavi, you're warm and insightful—you looked at me and saw my loneliness and pain. Everyone else thinks I'm so wrapped up in my work that I don't miss Brigid, but you knew differently, didn't you?"

"I know what it is to miss someone."

"Is it true that gypsies have second sight, do you think?"

She looked at him in surprise, since medical men were usually the first to scoff at such notions. "Oh, yes, it's true, when we really try."

"You know, I've been thinking about what you said . . . about a man not truly knowing what's in a woman's heart. I have a particularly difficult patient I'm attempting to psychoanalyze. Would you like to sit in with us at our next session? Use your gift of understanding to connect with another woman's heart? You could wear a nurse's uniform."

"Why, yes, I'd be glad to."

"I'll give you some of the notes I took last year when I studied with Doctor Freud. You could read them before her next appointment."

Chavi devoured the material that night, staying up until dawn to finish reading.

*   *   *

"This room is very uninviting," Chavi said two days later, looking around his parlor. "Couldn't you brighten it up a bit? Some nice curtains, a table and some flowers, a few pictures? I think your patients would be able to relax and talk easier."

Noel glanced about as though seeing the bare room for the first time. "You may be right. But no time to do anything now. She'll be here any minute. You can sit in the windowseat after I introduce you. Don't make any comments while she's here. She was brought in by her parents because she suffers from chronic insomnia, palpitations, and the habit of dozing off frequently at inappropriate moments—in church, for instance."

A nurse brought in a pale, dejected-looking young woman with deep violet eyes like bruises in her haggard face. Noel said, "Felicity, my colleague is going to sit quietly over there in the windowseat. I think she might be able to help us find out why you can't sleep."

The young woman nodded, seemingly too weary to care. She sank down in the chair, her head hanging over her thin chest in an attitude of utmost despair.

For the next hour Chavi listened to a rambling recital of complaints about this young woman's life. Since her clothes were obviously expensive and she spoke of finishing school and her debutante ball, Chavi listened with growing impatience.

After she departed Noel asked, "Well?"

"She's afraid she's too plain to catch a husband. She's bored. She doesn't do enough to get tired and sleep at night, then dozes off in the day because she was up all night. Most of all, she enjoys coming in here and talking about it to you. I can't imagine anyone else wanting to listen to such whining, can you?"

Noel's shaggy eyebrows went up in surprise. "Yes, I was afraid she was wasting my time. I've been frustrated in my treatment for so long. Freud says that some patients take satisfaction from their own suffering and hold back recovery because suffering releases unconscious guilt. But I haven't been able to trace the origins of her guilt."

"Perhaps there aren't any," Chavi suggested. "Why not forget about the reasons she's behaving this way and offer her a different way to live?"

"What do you mean?"

"Suggest she starts giving instead of taking all the time. Doing something for charity—or helping old people, or visiting hospitals. She'd soon have her mind off her own ailments."

Noel scratched his head thoughtfully. "It might at least help her sleep until we find her hidden guilt."

As she left the room she ran into Ram Majumbdar. He looked her up and down in an insulting way and said, "So . . . you've inveigled your way into the sanctum sanctorum? What a clever little minx you are! I am not allowed to listen in on his mind-meddlings, but you lost no time in getting invited. What do you intend to do? Blackmail his patients later?"

"Why do you dislike me so?" Chavi asked, genuinely surprised, since she'd never met anyone who had reacted with such hostility toward her before.

"Have you considered taking up acting for a living?" he asked sarcastically. "I dislike you because you're unwanted baggage. You're in the way. Women with your looks always cause trouble, one way or another, eventually." He pushed past her rudely.

Chavi stuck out her tongue at his retreating back and thought that he should have been a dancer on the stage with his mincing gait.

The following day Noel again asked her to sit in on one of his psychoanalysis sessions, this time with a middle-aged woman with very real troubles. Her husband had left her without any means of support, her son was in trouble with the law, and she had a senile father to care for. Chavi could barely keep quiet until she was alone with Noel. "You must do something for her at once," she said. "Keep her here— don't let her go home. She's going to commit suicide."

Noel didn't question how she could be so sure. He raced after the woman.

One afternoon toward the end of Chavi's first month in London, when Garri was taking his nap and she was finishing balancing a page in the ledger, Doctor Majumbdar burst into the office.

"Come with me at once," he ordered in his singsong English. "All of the nurses are busy and I need another pair of hands."

Chavi hesitated. "What do you want me to do?"

He gave her a supercilious smile. "Mop blood, my dear. *Now*, please." He turned and hurried toward the staircase leading to the upper floor where the operating rooms were. Chavi followed with some apprehension.

He led her into a small windowless cubicle. A woman, her eyes wide and frightened, lay on a narrow examining table, a sheet over her.

"I'm not a nurse—" Chavi began.

"You'll hand me what I require. And you'll be ready with sponges and gauze as I need you. I'll tell you what to do. Put those restraints on her wrists for a start."

An hour later, Chavi wandered in a daze back down to the office. She collapsed into Noel's chair and stared into space. She knew now what those "minor operations" upstairs were. She also knew that one of the women, who had apparently lied to Noel about how far along she was, had precipitated an emergency that had required the presence of Noel and all of the other nurses. Otherwise Doctor Majumbdar would not have requested her help.

She sat very still, feeling drained and sick to her stomach as the afternoon shadows grew longer. At length, Noel came into the room. He didn't look embarrassed or contrite; in fact, his manner was brusque.

Perching on the edge of his desk in front of her he said, "All right, it's unfortunate that you had to undergo such a baptism by fire, and Ram should have postponed his operation rather than involving you. But what's done is done."

"I thought . . ." Chavi said slowly, "that old women on back streets did that. I didn't think doctors did it. It's against the law. Against God and nature. How can you—"

"Shut up," Noel said. "Listen to me. Since the beginning of time women have chosen, for various reasons, to terminate their pregnancies. Ask any anthropologist, there has never been a society in which culture and biology do not occasionally conflict and a pregnancy occurs that the society condemns. However, the reason for the women not wanting to continue with a pregnancy is usually economic—too many mouths to feed already, poverty so acute that an older child on the breast will die. We won't even go into the question of rape, incest, or a sour marriage, an abusive husband, or even an indiscretion with another man. Circumstances can and do exist where a woman believes she has no choice but to end her pregnancy." He paused, breathing heavily.

Chavi said, "I know all that. My first child was illegitimate."

"And here you are, with another child and no husband or means to support yourself. Tell me that having that first child didn't alter your life and have a great deal to do with your present state of affairs."

"I loved my daughter!" Chavi cried in anguish.

"Of course you did. That isn't the point. The point is that you could have chosen to abort the fetus—and many women do, and always have, and always will. That fact never changes. But society denies you legal access to proper medical care."

"I would never—"

"Shall I tell you some of the methods women have used through the ages? Women have had others roll logs over their abdomen, wrap increasingly tight cords around their bodies, pound them with heavy objects—or insert a horrifying variety of objects into the uterus with gruesome results. They have swallowed an incredible number of toxic and just plain revolting substances. We aren't debating *whether* women will have abortions, the fact is that they *will*. Rich women will pay discreet doctors, poor women will use a knitting needle. They will die of perforated wombs, terminal hemorrhages, raging fevers, and poisoning. They will maim themselves for life. They will die."

"You're setting yourself up as God!"

"No, my dear, you are. You want to impose your will on others. Nobody is insisting that you abort any of your own fetuses. All we're asking of you is that you not go to the authorities and divulge what you know about us. This hospital is maintained for all women who need our help, whether or not they can afford to pay for our services."

"But it's illegal—wrong."

"The law is wrong! Those who would impose their rules and standards on others are wrong. Do you know that it doesn't matter whether a society is devoutly Catholic or primitively atheistic—or anything in between—the abortion rates are the same. No one is going to stop it happening by simply saying it's against the law, don't do it."

"This is why your wife left you."

"Chavi, consider this: An unhappy woman who comes to

us can at least return to a family who is dependent on her, able to have more children in the future if she wishes. If she goes to a back-street abortionist, or attempts it herself, she may return maimed for life, or not return at all. What has society gained by denying her proper medical treatment?"

Chavi stood up, feeling like a sleepwalker. "I can't think about it any more today. I'm going to see to my son."

"Will you at least tell me whether or not I should prepare for the arrival of the peelers?" Noel asked with a ghost of a smile.

"I wouldn't dream of telling anyone."

"Now that you know all of our dark secrets, I wish you'd stay on. You'll never be asked to help out upstairs again, I promise you." He hesitated, then added, "I wasn't going to mention this yet, but I was very impressed with the way you interpreted the mental problems of the two patients you saw. I feel that with a course of study, you could be very valuable in the field of psychoanalysis."

She paused, one hand on the doorknob, and answered, "I'll let you know in the morning what I'm going to do."

38

Cornelia Dunstan paused before the oval mirror at the top of the staircase, searching her translucent complexion for possible wrinkles. Her brother appeared on the landing behind her and asked, "Well? Has he proposed yet?"

She tugged the décolletage of her gown lower, exposing the tops of her pale breasts above the dark red velvet. Nervously she pulled wisps of blonde hair out from behind her ears, fearing her earrings were too obviously paste. It certainly wouldn't do for the Merrins to realize how desperately both her age and her family's finances urged her toward marriage with James Merrin.

"Oh, do be quiet about it, Gil," she snapped. "His mother is ill. He's been spending so much time with her."

Gilbert lounged against the balustrade, his left hand fingering the empty right sleeve of his coat. "Well, at least you were able to talk them into having a Christmas party at Merrinswood. Perhaps you can reel him in tonight."

Nelia studied her reflection in the mirror, wondering if there was any way the plan she'd devised could possibly show in her face. She decided it couldn't. "I used my powers of persuasion on Robbie to get them to have a party." She smirked over her shoulder at her brother. "Robbie is madly in love with me. It's pathetic and quite amusing. He'd do anything for me."

"Yes, well, don't forget he's only the bastard son. Don't waste too much of your charm on him, sister dear. And keep your eye on that venomous little Emily—if there's any way for her to sabotage you, she will."

Nelia's green eyes glittered with malice. "I'll take care of little Emily the minute I'm mistress of Merrinswood, never fear. Out she goes."

"And Robbie?"

She considered. "It might be amusing to keep him around. He works hard for the estate and it would sort of be like having an adoring puppy following me around. And a way to keep James a little jealous."

Gilbert gave a knowing laugh. "I pity them all."

The gathering at Merrinswood was small—just the family, the Dunstans, and the American, Sam Rutherford. The dining room was festive with holly and a fir tree decorated with candles and ornaments, but Nelia saw no mistletoe. Well, she wouldn't need it. She would rekindle James's ardor without it, and when she had been compromised she would demand marriage or threaten a breach of promise suit.

After all, the rules had been changed—by James—and she could no longer rely on her beauty to maneuver him into marriage. After leading her to believe he was going to propose, he suddenly backed away and started pursuing that gypsy tart, who had fortunately vanished.

Seated beside Robbie, who stammered and shook and turned bright red every time she spoke to him, Nelia sipped port wine as they awaited the arrival of the Christmas pudding and mince pies. Catching James's eye, she deliberately turned and flirted with Robbie. "How clever of you to suggest we go upstairs and sing carols for Lady Moreland in her room. She'll be so cheered to think we haven't excluded her."

"Y-y-you th-think s-so? I h-hope we don't t-tire her."

"It's a wonderful idea." Out of the corner of her eye she looked across the table at James, who was in conversation with Sam Rutherford, while Philip Merrin tried in vain to coax a smile onto Emily's discontented face. Nelia heard snatches of the conversation between Sam and James, and badly wanted to turn to Robbie and tell him to shut up so she could hear more.

She strained to try to pick up the thread of what James was saying to Sam. ". . . and she's become obsessed with putting all of her notes into manuscript form. Her feeling of running out of time is worrying me."

"Me too. I've been thinking about it. Perhaps if someone were to work on her journals for her it would relieve her mind."

"Hire an emanuensis, you mean?"

"How about an anthropologist? Someone as passionately interested in the plight of the Indian as Sarah is."

"Your daughter? But I thought she was still in university."

Robbie sputtered in her ear, 'N-n-nelia, you l-look s-so b—"

"Do shut up," she hissed back, but it was too late, she didn't catch all of Rutherford's reply. Robbie looked crestfallen and chewed his lower lip as though he might cry. What a terrible sissy he was, she thought with a shiver of distaste. He was more sensitive than any woman.

At that moment a footman carried the flaming Christmas pudding into the room. Everyone applauded as the brandy-fed blue flames leapt up the rich moist sides of the pudding to lick at the sprig of holly on top. A second footman followed with rum sauce and a silver platter of mince pies.

The carol singing in Sarah's room was cut short by James, who saw that his mother, looking ghostly pale and unable to raise her head from her pillow, was too fatigued. The nature of her illness was still unclear, although James had brought in specialists.

Everyone drifted back downstairs, until only Nelia and James remained. He bent and kissed his mother's cheek, then took Nelia's hand and led her firmly from the room. He looked particularly handsome tonight, the candlelight gilding his hair as he carried himself like a prince. Merrin men always looked wonderful in evening clothes, she thought; even Robbie looked quite dashing tonight, despite his thick-lensed spectacles. Of course, when James had his portrait painted for the family gallery, she must insist that he wear his cavalry uniform.

She slipped her arm through his and said wheedlingly, "James, I must speak with you privately for a moment."

For a second she thought he might refuse, but good manners prevailed. "We could go down to the library—" he began.

She pushed open a bedroom door and said, "No, in here."

The room was dark, illuminated only by the glow of the lamps on the landing through the open door. Nelia closed the door, plunging them into deeper darkness.

James said, "I'll light a lamp." But before he could do so, she caught the lapels of his coat and began to cry softly.

She felt him try to pull away, so she held on more tightly and sobbed a little harder.

"Nelia, what is it? What's the matter?"

"Oh, James, I'm so unhappy . . . I wanted to tell you privately that I've decided to leave home."

There was a pause, then his hand patted her arm soothingly, like a father with a child. That was not the reaction she wanted, so she pressed herself closer to him and wrapped her arms around his neck.

"What happened at home?" he asked.

"Everything! Gil's life has been ruined by the war, Daddy thinks he might have to sell the house, everyone is being beastly to everyone else."

"But where will you go?"

"Away—anywhere!" she replied dramatically, and slipped her hands inside his coat. "My only regret is that you and I . . . we never . . . consummated our love. How foolish I was to deny you—that night on the terrace when you wanted me so badly."

Before he could speak, she raised her head and kissed him so heavily that he had to put his arms around her. He made a small sound that could have been resignation, but she preferred to think it was the expression of his passion.

"Nelia, we must go down to the others—"

"No, James, please, stay a moment . . . we may never see each other again. Oh, I can't bear it!"

She began to kiss him again and ran her hands up and down his back like frantic little animals. "Please, I want a beautiful memory to take away with me . . . make love to me."

He was aroused, she knew. Her tongue darted along his lower lip and she became more bold with her hands. James picked her up and carried her to the bed, then returned to lock the door. In that moment she turned back the coverlet and pushed the blankets into a heap at the foot of the bed. She wanted the linen left in as much disarray as possible for the eyes of a servant.

As he undressed, she carefully removed her velvet gown, and wondered how she could keep her coiffure from being crushed. Her own excitement mounted as she recalled all of the stories she and her friends had concocted about the "wild Indian" when they had been children. She wondered if his lovemaking would be primitive and perhaps just a little savage.

At first he seemed almost too civilized, perhaps even a trifle offhand. Her fingernails clawed his back and she arched her body toward him. Then he was inside her with a swift thrust that brought a cry to her lips. It was quickly evident that he was an accomplished lover, and her pleasure was far greater than she had expected. Yet throughout the entire experience she had the uneasy feeling that he was obliging her rather than receiving her most priceless treasure. She rationalized that a man would naturally be less reverent with a widow than with a virgin.

When it was over he held her for only a moment before saying, "We really ought to return to the drawing room. They'll wonder what we're up to."

"Darling, they'll *know* what's happening," Nelia purred contentedly. "They'll understand that you got me alone in order to ask me to marry you." She paused. "After all, a gentleman doesn't compromise a lady unless his intentions are honorable, does he? Indeed, there are specific laws on the subject. You may have heard of breach of promise? In view of all the time we've spent together, and tonight's explosion of passion . . . well, after all, one wouldn't want a scandal, would one? When we go downstairs you must speak with my father. He can make the announcement tonight."

James rolled away from her. The bed creaked as he stood up and began to dress. She added, "We should have an early spring wedding. I do hope your mother lasts until then. Oh, dear, I don't mean to sound heartless, but she is awfully ill. A wedding during the mourning period is considered to be in frightfully bad taste."

"Nelia," James's voice interrupted, low and controlled. "Let me see if I understand what it is you want. You would, I take it, like to become the Countess of Moreland. Tell me, if I were not the Earl of Moreland, but was merely the master of Merrinswood, would you still want to be mistress of Merrinswood, without the title?"

"Darling, what nonsense you're talking. You *are* the Earl—and your fortune encompasses a great deal more than this house."

"The income from the estate farmland supports the house. You haven't answered my question. Would you still want to marry the master of Merrinswood," he persisted, "if there were no title? If there were no real fortune?"

"Oh, I see, it's a hypothetical question. You want me to prove that I love you for yourself alone. Well, darling, of course I do. Neither the title nor the family fortune mean anything to me. Yes, I would marry the master of Merrinswood, even if there were no title, no fortune."

"Good. Then we must let Robbie know at once."

"*Robbie*? What has he to do with it?"

"Everything. Merrinswood is Rob's home. He loves it as I loved my home in the mountains and desert. This estate is now the property of Robert Leighton, esquire. I had our solicitor put everything into Robbie's name."

Andrew looked into the hideously scarred face of the man who stood in the vestibule, steeling himself not to betray by so much as a twitch of his eyebrow the apprehension he felt.

"I've explained to you several times, Mr. Chambers, that it is my belief that Chavi has rejoined her Romany family."

"I found the gypsies in Somerset and she and the boy were not with them. Since you were the last person she talked to before leaving, I'm quite sure you know where they are. I ask you again, where did they go?"

"Mr. Chambers, please! It's Christmas and we were just about to carve the bird."

"Andrew? Who is it, dear?" Jean's voice called. "Why don't you invite—oh!" She broke off as she reached the vestibule door and saw their visitor. Andrew said quickly,

"Mr. Chambers was just leaving. Please go back to our guests, Jean, I'll be along in a moment."

He could see that Jean was frightened, not for herself, but for him. She was well aware of how Chambers had badgered him about Chavi.

Chambers said, "I'm not leaving this house until you tell me where my wife is." He took a threatening step forward and Jean cried, "Why don't you go and ask Lord Moreland?"

Andrew was aghast, but it was too late to cover up. Chambers's eyes, which were the most disturbingly intense he'd ever encountered, seemed to burst into black flame. "*Lord Moreland?*" The words on his lips sounded like a curse. "Richard Merrin is dead."

"I meant his son, James, who inherited his title." Jean said. "The Merrins befriended both Chavi and her brother, Danior. Perhaps Lord Moreland knows where Danior is— you might find Chavi with him."

As the man turned and stormed out of the house into a raw Christmas evening, Andrew said with real regret, "I wish you hadn't sent him to Merrinswood."

"Andrew, that man is desperate, didn't you see his eyes? There's no telling what he might have done. We know that Danior is traveling the country with his organ-grinder friend, and Chavi is safe with Noel—at least until they're all arrested for breaking the law. Come along, dear, and let's have dinner. We can't solve all of the world's problems tonight."

Pas kissed his fingertips and chuckled appreciatively. "*È stato veramente un bel pranzo.* A fine meal, Danior. A Christmas dinner worthy of a king, yes? We are indebted to the signora, sì?" He beamed at the plump and blushing woman across the table. A farmer's widow, she had brought Pas every knife and scissors she owned, keeping him in the Lancashire village longer than they customarily stayed anywhere. Then, two days ago, she had invited them to spend Christmas day with her.

Alphonso II, who was younger and less inclined to bite than his predecessor, slept contentedly on a chintz-covered chair by the fire while the widow's dog watched suspiciously from the hearth rug.

"Indeed, yes, Mrs. Fleming," Danior said. "I can't remember when we dined so well."

"Perhaps later you'd sing for me?" she asked shyly. "Your voice . . . I can't tell you what it does to me. It's spellbinding."

Danior stared at his plate, but Pas said quickly, "Of course, he'll sing. He lives to sing. He is only alive when he sings."

Mrs. Fleming, sensing Danior's discomfort, rose to her feet. "Now, why don't you two just go into the sitting room and have a nice after-dinner drink? I've got a couple of cigars, too. I'll just pop the dishes into the kitchen and join you in a bit."

Danior followed Pas into a tiny cluttered room, fussy with bric-a-brac and aspidestras, the chairs and sofa draped with embroidered antimacassars. A yule log sputtering in the narrow tiled fireplace had not yet warmed the room nor disguised its musty, unused smell.

When Mrs. Fleming withdrew, Danior said, "What the hell are we doing here, Pas? You planning to marry her?"

Settling himself down comfortably in a fireside chair, Pas grinned. "It'sa nice to spend Christmas in a real house for a change, that's all. She's lonely, glad of our company. A good bargain for us all." He scratched his nose with his forefinger in a sly way that alerted Danior to an ulterior motive.

"What else?" Danior asked.

"Well, we're close to Liverpool. An Italian opera company is performing there." He reached into his inside pocket and pulled out a folded newspaper clipping. Smoothing it out, he handed it to Danior.

Danior read: *Famous Italian baritone Mazetti to appear in new production of* Rigoletto. He looked up. "I don't want to go to the opera."

"Then I shall go alone. Mazetti is an old friend."

"What? You knew Mazetti?" Danior was impressed. "When?"

"We were apprentices together, back in the old days. We sang in the chorus, shared a terrible little flat. Two young men with no money, little prospect, but high hopes." Pas shrugged philosophically. "Mazetti realized his dream, I did not. It was never meant to be for me, I see that now. But it was for him, as it is for you."

"You promised not to lecture me again."

"So? I'm getting old. I no longer feel bound to tell the truth. And I demand favors. This one I ask of you—come with me to hear Mazetti sing. It will do us both good to hear *Rigoletto* as Verdi intended it to be sung."

"And after the performance you'll introduce me to Mazetti?" Danior felt a thrill of anticipation in spite of himself.

"But of course! He will be able to convince you to go back to the beginning and start again."

"Pas! What's the use? I'm a gypsy who temporarily suffered from delusions of grandeur. Wanting something doesn't necessarily mean you have the talent for it. How many Mazettis came out of *your* opera company?"

"Danior, listen to me. You went too far, too fast. *In men che non si dica*—in no time. That was your trouble. No sooner you get a job in the chorus than you're an understudy. Then you're singing a major part. Long before you were ready for it. It was all too easy for you. Nothing worthwhile ever comes so easy. You have to work, practice, study, *sweat* . . . step by step, day in and day out with maybe not a kind word, or even enough to eat. You have to learn to suffer disappointments, yes, and even ridicule and insults. You have to fall on your face a few times. Then when you get your big chance, you'll know you've earned it and no one can take it away from you."

Danior was silent.

Pas said softly, "With work, dedication, you can be as good as Mazetti. It'sa time for you to go forward now. Forget what that critic wrote—ah, *ne ferisce più la lingua che la spada*! The tongue wounds more than the sword. Danior, for me you will come talk to Mazetti, sing for him?"

"For you, anything, Pas." Danior picked up a brass poker and prodded the log, feebly attempting to burn in the widow's fireplace.

"Now," Pas said, "you can tell me why today you feel such sadness. Christmas is a joyous time."

"I was thinking about my sister, Pas. I've dreamed of her the past several nights and feel great worry for her. I think she might be in danger."

"You must go to her then, at once."

"The caravans will be in the south now. I'd have a hard time finding them. Besides, I don't think she wants to see me. I'm the reason Brenna died."

Pas shook his head sadly. There was no point in going over the same ground again. The death of the child, Pas thought, had brought not only terrible grief, but had sent two lives spinning off in directions they'd never intended to take. He hoped Danior's intuition that his sister was in danger was wrong, but Pas had come to respect gypsy second sight.

39

Barlow's immobile features showed no sign of shock, or even surprise at Lysander's appearance. The butler showed him into the library and said he would see if Lord Moreland was at home.

The moment Barlow left the room, however, he felt beads of perspiration form on his brow. The butler walked as quickly as his arthritic limbs would allow up to Lady Moreland's bedroom, where he knew he'd find her son. Knocking on the door, he suggested by gestures that they should speak out on the landing.

"What is it, Barlow?" Hakan asked.

"A visitor. I've put him in the library. He wants to see you—but I think we should send for the police."

"Why?"

Barlow lowered his voice even further. "I never mentioned it to anyone, because I was afraid I had imagined such a face, but I've seen this man before. The night your father died. I looked up and saw his face—it's not one anyone would be likely to forget—at the window."

"Who is he?"

"A Mr. Chambers, sir."

"I'll go down and see what he wants."

"Lord Moreland . . . I think the man downstairs may have killed your father."

"*What?*" Hakan spun around.

"I helped lay your father out that night. There were

bruises on his face and his lips were blue." Barlow maintained an impassive stare, but the palms of his hands were
damp. He had also seen Jean Leighton, who in his mind was
the true mistress of Merrinswood, leaving Lord Moreland's
room that night. And that was hours after he'd seen the
scarred face at the window and several grooms had searched
the grounds, at which time Lord Moreland was still alive. Of
course, they had all gone up to wish him happy birthday and
good-night, but Jean was the last one to enter the sickroom,
before Sarah went to bed in the adjoining room. God knew
that poor little Jean Leighton had reason to wish him dead.
Barlow had said nothing when her doctor-husband signed the
death certificate, and Lady Moreland didn't question the
cause of death. But Barlow had worried, all this time, that
sometime, somehow, someone would find out that Jean had
held a pillow over the face of the man who had tormented
her so. There had been the added evidence of that extra
pillow case that a maid had discovered stuffed under the bed.

Had Barlow known where to find that hideously scarred
prowler at the time, the man would have danced on the end
of a rope then. But it wasn't too late to do something for
dear kind Jean now. To make her safe forever. Her husband
had tried to protect her when he had signed the death certificate, but the only way to close the books on a murder was to
hang somebody for it. The young Lord Moreland was staring
at him strangely, and it occurred to Barlow that perhaps he'd
asked a question. "Beg pardon, sir?"

"I asked why you didn't say anything at the time." Hakan
was careful not to show any emotion. "I'm sure Doctor
McGreal would have given you an explanation."

"The doctors were *expecting* your father to die from his
illness," Barlow answered carefully. "I do beg of you, sir, to
exercise caution with this man Chambers. And to allow me
to send for the police. He's up to no good, I can feel it."

"I'll go and speak with him." Hakan went slowly down
the stairs, feeling the walls close in on him again. So Barlow
suspected. Why had he kept quiet, really? And why did he
now want to try to place the blame on Chambers? Why
would Chambers have lurked outside at the window that
night rather than accompanying his wife to the party?

Chambers stood in front of the library fire. He was an
imposing figure of a man, once one got over the shock of his

scars, which were partially hidden by a neatly trimmed beard. Hakan's practiced eye recognized that those scars were the result of torture, of mutilation at the hands of another man. He'd seen such scars before, although nothing as bad as these. He wondered about the scars that were not visible. Chambers's eyes were fierce, unrelenting. Rage was ready to burst from him like a wild beast.

His voice was a low growl. "You look like your father."

"What is it you want?"

"I suppose I should have inquired around here before dashing off on a wild-goose chase to the south. If I had, I would have found that like your father, you were after my wife. You hung around the gypsy caravans, did you not? Forcing your attentions on my wife."

"Perhaps you should have been here to protect her, instead of abandoning her." Hakan felt his own anger simmer to boiling point. He turned his body slightly sideways, his arms curving at his sides without conscious effort. His feet were spread, poised to spring.

Chambers noted the change of posture and flung off his coat. "Your bloody swine of a father ruined that girl's life. Now you dare to seduce her, too. They tell me that you were brought up among savages. I presume you wish to fight like a savage rather than be called out like a gentleman. Therefore I'll be glad to oblige you."

Not wishing to brawl in the house, Hakan turned to leave, but Chambers grabbed his shoulder and spun him around. "Damn you, don't turn your back on me."

The fist intended for his chin missed its mark as Hakan moved slightly to the side, taking most of the force of the blow just below his ear. As he staggered, trying to regain his balance, Chambers swung his fist again, but this time Hakan blocked the blow with his forearm, crouched and used his opponent's momentum to send him crashing into the wall.

Chambers came back at him and fastened his hands around Hakan's throat. They swayed back and forth as Hakan tried to break the hold, cursing the weakness in his leg that threw him off-balance.

They were evenly matched. Although the lighter of the two, Hakan was younger, lithe, his reflexes swifter. Before he was wounded he would have ended the fight much more rapidly, despite Chambers's size.

A bookcase toppled over with a crash and a minute later the doors burst open. Barlow appeared, followed by three of the burliest young grooms. Out of the corner of his eye Hakan saw the grooms moving in. He wanted to yell at them to stand back, that he would prevail over this man. But it was too late. They seized Chambers's arms and dragged him away, forcing him to the floor and pinning him there.

Barlow said, "I've sent for the police, sir."

Hakan sat at his mother's bedside, watching her slip slowly away from him. He picked up her limp hand and held it. Her eyes had flared to life briefly, but she hadn't spoken. Her skin was as pale and fragile as gossamer. Two long plaits of silvery gold hair lay on her wasted shoulders.

Doctor McGreal had said she probably would not live to see in the New Year. He and Harkness and three other doctors had been baffled by her illness and it remained undiagnosed. But it didn't take a doctor to see that Sarah was dying. Hakan felt the weight of great sadness press upon him.

He wondered how she would feel if she knew that a man might possibly be brought to trial for killing her husband. If only he could talk to her about it. If only he could talk to somebody about it. Hakan, son of *Tonsaroyoo*, would not have had the moral dilemma to face that James, Lord Moreland, now agonized over. The man who called himself Dirk Chambers was apparently an escaped double-murderer.

The web had closed swiftly and inexorably about Chambers. Before the police arrived to take him into custody, Robbie had already sent for Hilliard Stoughton, their solicitor, in order to determine the charges to be filed. Stoughton recognized the man he'd sent to meet Richard Merrin all those years ago, although he didn't reveal anything other than that he knew this man had escaped from prison, where he had been serving a life sentence for murder. A guard had been killed during the escape.

Hakan would simply have let Chambers go, but the matter was taken out of his hands. Now Hakan considered the fact that if Chambers were convicted of murdering his father, there would be no doubt that he'd hang. The earlier murders, perhaps, if he'd lived a law-abiding life in the meantime, would draw prison sentences instead of the ultimate penalty.

Someone knocked at the door and Hakan uncoiled him-

self from his chair. He'd been at his mother's bedside all
night and his body still ached from the fight with Chambers.

A footman waited respectfully until Hakan closed the
bedroom door, then said, "Mr. Rutherford and Miss Rutherford have arrived, sir."

"Have the nurse go to Lady Moreland. I'll return in five
minutes."

Hakan knew he looked disheveled after the sleepless night,
but didn't care. Sam was an old friend and although Hakan
wasn't looking forward to a reunion with the sharp-tongued
and tomboyish Bly Rutherford, perhaps her presence would
set his mother's mind at rest. Sam's daughter had published a
number of articles on various Indian tribes, and know-it-all
shrew that she was, with Bly's superior intelligence and passionate interest in the North American Indian, she was the
perfect editor for Sarah's book.

They were waiting in the morning room. Sam looked
tired and worried as he paced up and down in front of the
wall of windows overlooking the winter-bare grounds. But it
was the young woman seated quietly near the door who
commanded Hakan's immediate attention.

She was dressed in a neat fawn-colored traveling suit, with
a soft cream satin blouse. Her straight dark hair swept smoothly
from a high intelligent brow to a burnished coil on her
crown. Questing eyes of a light golden-brown met Hakan's
surprised gaze and she gave him a tentative smile that deepened the dimples in her cheeks and emphasized her cleft chin.

"Hello, Hakan," she said softly. "I'm so sorry your
mother is ill." There was no hint of the strident tone he
remembered. In fact, Bly's voice reminded him of warm
honey flowing freshly from a sun-drenched hive.

Noel Brannock put the newspaper down on his desk and
looked up at Chavi. "I presume this is your Lysander?"

She nodded. "It says there's to be an investigation into
Lord Moreland's death, that Lysander was in Yorkshire and
was seen that night. After all this time, could they do an
autopsy and find out how Richard died?"

"No, I don't think so. A paralyzed stroke victim . . . it
would be easy to simply stop him from breathing. There'd
probably be no evidence of wounds or poison. But in any
case, it says here that your Lysander—they call him Keir

Chambers in the paper—is an escaped felon. He'd already been convicted of murder, so I don't believe you need worry about him being released to come and look for you and Garri."

Chavi drummed her fingernails on the paper distractedly. "I have a letter Lysander wrote telling me that he went to Merrinswood the night of Richard's party, the night he died, to spy on me."

"You realize that that letter, along with a possible witness who can place him there, and your testimony that he wanted you to demand money for your daughter from the Merrins could hang him?"

"I don't want him to hang," Chavi said, and burst into tears.

Noel came around the desk and took her into his arms. He held her until her sobs diminished, then offered her his handkerchief. "Just when I think I'm starting to understand your sex, one of you destroys every one of my theories and beliefs. I thought you ran away from this man. That you hated him, were afraid of him."

Chavi wiped her eyes. "I don't hate him. He's my dear friend, but he shocked me by suddenly wanting to be my husband. He had no right to make decisions that included me without consulting me. Especially in view of the way we parted after Brenna's funeral. It was a bad time for both of us. I was wild with grief, I didn't want to go on living. It was a sort of madness . . . a rage at God and humanity. I look back now and see the misery I was in when I met Hakan. I was crawling through my life on my hands and knees and he forced me to stand up again."

"So you believed yourself in love with him?"

"Yes, I suppose so. But I see now that my feelings for him were more complex than either love or gratitude. In some remote part of my mind I think there was perhaps some sort of strange desire to go back and create Brenna again. Hakan looks so much like his father . . . like Brenna's father. It was a way to go back to the beginning and start again and maybe have it turn out differently. Oh, God, what am I saying? Why did you teach me so much about my own mind? It hurts too much to think these thoughts."

"A good doctor never treats himself, Chavi. Nor should a psychoanalyst. Your gift is to connect with other people's minds. And it is a gift, one that I feel will carry you far in the

profession. But tell me, what happened at Brenna's funeral to
cause a rift between you and Lysander?"

"He criticized me for giving her a gypsy's funeral, for one
thing. But . . . well, he'd been writing letters demanding that
I take both children to Ireland to visit him. He wanted to see
Garri so badly. But I ignored his letters. Then, when he
arrived for the funeral, he immediately wanted to see Garri.
The baby was asleep, and of course when he woke up to find
Lysander looming over him, he screamed in fright. There
was no point in trying to convince Lysander it wasn't his
disfigured face that terrified the child, he'd have cried at any
stranger. He was only fourteen months old. Lysander made
me angry by seemingly being more interested in making
friends with Garri than in grieving for Brenna. I'd seen him
cry over her in the Australian Outback because he was afraid
for her—yet he never shed a tear at her funeral."

"Perhaps he was holding his grief in?" Noel suggested.
"You told me he'd loved your daughter from the time she
was a couple of weeks old. He'd already lost his own young
son years before. Perhaps his way of dealing with a second
dose of grief was to imagine that he had married you, rather
than his brother, and that Garri was his child—in a sense a
replacement for the lost children. And then act upon that
fantasy?"

Chavi pushed her hair back from her brow, her hand
lingering to press her temples. She hadn't told Noel about the
night of the fire, nor her ultimate realization that Garri was
indeed Lysander's son.

"I was unkind to him, Noel. I was so hurt and lost and I
wanted someone to pay for how I felt, so I was cruel to my
dearest friend. If you could see what that monster had done
to his face—you'd never condemn Lysander for killing him.
But now he's been caught and he'll hang and it's all because
of me. . . ."

"Ah, guilt!" Noel said knowingly. "The whip that impells
us all. But what if in fact he did murder Brenna's father?"

"I don't believe he did. I did wonder, for a little while,
but when I really thought about it, I knew he hadn't. There
was no reason for him to. Lord Moreland was enduring a
living death."

"What about the letter Chambers wrote, admitting he
was on the scene?"

"I'm going to my room to burn it."

Sarah had rallied, to the delight of her doctors and family, after Bly and Sam arrived. But while they made plans for the future which included her return to full health, Sarah knew that she had only a short time left. Despite her weakness, she insisted that her journals and notes be spread upon her bed and that Hakan and Sam read the manuscript and offer advice as Bly began the task of organizing what had become a mammoth pile of notebooks and papers.

With her keen journalistic mind, Bly had echoed Hakan's feelings that the book should be an historical text, but Sarah was adamant that it would be a novel. "I want my reader to experience the Life-way, not simply be told about it."

She swiveled her head slowly and painfully toward her son. "Hakan, tell Bly about the first raid you went on. I've already written how boys between fifteen and seventeen would be instructed by an old man about what was expected of him on the warpath, and of the fasting before the raid. Then for the first raid the boy would simply observe the warriors. But this afternoon while I'm resting, I want you to tell her how you felt—the excitement, the fear, the elation of coming back safely. How the blood pounded through your veins during the war dance the night before the raid."

Sarah's head felt too heavy for her neck, and turning to look at Bly took what seemed an age. "Bly, you must coax everything he remembers out of him."

This strange new Bly with her gentled manner and soft-spoken charm smiled and said, "I'll get every detail out of him, Sarah, don't worry. If coaxing doesn't work there's always torture."

As she and Hakan launched into good-natured bandying back and forth, Sarah's eyes met Sam's across the paper-strewn bed. In his gaze deep grief had already joined the yearning for what he knew could never be. Sarah wanted to hold him, comfort him, but it was better if he believed his love was not returned, that she looked upon him only as a friend. To let him know now that she had loved him would only be to add to his pain when the inevitable parting came. Instead she strove to convey with her glance that perhaps their love would live on in their children.

Look at them, Sam, Sarah said with her eyes, *they're*

really meeting for the first time as complete adults. They're attracted to one another, although they haven't realized it yet.

Sam's eyes misted visibly, and to cover his feelings, he picked up one of her journal pages. He read aloud, "Killer of Enemies. White-painted Woman and Child of the Water. Owl-man Giant, Buffalo Monster, Eagle Monster, Antelope Monster . . . you've remembered them all, Sarah." His voice was a little unsteady.

Bly said, "Oh, let me look at that, Dad. I've been working on a piece about Chiricahua myths and legends."

Sarah rested, watching Bly devour her notes with an eagerness that confirmed her suitability for the task of completing Sarah's book. It was more than Bly's intelligence and education; there was a vitality, an indefatigable stamina, as well as an intense compassion about this young woman that said she not only had strong beliefs, but would be willing to fight for those beliefs at great personal cost. Sarah's instincts told her that Bly could very well be as brave as Hakan. When she was a child they'd mistaken that feistiness, constant questioning, and outspoken outrage for an overbearing personality. In a boy it would have been commended, but it was not surprising that Bly's grandparents and teachers and everyone else had tried to stamp it out of her. Luckily, like a spirited horse, she'd remained proud and unbroken. Sarah was not fooled by Bly's present ladylike pose. Her true self was still evident in her quick, knowing glances and the restlessness of her hands if someone made a stupid remark.

Feeling herself begin to drift off to sleep, Sarah studied Bly carefully. Slender, but with a tensile strength about her that said she would endure. Her features were even, not pretty but pleasantly vivacious, especially when she smiled and her dimples deepened. When she laughed, or was angry, or any of her feelings ran rampant, which was all the time because she seemed to live life on the keen edge of awareness, her eyes became golden. Sarah had only ever seen one other person whose eyes flashed with golden fire. *Tonsaroyoo . . .* her beloved Lone Wolf. She fell asleep thinking about him as Bly read aloud from the notes Sarah had written so long ago.

"When Y'sun had set people out onto the world, he decided there had to be two kinds. He called the children of White-painted Woman before him and said, 'Here are two weapons. Choose which you want to live by.'

He laid before them a gun, and bow and arrows. Killer of Enemies was older and he got first choice. He took the gun. Child of the Water was left with the bow and arrows.

Killer of Enemies became leader of the white-eyes, and Child of the Water became leader of the Indians. That's how they got to be different. Some say that Killer of Enemies nearly took the bow and arrows . . . then we would have been whites, I suppose."

40

Noel and Chavi waited in the now brightly wallpapered and plant-filled parlor for the arrival of their patient.

"Doctor Freud says that just as there's a wish for life, so too is there a desire for death," Noel said. "An urge to escape the stress of living by becoming inanimate. That there is a conflict submerged in the unconscious between the death instinct and the wish for life. Some people turn their selfdestructive impulses outward. A man obsessed with his own death may turn his aggression on someone else and commit murder."

"I don't want to talk about Lysander today," Chavi answered. "I was up all night trying to decide what to do."

"There's nothing you can do. The man was doomed from the start."

She went to the window and stared out at the gray slate roofs, silvered with a slashing January rain. "You know, not everything your wonderful Doctor Freud says is true. All that nonsense about women envying men's sexual organs, for instance. It would make more sense if men envied women's ability to bear children—that's a greater feat than having an organ that acts without conscious effort on the man's part."

Noel laughed. "How I shall miss you when you're gone, Chavi. You say exactly what's on your mind and don't give a tinker's toss about who might be shocked. I've never met anyone else, man or woman, with whom I could talk so freely."

"What do you mean when I'm gone? I told you that I would stay as long as you'll have me. I won't have anything to do with your illegal activities upstairs, but I do want to learn more about why people behave as they do—and perhaps help them see a better way of handling their problems."

Noel's metallic-gray eyes crinkled around the corners and he looked at her fondly. "I wish I could teach you all you need to know. But I can't. You must go to Vienna soon, and study with Doctor Freud and the others. You have a calling, I believe, Chavi. Perhaps that was why the fates led you along your torturous path to me."

He was right, of course. She wanted it with all her heart. She was so eager to absorb knowledge of the human mind that she became impatient with anything that got in her way. Even Garridan had learned to play quietly when his mother buried her head in her books. Fortunately, the appealing little boy was the darling of nurses and patients alike, and never lacked for companionship. He spent so much time with adults that he was rapidly expanding his vocabulary and often made Chavi laugh with his grown-up expressions—not all of the meanings of which he understood. With a gypsy's instinct for survival, however, the child steered clear of Doctor Ram, as he called him.

"There's nothing I'd like better than to go to Vienna, Noel. But it's out of the question just now."

"If you're worried about the cost, I've been giving the matter some thought. When I studied with Doctor Freud I stayed at the home of a retired neurologist. He and his wife are both partly incapacitated, and they offer food and lodging and help with fees in return for students caring for them and running their household. It's a lively place, overrun with students. You'd like it, and there would always be someone to watch Garri when you were gone. I've already written them about you and received an enthusiastic response. I'll give you their reply when we get back to the office. You can put it away and think about it."

Chavi said quietly, "I can't go anywhere until I know what's to become of Lysander."

Noel said, "The wheels of justice grind slowly, so your Lysander is probably not in imminent peril of the noose."

"Perhaps not. But he's locked up. I wonder if he's missing the stars more than the sunlight."

"What?"

"Oh, nothing. Something he once said to me."

Their patient arrived, an interesting case. A woman obviously well past childbearing age, she nevertheless insisted she was pregnant. Noel fussed with the woman's chair as he greeted her. His mind kept darting to another patient he wanted Chavi to see, although he hadn't told her yet. Perhaps when she listened to the heartbreaking story of the thirteen-year-old child, pregnant with her stepfather's baby and too far along for the fetus to be aborted, Chavi might begin to understand why they had those upstairs rooms.

Ram Majumbdar tapped on Noel's bedroom door, opened it, and went inside. Noel, clad in a nightshirt, was in bed reading.

"I must speak with you privately. I've been trying to get you alone all day," Ram said, "but, of course, your protégée is never far from your side. What a catalogue of information about us and our work she's storing up. God help us when she decides to betray us."

"Now, now, Ram. I'm well aware that you don't like Chavi, but what you're suggesting is ridiculous. I'd trust her with my life."

"I've known from the start that when she could no longer learn anything from you she would betray you merely to destroy me. She hates me, I feel it. Everytime I go upstairs to do a curettage she fixes those big eyes on me accusingly."

"You're imagining things, Ram. You surely didn't come to me at this hour with such a childish complaint?"

A slow flush appeared under Ram's creamy coffee complexion. He was an exceedingly handsome young man, Noel thought, and a competent medical doctor, but like many other physicians, Ram was opposed to the new science of psychology. Noel had never been able to inspire the interest in Ram that Chavi had exhibited from the start.

"No, I'm leading up to something much more serious." He hesitated. "It's going to be painful for you, Noel, but you must be told. You see, you've allowed her to take over the running of your office and you never look at your accounts anymore and . . . well, she's stealing from us."

Noel said quietly, "That's a very serious accusation."

"I have proof. The money she's stolen from you is hidden

in her room. I observed where she put it earlier today. I wouldn't have come to you at this hour, but I believe at this very minute she's packing, ready to leave."

Noel's face was ashen. "No . . . no, I don't believe it. I couldn't have been so wrong about her."

"The nurses collect fees from the patients and drop them in the cashbox. But as you well know, many patients do not pay. You used to take care of the money, but you never bother to even check on it since she came. I tell you it was simply too great a temptation—especially for a gypsy. They're renowned thieves."

Noel leapt from the bed. "You're wrong about her. I won't believe it."

"Come and see for yourself," Ram suggested.

Chavi had packed Garridan's belongings and was folding the last of her own clothes when Ram flung open her door. She looked up in surprise to see Noel, still in his nightshirt, push past the other doctor into her room. "So it's true— you're leaving."

Garridan stirred and murmured in his sleep. His cot was pushed against the wall on the other side of Chavi's bed. She said, "Yes, in the morning." Taking in Noel's anguished expression and Ram's gloating sneer, she added, "I intended to tell you at breakfast tomorrow. I didn't decide until late this evening."

"She would have been gone before we were up," Ram said. "Fortunately, I saw her bring her bags down from the boxroom."

Chavi addressed Noel. "Why did you come bursting in here like this? You must have guessed I was planning to go north. I have to go and see Lysander."

"I'll tell you why." Ram walked across the room toward Garridan's cot. Chavi cried. "No!" But it was too late. Ram seized the child and tossed him onto her bed. The little boy woke up with a whimper of fright. Ram was foraging under the mattress on the cot. With a cry of triumph, he produced a bundle of well-worn banknotes.

Chavi looked at the money in complete bewilderment. "Where did that come from?"

"Oh, well done!" Ram said sarcastically. "I always said you ought to be on the stage." He turned to Noel, who stood rooted to the spot, one hand raised in supplication. "I suggest we let her go on the condition that she never comes near us again. After all, we wouldn't want the police snooping around, would we?"

"Chavi?" Noel said pleadingly. "There's an explanation, I know there is."

"You think I stole that money?" Chavi said in amazement. "I've saved more than enough from what you've been paying me to take Garri and me to Yorkshire."

At the mention of his name, Garridan sat up in the middle of her bed and rubbed his eyes. He looked at his mother and then Noel, and finally turned to look at Ram, who still clutched the bundle of banknotes. Garri said distinctly, "Doctor Ram hiding money in my bed again."

Noel's face burned an angry red. For a moment Chavi was afraid he was going to fling himself on the other doctor and strike him. Instead Noel said, "Get out. I never want to lay eyes on you again. Go now—before I take a horsewhip to you."

Ram Majumbdar opened his mouth to speak, thought better of it, and fled from the room. Chavi stood still for a moment. Noel came to her and put his arm around her shoulder. "I never really doubted you, my dear."

"I know. But because of me you've lost your colleague. You can't run this place alone."

"Please don't look like that. I don't need that young scoundrel. I'll find someone else to assist me. But Chavi, I do need you to come back, and I shan't rest until you've gone to study in Vienna with Doctor Freud."

Chavi said in a small voice, "I'll come back—and I will study in Vienna. That's not what's worrying me. What I'm afraid of is what he will do now. Noel, I don't think we've heard the last of Doctor Ram."

"If you're afraid he might go to the police about our upstairs business, don't worry. He would implicate himself, too."

"I suppose you're right. Still, I have a terrible premonition of danger."

"I'm quite sure it's waiting for you in a Yorkshire prison. Do you really think it's wise for you to see Lysander?"

"I have to," Chavi said simply.

The theater was empty, lights dimmed, but the excitement of the performance still hung in the air. *Rigoletto* had

been performed by masters. A musical drama both poignant
and chilling, a gothic-horror story that occasionally made the
audience smile, it was all fused together by the magnificence
of the music and the overwhelming presence of Mazetti.

Still caught in the magic, Pas wiped his eyes. His body
stood in this quiet theater, but his mind soared to the Teatro
Farnese, the Palazzo del Te, the Teatro Olimpico in Vicenza.
All the years of his exile hung on his shoulders like a great
fisherman's net in which he'd been caught, and now he
longed to be free.

On stage a lamp glowed and a pianist was seated at the
keys. Danior, looking nervous, walked toward the darkened
footlights. "He's changed his mind, Pas."

"No, he's changing only from his costume. He'll be here
in a moment."

Mazetti strode from the wings, spoke briefly to the ac-
companist, waved for them to begin, then descended to the
orchestra stalls to sit with Pas.

Danior began to sing Figaro's aria "Largo al factotum."

They listened in silence, and when it was finished Mazetti
called to Danior. "Choose something else now." Danior
went to speak with the pianist.

Words tumbled from Pas. Speaking in his own language
again at last was like starting to run after a slow and laborious
walk. "The first time I heard him sing, I think I knew. He
was just a little boy, but there was such passion in his voice. I
knew some day there would be this power, this force. How
formidable a hold a great artist can place on our souls! I
wanted to keep him with me—to be a guardian of his talent—
but I love him like the son I never had so I have to let him
go. You will help him? Convince him what he must do?"

Mazetti's handsome face, crowned with a mane of jet
black hair, crumpled into an exaggerated grimace of dismay.
"You want me to help you launch the man who might take
Mazetti's place? Hey, old friend, you forget how once we
plotted to poison—what was his name?—to get his part in *La
Traviata*?"

They chuckled together, but neither of them took their
eyes off Danior.

"So what about you, Pasquale? What have you been
doing all these years?"

"Oh, a little of this, a little of that."

"You know, I looked for you everywhere after you disappeared. I looked for a long time. It was months before I found out about the operation on your throat. Why didn't you tell me? Why didn't you let me know where you were going?"

"You couldn't have helped me. No one could. My singing life was over forever. But now . . . ah, now you can do me a great favor. You can help Danior, and through him I can live again."

"Sh . . . he's ready to sing again."

They listened in rapt silence, and when Danior finished the second aria, Mazetti said, "I know where you've been and what you've been doing all these years, Pas. The young man told me. Oh, foolish Pasquale, you couldn't sing anymore so you punished yourself by this exile—"

"What are you saying? You make no sense."

"Come home with me, Pasquale. It's time. And bring your gypsy. He's a diamond in the rough, I think. We'll smooth him out and then . . . we'll see."

As the train came slowly to a halt in Carisbrook station, Chavi saw to her surprise and joy that instead of Andrew McGreal standing on the platform as she expected, Danior awaited her arrival.

They flung themselves into each other's arms and Garri bellowed his outrage at being crushed between them. Laughing, Danior grabbed the little boy and swung him up in the air.

"Hello Garridan Chambers, what a pair of lungs you have! Are we to have another singer in the family? Come on, give your uncle Danior a kiss."

"Oh, Danior, how wonderful it is to see you. How well you look. Where did you come from? How did you know I was coming? Where's Pas, is he with you?"

"I came from Liverpool. Pas is there, seeing about a ship to Italy. Your letter to Andrew arrived the day before I went to him to get your address. Lucky for me, or I'd have passed you on a train bound for London. Come on, I've a carriage waiting, and a lot to tell you."

As their carriage journeyed to the McGreals' cottage, Chavi learned of Danior's meeting with the great Mazetti, and his plans to go back to Italy with Mazetti and Pas to study and eventually join Mazetti's opera company.

"How could I argue with Mazetti?" Danior exclaimed.

"He convinced me I have a future as an operatic baritone. It's the only thing I've ever wanted, of course, but . . ."

"You thought you had to give up the dream because I lost Brenna," she finished for him. "You punished yourself because of your completely unfounded guilt. Danior, you do understand that now, don't you? Her death was an accident. It had nothing to do with you."

"I suppose I always knew I couldn't have prevented it. Pas said I used it as an excuse not to go on because the critics tore me to pieces. He may have been right."

"There's never a single reason any of us do anything, Danior. The main thing now is that you're going to go on. You're going to be the greatest singer the world has ever known. Someday people will breathe your name with awe. I see it in your future so clearly, and you know I have second sight!"

Her eyes shining with pride, Chavi hugged him, temporarily forgetting her own mission to Yorkshire as she listened to her brother's hopes and plans. His joy at singing again was evident in every word and glance.

Just before they reached the McGreal cottage Danior paused. "Oh good lord, Chavi, I've been so full of my own news I haven't even asked how you feel about the situation with the Merrins. What about this man Chambers? I take it he's the Lysander you told me about? Did he kill Richard, do you think?"

Chavi did not have time to answer, as they had reached the cottage and Jean and Andrew came rushing out to greet them. Noel's wife waited inside, and Chavi took note of the wistful way Brigid questioned her about Noel's health and well-being. Chavi wanted to shake the woman and tell her to go home to her husband—church and principles be damned, the love and loyalty of a man and woman should come before either—but she didn't.

Eventually Jean and Brigid took Garri away, amid much cooing and baby talk, to put him down for a nap. Andrew asked, "Chavi, are you really going to the prison to see Chambers?"

Danior added. "You don't owe him anything. Whether or not he killed Richard Merrin, he's guilty of other murders, other crimes. Stay away from him. Let the law deal with him."

Chavi replied, "I've no wish to argue with either of you about Lysander just now. Besides, first there's someone else I want to see."

What changes even a short span of time could bring about, Hakan thought as he regarded Chavi across the table in the ladies' saloon of the Carisbrook Inn. People move on, meet new people, experience other events, lose touch. They never remain the same, not while they live.

She wasn't the same woman he'd fallen in love with and had longed for every minute since she'd left . . . and he wasn't the same either. He still loved her and wanted her, but was the woman he yearned for this intelligent, self-possessed creature who spoke to him in language he scarcely understood? Or was it the memory of the wildly beautiful, heartbreakingly sad young woman she used to be that tormented him still?

Chavi had expressed her concern over his mother's illness, they'd rejoiced over Danior's return to his singing, but she had not yet broached the subject he knew she wanted to discuss when she'd sent Danior to arrange this meeting. Before she brought it up, though, Hakan had other things he wanted to say to her.

"I was . . . less than kind when we met last. I'm sorry. I was stunned by what you told me about my father, and . . . I think it had less to do with you than with my feelings about him."

"I know. It's all right. I understood."

"I love you, Chavi. I loved you then and I do now. I've missed you, thought about you constantly. When I eventually came to grips with . . . your relationship to my father . . . I would have come after you. But by then my mother was so ill I couldn't leave her. I'm so glad you're back and I—"

"Hakan, don't say anymore, please. We both knew that we were meant to be together for only a little while."

"I won't accept that. I'll never love another woman as I love you."

She smiled sadly. "Yes, you will. We're all capable of loving many people in our lifetimes."

"Please don't start telling me your Doctor Freud's theories. Danior warned me what will happen if I let you get started about the power of the human mind."

"Then tell me about Bly Rutherford. Danior says she's

helping your mother write her memoirs. He also says that you and she have become close friends."

"Bly is all right. I suppose you could say we're friends."

"That's the best beginning for a man and woman, Hakan. You should open your heart and let her in."

"With you I had magic. That's what I want with a woman." His arms ached with wanting to hold her. "Could we go somewhere to be alone?"

"No, we can never be alone again in the way you mean. That belonged to another time. Be patient, you'll come to understand as I did. After we parted, I cried myself to sleep every night. I would have done anything to bring you back . . . but something, perhaps in you, perhaps in me, was wiser than either of us. We were wrong for each other then, and we're even further apart now."

"Because I am the Earl of Moreland? A man of title and wealth and property? If that's the reason, then there is something I must tell you."

"No, that isn't the reason. It's not who we are, but what we truly want out of life, without which we can't be complete, that matters. That can't be attained if we're together."

"You're not making sense. I don't know what you mean. Weren't we happy together?"

"Oh, yes. We were. I'll always think of you fondly, with love and gratitude, because I do believe you saved my sanity. You gave me a reason to live again after I lost Brenna. But after I went to London and became interested in Freud's teachings, I realized that . . . as much as I cared for you, you were my bridge from the dark place in my life back into the light. I think perhaps I was the same for you, a transition from despair to hope. Don't you see? In loving one another, we learned to love again. Now we can move on, perhaps even love others. But we can't stay back there, forever crossing that bridge together. Our lives must move forward, and in different directions. We can't stand still."

"You sound like my mother," Hakan said bitterly. "I say that we should seize our happy times."

"Even if in doing so we miss the opportunity to be even happier?"

"I couldn't be happier than I was with you . . . and could be again."

"Happiness doesn't come from another person. It comes

from within ourselves. You haven't discovered what you really want out of life yet. When you do, you'll find the woman who can share it with you. That woman isn't me, I know."

"Only because you won't let it be."

Her hand crept across the table and closed over his. She squeezed his fingers. "At the moment you're worried about your mother. Give her all your love and attention and don't think about anything else for a while. Soon everything will be clear to you, I promise."

He gave her a small smile. "Shall I turn over my hand so you can read my palm?"

"I don't have to. I know it in my heart. Hakan, we've spent so much time talking about ourselves, we haven't discussed the man who was arrested in connection with your father's death."

"Ah, the fearsome Mr. Chambers. He is also charged with assaulting me, although it wasn't my idea to press charges. Poor devil was consumed with jealousy over you, understandably so."

"Hakan, if you ever cared for me, please listen carefully to what I have to tell you now. . . ."

Sarah tried valiantly to swallow the soup that Hakan fed her. At last, exhausted by the effort, she whispered, "Please . . . no more."

"Are you up to seeing Rob?" he asked. "I can tell him you're too tired—"

"No—no, I want to see him. Send him up to me now."

A few minutes later Robbie came into the room. Sarah watched him approach her bed on tiptoes. He was a handsome young man, despite his thick-lensed glasses. Not quite so tall, nor as golden-haired and blue-eyed as Hakan, but still the good looks of Merrin males were very much in evidence.

He sat beside her bed. "How are you f-feeling today, Sarah?"

She smiled at him fondly. "Much better. Now, before you burst, tell me what it is you want to tell me."

Robbie drew a deep breath. "I've asked Nelia Dunstan to be my wife and she's accepted."

Sarah was astonished. Not at the news, since Hakan had already told her what to expect, but at the fact that Robbie did not stammer during his declaration. She said, "I'm so happy for you both. Have you set a date?"

"In the spring. Nelia wanted to have the banns called at church right away, but I told her that would start gossip about us . . . having to get married. So we shall wait until spring."

There was authority in his voice, and a certain new self-confidence in his manner. Sarah supposed that having the most beautiful girl in the county agree to marry him, especially since he'd won her away from Hakan, was probably reason enough for Robbie's new-found aplomb. But she couldn't help feeling that Robbie would perhaps surprise everyone—especially Nelia—by becoming a great deal more self-assured in the future. Sarah knew that Hakan was making legal provision to share the estate with Robbie, although he hadn't troubled her with the details. Having a lovely bride and being a man of property would do much for Robbie's self-esteem.

Sarah smiled contentedly as he bent to kiss her cheek. The people she cared about would go on quite well without her, and through Bly Rutherford, who was doing an excellent job of editing Sarah's book, people would be made aware of the terrible injustice done to the Apache.

Hakan was certainly aware of Bly . . . she had seen him watching her in silent amazement, in the same manner, in fact, that as a small boy he had watched a butterfly emerge from a chrysalis. Yes, everything was going so well that Sarah knew she could soon let go and rest.

"Send Hakan back, will you, Robbie? There's something I forgot to tell him."

She lay still, watching the bare branches of the trees move against a pewter sky in a rising north wind. If she were still in the Chiricahua mountains, and if an Apache spirit bell had been hanging there, the north wind would have rung the chimes. An omen of possible disaster . . . a warning of approaching doom. But there was no spirit bell, and death would not be a disaster.

"*Sons-ee-ah-ray,*" Hakan's voice said softly. "Where are you now?"

"You always know when I've reverted back, don't you? Yes, I was thinking about the old days. Hakan . . . do you think about *Tonsaroyoo?* Do you still grieve for him?"

Hakan said, "Let me answer you by telling you the story that he told me once. We had gone hunting—it was one of the earliest hunts I remember. The summer was hot and game scarce. We were far south that year, in the land of the giant saguaros. Lightning had struck one of the big cactus, felling it. The saguaro must have been fifty feet tall, strong and healthy—and there it lay, broken on the desert floor. I was deeply saddened. I'd thought they lived forever, that nothing could destroy them. Then *Tonsaroyoo* told me that the dead saguaro would still give life to the desert. It would be a home for small animals, and as it slowly decayed it would provide nourishment to the soil and feed new plants. But most important of all, a saguaro seed cannot survive unless it is shaded by another plant. If it falls on the open desert sand the sun will kill it. He showed me the tiny saguaro pup that was already growing in the shade of the fallen giant."

Sarah was weeping. Hakan said, "I didn't mean to make you sad. I just wanted you to know that although he's gone, I'm still growing in his shadow."

"Yes, I know."

They were silent for a while as Sarah gathered her strength. At length she reached for his hand and held it. "I loved him so. When I was with him I knew . . . without a shadow of a doubt . . . that he would care for us always, protect us with his own life . . . that where he went, we would go. He never wanted to be parted from us. I think perhaps that's the measure of real love . . . the being there, always. Lone Wolf's devotion was complete, unconditional."

"The day he was killed, I thought our lives had ended," Hakan said. "I didn't know then that he would live with us forever, in our memories."

"I used to marvel that he could be so gentle with us when he was so fierce in every other way. I worried once that he'd take another wife, because I was never able to bear another child. But he said he had me and he had you and that his world was already complete. When I was with Lone Wolf, I always felt cherished . . . whole in a way I can't explain."

"There was no pretense," Hakan said. "We didn't wear masks like we do here."

They lapsed into a thoughtful silence. After a few moments she said, "I suppose you remember where we buried him."

"Yes, I remember."

"Hakan, I don't want you to take me to him. I want to be buried here, with Richard."

He looked at her in disbelief. "Surely you don't feel guilt about his death? I still remember his eyes . . . oh God, that look in his eyes after his stroke when he was so helpless. He was begging us to end his misery."

"There was a time, shortly afterwards, that I questioned my motives," Sarah said. "Had I acted purely out of pity? Was it an act of love, or was it a kind of revenge? I'd recently learned what he did to Jean McGreal and to Chavi . . . had that influenced me?" She remembered, but did not give voice to the memory, how she had worried too that Hakan might also have been considering the way of the *Tin-ne-ah* in dealing with the helpless aged.

She went on quickly, afraid he might read her thoughts. "Then I remembered waking that night and feeling impelled to go into Richard's room. When I lit the lamp I saw that he was lying there wide awake . . . staring. The full horror of his existence struck me then. To awaken in the darkness and be forced to wait for the dawn . . . for people to come. The unutterable loneliness . . ."

"I'm sure he welcomed death," Hakan said.

"I was very calm. Afterwards I asked *Y'sun* to be merciful, to both Richard and myself. Hakan, that night I did not for one minute think, act, or behave as an Englishwoman. Later, realizing the enormity of what I'd done, I was overwhelmed with guilt. I was afraid too that someone would find out that Richard did not die naturally. But my worst fear of all was that someone else might be blamed for his death. So many people hated him. That was why I believed I had to stay at Merrinswood, so that if that happened I'd be here to confess."

"But why do you feel you must spend all eternity here? There is no need. You just told me how much you loved *Tonsaroyoo*. Surely you want to go to the hunting ground where he is—" Hakan broke off as he realized that he'd spoken like a Chiricahua. For a moment his English self had battled the Apache, and the Englishman had lost. He went on. "The Merrins are all buried together, their graves clearly marked. How different were the *Tin-ne-ah*, who carefully concealed the burial places of their dead. Members of the burial party left the place individually, covering their trails as they went. Some of the dead person's goods were buried with him, his horse shot at or near the grave and sometimes it too was buried. Back at the rancheria, his remaining possessions and his wickiup were burned and the site abandoned."

"I want to stay here," Sarah repeated. "I want you to stay here also. There's nothing left for you there."

"But why do you want to stay here?"

"I believe my spirit will be reunited with Lone Wolf, no matter where my body is buried. But if my grave is here, then I think that you, my son, will remain, or that if you leave, you will return. Besides, I would like to think that future generations of Merrins will wonder about their ancestor who lived as a Chiricahua Apache. That in some obscure way the years I spent with Lone Wolf will send a message . . . a plea for tolerance of other ways of life. I want to be buried here, my gravestone clearly marked. Hakan, promise me—"

"I promise that I'll respect your wishes about leaving you here. But I can't promise I shall stay. Don't ask that of me, please."

"Hakan, you can't go back. None of us can ever go back to what we were. Find a wife, one who understands you. Stay here and have a family. I promise you that when your own son is born you'll see everything differently than you do now . . . no man truly learns what life is about until he has a child."

"If I have a son," Hakan said slowly, thinking suddenly of Chavi's bright-eyed little boy, "I'd want to give him the boyhood I had."

Sarah sighed, her breath fluttering away from her like a dying breeze. "How can I make you understand the impossibility of that yearning?"

"And how can I explain to you the sheer horror of an English schoolboy's life? Beleaguered by brutal masters, bullied by older boys, useless knowledge crammed into his brain . . punished if he doesn't learn, ostracized if he doesn't conform or shows a lack of team spirit . . . taught incomprehensible rules of behavior, given values that are contrary to nature—" He stopped abruptly, wondering how long he'd bottled up those thoughts.

She stared at him with horrified eyes. "Oh, God, Hakan, what have I done to you?"

Quickly he gathered her into his arms and held her. "I'm being unfair. I chronicled all that was wrong, without admitting that much that I found here was good and noble. I saw so many heroic, selfless acts among the soldiers I served with, so much bravery and compassion; I suppose they learned those values during their boyhoods here, too. And here in England I see men striving to cure social ills and eliminate disease. . . ."

She was very limp in his arms. Carefully he laid her back on the pillow. "Hakan . . . forgive me."

"There's nothing to forgive. Oh, God, I'm a clumsy fool. My beloved *Sons-ee-ah-ray*, I didn't mean—I was only trying to make you understand that I can't promise to remain here. I never felt your attachment to Merrinswood. And while the moors and meadows are beautiful, I feel more of an affinity for the desert."

She nodded, trying to catch her breath, and he was unsure if she nodded that she understood, or that she gave her blessing for him to leave. She was quiet for a long time after that, drifting in and out of sleep. Hakan sat at her bedside and willed himself not to let her see him weep.

Just before dusk she stirred and her lips moved. He had to bend close to hear her whisper, "Is Sam still here?"

"Yes, he's downstairs. Shall I bring him?"

"No . . . tell him . . . tell Sam that I . . ."

Could she really hear the spirit bell ringing in the north wind, or was it just the echo of a forgotten time that chimed so mournfully in her ears?

41

As the guards dragged Lysander along the dank prison corridor, even the most hardened of the inmates or murderers' row looked away.

His beard and his head had been shaved, baring his scars

He snarled like an animal as another inmate shrank away from the bars of his cell.

One, more bold than the rest, shouted as he went by, " 'Bout time they stretched your ugly neck. Now maybe the rest of us won't get no more nightmares."

Lysander's chains chafed his wrists and ankles, and his belly growled its revolt at the food he'd forced down. He blinked as they took him out into the daylight, across the bleak windswept yard where the icy air burned his throat and nostrils, then led him into the administration building.

These rooms smelled cleaner, the lighting was better, there was an absence of something . . . something was missing, what was it? Fear, probably.

A door was opened and Lysander was thrust, stumbling, into a comfortably furnished office. Seated around the desk were the prison governor, the chaplain, two strangers, and . . . Chavi?

Lysander shook his head, unsure if he were dreaming. She was like a beautiful vision. She wore a soft green dress and matching coat and looked like springtime on the moors. She had tried to coax her mane of hair under a pretty black bonnet with a jaunty feather, but several long curly strands escaped. Lysander had an overwhelming urge to grab her hair and run his fingers through it. He decided it was a ridiculous thought.

The governor cleared his throat and then turned to Chavi. "Mrs. Chambers?"

She looked Lysander full in the face. He wanted to turn away, but her eyes caught his and wouldn't let go. So much passed between them in that split second that he felt a surge of energy race through his entire body.

Then she was speaking, using that well-modulated tone he'd taught her so long ago, her educated lady's voice. She was so sure of herself, of her effect on the men, and there was something else. A certain gleam in her eye that seemed to indicate she knew exactly what each of them was thinking. She said, "Yes, this is my husband, Dirk Chambers."

The ensuing silence rocked the room. The men looked at each other, at her, at the papers on the desk, at the window and the ceiling. Everywhere but at Lysander.

Chavi went on. "It's true that his brother Ly—Keir came to us in Australia after he escaped from prison. There was a terrible brush fire—you can verify this, it burned thousands of acres of New South Wales. That's when my husband, Dirk, received those scars you see now. He was burned saving me and my daughter. I suppose it was a strange coincidence that in separate events both brothers were so badly scarred, but that's what happened. The man you're looking for, Keir Chambers, was killed in the Northern Territory last year. He was struck by lightning. You've arrested the wrong brother."

The governor muttered something to one of the men. Lysander didn't hear what it was, he was mesmerized by Chavi. She held her head high and continued to speak in that incredibly cool way. "Dirk and I had a quarrel. I went to stay with friends in London. It was all a misunderstanding. I know he shouldn't have gone bursting in on Lord Moreland like that, but I've already spoken to him and he's willing to withdraw the assault charges. Lord Moreland is a close friend of my brother and Dirk misunderstood my friendship with him."

Her thick black eyelashes fluttered, almost imperceptibly, and she looked modestly at her hands, folded in her lap. "My husband is a little jealous of me."

Lysander held his breath. This, surely, was a situation these men could understand. Nor did it hurt matters to mention Lord Moreland's friendship with Danior. But would they believe her claim that they'd arrested Dirk?

One of the men murmured, "Lord Moreland's solicitor has been in touch with us, and the charges have been dropped."

"Then I don't understand why you are hesitating," Chavi said tartly. "You're holding my husband illegally if there are no charges against him."

The man who had spoken earlier leaned closer to the governor and said, "What about the butler's allegations about the present Lord Moreland's father?"

Hearing him, Chavi said, "I have Doctor McGreal waiting outside. He is the doctor who signed the death certificate. He says Barlow, the butler, was mistaken about seeing bruises on his lordship's face." She lowered her eyes delicately. "Doctor McGreal said that in any case, with a paralyzed stroke patient it wouldn't be necessary to inflict bruises—say, by smothering with a pillow—because all that would be necessary would be to pinch the nostrils closed and cover the mouth."

All of the men stared at her in fascination.

She went on, "The doctor further states that in any event, after all this time an autopsy would be of no value." Chavi looked down at her gloved hands, recalling Andrew McGreal's exact words, prodded out of him by his belief that she had already discussed the possibilities in detail with Noel Brannock. *Of course, a person who wished to kill a man formerly so strong and powerful might not have known that they could pinch his nostrils closed and cover his mouth—they might have believed it necessary to use enough force to produce bruises, perhaps even break facial bones. But there were no such bruises. Chavi, does anyone other than Barlow wish to drag all of this up again, after all this time? Sarah—Lady Moreland is dead, her family in mourning. They have enough to contend with just now without the nerve-racking ordeal and publicity attendant upon an investigation.*

Chavi had looked into the doctor's soul and seen his fear. Wheels within wheels, she'd thought, worlds within worlds. All of them had their secrets. Richard Merrin had bound them all to him, like links in a chain. Andrew McGreal knew someone killed Richard—she could feel it. Perhaps he was afraid it was his wife.

Aloud, she said to the prison governor, "As far as my husband coming to Merrinswood the night Lord Moreland died is concerned—it's true Dirk was there, but he was too uncomfortable about his scars to come in with me. He just looked in the window to see that I was being properly received. You must realize that it's rare for a gypsy to move in such circles."

Lysander watched her with admiration and pride. What a woman she was, worth every moment of rage and longing and frustration. He'd treated her abominably more than once since he'd known her, and so had other men. But she was as resilient as the earth. The fact was, although Lysander was reluctant to admit it, she was strong enough to manage her life without any man. Perhaps that was what had always attracted him to her. Even when she'd been most vulnerable, she had that inner core of self-sufficiency that was a part of her being, like the grain of sand in the center of the pearl.

The man seated next to the governor said, "It's a great pity Sir Edward Richard Henry hasn't yet completed his investigation into the advisability of adopting fingerprinting as a method of identifying criminals, isn't it? You know there's a British official in Bengal who says he's been using the method for years."

"Unfortunately, Mr. Chambers's fingerprints were never taken, so it doesn't help us much."

Chavi said, "But you have me, his wife, to identify him. What more do you need?"

Lysander found his voice. He looked at Chavi. "I'm sorry I behaved so badly to you. It won't happen again, I promise."

She gave him a cheeky grin and said, "Dirk, dear, you smell like a dead bull."

Andrew McGreal stopped pacing and looked at Chavi as she was ushered by the prison chaplain into the room where he waited. She said, "He's to be released, but not right away. They have what they call formalities to go through."

"Let's get out of this terrible place then, as quickly as we can." Andrew shivered. "I feel as though I'm sealed in a tomb, and I'm not even a prisoner."

When they were safely outside the gates, Andrew said, "Will you return to meet him?"

"Yes, I'll come back tomorrow."

"What are your plans then?"

"We'll go our separate ways."

"Chavi, when you left to go to Noel in London, you were quite afraid of this man. Perhaps I'd better accompany you tomorrow."

"You've been very kind, but you don't have to worry Lysander won't hurt me." She had paid him back today a little of what she owed him, and he'd respect that.

Andrew shivered. "Let's get back home as quickly as we can. I don't think I shall ever be warm again. There was an icy atmosphere in that place that had nothing to do with the weather. Besides, if we don't get back soon I'm afraid Jean will have become too attached to your son."

When they reached the cottage in Carisbrook, however, they found Garridan asleep and Jean wringing her hands, her face desolate. Brigid sat on the sofa, sobbing into a soaked handkerchief.

"What on earth has happened?" Andrew asked, going to his wife to embrace her. Chavi stood in the doorway behind him, and it was to her that Jean addressed her reply.

"We've just heard . . . a wire from London. Noel has been arrested and taken into custody for performing illegal operations. The hospital has been shut down."

"Ram Majumbdar," Chavi said, squeezing her eyes shut as if to make the unthinkable go away.

"Yes," Jean said. "According to the telegram from one of Noel's nurses, he has returned to India, but he informed the police in a letter about Noel before he left. Andrew, I hate to ask you to leave again, but Brigid wants to go to her husband right away. Will you take her to the station?"

"I'll go, too," Chavi said.

"No, Chavi," Andrew said sharply. "That's not a good idea at all. There's nothing you can do to help Noel and your presence might even hurt his case. After all, you've been working with him . . . you might be called upon to testify, which would further incriminate him. Stay away from London at all costs. You can stay with us, if you wish."

Chavi considered. Her heart ached for Noel Brannock, but Andrew was right. She would only make matters worse for him. "Thank you, but I have somewhere else I must go. I hadn't intended to go quite so soon, but I might as well get started."

"To Vienna, to study with Doctor Freud," Andrew said. "I know, Noel wrote me how excited he was about your natural gift for psychoanalysis."

Chavi sighed. "It's what I want more than anything, but I wish I weren't leaving at such a bad time."

She wondered what would happen to Lysander. Where would he go, what would he do now? Her thoughts kept pulling her back to what she had lost with him . . . the old days . . . the companionship that was oddly comfortable yet exciting at the same time. The memory of the night he'd made love to her. She was confused and sad about parting from him, even though she knew it had to be.

Andrew said gently, "If there's one thing you must have learned by now, Chavi, it's that there's *never* a perfect time to begin any new endeavor. We can always find a dozen reasons to stay where we are. Life doesn't tie up each little episode for us in a neat bundle and say, there, that's finished, now you can go on to what's next. Even as we're unraveling one situation, the thread of another has us in its grip, pulling us toward whatever's next in our lives. If you were to wait for everything to come to a stop before you went to Vienna, it would be the end of the world, wouldn't it? I know I speak for Noel when I tell you that he would want you to get on with it and let him deal with his own problems."

Chavi looked from Andrew to his wife, who was smiling her encouragement. "You've both been so kind to me," Chavi said. "I don't know how to thank you."

Brigid Brannock stopped crying and said, "Don't worry about Noel, Chavi. I'll see him through this, no matter what happens."

Chavi asked, "May I write to you so that I'll know how Doctor Brannock is faring?"

"Of course," Andrew said. "Rest assured we'll rally around him and do all we can. I'll follow Brigid to London as soon as I can find someone to come in and look after my patients here."

"There's no way I can properly thank you," Lysander said. They sat in the dismal snack bar of the railway station, drinking strong tea and watching one another warily, as Garridan curled up in Chavi's lap and slept.

"Yes, there is," Chavi answered. "You can stay out of England in the future so you don't get caught again."

"So you're actually going to Vienna. Do you really believe all this psychoanalytical mumbo jumbo?"

"No, not all of what I've heard so far. But it's a beginning. Someone had to start somewhere. Sigmund Freud opened the door and the rest of us must follow through. Before he came along, neurologists believed that mental illness must be caused by a lesion on the brain, then were baffled when many of their patients had no organic problem."

"Tell me, what is it you hope to learn in Vienna?"

"About life. About people. How to help them live with their problems. No great hopes, Lysander. Just that." She settled Garri more comfortably in her arms, paused for a moment to gaze at the innocent beauty of her sleeping son. "But mostly, I think, to learn about myself. To find a way of living that's mine alone."

Lysander's hat covered his shaved head, but the brim cast shadows on his scars, emphasizing them, to the dismay of those seated nearby. Scowling at a staring youth, Lysander said, "And must your new life of necessity exclude old friends?"

She looked him straight in the eyes. "But we can never go back to being just friends, Lysander. You know that as well as I do."

He was silent for a long time, then sighed in acceptance of what couldn't be changed or erased. "If you had to get involved with medical men and new treatments, I wish I would have met a doctor working on ways to eliminate scars and deformities."

"You know that it's not possible to give you new skin on your face. You were lucky that doctor was able to reshape your mouth a little by cutting away the scar tissue."

He gave an ironic laugh. "Do you remember when I went to London to see my investment bankers, but returned early, after only a couple of days?"

"Of course. You came storming into Doctor McGreal's office, spying on me, ordering me to go home and take care of Garri. As though I'd ever neglect him! I couldn't stand that. That was the day I left."

"I wasn't spying on you, Chavi. I suppose I was angry because I was afraid of losing you. But I'd already lost you, hadn't I? I of all people should know how a caged bird yearns to be free."

He pushed the tea mug away from him, studied its misshapen ugliness and the tannin-stained chip on the rim. "I never told you why I came back early. I hadn't seen my bankers at all. A doctor approached me while I was eating in a cafe. He told me that a few medical men have been experimenting with transplants of bits of epidermis from one part of the body to another."

"Skin transplants?" Chavi asked, amazed.

"He seemed quite hopeful that I would be a good candidate for such treatment, that he might be able to cover the worst of my scars. I was so excited at the prospect that I dropped everything to rush back to Yorkshire to tell you."

Chavi stared at him. "And instead of telling me, you flew into a rage because I was working for Doctor McGreal. Oh, Lysander!"

"Would you have stayed, had you known?"

She considered carefully. "No. I was too angry that you'd decided to be my husband without even asking my feelings on the subject. But I do think you should take a chance and see if that doctor can transplant skin to your face. Not for me, for yourself."

"Perhaps I will. I haven't decided yet."

"Lysander—" She paused, contemplative, feeling the weight of all her concern for him, and the insistent tug of shared memories, of small pleasures and great hardships. "What will you do now, where will you go?"

He shrugged. "Abroad, somewhere, I suppose. A fresh start. I'll look for something to help me get through the next fragment of my life. Have you noticed how we seem to live our lives in pieces? There's no constancy in the world. Nothing ever lasts, does it?"

"For some people it does. But I'm not sure that they're fortunate. Lysander, you do understand that because I got you out of prison . . . that doesn't change anything between us. I want a life of my own now, not one dictated by anyone else, or any circumstances over which I have no control."

Watching her with hooded eyes, he made no comment. A mask had slipped firmly into place to conceal what he might be thinking or feeling. Chavi plunged on, speaking the words she'd so carefully rehearsed. "Perhaps we'll meet again one day and be friends. But in the meantime I have to lead my own life and go where my heart takes me. I really feel I have a calling."

She felt vaguely disappointed when he nodded, as if in complete agreement. Reaching across the table, he touched her hand lightly. "Someday perhaps I'll present myself to you for psychoanalysis."

She laughed softly. "I doubt that. But it's an interesting thought."

A train entered the station in a burst of steam. She said, "That's my train. There's no need for you to wait with me until it leaves, it will be on the platform for a little while."

"I'll carry the boy to the train for you."

"All right," Chavi said. "But then you must leave us."

They walked along the platform, and when Chavi found an empty second-class compartment she got in, took Gar and placed him on the seat, then dropped the window to say good-bye to Lysander.

Before she could speak, he put his hands on her cheeks, holding her face. He studied her for a moment, staring as absorbing every detail of a picture. He was completely unaware of himself, of the curious, horrified glances of passersby.

It would have been easy to tell herself he was committing her face to memory, or even that in his mind he was seeing her once more as a half-wild, half-starved gypsy girl. But she sensed much, much more than that in the way his gaze traveled over her features.

Suddenly he pulled off her hat, found the pins in her hair, and freed the tumbling mass. He ran his fingers through the dark waves, wrapped a thick strand around his fist. "Do you remember when we sailed for Australia and you asked me to teach you to read?"

"And you asked me when gypsies put up their hair. I said they didn't, and you asked if I'd like you to teach me to be a lady."

"That was my big mistake."

She gave him a small smile. "All I really wanted was to learn how to read."

"I should never have taught you that either. Look where it's led you."

"If you hadn't, I'd have found a way to teach myself." She felt the smile tremble on her lips. "But I am grateful to you."

"When we met in Liverpool," he said quickly, aware they were running out of time and there was so much still unsaid between them, "I had to tell you I was posing as Dirk. You had to know that right away. It wasn't something I could conceal from you until a more opportune moment."

"Yes, I know."

"If there'd been time, and I could have . . . perhaps accustomed you to the idea, convinced you that I—" he broke off. "But it's too late for that now, isn't it?"

"Lysander, the train will be leaving any minute. We have to say good-bye."

"It isn't finished between us, Chavi."

"Perhaps not. But it looks as if it's finished for now. Good-bye, Lysander."

"Chavi . . ."

"Yes?"

His lips brushed hers lightly, then his fingertip touched her cheek and lingered there. "My life would have been much less if I'd never known you."

"Mine too, Lysander. Mine too."

The conductor walked by, slamming doors and blowing his whistle. The train began to inch down the line, and Chavi stood at the window, her eyes slowly filling with tears.

Lysander watched the carriages roll slowly by for a moment, then turned to leave. A cloud of steam followed him. He blinked, feeling more empty than ever before in his life.

So this, finally, was to be the punishment for all his sins. Better they would have hanged him, or kept him locked away from humanity forever. He cursed himself for a fool not to have foreseen that one day he'd have to pay more dearly than he could ever have imagined. There was to be no redemption for him, after all, no second chance at life. Because without Chavi and his son, there was nothing to live for.

At the end of the platform he stopped, unable to keep from prolonging his agony by turning to watch the train vanish from view. There, it was gone, leaving behind a dense smokescreen like the last breath of a mythic dragon bearing those he loved out of his life forever.

Blinking, he brushed his fist across his eyes as the steam from the departing train cleared, drifting upward to the sooty dome of the station.

A solitary figure stood at the far end of the platform holding a child in her arms.

Lysander took a step, then another. Then he was running toward them, not daring to hope, unable not to hope.

When he reached her, Chavi gave him a dimpled grin, shoved a corkscrew curl behind her ear with her free hand and shrugged her slender shoulders philosophically.

His voice rumbled up from some newly discovered core of intense feeling inside him, harsh and rasping, yet ragged with relief. "You could have both been killed, jumping off moving train. Must you always act on impulse?" Damn, why did he have to react with fear and anger even now?

"Don't stay out of pity," he said sharply. "Don't stay because I love you. Don't stay unless *you* feel love for *me.* Otherwise we're both bound for hell."

Her gaze moved over his scarred features. In her eyes there were too many emotions for him to isolate and define a single overriding passion, yet he felt it and knew he was part of it. She said, "I'm not staying. I am going to Vienna.

But . . . well, if you've nothing better to do, why don't you come with me? We can find a doctor there who is performing skin transplants. We might as well be together while we find out what's next for us."

He closed his eyes briefly, let out a long breath. "You're not telling me what I want to hear."

She smiled. "What does any of it mean, Lysander, without love?"

42

The Merrin cemetery was situated in a secluded part of the estate, lovingly tended by gardeners and surrounded by trees to shield the headstones from any casual passerby who wandered this way.

Hakan stood at the foot of his mother's grave, oblivious to the chill of the wind coming down from the north. There had been a north wind blowing on the day she died, too. She had been buried with her head to the west, her feet to the east, as was the Chiricahua custom, and except for her journals, he had ordered all of her possessions burned. Her grave was not in a secret place, as it should have been, but he was going away and would not return to the site, and that was as it should be.

She had told him, just before she died, that if she were buried here he would feel an attachment to this place and would perhaps remain or at least return, yet it was not the Apache way to mark a grave or return to it. Had she forgotten? Had she died as a white-eyes woman, or in her last drifting thoughts had the Apache in her wanted to set him free?

"Good-bye, *Sons-ee-ah-ray*," he said softly. "This is the last time I'll come to you. But know that you'll live within my heart and soul forever. I can't be the man you wanted me to be, but I promise you that my footsteps will not mar the earth upon which they tread."

He smiled sadly at the mound of winter-bare earth. "Do

you remember? *Tonsaroyoo* said that if a man accomplished only that much, his soul would not go into that of an owl, and he would be welcome in the warm underground where you now sleep."

The weight of his grief still felt like a heavy mantle upon his heart, but he had dealt with those first agonizing questions that had arisen after her death. His immediate reaction had been to curse the waste of the years they'd spent in the pursuit of a worthless dream. Most of the time they had not even been together to share the burden.

But, looking back, he realized that their lives might have been even worse had his mother not chosen to return to England. Their choices had been few. A stinking reservation in a Florida swamp with Geronimo, or life among the American settlers who cluttered Apacheria with their farms and towns; and if the latter, how could they have supported themselves? With the stigma of having ridden with Geronimo hanging over them, would they even have been accepted by the settlers? Sarah had made what she believed to be the best choice for them at that time, just as he would endeavor to make the right choice for himself now.

Something caught his eye, and he bent over the grave. A tiny green shoot was pushing through the frozen soil. The first crocus, bravely facing a hostile world. Carefully he brushed the particles of frost away from the delicate leaf.

He straightened up, glanced once more at the headstone. Her name, dates, and, carved near the earth in smaller script, *Sons-ee-ah-ray.* He supposed at some distant future time someone might read the inscription and wonder what that meant. Sam had suggested he add "Morning Star," but Bly supported Hakan's decision not to translate for curiosity-seekers. He turned away and walked back down the path.

The walls of Merrinswood were golden against the pallid morning sky. Inside the house the bustle of the day's activities would have begun. Hakan felt a quickening of his senses as he contemplated the day. There was much to be done.

Robbie and Emily looked up as Hakan entered the breakfast room. Emily said quickly, "I'll ring for hot food for you, James."

Robbie smiled. "Good morning. You haven't forgotten that Hilliard Stoughton is c-coming over today with the papers?"

"No, I haven't forgotten. This is the day everything becomes your responsibility, Rob. Thank God. And I can make arrangements to go back where I belong."

Emily poured him a cup of tea. "James, I want you to know that I think this is a very noble gesture on your part."

Hakan maintained a carefully noncommittal expression. "Actually, it's Rob who is being noble. He's relieving me of several burdens."

He thought of Nelia Dunstan and how quickly she'd switched her affections to Robbie. At the time Hakan had not actually turned the estate over to his half brother, since Sarah was still alive and she was the trustee of his inheritance. Only his father's title had automatically passed to him. At that time giving Merrinswood to Robbie was merely an idea that had yet to be put into effect. But Nelia hadn't known that. Nor, fortunately, had Robbie. When Nelia suddenly began to flirt with him and seek out his company rather than Hakan's, Robbie had looked at his own attributes and decided that, yes, they were enough to attract a beautiful woman. Hakan was glad about this, because with Robbie's new-found self-confidence, he was not only more forceful with Nelia, but had quickly assumed control of every other aspect of his life, including his bullying twin.

"Danior w-went to post a letter to his f-friends in Italy. He said he'd b-be back shortly. You know he booked passage to Genoa? He s-said you'd persuaded him it was time for him to go."

"I was grateful he stayed until after the funeral," Hakan replied.

"He loved your m-mother. As I did."

"Yes, Rob. I know."

"I told Nelia last n-night that the w-wedding won't take place for a full year out of respect for your mother."

Hakan was about to protest that Sarah wouldn't have expected such a postponement, but almost simultaneously an intuitive voice at the back of his mind whispered that perhaps Rob needed a year with Nelia to really get to know her and decide if he indeed wanted to spend the rest of his life with her. Hakan could tell from the gleam in Emily's eye that the same thought had occurred to her.

Emily said, "If you'll both excuse me, Uncle Philip asked

me to go over to the guest house this morning and discuss the renovations."

Robbie's eyes met Hakan's after she left and they both grinned. Emily was much less waspish these days. Hakan asked, "Do you think Philip is going to take pity on her and suggest she move in with him after you and Nelia are married?"

"Probably. Philip's been the f-family peacemaker for years. But Emily's my twin and even though she's got a terrible disposition and I'm the first to admit it, she stays here, in the main house with us."

"And what will your beautiful bride-to-be think about that?"

"Nelia will do as she's told."

Hakan looked at Robbie in wonder. He spoke with the conviction of a man who knew he had the upper hand.

"I won't ask you what you did to Nelia, Rob, because it would be indelicate of me. But I must say I admire the way you've apparently tamed her."

Robbie's grin widened. "Well, I haven't t-tamed her in *all* respects."

They were both laughing when Bly came into the room. She brought with her, Hakan decided, a warm breeze, a promise of sunshine.

"What are you two up to?" she asked. "No, don't tell me, I don't want to know. It's enough to start the day with laughter. There's been far too much gloom in this house for too long. Sarah wouldn't have wanted it, I'm sure. You know, Hakan, I think the Chiricahuas had the right idea about death. They didn't view it as the tragedy that we do, did they?" She turned to Robbie. "They called it going to the Happy Place. They never spoke the name of a dead person because that would summon his ghost, who might be annoyed if he were interrupted in some pleasant activity."

"How charming," Robbie commented. "Y-you never cease to amaze me with your knowledge, Bly."

Hakan said, "You'd think she had been brought up by the Apache, wouldn't you? You know, sometimes she tries to tell me how we lived!" He smiled at her to show there was no malice and added, "I did intend to talk to you about the Life-way today, Bly. I was wondering if it wouldn't be easier for you to write Mother's book in the setting where it took place."

"Go to Arizona, you mean?"

"The Chiricahua mountains. I've already spoken to your father and he's ready to go back, too. He agrees that we're both grieving too much for my mother here and it's time to go. I've intended to return for some time, although I always hoped I'd be able to persuade her to go with me."

Bly's face lit up, her eyes shining like golden lanterns. "Oh, yes—yes, I'd love to do that. Reading her journals here, in this setting, makes her life with the Apache seem so remote, so inaccessible. I lose track of her thoughts and feelings."

"Good. Then we'll start making plans today."

"M-my goodness, am I to lose all of you?" Robbie asked.

"Not permanently, Rob," Bly said. "Either we'll be back for a visit, or you'll come to America."

She turned to Hakan and said, "There's just one thing . . . you've given everything away, Dad never saved much, and I'm a penniless anthropologist. What do we use for money?"

Robbie discreetly rose. "I'll leave you two to your plans. I must go and see that I have everything ready for Hilliard Stoughton."

When they were alone, Hakan said, "Apart from the cost of three passages aboard a liner, train fare, three horses and perhaps a couple of mules, what do we need? I'll show you how the Chiricahua lived off the land. Of course, you'll have to learn to build my wickiup and tan hides to make my clothes and moccasins—"

Laughing, Bly placed her serviette on top of his head, where it hung down to cover his face, to make him disappear. The linen square was snatched away and he leaned forward and kissed her mouth. It was a playful, impulsive act, and they stared at each other in amazement that an unpremeditated action should have such an impact on their senses.

Her expression became suddenly serious. "Hakan, if you can get us those passages to New York, and train tickets to the West, that's all we'll need. I can write articles for newspapers and Dad has always been able to take care of himself. I can live as your mother did. In a way, I've been getting ready for it all my life. My grandmother always said—"

Hakan placed his finger against her lips to silence her.

"Don't romanticize what we're planning to do beyond the realm of reality. You may find yourself running screaming back to New York after a few weeks in the wilds."

"You don't know me very well yet, do you?"

"Perhaps it's myself I'm still discovering. There's one thing I've learned, Bly, from my life. That we're always changing. Yesterday's goal becomes today's reality. Old disappointments give way to triumphs that no longer seem quite as important as we once believed they were. The people we thought we couldn't live without fade in our memory. And sometimes we look back with regret at what we feel we missed in the past, and we go back and try to find it again. Some say it will never be there, but I think perhaps for me *something* will be there—perhaps something better, more lasting than what I had before."

She took his hand and kissed the finger that had silenced her. "I'm glad you want me to go with you. I think that I'd hate to have you leave me behind again. I remember when I first saw you—in New York, right after Dad had brought you and your mother there to put you aboard the ship for England. I was completely bowled over by you. There was a splendor about you that took my breath away. Your hair was still long then, and shining clean because you washed it so frequently, in the Apache custom, and you were so handsome and so fierce you made my knees turn to jelly."

He looked at her in astonishment. "But you were a little horror. You treated me like an ignorant savage."

She shrugged. "In order to hide the beginning of a tremendous crush on you. Ah, Hakan, how I secretly pined for you over the years. I used to dream about you."

"When you came to England and we met at the wild West show, were you still pining? As I recall, you were a sharp-tongued shrew then, too. Berating me for living in luxury and doing nothing for the Chiricahuas who brought me up."

"You were with Nelia Dunstan. God, how I hated her! She was the most beautiful thing I'd ever laid eyes on. As cool and remote as some white goddess. When she opened her mouth and spoke with that aristocratic drawl, I was so intimidated I didn't know what to do other than be a brat. I certainly couldn't compare with her for looks and breeding, now could I?"

Hakan leaned forward and kissed her again. "I'm glad

you've told me this. I can't say I felt the same way about you, but perhaps I had to wait until you grew up. And oh, Bly, how nicely you grew up!"

She dimpled, laughing. "Don't count on me being quite so well-mannered when we get to Arizona. It's only been an act, since I came here."

He smiled. "I know."

"Have you talked to Dad yet? About going home, I mean."

He nodded. "And by the way, there's no need for you to worry about financing our expedition. I'm not leaving myself penniless. Although Merrinswood will today officially pass into Robbie's keeping, I decided to hold on to the land in the south of England, and to the bank we own. After all, if the white-eyes are settling the West in droves, as I hear they are, then if the worst comes to the worst, I can always buy back some of our Chiricahua lands and have a place of my own in which to wander."

"Oh, no!" she exclaimed. "There'll be no settling down for you for a while. We must fight to have the Chiricahua brought back from Florida and Oklahoma—they must have a reservation on their own hunting grounds. Do you realize the Chiricahuas have been held as prisoners-of-war for nearly fifteen years? It's an outrage, a tragedy—it's . . . genocide. They're dying of despair. You'll have to go to Washington and fight for them. You were born in the Arizona Territory . . . we'll have to check on your citizenship status. But as soon as your mother's book is finished, we have work to do."

Grinning at her fervor, Hakan said, "I fully intend to do all I can for my Chiricahua friends. But perhaps you'll allow me to invest my money, if not my time, in land in Arizona—just in case we ever need it?"

Bly shook her head in mock regret. "I suppose it was inevitable that English upper-class life would corrupt you a little bit. Oh dear, I really hoped you'd give everything away. You're just not perfect, are you? Just as well, since I'm only human too. Besides, if you hang on to part of your fortune perhaps you can do something for your people. Or for my mother's people, who are living in absolute squalor in Texas. Hakan, did I tell you that the Kickapoo Indians hide in Mexico every winter in order to practice and preserve the rituals of their culture, keeping them from prying eyes in a secret mountain stronghold? They wouldn't even tell me where it is, because I'm only one-quarter Kickapoo. But with your tracking abilities, perhaps we could follow them one winter. If I could record . . ."

Hakan listened and watched her face take on that animated, passionate expression he had begun to admire so much. Could this woman make his life complete? Would it be possible for them to journey together on a voyage of discovery, to link the past to the future while they lived in a glorious present?

Perhaps it was too soon to determine how he felt about her. Perhaps his mother's death and his parting from Chavi were too fresh in his mind to allow him to pledge that kind of covenant to Bly. But if it were destined to happen, then it would come later.

Lysander stirred restlessly in bed, anxious for the dawn to break, yet dreading the new day. Somewhere in the sleeping city, a piano played softly. The sad sweet music drifted in through the open window. Liszt's *Liebesträume* . . . dream of love. Like the nocturnal pianist, Lysander too had a dream of love. He wondered if that dream would become reality in the morning, or would be lost forever.

Within the enclosing cocoon of his facial bandages he sensed the outer darkness rather than saw it. His doctor had covered his eyes fearing he would blink and disturb his new skin. The bandages on his chest and left arm had already been removed, and the doctor was pleased with the condition of the sites of the donated skin. But tomorrow's unveiling would tell the real story, revealing not only either a new face or a botched medical experiment, but also the truth of his relationship with Chavi.

For no matter how many times he told himself he was content merely to be a part of her life again, Lysander was convinced that the only reason she had invited him to accompany her to Vienna was because he had told her of the new medical procedure.

If the operation was a success, then perhaps there would be a chance for a real life together. But if not . . . how could he reasonably expect a woman to go through life tied to a man with a monstrous parody of a face? It was one thing to be isolated in the Australian Outback with him, but no woman could tolerate for long the rest of society's horrified reaction to him.

It had been Chavi who had taken time from her studies at the university and with Doctor Freud, to try to track down a doctor performing the new surgical procedure. It was she who had insisted that Lysander must have the operation as soon as possible.

He had taken a flat within sight of the graceful spire of Saint Stephen's Cathedral, hired a cook-housekeeper, and settled down to get to know his son, and to court Chavi. But he rarely saw her in those first days as she plunged wholeheartedly into her studies.

The romantic ambiance of the lovely city of Vienna seemed to mock him at every turn, surrounding him with music and springtime blossoms and the sight of couples in love; making him feel even more of an outcast than ever before. He cursed himself for a fool for wanting what other men had, no, even more than most men aspired to . . . a woman so excitingly beautiful, so infinitely desirable that she surely deserved a princely consort, not a human gargoyle. He had to remind himself daily that Chavi had invited him to accompany her to Vienna.

Their former easy camaraderie had returned but, fearing he might lose her again if he forced the issue of their future status or tried to become her lover, Lysander held back. Everyday he looked at her and longed to tell her all that was in his heart, of all the love he had stored up over the years and how he yearned to express it in every way that was possible between a man and a woman.

Once, her arms full of books and ink stains on her fingers, she had paused long enough to smile and say, "Even when I've a thousand other things to think about . . . at the back of my mind I'm always glad that you'll be here when I come home. One day I won't have to study quite so hard just to keep my head above water."

And then what? he wondered. Will you have to face what I am, and deal with the knowledge that I can't live with you in brotherly celibacy indefinitely? Do you know how many nights I stand outside your bedroom door after you've fallen asleep over your books, and with what superhuman effort I remain out there, straining to hear the sound of your breathing, imagining your hair in wild disarray on your pillow, feeling that hollow ache where my heart should be because we're together, yet still apart.

Then, less than a month after their arrival, she had come home bursting with excitement. "I've found him," she announced. "The doctor who can give you a new face."

The bandages smothered him in a way his scars had not, trapping in their gauzy folds false promises and concealed dread. The doctor had been frank in warning that the results of the operation might leave him even worse off than before. Reconstructive surgery was a dream that physicians had yet to have much success with, and often when they removed dressings they found rampant infection had literally destroyed the flesh beneath.

Oh, God, would this night never end, he thought, tossing the covers away from him and tentatively fingering the dressings on his face, desperate to know what lay under them, yet fearing the revelation. There had been moments when he felt that what lay beneath the gauze dressing was not flesh, not even dead flesh, not real in any sense, and the horror of the thought produced nightmares that rendered sleep impossible. At least the waiting was almost over. If he could just be acceptable to Chavi, he didn't want more than that.

He had insisted upon being sent home from the hospital a few days before the dressings were to be removed. He wanted Chavi to be present when the bandages came off, so he could see her immediate reaction, untainted by the doctor's forewarning description if she merely visited the hospital after the fact. Lysander knew her so well he'd be able to read the truth of her feelings in her eyes.

His bedroom door opened quietly and he was no longer alone. The faint, elusive fragrance of perfume, the rustle of silk . . . the unmistakable nearness of a woman . . .

Smooth fingers touched his neck, a soft voice whispered, "Lysander, are you awake?"

He didn't respond, although all of his senses had quickened. He wanted to savor the anticipation of what she might say . . . then, too, if he spoke, her caressing fingers might depart.

Perhaps he was only dreaming. If so, might he never awaken. He lay still, feigning sleep, while she gently stroked his shoulder, then touched his hair above the bandages, her fingers making small comforting circles on his scalp. "Are you asleep?"

Her hand dropped to the open neck of his night shirt, resting as lightly as a butterfly. A second later he felt her lips graze his throat. He trembled and wanted to put his arms around her but didn't dare move in case the dream ended.

He heard the whisper of a garment sliding from a naked body, then her fingers were busy with the tapes that fastened his nightshirt.

The blood pounded in his head, surged along his veins and throbbed in his loins as her hands traveled slowly down his body. He felt her hair brush his chest as her lips encircled his nipple. He bit back a groan of pleasure as her hands found his pulsing organ, but he forced himself to remain still.

Once, long ago, he had come to her in the night and made love to her, and if tonight were not a dream, then it was she who wished to be the one to give joy, or she would not have waited until she believed he was asleep. Perhaps in recreating that other magical night when Garri was conceived she sought to discover a truth about the two of them that words alone could not reveal.

How he wished he could see her! But his mind's eye remembered every detail of her loveliness and his nostrils inhaled the sweet scent of her. He felt her breasts press against him, soft and full and tantalizing in their demand that he caress them. But when he raised his hand she pushed it back to the bed and whispered, "Lie still and let me make love to you."

She explored him with such tenderness that he felt his desire surge to a scalding need, but she would not be hurried. Once she laughed softly and nibbled the skin near his navel, then teased him with her tongue. Her mouth was eager, hungry, and because his own mouth was lost in the thick padding of bandages and therefore denied her, she rained kisses on his chest, his stomach, even his fingertips and toes. Her lips and hands were everywhere, as if he were an instrument and she must seek and play every chord.

When at last her lovely mouth found his manhood and bore him away to ecstasy he could no longer contain himself. He seized her head in his hands and gasped her name. "Chavi, my love. Oh, my dearest, I love you more than life. I want you as no man has ever wanted a woman before or will again.

I need you more than I need air to breathe . . . oh, Chavi, my love . . ."

Did she hear? Were his words smothered by the bandages, heard only inside his head? She climbed on top of him and guided him into her moist warmth. Then they were rising and falling together and the moon and the tides and the spinning earth were part of their rhythm. He could hear her breathing rapidly, making soft little sounds of pleasure, and he wanted to stay inside her forever, but she was straining, squeezing him, and each stroke brought them closer to their zenith. He felt his climax approaching, and they were so attuned that she responded instantly.

She lay beside him afterwards in blissful satiety, her fingers tracing languorous patterns on his chest and occasionally detouring to caress the part of him that had brought her so much pleasure.

He still breathed heavily, and was so happy he was afraid to speak, lest the spell be broken. She said, "What a beautiful body you have, Lysander."

"You can see me?" His voice was muffled by the bandages and he was unsure if she could hear him. "I thought it was still dark. Is the night over?"

She chuckled. "It's almost dawn, but I brought a lamp. Yes, I can see you and surely no man has a finer physique than you. I could lie here and look at you for hours. Your body is as beautiful as a Greek statue. Oh, Lysander, let's sleep together every night from now on. I want to make love to you and fall asleep in your arms every night and wake up with you beside me every morning. I had to come and ravish you tonight, because I couldn't wait any longer for you to come to me. We've been so busy since we came to Vienna, but now we must make time for each other."

"Chavi . . . I love you so much . . . but . . . please, don't say things tonight you might regret in the morning."

"Do you know what Doctor Freud says? He says we all need two things in order to be happy. We need our work, and we need love. That no human being can be complete without both. Men have always known this, but women have always believed they had to sacrifice one for the other. When I decided to come to Vienna I thought it was a choice I had to make, too. Then when we said good-bye and the train began to move away from you, I couldn't bear the thought you'd be gone from my life forever. I didn't know how I could have my work and you, but I was damn well going to try!"

"I never suggested you give up your work. Well, at least not since we came to Vienna. I see what it means to you. I've been happy to spend time with Garri."

"He grows more like you everyday. I see him throw back his head and square his shoulders in that same challenging way you have . . . and sometimes his eyes burn with that same ferocity yours do. Lysander, if he grows up to be half the man his father is, I'll be the proudest mother on earth."

"That is the first time you've told me that you believe I'm his father."

"There was little doubt in my mind before, but after tonight I know it. You know, I was almost afraid of making love with you tonight, in case it wasn't as wonderful as that night in Australia. But it was even more so, because you won't be gone from me in the morning."

"Chavi, in the morning . . . if the operation is unsuccessful, there is no need for you to feel bound by any implied promises to me. Over the last few years I've made investments in several different countries. I have places I can go, things I can do to fill my life."

"Lysander, you're never going anywhere without me. Haven't you heard what I've been trying to tell you? I love you. I think I have for a long time now."

He was sure he didn't deserve to be this happy, so perversely had to test her. He asked, "Is it just my physique you love, Chavi? Are you confusing making love with loving? Tomorrow you'll have to look at my face again. At best it will be ugly, at worst it could be even more grotesque than it was before. The doctor warned us what could happen if the grafts don't take, or if they become infected . . ."

"Stop it!" Her voice was angry, commanding. "Don't you understand? It's you I love, the essence of you, what you are . . . not what you look like. I admire everything about you, your strength, your courage, your mind. I won't even mention the tiny portion of my love for you that is born of gratitude. My God, Lysander, you gave me my life!"

"Chavi, you have my love, always and forever, but please don't say any more tonight. Wait until tomorrow . . ."

"I don't care about tomorrow!" Chavi was almost scream-

ing. "That's why I came to you tonight, before the bandages
are removed, because it doesn't matter what the result of the
operation is. I want to spend the rest of my life with you. I
want us to have more children together. To laugh and love
and live and quarrel and make up and be best friends and
lovers and even parents to each other sometimes. To be all
the things a loving couple can be to one another. I love you,
Lysander. I want you . . . and I always will, even if you have
no face at all in the morning."

She gathered up his hands and drew them to her lips, then
laid her cheek against his palm. After a moment she asked,
"Lysander? Are you all right? You're trembling."

He couldn't speak, as he was afraid if he did the tears that
had welled up in his eyes would spill over. She said, "I wish
we didn't just have to pretend that we are Mr. and Mrs. Dirk
Chambers. I wish we could really be married, but you have a
wife somewhere so we can't . . ."

He found his voice at last. "She divorced me, Chavi . . .
years ago while I was in prison. I didn't learn of it until
recently, after we came back to England."

"Well, then, Lysander, my true love, will you consent to
marry me?" she asked solemnly.

"It would be my very great pleasure," he responded. "If
you still feel the same way tomorrow."

"A pox on tomorrow! I shall bring a justice of the peace
to your bedside before daybreak and he'll marry us before
the bandages come off."

He wasn't sure if he wanted to laugh or to cry, but did
neither because he had to preserve his new face. Oh, God, it
had to be better than before, but if it was not, he was still
more blessed than any man on earth. He held happiness in
his arms and it had been too dearly won to lose it now.
Chavi meant what she said, she always had. The miracle had
happened. She loved him, and he . . . why, he worshiped her.

Robbie clasped Danior in a fierce hug, then took off his
glasses and unashamedly wiped tears away. "B-be absolutely
wonderful, or I shan't forgive you for leaving us."

In the cramped space of the tiny cabin aboard the ship
bound for Genoa, Hakan waited for Robbie to leave. Already the stewards were calling for all visitors to go ashore.
Hakan said, "I'll be along in a moment, Rob."

When they were alone Danior embraced him. Hakan said, "Thank you for delaying your journey until now. It was a comfort to have you at Merrinswood after Mother died."

Danior sighed. "Is this our last good-bye? Shall we ever meet again, my friend?"

"Of course," Hakan said firmly. "When you're a great opera singer you'll perform all over the world, and we, your family, will be your most appreciative audience."

Danior's dark eyes shone with appreciation and joy. "Can you know how proud I am to have you think of me as a member of your family?"

"Speaking of family," Hakan said carefully, "I wanted a moment alone with you to ask if you'd heard from Chavi. Apart from a note of sympathy with the wreath she sent for my mother's funeral, I haven't heard from her nor seen her since she went to the prison to obtain the release of . . . her husband."

"That wasn't her husband, it was Lysander."

"Yes, I know. But I wasn't sure if you did. Chavi told me what she intended to do that day we met at the inn."

"And you didn't try to stop her? Even though he may very well have killed your father?"

"He didn't kill my father. Don't ask me how I know, but I do. I did then. That was why I couldn't ask Chavi not to pretend Lysander was her husband."

Danior was silent, wondering if Hakan knew that Lysander had accompanied Chavi to Vienna. Had he been wrong in believing Hakan had fallen in love with her? "No, I haven't heard from her. But you know how she is. She will have plunged into her studies with Doctor Freud and be oblivious to everything else for a while. If I hear from her I'll send her letter on to you."

"No," Hakan said quickly. "Don't, please." It would be easier, he thought, not to be reminded of her for a while.

"You loved her, didn't you?"

"How could I help it? But she was wiser than I. She saw what we had together for what it really was. An interlude of healing, for both of us." He sighed. "For me she was the rainbow that vanishes in the misty air. Our love for each other was as beautiful as the petals that fall from a blossom . . . but falling petals signify death for the flower."

"Hakan, stop, you're breaking my heart. You always did manage to conjure up images of nature that devastated me. I suppose it's a legacy of your Apache childhood." He paused. "Lysander went to Vienna with her."

"I thought he might. I knew—that day we met while he was still in prison—that she loved him. I'm not even sure if she knew it herself then, but she wore the look of a woman desperately afraid for a man, and for herself, for the bleakness of her life if she lost him."

"He'll have to share her, though," Danior said thoughtfully. "If he tries to dissuade her from studying with her mind-doctor she'll always feel she missed an important part of her life."

"Perhaps he'll be wise enough to realize that. Besides, I imagine a woman with interests of her own would be the best kind of partner for a man. What a burden it must be to have a woman's whole existence revolve around only you."

Danior grinned. "Is that what attracts you about Bly? She certainly has enough interests of *her* own."

A steward stuck his head around the cabin door. "Begging your pardon, sir, but you must go ashore now. They're already pulling up the gangways."

"Bon voyage, Danior," Hakan said, embracing him.

"And to you too, my friend. I shall expect long letters about your Apacheria, and of course an invitation to the wedding after Bly reels you in . . . which I'm sure she has every intention of doing."

Hakan laughed as the steward rushed him out of the cabin, and he wondered if Danior's gypsy second-sight had glimpsed the future.

The three riders traversed a dense thicket of manzanita, cantered into a sandy arroyo, and followed its path toward the sloping approach to the Chiricahua mountains, their rocky peaks carving the sky into a new horizon.

A spring breeze, already warm with the promise of summer and rebirth, moved down the foothills, bringing the clean scent of juniper and piñon pine from the higher slopes.

There had been good winter rains and wildflowers were sprouting in the seemingly barren sand of the washes. Desert mallow and baileyea and tiny fragile white daisies like stars sprinkled on the ground.

A Gila monster observed them from the top of a boulder, flaunting his gaudy colors, then turned disdainfully away. A wren chattered in a nearby clump of yucca, proclaiming his territory, or perhaps warning off the Apache, who used the yucca for many things—rope and brushes from split fibers, the fruit eaten, the flowers to sweeten a drink, and the roots for a rich shampoo.

With the approach of sunset the nocturnal animals stirred in the chapparral and the scarlet-slashed sky painted vermilion shadows on Dos Cabezas, the twin heads of the highest mountain peaks. It was time to look for a campsite and to anticipate food and a leisurely discussion of the day's events around a crackling fire.

Hakan felt something inside him bursting free, expanding, soaring, as the layers of conformity and restraint dissolved, disappeared. His feelings were new, yet as old and familiar to him as the feel of the rippling muscles of his horse beneath the blanket.

He dug his heels into the flanks of the Appaloosa and galloped toward a cluster of sandstone pinnacles rising to the heavens in silent beauty, like cathedral spires.

Sam and Bly followed as Hakan's full-throated yell echoed about the canyons. It was a cry of triumph, of joy in being. A reunion with all that he'd thought lost but had now regained.

His voice sang to the mountain spirits that he was coming home.

Joan Dial was born, raised and educated in England. She has been writing for ten years and is the author of a number of original paperback romances and historical novels. Her books have been published around the world. She lives in Elsinore, California, with her husband and is the mother of two sons and a daughter. Her hobbies include bodysurfing and ballroom dancing.

BANTAM BOOKS
GRAND SLAM SWEEPSTAKES

Win a new Chevrolet Nova . . .

It's easy . . . It's fun . . . Here's how to enter:

OFFICIAL ENTRY FORM

Three Bantam book titles on sale this month are hidden in this word puzzle. Identify the books by circling each of these titles in the puzzle. Titles may appear within the puzzle horizontally, vertically, or diagonally . . .

This month's Bantam Books titles are:

INDIAN COUNTRY

SOMETIMES PARADISE

BE HAPPY YOU ARE LOVED

In each of the books listed above there is another entry blank and puzzle . . . another chance to win!

Be on the lookout for these Bantam paperback books: FIRST BORN, CALL ME ANNA, SAMURAI STRATEGY. In each of them, you'll find a new puzzle, entry blank and GRAND SLAM Sweepstakes rules . . . and yet another chance to win another brand-new Chevrolet automobile!

MAIL TO: GRAND SLAM SWEEPSTAKES
                Post Office Box 18
                New York, New York 10046

Please Print

NAME _____

ADDRESS _____

CITY _____ STATE _____ ZIP _____

OFFICIAL RULES

NO PURCHASE NECESSARY.

To enter identify this month's Bantam Book titles by placing a circle around each word forming each title. There are three titles shown above to be found in this month's puzzle. Mail your entry to: Grand Slam Sweepstakes, P.O. Box 18, New York, N.Y. 10046

This is a monthly sweepstakes starting February 1, 1988 and ending January 31, 1989. During this sweepstakes period, one automobile winner will be selected each month from all entries that have correctly solved the puzzle. To participate in a particular month's drawing, your entry must be received by the last day of that month. The Grand Slam prize drawing will be held on February 14, 1989 from all entries received during all twelve months of the sweepstakes.

To obtain a free entry blank/puzzle/rules, send a self-addressed stamped envelope to: Winning Titles, P.O. Box 650, Sayreville, N.J. 08872. Residents of Vermont and Washington need not include return postage.

PRIZES: Each month for twelve months a Chevrolet automobile will be awarded with an approximate retail value of $12,000 each.

The Grand Slam Prize Winner will receive 2 Chevrolet automobiles plus $10,000 cash (ARV $34,000).

Winners will be selected under the supervision of Marden-Kane Inc., an independent judging organization. By entering this sweepstakes each entrant accepts and agrees to be bound by these rules and the decisions of the judges which shall be final and binding. Winners may be required to sign an affidavit of eligibility and release which must be returned within 14 days of receipt. All prizes will be awarded. No substitution or transfer of prizes permitted. Winners will be notified by mail. Odds of winning depend on the total number of eligible entries received.

Sweepstakes open to residents of the U.S. and Canada except employees of Bantam Books, its affiliates, subsidiaries, advertising agencies and Marden-Kane, Inc. Void in the Province of Quebec and wherever else prohibited or restricted by law. Not responsible for lost or misdirected mail or printing errors. Taxes and licensing fees are the sole responsibility of the winners. All cars are standard equipped. Canadian winners will be required to answer a skill testing question.

For a list of winners, send a self-addressed, stamped envelope to: Bantam Winners, P.O. Box 711, Sayreville, N.J. 08872.